Frontier by Starlight

A Western Fiction Novel

Ken Cannon

Shadowplay Communications, LLC

Contents

Chapter One.

When Vienna Florentino stepped off the train in New Mexico, it was close to midnight. Her initial impression was of a vast, dark area of chilly, windy emptiness that was unfamiliar and silent, extending out beneath the bright, blinking white stars. "Miss, there's nobody here to meet you," the conductor said, rather nervously. "I wired my brother," she replied. "Perhaps he grew tired of waiting due to the train being so late. He will be here soon. But if he does not arrive, can I find a hotel?" "There are places to stay. Ask the station agent to show you. If you'll excuse me, this is not a place for a lady like you to be alone at night. It's a rough little town mostly filled with Mexicans, miners, and cowboys. They often carouse. Furthermore, the revolution across the border has stirred up some excitement along the line. Miss, I suppose it's safe enough if you—" "Thank you. I'm not afraid at all."

As the train began to move away, Miss Florentino walked towards the dimly lit station. As she was about to enter, she encountered a Mexican with a sombrero covering his face and a blanket draped over his shoulders. "Is there anyone here to meet Miss Florentino?" she asked. "No sabe, Senora," he responded from under the blanket and shuffled away into the shadows. She entered the deserted waiting room. An oil lamp emitted a thick yellow light. The ticket window was open, and through it, she saw that there was no agent or operator in the small compartment. A telegraph machine clicked faintly. Vienna Florentino stood tapping a shapely foot on the floor, and with some amusement, she contrasted her reception in El Cajon with her current situation.

The last time she found herself alone like this was when she missed her maid and train at a place outside of Versailles. It was an adventure that had been a novel and delightful break in the prescribed routine of her much-chaperoned life. She walked across the waiting-room to a window and, holding aside her veil, peered outside. At first, she could only make out a few dim lights that were blurred in her sight. As her eyes grew accustomed to the darkness, she saw a superbly built horse standing near the window. Beyond that, was a bare square, or if it was a street, it was the widest one she had ever seen. The dim lights shone from low, flat buildings, and she made out the dark shapes of many horses, all standing motionless with drooping heads. Through a hole in the window-glass came a cool breeze, and on it breathed a sound that struck coarsely upon her ear a discordant mingling of laughter and shout, and the tramp of boots to the hard music of a phonograph. "Western revelry," she mused to herself as she left the window. "Now, what to do? I'll wait here. Perhaps the station agent will return soon, or Ken will come for me."

As she sat down to wait, she reviewed the causes which accounted for the remarkable situation in which she found herself. That Vienna Florentino should be alone, at a late hour, in a dingy little

Western railroad station, was indeed extraordinary. The close of her debutante year had been marred by the only unhappy experience of her life - the disgrace of her brother and his leaving home. She dated the beginning of a certain thoughtful habit of mind from that time, and a dissatisfaction with the brilliant life society offered her. The change had been so gradual that it was permanent before she realized it. For a while, an active outdoor life of golf, tennis, and yachting kept this realization from becoming morbid introspection.

At a certain point, even the glitz and glamour lost its appeal for Vienna Florentino. She couldn't shake the feeling that something was wrong with her. Traveling didn't help either. She had been restless for months, feeling like her position, wealth, and popularity just didn't cut it anymore. She had grown out of her girlhood fantasies and had become a worldly woman. She continued to put on a show, but deep down, she knew that her luxurious lifestyle lacked significance. She had moments where she felt a future rebellion brewing within her. One particular night at the opera, she was struck by the scenery of a vast, lonely landscape under a sky full of stars. It brought her an unexplainable sense of peace, but when the scene changed, she lost it and became irritated. She glanced around at the glittering boxes filled with the wealthy, cultured, and beautiful people who represented her world. Vienna was a part of it, but she didn't feel natural or true to herself. She wondered if there was a way for these people to be different, but she couldn't quite put her finger on what she wanted them to be. If they were different, they wouldn't belong in that world. Despite this, she couldn't help but feel that something was missing.

As she sat among the polished, imperturbable men who sought only to please her, Vienna suddenly realized that she would marry one of them if she did not revolt. A great weariness washed over her, an icy-sickening sense that life had become dull and uninspiring. She was tired of the fashionable society she found herself in, tired of being feted, admired, loved, followed, and importuned. She longed for something more, something real.

In the distance, she glimpsed boldly painted stage scenery that stirred her soul. The rugged beauty of nature called to her, and she knew that she needed to be alone, to find her real self. She thought of visiting her brother, who had gone West to cast his fortune with the cattlemen. When she calmly announced her intention of going out West, her mother was consternated, and her father was reminded of the black sheep of the family. He forbade her from going, but Vienna stood her ground, reminding them that she was twenty-four and her own mistress. She had never exhibited such will before.

As luck would have it, she had friends who were on the eve of starting for California, and she made a quick decision to travel with them. She was tired of people, tired of houses, noise, ostentation, and luxury. She longed for the lonely, silent, darkening stretches of the West, where she could brood for long hours, gaze out at the stars, and face her soul.

She had ultimately triumphed, concealing her true emotions throughout the journey. Her decision to visit her brother was made in haste, leaving her no time to inform him of her plans. Instead, she sent telegrams from both New York and Chicago, the latter due to her companions' illness causing a delay. She was determined to reach El Cajon on October 3rd, her brother's birthday, and despite her train being several hours late, she arrived on time. She had no way of knowing if her brother had received her message, but her concern now was that he was not there to greet her upon her arrival.

Vienna's thoughts quickly shifted from the past to the present. "I hope Ken is okay," she whispered to herself. "He was doing well the last time he wrote. It's been a while, but he never wrote often. He must be fine. He'll be here soon, and I'll be so happy to see him again. I wonder if he's changed."

As Vienna waited in the dimly lit room, she heard the faint clicking of a telegraph machine, the soft hum of wires, the occasional sound of a horse's hooves, and the distant laughter of a party. These sounds were unfamiliar to her, and she felt her heart race with excitement. Vienna was not well-versed in the ways of the West. Like others of her social status, she had explored Europe but neglected her own country. Her brother's letters had only added to her confusion about the plains, mountains, cowboys, and cattle.

Vienna had been amazed at the endless distance she had traveled. If there had been anything worth seeing during her journey, she had missed it in the darkness of night. Now, she found herself in a dreary little station, with only the mournful sound of telegraph wires to keep her company. Suddenly, she heard a faint noise that sounded like chains rattling. At first, she thought it was just the telegraph wires again, but then she heard footsteps. The door creaked open and a tall cowboy walked in, his spurs clinking with every step. Vienna couldn't help but think of Dustin Farnum's entrance in "The Virginian."

"Excuse me, can you tell me where the hotel is?" Vienna asked, standing up. The cowboy removed his hat and made an exaggerated bow, but there was still a certain grace to his movements. He took two long strides towards her and asked, "Ma'am, are you married?"

Vienna tried to keep a straight face, but it was difficult. She had heard about cowboys and their ways, but she never expected this. Before she could say anything, the cowboy took her left hand and removed her glove. "Nice ring, but no wedding band," he drawled. "I'm glad to see you're not married, ma'am."

He handed her back the glove and continued, "You see, the only hotel in this town doesn't allow married women. It's bad for business, keeps the boys away."

Vienna was taken aback by this news. "Really?" she asked, trying to make sense of it all.

The cowboy nodded. "Yep, it sure is. Married women just don't belong in a place like this."

"This ain't Reno," the cowboy slurred, laughing boyishly. Vienna could tell he was half drunk from the way he slouched on his sombrero. She instinctively recoiled, but also took a better look at his face in the light. It was sharp and raw, like red bronze. He laughed again, but it didn't soften the hard set of his features. Vienna had developed a delicate perception of men and their intentions, thanks to her beauty and charm. She knew this cowboy meant no insult, but his crude behavior still offended her. "Can you show me to the hotel?" she asked, hoping to end the interaction. "Lady, you wait here," he replied slowly, his thoughts muddled by the alcohol. "I'll go fetch the porter." Vienna thanked him and waited in relief as he left and closed the door. She realized she should have mentioned her brother's name, and wondered what living with cowboys had done to Ken. She had always believed in his latent goodness, but her faith had dwindled during their two years of silence. As she waited, the wind moaned through the wires and the horse outside grew restless. Suddenly, Vienna heard the galloping of horses approaching. She rushed to the window, hoping it was her brother.

The noise grew louder and louder until it became a deafening roar. Vienna Florentino watched in awe as lean horses with flying manes and tails galloped past, carrying sombreroed riders who seemed strange and wild to her. She remembered what the conductor had told her and tried to calm her unease. The dim lights in the windows were shrouded by dust clouds. Suddenly, two figures emerged from the gloom - one tall and the other slight. The cowboy was leading a porter back to the room. Heavy footsteps and dragging sounds could be heard outside, and then the door opened with a loud rasp, shaking the whole room.

The cowboy pulled a disheveled figure into the room - a priest, or padre, whose mantle was in disarray from the rough treatment. It was clear that the padre was extremely frightened. Vienna looked on in confusion at the little man, so pale and shaken, and was about to protest when the cowboy, who now seemed half-drunk, turned into a cool, grim-smiling devil. He reached out and grabbed Vienna, pulling her back to the bench.

"Stay there!" he ordered. His voice wasn't brutal, harsh, or cruel, but it made Vienna feel powerless to move. No man had ever spoken to her like that before. Despite her pride, Vienna obeyed. The padre lifted his clasped hands as if begging for his life and began to speak in Spanish, which Vienna didn't understand. The cowboy pulled out a huge gun and pointed it at the priest's face. Then he lowered it, aiming at the priest's feet. There was a red flash, followed by a thundering report that stunned Vienna. The room filled with smoke and the smell of gunpowder. Though she didn't faint or close her eyes, Vienna felt as though she was trapped in a cold vise.

As the smoke cleared, Vienna let out a sigh of relief. The cowboy hadn't shot the padre. But he still had the gun and was dragging the priest towards her. What was his intention? She thought it might be some cowboy trick, like the ones her brother Ken had described in his letters. She remembered a movie where cowboys played a joke on a teacher. Maybe this was just another prank.

But as the cowboy barred her passage and grabbed her arms, Vienna realized this was no joke. She fought back, using all her strength, but the man was too strong. And his strange smile and cool demeanor unnerved her more than his physical strength. She trembled as she asked him what he wanted.

"Dearie, ease up a little on the bridle," he replied, gaily. Vienna couldn't believe what was happening. She felt like she was in a dream, unable to think clearly.

The events had happened so quickly that Vienna couldn't fully comprehend what was going on. However, she was aware of the man's imposing presence, the trembling priest, the blue smoke, and the smell of gunpowder. Suddenly, there was another red flash followed by a deafening report. Vienna couldn't stand and collapsed onto a nearby bench. Her mind was foggy, and she struggled to process what was happening. She heard the priest's voice, but it sounded distant and dreamlike. Then, the cowboy's voice brought her back to reality. "Lady, say Si Si. Say it quick! Say it Si!" he urged. Vienna felt compelled to comply with his request, and she spoke the word.

The cowboy then asked for her name, and she told him mechanically. He seemed to recognize her name and leaned back unsteadily. Vienna heard him exhale sharply, which sounded like something a drunk person would do. He demanded to know her name again, and she repeated it, adding that she was Ken Florentino's sister. The cowboy reached out to touch her veil, but Vienna removed it before he could lay a hand on it. She revealed her face, and the cowboy was surprised to see that she was not Princess Florentino. Vienna was taken aback by the mention of her nickname by this stranger. It was a name reserved for only her closest family members. She gathered her wits and corrected him, "You are Princess Florentino," he affirmed, more in wonder than in question.

Vienna turned to face the man standing before her. "Yes, I am," she replied. He quickly holstered his gun and said, "Well, I reckon we won't go on with it then."

"With what, sir? And why did you force me to say 'Si' to this priest?" Vienna demanded.

"I reckon that was a way I took to show him you'd be willing to get married," he explained.

"Oh!... You, you!..." Vienna was at a loss for words. The cowboy seemed to be spurred into action by her outburst. He grabbed the priest and led him towards the door, cursing and threatening him, most likely instructing him to keep quiet. He then pushed the priest outside and stood there, breathing heavily and struggling with himself.

"Wait a minute, Miss Florentino," he said, his voice husky. "You could fall into worse company than mine, though I reckon you sure think not. I'm pretty drunk, but I'm all right otherwise. Just wait a minute."

Vienna stood there, seething with anger, watching the cowboy battle his drunkenness. He seemed to be a man who had been suddenly jolted into a rational state of mind and was now fighting to maintain it. She watched as he lifted his dark, damp hair from his forehead to let the cool wind blow through it. Above him, she saw the white stars twinkling in the deep blue sky. They appeared to her as unreal as any other thing in this strange night. They were cold, aloof, and distant. Looking at them, she felt her anger dissipate and leave her feeling calm.

The cowboy turned back to her and began to speak. "You see, I was pretty drunk," he explained. "There was a fiesta and a wedding. I do foolish things when I'm drunk. I made a bet that I'd marry the first girl who came to town... If you hadn't worn that veil, the guys were teasing me, and Ed Linton was getting married, and everybody always wants to gamble..."

"I must have been pretty drunk," he muttered, wiping the sweat from his forehead with his scarf. He couldn't bring himself to look at her after that first glance. The boldness he had shown earlier had disappeared, replaced with either excessive emotion or the drunken stupor some men experience. He fidgeted, breathed heavily, and couldn't stand still. "You see, I was pretty..." he trailed off.

"Explanations are not necessary," she interrupted, her voice tired and distressed. "I am tired, and it's late. Do you have any idea what it means to be a gentleman?"

He blushed, his face turning a bright red. "Is my brother in town tonight?" she asked.

"No, he's at the ranch," he replied.

"But I wired him," she said.

"He might not have gotten the message yet. He'll be in town tomorrow. He's shipping cattle for Stillwell," he explained.

"Meanwhile, I need to go to a hotel. Will you please..." she started, but he didn't seem to hear her.

A commotion outside caught his attention, and Vienna listened as well. She heard men's voices, a woman's softer tones, and they were speaking in Spanish. The voices grew louder, and the sound of footsteps on gravel approached the station. Suddenly, there was shouting, and then a muffled shot. A body fell, and a woman's cry pierced the air.

Vienna was afraid, and the cowboy's demeanor only added to her fear. She knew something terrible had happened. The sound of footsteps retreating in the distance confirmed her worst fears.

Vienna Florentino slumped back in her seat, feeling cold and queasy. The thumping beat of the dancers and the tinny music only made her feel worse. Suddenly, a girl's face appeared in the doorway. Her features were tragic, framed by dark hair and lit up by even darker eyes. The girl clutched the doorframe with a slim, brown hand, as if she needed support. She wore gaudy clothes, with a long black scarf accentuating her outfit.

"Senor Gene!" the girl exclaimed, relief breaking through her fear. "Bonita!" The cowboy, Gene, leaped up to her. "Girl! Are you hurt?"

"No, Senor," she replied.

"I heard someone got shot. Was it Danny?" Gene asked.

"No, Senor," Bonita replied.

"Did Danny do the shooting? Tell me, girl," Gene persisted.

"No, Senor," Bonita repeated.

"I'm sure glad. I thought Danny was mixed up in that. He had Stillwell's money for the boys. I was afraid..." Gene trailed off. "Say, Bonita, you'll get in trouble. Who was with you? What did you do?"

"Senor Gene, the Don Carlos vaqueros quarreled over me. I only danced a little, smiled a little, and they quarreled. I begged them to be good and watch out for Sheriff Hawe... and now Sheriff Hawe put me in jail. I'm so frightened. He tried to make a little love to Bonita once, and now he hates me like he hates Senor Gene."

"Pat Hawe won't put you in jail. Take my horse and hit the Peloncillo trail. Bonita, promise to stay away from El Cajon."

"Si, Senor," Bonita agreed.

Gene led her outside. Vienna heard the snort and stamp of a horse. Gene spoke in a low voice, and Vienna could only make out a few words: "stirrups... wait... out of town... mountain... trail ... now ride!"

There was a moment of silence, then the pounding of hooves and the sound of gravel. Vienna caught a glimpse of a big, dark horse running into the open space. She saw Bonita's scarf and hair whipping in the wind, her small form low in the saddle.

The silhouette of the horse stood out in black against the faint lights. Its flight was magnificent and untamed. The cowboy appeared once more in the doorway. "Miss Florentino, we oughta leave now. Things ain't been good here, and there's a train comin'." She rushed outside, too scared to look behind or to either side.

Her guide walked quickly, and she had to run to keep up with him. A jumble of emotions filled her. She had a peculiar feeling about the towering figure next to her, who only made noise with his spurs. She felt the breeze on her face and saw the bright stars. Were they really blinking, or was it just her imagination? She had a strange thought that she had seen these stars before, in another life. The night was dark, yet there was a dim light from the stars that seemed to follow her. She suddenly realized that they had gone past the houses and asked, "Where are you taking me?" "To Florence Kingsley," he replied. "Who's she?" "She's your brother's best friend out here." Vienna walked with the cowboy for a few more moments before stopping to catch her breath and calm her nerves. She realized her training had not prepared her for this experience. The cowboy noticed her absence and walked back a few steps, standing next to her in silence. "It's so dark and lonely," she murmured. "How can I trust you? What guarantee do I have that you won't harm me?" He replied, "None, Miss Florentino, except that I've seen your face."

Chapter Two.

With that one response, Vienna gained the confidence to continue her journey with the cowboy. Despite her initial reservations, she felt a newfound trust in him. The two of them rode on through the rugged terrain, their horses pounding the ground with each stride. They encountered various obstacles along the way, but the cowboy's expertise and Vienna's determination kept them moving forward. As they rode, they shared stories of their pasts and dreams for the future. Eventually, they arrived at their destination, exhausted but victorious. The experience had brought them closer together, and Vienna knew that she had made the right choice in trusting the cowboy.

In that moment, Vienna didn't even register what the cowboy had said. Any response would have sufficed, as long as it was kind. His silence only made her more anxious, forcing her to voice her fears. Despite his lack of reply, she knew she would follow him anyway. The idea of returning to the station, where she believed a murder had taken place, was too dreadful to consider. She couldn't bear the thought of wandering around alone in the dark, either. As they continued walking into the windy darkness, Vienna was relieved that he had finally spoken, but also realized that he had yet to prove himself. She felt a renewed sense of pride, as if she should scorn to even think about such a man. However, Vienna couldn't help but acknowledge that she was experiencing feelings she had never felt before.

Eventually, the cowboy led Vienna off the path and knocked on the door of a small house. "Hello, who's there?" a deep voice answered. "Gene Norris," said the cowboy. "Call Florence quick!" Footsteps could be heard, followed by a tap on a door and voices. Vienna overheard a woman exclaim, "Gene! You're here when there's a dance in town! Something wrong out on the range." A light shone brightly through a window, and soon after, a woman holding a lamp opened the door. "Gene! Al's not--" "Al is all right," interrupted the cowboy. At that moment, Vienna was struck by two sensations: wonder at the alarm and love in the woman's voice, and relief at being in the company of a friend of her brother's. "It's Al's sister who came on tonight's train," the cowboy explained.

"I was at the station and I brought her to you," said Norris, as Vienna stepped out of the shadows.

Florence Kingsley was shocked beyond belief. "You're not really Princess Florentino!" she exclaimed, almost dropping the lamp in her hand.

Vienna replied, "Yes, I am really she. My train was late and for some reason, Ken did not meet me. Mr. Norris saw fit to bring me to you instead of taking me to a hotel."

Florence welcomed Vienna warmly and invited her in, surprised that Al had not mentioned her arrival. The cowboy who came in with Vienna's satchel had to stoop to enter the door, and once inside, he seemed to fill the room. Vienna saw a young woman with a friendly smile and fair hair hanging down over her dressing-gown.

Florence noticed that Vienna looked pale and tired. "You must be tired. What a long wait you had at the station! That station is lonely at night. If I had known you were coming! Indeed, you are very pale. Are you ill?" she asked.

Vienna replied, "No, only I am very tired. Traveling so far by rail is harder than I imagined. I did have rather a long wait after arriving at the station, but I can't say that it was lonely."

Florence searched Vienna's face with keen eyes and then took a long, significant look at the silent Norris. She closed a door leading into another room and lowered her voice, asking, "Miss Florentino, what has happened?"

Vienna replied, "I do not wish to recall all that has happened."

"I'd rather have met a hostile Apache than a cowboy," Ken said to Florence.

"Don't tell Al that!" Florence cried, pulling Norris close to the light. "Gene, you're drunk!"

"I was pretty drunk," he replied, hanging his head.

"Oh, what have you done?"

"Now, see here, Flo, I only-"

"I don't want to know. I'd tell it. Gene, aren't you ever going to learn decency? Aren't you ever going to stop drinking? You'll lose all your friends. Stillwell has stuck to you. Al's been your best friend. Molly and I have pleaded with you, and now you've gone and done God knows what!"

"What do women want to wear veils for?" he growled. "I'd have known her but for that veil."

"And you wouldn't have insulted her. But you would the next girl who came along. Gene, you are hopeless. Now, you get out of here and don't ever come back."

"Flo!" he entreated.

"I mean it."

"I reckon then I'll come back tomorrow and take my medicine," he replied.

"Don't you dare!" she cried. Norris went out and closed the door.

"Miss Florentino, you don't know how this hurts me," said Florence. "What you must think of us! It's so unlucky that you should have had this happen right at first. Now, maybe you won't have the heart to stay. Oh, I've known more than one Eastern girl to go home without ever learning what we really are cut here. Miss Florentino, Gene Norris is a fiend when he's drunk. All the same, I know, whatever he did, he meant no shame to you. Come now, don't think about it again tonight." She took up the lamp and led Vienna into a little room. "This is out West," she went on,

smiling, as she indicated the few furnishings. "But you can rest.
You're perfectly safe."

"Can I help you undress? Is there anything I can do for you?"
asked a kind voice. Vienna replied, "Thank you, but I can manage."
With that, the person left, telling Vienna to forget what happened
and focus on the surprise she would give her brother tomorrow.
Vienna noticed that it was past two o'clock when she looked at her
watch. She felt exhausted and could barely move, but her mind was
racing. Memories of the train, being lost, pounding hoofs, and her
brother's face from five years ago flooded her thoughts. She also
remembered a long line of lights, the jingle of silver spurs, and the
darkness of the night. She recalled the gloomy station, the shadowy
Mexican, and the empty room with dim lights across the square.
The sound of dancers and discordant music echoed in her mind,
followed by the entrance of a cowboy. She couldn't remember his
appearance or what he had done. One moment he seemed cool and
devilish, and the next his physical being was vague as outlines in
a dream. The white face of the padre flashed into her thoughts,
bringing with it a dull, half-blind state of mind. Memories of
strange voices, furious men, a deadened report, a mortal pain, and
a woman's cry followed.

Vienna gazed at the girl's tragic eyes, wild with fear, as the big
horse bolted into the darkness. A silent cowboy followed, his dark
figure stalking through the night. The white stars above seemed to
look down remorselessly. The memory of that scene washed over
Vienna repeatedly, but eventually faded, leaving her feeling adrift.
The room was pitch black, and the silence was suffocating. It was

as if she had been transported to another world. Thoughts of her fair-haired friend Florence and her brother Ken drifted through her mind, and eventually, she drifted off to sleep.

When she woke up, the room was bathed in sunlight and a cool breeze blew across the bed. She lazily contemplated the mud walls of her small room before remembering where she was and how she had gotten there. The shock of the previous night hit her again, and disgust overwhelmed her. She felt contaminated. Vienna had never experienced such emotions before, but she exercised her self-control and managed to compose herself. Her life had always been tranquil, luxurious, and uneventful. She could barely remember the last time she had to control her emotions.

As she was about to inquire about her brother, a voice stopped her in her tracks.

As she stepped outside, she recognized Miss Kingsley's voice and noticed a sharpness to it that she hadn't heard before. "So you came back, did you? Well, you don't look very proud of yourself this morning. Gene Norris, you look like a coyote."

"Say, Flo, if I am a coyote, I'm not going to sneak," he responded. "What did you come for?"

"I said I was coming round to take my medicine."

"Meaning you'll not run from Al Florentino? Gene, your skull is as thick as an old cow's. Al will never know anything about what you did to his sister unless you tell him. And if you do that, he'll shoot you. She won't give you away. She's a thoroughbred. Why, she was so white last night I thought she'd drop at my feet, but she never blinked an eyelash. I'm a woman, Gene Norris, and if I couldn't feel like Miss Florentino, I know how awful an ordeal she must have had. Why, she's one of the most beautiful, the most sought after, the most exclusive women in New York City. There's a crowd of millionaires and lords and dukes after her. How terrible it'd be for a woman like her to be kissed by a drunken cowpuncher! I say it-"

"Flo, I never insulted her that way," Norris interrupted.

"It was worse then?" she asked, sharply.

"I made a bet that I'd marry the first girl who came to town. I was on the watch and pretty drunk. When she came, well, I got Padre Marcos and tried to bully her into marrying me."

"Oh, Lord!" Florence gasped. "It's worse than I feared... Gene, Al will kill you."

"That'll be a good thing," the cowboy replied, dejectedly.

"Gene Norris, it certainly would, unless you turn over a new leaf," Florence retorted. "But don't be a fool." Here, she became earnest and appealing. "Go away, Gene. Go join the rebels across the border. You're always threatening that."

"Don't hang around here and risk getting Al all riled up. He'd kill you just like you'd kill a man for insulting your sister. Don't go causing any trouble for Al. That would only bring grief to her, Gene," Flo warned.

Vienna couldn't help but overhear their conversation and it upset her. She tried to tune it out, but it was no use. "Flo, you can't see this from a man's perspective," Gene responded calmly. "I'll stay and face the consequences."

"Gene, I could swear at you or any other stubborn cowboy. Listen, my brother-in-law, Jack, overheard some of our conversation last night. He doesn't like you. I'm afraid he'll tell Al. Please, for the love of God, go downtown and shut him up and yourself up too."

Just then, Vienna heard Flo enter the house and knock on the door. "Miss Florentino, are you awake?" she called softly. "Awake and dressed, Miss Kingsley. Come in," Vienna replied.

"You look so different, I'm glad you got some rest. Let's have breakfast and get ready to meet your brother," Flo said cheerfully.

"Wait, please. I overheard your conversation with Mr. Norris. It was unavoidable, but I need to speak with him. Can you ask him to come into the parlor for a moment?" Vienna requested.

"Of course," Flo replied quickly, giving Vienna a meaningful look as she left the room. "Make him keep his mouth shut!"

After a few moments, Vienna heard slow footsteps outside the front door. The door opened and Norris stood there, bareheaded in the sunlight. Vienna couldn't help but notice his embroidered buckskin vest, red scarf, bright leather wristbands, wide silver-buckled belt, and chaps. She quickly scanned his face but didn't recognize him. His presence made her feel uneasy and rebellious.

Vienna couldn't quite understand why she was drawn to this rugged, dark-skinned man before her. "Mr. Norris, will you please come in?" she finally asked after a long pause. "I don't reckon so," he gruffly replied. His hopeless tone indicated that he knew he wasn't good enough to be in her presence, and he either didn't care or cared too much. Vienna walked towards the door, noticing the hardness and sadness in his face. Despite her loathing for him, she couldn't help but feel a sense of kindness and pity towards him. "I won't tell my brother about your rudeness towards me," she began, struggling to keep the chill out of her voice. "I choose to overlook it because I know you weren't fully accountable and I don't want any trouble between Ken and you. Can I rely on you to keep quiet and not tell anyone about what happened? There was a man killed or injured last night, and I want to forget about it."

"The Greaser didn't die," interrupted Norris. "Well, that's a relief. I'm glad for the sake of your friend, the little Mexican girl," Vienna replied. She noticed a slow scarlet wave spread across his face, and she couldn't help but feel that if he was a heathen, he wasn't completely bad. It made such a difference that she even smiled at him. "Will you spare me any further distress, please?" she asked. His hoarse reply was incoherent, but she could see the remorse and gratitude on his face. Vienna returned to her room and soon Florence came to take her to breakfast.

In the morning light, Vienna Florentino had to reconstruct her impression of her brother's friend. She found Florence Kingsley to have a wholesome, frank, and sweet nature, and she enjoyed her slow Southern drawl. Vienna was puzzled as to whether Florence

was pretty, striking, or unusual. Her face lacked the soft curves
and lines of Eastern women, but she had a youthful glow and
flush, the clear tan of outdoors, light gray eyes like crystal, and
beautiful bright, waving hair. Florence's sister was the elder of the
two, a stout woman with a strong face and quiet eyes. They served
a simple fare and made no apologies for it. Vienna found their
simplicity to be restful and was pleased to see that they treated
her like any other visitor. They were sweet and kind, and Vienna
thought she would like to have them near her if she were ill or in
trouble. However, she reproached herself for being too fastidious
and hypercritical, unable to help distinguishing what these women
lacked.

Florence was breezy and frank, while her sister was quaint and not
much of a talker. Florence asked Vienna if she could ride, which
was a question Westerners always asked anyone from the East.
Vienna replied that she could ride like a man astride, and Florence
was pleased, saying they had some fine horses out there. When
Al arrived, they would go to Bill Stillwell's ranch, whether they
wanted to or not, because when Bill learned Vienna was there, he
would pack them all off. Florence assured Vienna that she would
love old Bill.

The ranch may not be in the best condition, but the view of the
mountains from up high is breathtaking. Hunting and climbing
are all well and good, but it's riding that I love the most. Feeling
the wind in my face as I gallop across wide open spaces with the
mountains calling out to me is pure bliss. Of course, having the
best horse on the range is crucial, and that often leads to disagree-

ments between cowboys like Al and Bill. However, there is one horse that everyone can agree on - Gene Norris's iron-gray.

Vienna couldn't help but feel a thrill run through her as she thought back to the wild ride she had witnessed Norris and his horse take. "Does Mr. Norris really have the best horse in the country?" she asked Florence.

"He sure does," replied Florence. "But that's about all he has. Gene can't even keep hold of a quirt, but he loves that horse like it's his own child."

Their conversation was interrupted by a sharp knock at the door. It was Gene, who had been waiting on the porch and wanted to let them know that Florence's brother was on his way. As they looked out, they saw a cloud of dust approaching, with the outlines of horses and riders becoming clearer as they got closer.

Vienna felt a warmth spread through her as she thought about seeing her brother again after so many years. But there was also a hint of worry in the air. Florence asked Gene if Jack had kept his mouth shut, to which he replied that he hadn't. Florence pleaded with Gene to avoid a fight, knowing that Jack and his friends would not hesitate to cause trouble.

"There won't be a fight," Gene reassured them. But Florence wasn't convinced. She gently pushed Vienna back into the parlor, reminding Gene to use his brains.

Vienna watched in dismay as the warmth of Vienna quickly turned to fear. She couldn't believe that her brother was about to act with the same violence that she associated with cowboys. Suddenly, the clatter of hooves stopped before the door. As she looked out, she saw a group of dusty, wiry horses pawing at the gravel, and their riders with their rough dress and hard aspect that characterized the cowboy Norris.

One of the riders dismounted and came bounding up the porch steps, calling out to Florence, "Hello, Flo. Where is she?" Florence stepped aside, and he caught sight of Vienna, jumping at her with excitement. Although she hardly recognized him, the warm flash of blue eyes was familiar, and he threw his arms around her, holding her off and looking searchingly at her.

Before he could say anything, Florence interrupted, "Al, I think you'd better stop the wrangling out there." He suddenly appeared to hear the loud voices from the street, and releasing Vienna, he said, "By George! I forgot, Flo. There is a little business to see to. Keep my sister in here, please, and don't be fussed up now."

He went out on the porch and called to his men, "Shut off your wind, Jack! And you, too, Blaze! I didn't want you fellows to come here. But as you would come, you've got to shut up. This is my business."

Vienna watched in alarm as he turned to Norris, who was sitting on the fence. "Hello, Norris!" he said. Vienna couldn't help but feel uneasy at the greeting and the tone of his voice. Norris leisurely got up and advanced to the porch, drawling, "Hello, Florentino!"

"Hey, Norris, were you drunk again last night?" asked Al.

Norris replied, "If you really want to know, then yes, I was pretty drunk."

Norris's response showed that he was in control of himself and the situation. There was a brief silence until Al spoke up, "Listen, Norris, here's the situation. Everyone in town is saying that you insulted my sister last night when you met her at the station. Jack and the other boys are after you, but this is my problem. I didn't bring them here. They want to see you make things right, or else they think you're on the wrong path, drinking and all. But Bill and I still believe you're a good man. We've never known you to lie. So, what do you have to say for yourself?"

Norris drawled, "No one is saying that I'm a liar, right?"

Al confirmed, "No, that's not it."

Norris continued, "Well, I was pretty drunk last night, but not so drunk that I can't remember what I did. I told Pat Hawe this morning when he asked. And that's saying something, considering how I feel about Pat. Anyway, I found Miss Florentino waiting alone at the station. She had a veil on, but I knew she was a lady. I think she was taken aback by my gallantry, but that's just my guess."

At this point, Vienna, who had been listening in, couldn't hold back anymore and stepped out onto the porch. She said, "Gentlemen, I'm new to these Western ways, but I think you have the wrong idea about Mr. Norris. I want to correct this mistake in fairness to him."

He was a bit brusque and unusual when he approached me last
night, but now I comprehend that it was due to his chivalry. He
was a tad impetuous and emotional in his desire to safeguard me,
and it wasn't evident if he intended to protect me just for that
night or for all time. However, I'm pleased to say that he didn't
utter a single dishonorable word to me. Additionally, he escorted
me safely to Miss Kingsley's residence.

Chapter Three.

V ienna returned to the small parlor with her brother whom she had barely recognized. "Princess!" he exclaimed. "I can't believe you're here!" The warmth flowed back
into her veins. She remembered how that nickname had sounded when her brother had given it to her. "Ken!" she replied.

His words of joy at seeing her again, his regret at not being
at the train station to greet her, were not as memorable as the
way he hugged her. He had held her that way the day he left
home, and she had never forgotten. But now he was so much
taller and bigger, so dusty and different and forceful, that she
could hardly believe he was the same man. She even had a
funny thought that this was another cowboy trying to boss her
around, and this time it was her own brother.

"Dear old girl," he said more calmly as he let her go, "you
haven't changed at all, except to become more beautiful. You're
a woman now, and you've lived up to the name I gave you.
God! Seeing you brings back memories of home! It feels like a
hundred years since I left. I missed you more than anyone else."

Vienna felt like she was rediscovering her brother with every word
he said. She was so amazed by the transformation in him that
she couldn't believe her eyes. She saw a tanned, strong-jawed, ea-
gle-eyed man, tall and magnificent, dressed like the cowboys with
a belt, boots, and spurs.

There was a steely determination etched onto his face that trembled with every word he spoke. Only when those hard lines softened could she see the faint resemblance to the boy she once knew.
It was his mannerisms, the way he spoke, and the little quirks
that convinced her that he was truly Ken. She had said goodbye
to a disgraced, disowned, and dissolute boy. She still recalled his
handsome, pallid face with its weaknesses and shadows, the careless
grin, and the ever-present cigarette dangling from his lips. Years
had passed, and now she saw him as a man, molded by the West.
And Vienna Florentino felt a powerful, passionate happiness and
gratitude, and a direct challenge to her newfound hatred of the
West.

"Princess, it's good to see you. I'm a mess. How did you manage to
come here?" he asked, overcome with emotion. But he didn't dwell
on that. "Tell me about my brother," he said.

Vienna told him everything, including tidbits about their sister
Melissa. He fired question after question at her, and she answered
them all, telling him about their mother and Aunt Grace, who had
passed away a year ago, and his old friends who had married, moved
away, or disappeared. She didn't mention his father, and he didn't
ask. Suddenly, the rapid-fire questioning stopped, and he choked
up. He was silent for a moment, then burst into tears. It felt like

a long-held bitterness was finally being released. It pained her to see him like this, and it hurt even more to hear him cry. In those few moments, she felt closer to him than she ever had before. Had their parents treated him right? Her heart raced at the thought. She didn't say anything, but she kissed him, something that was out of character for her. And when he regained his composure, he didn't mention his breakdown, nor did she. But that scene stayed with Vienna Florentino for a long time.

got around to it." Vienna was sympathetic to Ken's troubles and listened as he told her about his ranch and how he had lost most of his cattle due to a drought. He had to sell off his land to pay his debts and was now working as a cowboy on someone else's ranch. Vienna could see the sadness in Ken's eyes, but also the determination to make things right again. She offered to help him financially, but Ken refused, insisting that he would work hard and earn his own way back to success. As they parted ways, Vienna knew that Ken would make it through his hardships and come out stronger on the other side.

Chapter Four.

"Spill the beans, Ken. What's going on?" Princess Vienna pressed him, sensing something was off.

"Vienna, don't trouble yourself with my problems. I want you to enjoy your stay here," Ken replied, trying to deflect her.

"I knew it. Something's not right. That's why I came out here," Vienna insisted.

Ken sighed, but it seemed like a weight had been lifted as he decided to tell her. "Remember my ranch and how I was doing well raising stock? Well, I made some enemies. A cattleman named Ward and I had some trouble. Then there's Pat Hawe, the sheriff, who has been hurting my business. He has influence in Santa Fe and El Paso. He hates Gene Norris and me because I spoiled his plan to get Gene. But the real reason he hates me is because he loves Florence, and she's going to marry me," Ken explained.

"Ken!" Vienna exclaimed, surprised. "I like her, but I didn't think of her that way. Is she from a good family?"

"What connections?" Ken asked with a laugh. "Florence is just a regular girl, born in Kentucky and raised in Texas. My fancy and wealthy family would probably look down on her."

Vienna lifted her head, her tone haughty, "Ken, you are still a Florentino."

Ken shrugged, "We won't argue about that, Princess. I remember you, and despite your pride, you have a heart. If you stay here for a month, you'll come to love Florence Kingsley. She's had a big hand in turning my life around."

He continued, "But let me get back to my story. There's Don Carlos, a Mexican rancher, and he's my worst enemy. He's just as bad for Bill Stillwell and other ranchers. Stillwell is my friend and one of the best men I know. I got myself into debt with Don Carlos before I realized how crooked he was. I lost money playing faro when I first came out West, and then I made some bad cattle deals. Don Carlos is sneaky, he knows the land, he controls the water, and he's dishonest. So he outsmarted me, and now I'm practically broke. He hasn't taken over my ranch yet, but it's only a matter of time with the lawsuits in Santa Fe. Right now, I have a few hundred head of cattle grazing on Stillwell's land, and I'm his foreman."

"Foreman?" Vienna asked.

Ken nodded, "Just the boss of Stillwell's cowboys, and I'm happy to have the job."

Vienna felt a burning inside her. She struggled to keep her composure, realizing how sheltered her life had been. "Can't you get your property back?" she asked. "How much do you owe?"

"Ten thousand dollars would clear my debt and give me a fresh start," Ken replied.

"But, sis, that's a lot of money in this country, and I can't come up with it. Stillwell's even worse off than I am," Ken lamented.

Vienna walked over to him and placed her hands on his shoulders. "We can't be in debt," she stated firmly.

Ken looked at her with surprise, as if her words had triggered a memory. Then he grinned. "You're quite the bossy one, aren't you? I almost forgot who my beautiful sister really is. You're not seriously suggesting that I take money from you, are you?"

"I am," Vienna replied without hesitation.

Ken shook his head. "No way. I never have, not even when I was in college. And back then, there wasn't much I couldn't handle."

"Listen, Ken," Vienna began earnestly. "This is different. Since the last time I wrote you, I inherited a large sum of money from Aunt Grace. It's mine, not father's. I haven't even been able to spend half of it. Please, let me help you. It would make me so happy."

Ken kissed her on the forehead, taken aback by her sincerity. Vienna was surprised herself at how passionately she had spoken. "You've always been the best, sis. And if you really want to help me, I'll gladly accept. It'll be great. Florence will be ecstatic. And that

Greaser won't bother me anymore. You know, pretty soon some fancy guy will be spending all your money anyway. Might as well let me have a little before he takes it all," he joked.

Vienna laughed lightly. "And what do you know about me?"

"More than you think," Ken replied with a grin.

Even out here in the wild West, news travels fast. Everyone knows about Anglesbury and the Dago duke who chased Vienna all over Europe. But now Lord Mountcastle has taken the reins and it seems like he may win the race. Vienna detected a hint of scorn in his speech and a flame in his eyes. She became thoughtful, realizing she had forgotten about Mountcastle and New York society.

Ken, her brother, cried out passionately, "I don't care about the money, it's you! You're so splendid and wonderful. People call you the American Beauty, but you're more than that. You're the American Girl! Princess, don't marry any man unless you love him and love an American. Stay away from Europe long enough to learn to know the real men of your own country."

Vienna replied, "Ken, I'm afraid there aren't always real men and real love for American girls in international marriages. But Melissa knows this. It'll be her choice. She'll be miserable if she marries Anglesbury."

"It'll serve her right," declared Ken. "Melissa was always crazy for glitter, adulation, and fame. I'll bet she never saw more of Anglesbury than the gold and ribbons on his chest."

Vienna was surprised that Ken knew about her, "way out here."
He explained, "I told Florence about you and gave her a picture of
you. And, of course, being a woman, she showed the picture and
talked. She's in love with you."

Occasionally, my dear sister, we receive New York papers out here,
and we are able to read and keep up with the happenings. You may
not be aware that you and your high society friends are subjects of
intense interest in the United States, particularly in the West. The
papers are filled with stories about you, and perhaps even some
things that you never did.

"That Mr. Norris knew too," he said. "He asked, 'You're not
Princess Florentino?'"

"Never mind his impudence!" exclaimed Ken, laughing. "Gene is a
good guy, you just have to get to know him. Let me tell you what
he saw in the Times. He took it from here, and despite Florence's
objections, he wouldn't bring it back. It was a picture of you in
a riding outfit with your blue-ribbon horse, White Stockings, remember? It was taken in Newport. Well, Norris tacked the picture
up in his bunkhouse and named his horse Princess. All of the
cowboys knew about it. They would see the picture and tease him
relentlessly, but he didn't care. One day, I happened to visit him
and found him recovering from a wild night. I saw the picture too,
and I said to him, 'Gene, if my sister knew you were a drunkard,
she wouldn't be proud of having her picture hanging up in your
room.' Princess, he didn't touch a drop for a month, and when he
did start drinking again, he took the picture down and never put
it back up."

Vienna smiled at her brother's amusement, but she didn't respond. She simply couldn't adjust herself to these strange, free Western ways. Her brother had begged her to stay away from a materialistic and flashy marriage, but he not only allowed a cowboy to keep her picture in his room, but he also spoke of her and used her name in a temperance lecture. Vienna couldn't help but feel disgusted.

She was saved from her brother's plan to reform Norris for a month by a series of events. First, Norris's audacity towards her, then Florence Kingsley treating her as an equal, followed by her elder sister's easy acceptance of the visitor who had hobnobbed with royalty. Ken's slight scorn and amused comment about her picture and the name "Princess" compounded her feelings of alienation, but also piqued her interest in the West. She resolved to learn more about this incomprehensible place.

"Princess, I must run down to the siding," Ken said, checking his watch. "We're loading a shipment of cattle. I'll be back by supper-time and bring Stillwell with me. You'll like him. Give me the check for your trunk."

She went into the little bedroom and picked up her bag, taking out several checks. "Six! Six trunks!" he exclaimed. "Well, I'm very glad you intend to stay awhile. Say, Princess, it will take me as long to realize who you really are as it'll take to break you of being a tenderfoot. I hope you packed a riding-suit. If not, you'll have to wear trousers! You'll have to do that, anyway, when we go up in the mountains."

"No!" she protested.

"You sure will, as Florence says."

"We shall see about that. I don't know what's in the trunks. I never pack anything. My dear brother, what do I have maids for?"

"How did it come that you didn't travel with a maid?"

"I wanted to be alone. But don't you worry. I shall be able to look after myself. I dare say it will be good for me."

She went to the gate with him. "What a shaggy, dusty horse! He's wild, too.

"Do you just let him stand there without being tied up? I'd think he'd run off," Vienna questioned.

"Tenderfoot! You'll be quite the entertainment, Princess, especially for the cowboys," Ken replied.

"Oh, really?" Vienna responded awkwardly.

"Yes, and in just three days they'll be fighting over you. That's going to worry me. Cowboys fall in love with any woman, young or old, pretty or ugly. And you, Good Lord! They'll go crazy for you," Ken stated.

"You're trying to be funny, Ken. I think I've had enough of cowboys, and it's only been one day," Vienna retorted.

"Don't judge too quickly. That was my mistake when I first got here. Well, I'll be going now. You should rest, you look tired," Ken advised.

Ken put his foot in the stirrup, and the horse started running as he slipped his leg over the saddle. Vienna watched in awe as he rode off. He moved with the horse, and she admired his cowboy style.

Vienna sat on the porch and observed her surroundings. The street was dusty and unappealing, and the houses were made of red cement. She realized that it was adobe, a building material she had read about. The street seemed endless, but she caught a glimpse of the dim, dark-blue outline of the mountains over the rooftops, which captivated her gaze.

She was a well-traveled woman, having seen the Adirondacks, the Alps, and the Himalayas. However, none of those majestic landscapes captivated her like the Rockies. The sight of these mountains cutting through the blue sky was enthralling to her. She couldn't help but think of them as distant and untouchable, like a mirage in the desert. Exhausted from the journey, she went to her room to rest and ended up falling asleep.

She was woken up by a knock on the door. It was Florence, who informed her that her brother had returned with a man named Stillwell. Vienna was introduced to Stillwell, a man who called himself the last of the cattlemen. He had lived in Texas and the Rockies his whole life. He greeted her with a booming voice and a handshake that almost crushed her hand. He was an old man with long furrows on his face and gray eyes that were almost hidden in wrinkles.

Vienna couldn't help but be fascinated by Stillwell's appearance and demeanor. He was unlike anyone she had ever met before.

In an instant, Vienna realized that the man's expression had changed from a smile to a hard, chiseled stone. Norris's toughness was intensified in this old man's face. "Miss Princess, it's a shame we weren't there to welcome you," Stillwell said. "Al and I went to the post office and exchanged a few pleasantries. Those messages should have been sent to the ranch. I'm afraid it was an uncomfortable situation for you last night at the station."

"I was a bit anxious and scared at first," Vienna replied.

"Well, let me tell you, there's no man in these parts except your brother that I'd rather have met you than Gene Norris," Stillwell said.

"Is that so?" Vienna asked.

"Yes, even taking into consideration Gene's weaknesses. I always say that I'm the last of the old cattlemen. Norris may not be a native Westerner, but he's my pick of the last of the cowboys. He's young, but he's the last of the old style, the charming and chivalrous kind. I dare say, Miss Princess, he's also the old hard-riding kind. People may not like Norris, but I'm speaking up for him because he's down, and maybe he scared you last night, being fresh from the East."

Vienna appreciated Stillwell's loyalty to the cowboy he cared for, but there was nothing for her to say, so she remained silent.

"Miss Princess, the day of the cattleman is coming to an end. The day of the cowboy, like Gene Norris, is over. There is no place for him. If it weren't for modern times, he would have been a gun-man, just like in Texas when I was ranching there in the '70s."

"He can't fit in anywhere now; he can't hold a job, and he's going down," lamented Mr. Stillwell.

"I'm sorry to hear that," murmured Vienna. "But Mr. Stillwell, aren't these modern days out here still a little wild? The conductor on my train told me about rebels, bandits, and raiders. I've had other impressions that were wild enough for me."

"Well, it's certainly more pleasant and exciting these days than it has been for many years," replied Stillwell. "The boys have taken to packing guns again. But that's owing to the revolution in Mexico. There's going to be trouble along the border. I reckon people in the East don't know there's a revolution. Madero will oust Diaz, and then some other rebel will oust Madero. It means trouble on the border and across the border, too. I wouldn't be surprised if Uncle Sam had to get involved. There have already been holdups on the railroads and raids along the Rio Grande Valley. And these little towns are full of Greasers, all disturbed by the fighting down in Mexico. We've been having shooting-scrapes and knifing-scrapes, and some cattle-raiding. I've been losing a few cattle right along. It reminds me of old times, and pretty soon, if it doesn't stop, I'll take the old-time way to stop it."

"Yes, indeed, Princess," added Ken. "You've come at an interesting time to visit us."

"Well, that sure appears to be so," rejoined Stillwell. "Norris got in trouble down here today, and I'm more than sorry to have to tell you that your name figured in it. But I couldn't blame him, for I sure would have done the same myself."

"Really?" asked Ken, laughing. "Well, tell us about it."

Vienna simply gazed at her brother, and although he seemed amused at her consternation, there was mortification in his face.

It was clear to Vienna that Stillwell loved to talk, as he sat with his hands spread over his knees, ready to make the most of this opportunity. "Miss Princess," he began, "now that you're in the West, you've got to take things as they come and worry about each thing a little less than the one before. If us old timers hadn't been that way, we wouldn't have lasted."

"Last night wasn't particularly bad, compared to some other nights lately. There wasn't much going on. But I had a hard knock. Yesterday, when we started with a bunch of cattle, I sent one of my cowboys, Danny Mains, ahead with money to pay off hands and bills. I wanted the money to get to town before dark. Well, Danny was held up. I don't distrust the lad. There have been strange Greasers in town lately, and maybe they knew about the money coming."

"When I arrived with the cattle, I was struggling to make ends meet. And today, I wasn't in any angelic mood. I went around poking my nose, trying to get a scent of that money. I happened to find myself in a hall that does duty as a jail, hospital, and election post. Last night was fiesta night for these Greasers, and one of them had been badly hurt and brought to the hall from the station. Someone had sent for a doctor, but he hadn't come yet. I've had some experience with gunshot wounds, so I took a look at him. He wasn't shot up much, but I thought there was a danger of blood poisoning. Anyway, I did all I could."

The hall was packed with cowboys, ranchers, miners, town folks, and even some strangers. Just as I was about to begin, Pat Hawe entered the room. "Pat's the sheriff," I explained to Miss Princess. "Sheriffs are probably new to you, but in the West, we don't have many real ones anymore. Garrett was the kind of sheriff that helped make a self-respecting country. He killed Billy the Kid, but was himself killed about a year ago. This Pat Hawe, well, I won't say what I think of him. He came into the hall, roaring about things. He was going to arrest Danny Mains on sight. I politely told Pat that the money was mine and he needn't get riled about it. If I wanted to trail the thief, I could do it just as well as anybody. Pat howled that law was law, and he was going to lay down the law. To me, it seemed like Pat was dead set on arresting the first man he could find an excuse to."

"Then he cooled down a bit and started asking questions about the wounded Greaser when Gene Norris walked in. Whenever Pat and Gene are together, it reminds me of the early days back in the '70s. Everyone shuts up because Pat hates Gene, and I don't think Gene is too fond of Pat either. They're natural enemies, and the events here in El Cajon have only made things worse."

"Hello, Norris! You're the feller I'm looking for," Pat said, as Gene walked in.

"Hey Norris, you're looking at me like I owe you money," said
Pat Norris, eyeing him with a sarcastic tone. "You seem to be in
quite a hurry to get away from me."Pat went red at the jab, but
he held his tongue. "Say, Norris, you think a lot of that fancy
horse you've got with the big name?""I sure do," replied Gene,
shortly."Well, where is he?""That's none of your business, Ha
we.""Oh really? Well, I think I can make it my business. Norris,
there were some strange happenings last night that you might
know something about. Danny Mains took Stillwell's money,
your roan horse is gone, that little Bonita girl is missing, and
this Greaser guy is almost gone too. Now, considering you were
up late and prowling around the station where this Greaser was
found, it's not unreasonable to think that you might know how
he got hurt, is it?"Norris laughed coldly and rolled a cigarette,
keeping his eyes fixed on Pat. "If I'd shot the Greaser, it wouldn't
have been such a sloppy job.""I can arrest you on suspicion,
Norris, but before I do that, I want some evidence. I want
to find Danny Mains and that little Greaser girl. I want to
know what's happened to your horse. You've never lent him
out before, and there aren't enough raiders across the border to
steal him from you. It's all very suspicious.""You sure are a great
detective, Hawe. I wish you the best of luck," replied Norris.Pat
was clearly agitated by Norris' nonchalant attitude and began to
pace and swear. Then he had an idea. It was written all over his
face as he pointed his finger in Norris' face."You were drunk last
night, weren't you?"Norris didn't flinch. "I met a lady on the
train," he replied in a menacing tone."You met Al Florentino's
sister, and you took her up to Kingsley's," accused Pat.

"I'm gonna go up there and ask this fine lady some questions, and if she's as tight-lipped as you, I'll haul her in!" Pat Hawe barked, his cowboy hat tilted back on his head.Gene Norris, who I expected to see fly off the handle like a bull in a china shop, surprised me with his calm demeanor. He was thinking hard before he spoke."Pat, that's a foolish idea, and if you go through with it, you'll regret it for the rest of your life. There's no reason to scare Miss Florentino, and trying to arrest her would be a grave injustice that won't be tolerated in El Cajon. If you're angry with me, throw me in jail. I'll go. And if you want to hurt Al Florentino, do it like a man. Don't take your anger out on us by insulting a lady who's come here for a visit. We're bad enough without stooping to the level of those Greasers."It was a long conversation for Gene, and I was as surprised as everyone else. It was strange to see Gene, who usually had a fiery temper, talking so softly to the red-eyed sheriff. Pat looked like a devilishly gleeful coyote, and if something about Gene hadn't held me back, I might have jumped in myself. It was clear to me and the others who talked about it later that Pat Hawe had forgotten about the law and the officer in the man, consumed by his hatred."I'm going, and I'm going right now!" Pat shouted, and afterward, you could hear a clock ticking a mile away. Norris seemed to be choking, bewildered by the idea of Hawe confronting Miss Florentino."And think about who she is, man! It's Miss Florentino! Even if you were crazy or drunk, you couldn't do it," Norris burst out finally."Couldn't I? Well, I'll show you real quick. I don't care who she is," Pat replied, his eyes flashing with malice.

I've heard of those fancy Eastern women, but they ain't all that great. Suddenly, Hawe stopped talking and went for his gun, his face turning from red to green. Stillwell paused to catch his breath and wiped his sweaty brow. His rough face softened and he smiled as he continued his story. "Then, Miss Princess, something amazing happened. Norris took Pat's gun away and threw it on the ground. It was the most beautiful thing I've ever seen, but it was over so quickly. Later, when the doctor came, he had another patient besides the wounded Greaser. He said the new patient would need about four months to recover. Gene Norris had already hit the trail for the border."

Chapter Five.

The following morning, Vienna was woken up by her brother
before dawn. The chilly air made her shiver, and in the dim
light, she had to search for matches and a lamp. Her usual lazy attitude disappeared with a splash of cold water. When Ken knocked
on her door and informed her that he was leaving a pitcher of
hot water outside, she replied, teeth chattering, "Th-thank y-you,
b-but I d-don't ne-need any now." However, she had to warm her
numb fingers before she could fasten her hooks and buttons. After
dressing, she noticed in the faint mirror that there were tinges of
red in her cheeks. "Well, if I haven't got some color!" she exclaimed.
The dining room was where breakfast awaited her, and the sisters
dined with her. Vienna swiftly caught the sense of brisk activity
that seemed to be in the air.

The sound of men's boots and voices echoed through the back
of the house, accompanied by the dull thump of hooves and the
creak of wheels outside. Ken burst into the room, announcing that
they were rushing Vienna off to the ranch for the fall round-up.
She would be riding in the buck-board with Florence and Stillwell,
while Ken rode ahead with the boys to prepare for her arrival.
Her baggage would follow, but not until tomorrow. The journey

would be a long one, nearly fifty miles by wagon-road. Florence reminded Vienna to bring a couple of robes to keep warm. They were waiting for her outside.

As they set off, the gray gloom slowly began to lighten. Horses champed their bits and pounded the gravel beneath them. Stillwell gruffly greeted Vienna from the front seat of the vehicle, while Ken bundled her up in the back with Florence and wrapped them in robes. With a crack of his whip, Stillwell urged the team into a trot and they were off.

Florence whispered to Vienna that Stillwell was always grouchy in the morning, but he would thaw out once it got warmer. As they left El Cajon behind, Vienna was glad to be leaving and found it easier to dispel the persistent memories that haunted her. Soon, a line of horsemen appeared from the right and fell in behind Ken, gradually drawing ahead until they disappeared from sight. The gray gloom lightened into dawn, revealing a barren landscape with no hills or trees to break the monotony.

The ground seemed level, but the road had its ups and downs, with little ridges to cross. Vienna looked back towards El Cajon and the mountains she had seen the day before, but all she saw was barren and dark ground, much like what lay before her. A gust of cold wind hit her face, causing her to shiver. Florence noticed and pulled up the second robe, tucking it tightly around Vienna up to her chin. "If the wind picks up, you'll definitely feel it," the Western girl said. Vienna replied that she was already feeling it. The wind seemed to penetrate through the robes, and it was cold, crisp, and biting. It was so thin that she had to breathe as if she were under normal exertion. It hurt her nose and made her lungs ache. "Are you cold?" Vienna asked. "Me?" Florence laughed. "I'm used to it. I never get cold." With ungloved hands on the outside of the robe, the Western girl sat confidently. Vienna thought she had never seen such a healthy, clear-eyed, and splendid girl. "Do you like watching the sunrise?" Florence asked. "Yes, I think I do," Vienna replied thoughtfully. "Honestly, I haven't seen one in years." "We have beautiful sunrises, and the sunsets from the ranch are absolutely glorious," Florence said. Long lines of pink fire ran parallel to the eastern horizon, which appeared to recede as the day grew brighter. A bank of thin, fleecy clouds turned rose-colored. To the south and west, the sky was dark, but it changed every moment, with the blue turning even deeper. The eastern sky was opalescent. Then, in one spot, a golden light appeared, slowly concentrating until it became like fire. The rosy bank of clouds turned to silver and pearl, and behind it rose a great circle of gold. Above the dark horizon, an intensely bright disk gleamed. It was the sun.

The sun rose quickly, illuminating the land between the ridges and adding depth and color to the landscape. "Well, well," drawled Stillwell, stretching his arms as if he had just woken up. "That's something." Florence nudged Vienna and winked at her. "Good morning, girls," continued old Bill, cracking his whip. "Miss Princess, it'll be an interesting ride all morning. But when we get a bit further, you'll enjoy it. Look over there, to the southwest, just beyond that ridge." Vienna scanned the gray horizon until she saw dark-blue spires rising in the distance. "Peloncillo Mountains," said Stillwell. "That's home, where we're headed. We won't see them again until afternoon when they suddenly appear." Peloncillo!

Vienna murmured the name, wondering where she had heard it before. Then she remembered. The cowboy Norris had told the little Mexican girl Bonita to "hit the Peloncillo trail." Vienna had a shiver, not from the cold wind. "There's a jack!" cried Florence suddenly. Vienna saw her first jackrabbit. It was as big as a dog, with enormous ears. It seemed to be almost tame, and the horses kicked up dust as they trotted past it. From then on, old Bill and Florence competed to point out various things along the way. Coyotes scurrying into the brush; buzzards flapping over the carcass of a cow that had been stuck in a wash; strange little lizards running quickly across the road; cattle grazing in the hollows; adobe huts of Mexican herders; wild, shaggy horses with heads held high, watching from the gray ridges. At first, Vienna was indifferent to these sights because indifference had become her habit. But as she rode on, her interest grew and flourished, almost without her noticing it.

As Vienna rode along the dusty trail, she couldn't help but feel a sense of restlessness. It wasn't until she spotted a young Mexican boy on a tiny burro that she felt a spark of excitement within her. The crisp air filled her lungs and she knew that something new was on the horizon. She couldn't quite explain it, but she felt a pull towards the wild and natural world that surrounded her.

As the sun rose higher, Vienna's companions chatted away and the horses kept a steady trot. They eventually came upon a group of cowboys who had stopped for a midday meal. Stillwell couldn't contain his hunger and suggested they do the same.

Vienna hopped off her horse and stretched her legs while Florence prepared lunch. She heard the sound of Stillwell unharnessing the team and urging his horses to roll around in the dirt. One of them finally succeeded and Vienna couldn't help but let out a small chuckle at the sight.

The rest of the day was filled with more riding and more sights to see. Vienna felt a sense of freedom and excitement that she had never experienced before. She knew that this trip was going to be a turning point in her life, and she was eager to see where the trail would lead her.

One of the cowboys couldn't manage to roll over and gave up, instead half-rising to his feet before lying down on the other side. Florence, smiling, remarked, "He's sure going to feel the ground." Vienna joined in, "Miss Florentino, I suppose that prize horse of yours, White Stockings, would spoil his coat if he were here to roll in this greasewood and cactus."

During lunch, Vienna noticed that the three cowboys were all very interested in her. She returned the attention, and it was clear that they were embarrassed by her gaze. Although they were grown men, one of them even sporting white hair, they acted like boys caught in the act of stealing a forbidden look at a pretty girl. Florence remarked, "Cowboys are sure all flirts," but Vienna could see the merriment in her eyes. The cowboys heard her and were suddenly ashamed, hurrying to perform their tasks. Vienna didn't see where they were being bold, but they seemed stricken with conscious guilt. She recalled the appraising looks of critical English eyes, the impudent French stares, and the burning Spanish glances that any American girl had to face abroad. Compared to foreign eyes, the cowboys seemed like smiling, eager babies.

"Haw, haw!" laughed Stillwell. "Florence, you hit the nail on the head. Cowboys are all plumb flirts. I was wondering why them boys were noonin' here. This ain't no place to noon. Ain't no grazin' or wood worth burnin' or nothin'. Them boys just held up, threw the packs, and waited for us. It ain't so surprisin' for Booly and Ned, they're young and coltish, but Nels there, why, he's old enough to be the paw of both you girls. It sure is amazin' strange."

A silence ensued. The white-haired cowboy, Nels, fussed aimlessly over the campfire and then straightened up with a very red face. "Bill, you're a dog-gone liar," he said.

"I ain't gonna be lumped in with Booly and Ned. Don't get me wrong, I love the ladies just as much as the next cowboy, but I ain't gonna go out of my way for 'em. I got enough riding to do as it is. Hey Bill, you see anything on the way out here with your sharp eyes?" Nels asked.

"Nah, I ain't seen nothin'," Bill replied bluntly. His demeanor changed as Nels drew him aside to show him some horse tracks in the dirt. "Take a look at these tracks," Nels said, pointing at the large hoofprints. "You recognize the horse?"

"Gene Norris's roan, if I'm not mistaken," exclaimed Bill as he dropped to his knees to scrutinize the tracks. "But they ain't fresh."

"I reckon they were made early yesterday morning," Nels said.

"What's the big deal?" Bill asked.

"It's clear as day that Gene wasn't riding his own horse," Nels replied. "Let's follow these tracks."

Bill walked slowly, muttering to himself, until he stopped and crawled about examining the horse tracks. "Whoever was riding Norris's horse met someone, but they didn't get down," Bill said.

"You're thinking straight, Bill," Nels replied.

Bill got up and walked swiftly to the left, then retraced his steps. "Nels, I don't like this one bit. These tracks lead straight to the Peloncillo trail," Bill said, looking at Nels with impatience.

"You know whose horse made those tracks?" asked one cowboy.

"I'm not sure," replied the other.

"It was Danny Mains's horse," said the first cowboy.

"How do you know that?" demanded the second cowboy.

"Bill, the left front foot of that little horse always wears a shoe that sets crooked. Any of the boys can tell you. I'd know that track if I was blind," explained the first cowboy.

The second cowboy kicked at a cactus plant, "Was Danny leaving or coming back?"

"I reckon he was heading across country for the Peloncillo trail. But I'm not sure without trailing him a ways. I was just waiting for you to come up," replied the first cowboy.

"Nels, do you think Danny ran away with that little hussy, Bonita?" asked the second cowboy.

"Bill, he sure was sweet on Bonita, just like Gene was, and Ed Linton before he got engaged, and all the boys. She's a real beauty. Danny might have run away with her. Danny was held up on the way to town, and then in the shame of it, he got drunk. But he'll show up soon," replied Nels.

"Well, maybe you and the boys are right. I believe you are. Nels, there's no doubt on earth about who was riding Norris's horse?" asked Bill.

"That's as plain as the horse's tracks," replied Nels.

"It's all amazingly strange. It beats me. I wish the boys would ease up on drinking. I was pretty fond of Danny and Gene. I'm afraid Gene is done for, sure. If he crosses the border where he can fight, it won't take long for him to get shot. I guess I'm getting old. I don't handle things like I used to," said Bill.

"Bill, I should hit the Peloncillo trail. Maybe I can find Danny," suggested Nels.

"I reckon you should, Nels. But don't take more than a couple of days. We can't do much on the round-up without you. I'm short of boys," replied Bill.

That ended the conversation.

Stillwell wasted no time in hitching up his team as the cowboys went out to retrieve their strayed horses. Vienna had been in-

trigued and Florence noticed. "Things happen, Miss Florentino,"
she said solemnly. Vienna pondered, but then Florence began
humming a tune and repacking what was left of the lunch. Vienna felt a strong admiration and respect for this Western girl. She
appreciated the consideration or delicacy or wisdom - whatever
it was that kept Florence from inquiring about her thoughts on
the recent events. They were soon back on the road, gradually
descending before ascending a long ridge that had blocked their
view for hours. It was a tiring climb, with the sun, dust, and
limited view. When they finally reached the top, Vienna gasped
in amazement. A beautiful, smooth, gray valley stretched below
them, rising up on the other side in little ridges like waves, leading
to the foothills dotted with clumps of brush or trees, and beyond, dark mountains, pine-fringed and crag-spired. "Well, Miss
Princess, now we're getting somewhere," said Stillwell, cracking
his whip. "Ten miles across this valley and we'll be in the foothills
where the Apaches used to run." "Ten miles!" exclaimed Vienna.
"It looks like half a mile to me." "Well, young woman, before you
go riding off alone, you need to get used to Western distance.
Now, what do you call those black things on the slope over there?"
"Horsemen. No, cattle," Vienna replied hesitantly. "Nope. Just
plain, everyday cactus. And look down the valley. A pretty forest,
isn't it?" he asked, pointing. Vienna saw a gorgeous forest in the
center of the valley to the south. "Well, Miss Princess, that's just
the deceiving air. There is no forest."

"It's a mirage," Vienna exclaimed, squinting her eyes towards a dark
shape in the distance. The shape seemed to float in the air, with
no distinct boundaries, flickering and fading until it disappeared

completely. The mountains receded once again behind the horizon, and the horses slowed to a leisurely walk. The road ahead led to a mile of rolling ridge and then foothills, with winding valleys and dry ravines filled with trees, brush, and rocks. Although there was no water, the sandy washes provided evidence of past floods. Vienna was exhausted from the heat and dust, but she kept her eyes open and saw beautiful birds, quails with crests, rabbits, and even a deer.

"Miss Princess," Stillwell said, "in the old days, this country was a dangerous place to live in. You probably don't know much about those times. You were hardly born then. I'll tell you about how I fought Comanches in the Panhandle, which used to be in northern Texas, and how I had some hair-raising scares with Apaches in this area."

He went on to tell Vienna about Cochise, the chief of the Chiricahua Apaches, who was the most savage and bloodthirsty tribe that ever terrorized the pioneers. Cochise had once befriended the whites, but he was betrayed and became their most implacable enemy. Geronimo, another Apache chief, had gone on the warpath as recently as 1885, leaving a trail of bloodshed along the New Mexico and Arizona border. Lone ranchers and cowboys had been killed, and mothers had even shot their children before killing themselves at the sight of the Apaches. The mere mention of the name Apache sent shivers down the spines of women in the Southwest during those days.

Vienna was unsettled, so she was relieved when the old frontiersman changed the topic to the Spaniards' settling of the country. He

spoke of legends of lost gold mines passed down to the Mexicans, stories of heroism, mystery, and religion. Despite the
spread of civilization to the Southwest, the Mexicans remained
superstitious. They still believed in the legends of treasures
hidden in the walls of their missions and that unseen hands
rolled rocks down the gullies onto the heads of prospectors
who dared to hunt for the lost mines of the padres.

"Up in the mountains back of my ranch, there's a lost mine,"
Stillwell said. "Maybe it's only a legend, but somehow I believe
it's there. Other lost mines have been found. And as for the
rolling stones, I know it's true. Anyone can find out if they go
up the gulch. Maybe that's only the weathering of the cliffs.
This Southwest is a sleepy, strange country, and Miss Princess,
you're going to love it. You'll call it romantic, and I reckon
that's correct. A person gets lazy out here and dreamy, and they
want to put off work until tomorrow. Some folks say it's a land
of mañana, a land of tomorrow. That's the Mexican of it.

"But I like best to think of what an educated lady said to me
once, a lady like you, Miss Princess. She said it's a land where
it's always afternoon. I liked that. I always wake up sore in the
mornings and don't feel good until noon. But in the afternoon,
I get warm and like things. And sunset is my time. I don't
want anything finer than sunset from my ranch. You can look
out over a valley that spreads wide between the Guadalupe
Mountains and the Chiricahuas, down across the red Arizona
desert clear to the Sierra Madres in Mexico."

"Miss Princess, we've come two hundred miles and everything's as clear as day," the old cattleman exclaimed. "And the sun sets behind it all. When my time comes, I want to be on my porch smoking my pipe and facing the west." Vienna listened as the old man talked, while Florence dozed in her seat. The sun began to set, and the horses climbed steadily up a steep ascent. Stillwell got out and walked, leading the team.

Vienna grew tired and closed her eyes. When she opened them again, the sky had turned from glaring white to a steel-blue, and the air was growing chilly. Shadows crept up out of the hollows. Stillwell returned to the driving seat and chuckled to the horses. "Well, Flo," he said, "I reckon we should finish the rest of that lunch before it gets dark."

Florence produced the basket from under the seat, and they ate as the short twilight shaded and gloom filled the hollows. Vienna saw the first star, a faint winking point of light. The sky changed to a hazy gray, and Vienna saw it gradually clear and darken to show other faint stars. The gray deepened, and the stars brightened, some new-born ones joining in. Night came on the cold wind, and Vienna was glad to have the robes close around her and to lean against Florence. The hollows were black, but the tops of the foothills gleamed pale in a soft light. The horses' steady tramp went on, and the wheels creaked and gravel crunched. Vienna grew so sleepy that she couldn't keep her weary eyelids from falling.

Vienna drifted in and out of consciousness as the buckboard bounced along the rough terrain. She was jolted awake by the oc-casional bump in the road, but there were moments when she lost all sense of where she was. Eventually, a jarring movement brought her back to reality, and she found herself leaning on Florence's shoulder. She laughed, apologizing for her drowsiness.

Florence reassured her that they were almost at the ranch, and Vienna noticed that the horses had started trotting again. The wind had picked up, and the night had grown darker. The hills were no longer as steep, and the sky was a gorgeous deep blue, illuminated by millions of stars. Vienna was struck by their beauty, marveling at how white and alive they looked. The stars seemed to call to her, stirring up vague but familiar emotions.

Chapter Six.

Vienna was abruptly awoken by the vigorous crackling and roaring of the fire. As she opened her eyes, she found herself staring at a colossal stone fireplace that contained a bundle of blazing sticks. Someone had kindled a fire while she was asleep. For a moment, she felt disoriented and lost. She could only vaguely recollect arriving at the ranch and being escorted into a colossal, dimly lit room. She had fallen asleep instantly and woke up without any memory of how she had gotten into bed. But the feeling of bewilderment vanished as quickly as it had arrived. Vienna was fully alert within an instant.

The bed was located near one side of a vast chamber. The adobe walls looked like they belonged to a hall in an ancient feudal castle, with stone floors, walls, and massive, darkened rafters that ran across the ceiling. The meager pieces of furniture were old and poorly maintained. The room was flooded with light from four windows - two on each side of the fireplace and another large one near the bed. As she looked out from the bed, Vienna could see a dark and slow up-sweep of mountain in the distance.

As she gazed at the crackling fire, Vienna mustered up the courage to leave her warm bed. The room was frigid, and her bare feet quickly retreated back under the covers. She was still contemplating getting up when Florence knocked on the door, holding a steaming hot water jug.

"Good morning, Miss Florentino. I hope you slept well. You were exhausted last night. This old rancho house can be as cold as a barn, but it'll warm up soon. Al's gone with the boys and Bill. We'll ride down to the range after a while when your baggage arrives," Florence said with a smile.

Florence wore a woolen blouse with a scarf around her neck, a short corduroy divided skirt, and boots. She energetically added wood to the fireplace while laying out Vienna's clothes and heating a rug for the floor by her bedside.

"Al told me you weren't used to being without your maid. Would you like me to help you?" Florence asked.

Vienna declined, insisting that she could take care of herself. After breakfast, Florence showed Vienna around the charming old Spanish house, which had a courtyard or patio, as Florence called it. The house was enormous, with doors opening into the courtyard. Vienna thought it would make a delightful home. She wondered if the house had been a Spanish barracks because of its immense size.

As Vienna entered the house, she noticed that many of the rooms were dark and empty, with no windows to let in any light. Others were filled with ranchers' tools and supplies, such as sacks of grain and bales of hay. Florence referred to the latter as alfalfa. Despite the lack of furnishings, the house itself was well-maintained and picturesque. However, the living rooms were sparsely furnished, with only the bare essentials that were worn out and uncomfortable.

Once outside, Vienna forgot about the dreary interior of the house. Florence led her to a porch and gestured towards a vast expanse of color. "That's what Bill likes," she said. At first, Vienna couldn't distinguish between the sky and the land. The sheer size of the scenery was overwhelming. She sat down on an old rocking chair, staring out at the view, knowing that she couldn't fully comprehend the reality of what lay before her.

"We're up at the edge of the foothills," Florence explained. "Remember when we rode around the northern end of the mountain range? Well, that's behind us now. If you look across the line, you'll see Arizona and Mexico. The gray slope you see is the head of the San Bernardino Valley. Straight ahead are the black Chiricahua Mountains, and to the south are the Guadalupe Mountains. The red gulf you see in between is the desert, and far beyond the dim, blue peaks are the Sierra Madres in Mexico."

Vienna listened intently and gazed out with wide eyes, wondering if what she saw was just a mirage. It seemed so different from anything else she had ever seen, so vast, grand, and endless. "It'll take some time getting used to being up high and seeing so much," Florence said. "That's the secret. We're up high, the air is clear, and we can see the whole world beneath us. Doesn't it somehow make you feel at peace? Well, it will. Now, see those specks in the valley? They're stations, little towns. The railroad goes down that way."

Chiricahua is the largest speck around here, and it's a good forty miles away by trail. Just north of here, you can see Don Carlos's rancho, which is about fifteen miles away. I sure wish it were a thousand miles away though. That little green square about halfway between here and Don Carlos's place is Al's ranch. If you look below us, you'll see the adobe houses of the Mexicans. There's even a church down there. And if you look to the left, you'll see Stillwell's corrals and bunkhouses, as well as his stables, which are all falling apart. The ranch has gone to ruin, just like all the other ranches around here. But most of them are little one-horse affairs. See that cloud of dust down in the valley? That's the round-up. The boys and the cattle are down there. Wait, let me grab my glasses.

By using Vienna's glasses, she could see a massive herd of cattle in the foreground. The cattle were moving in every direction, creating dark, thick streams and dotted lines. She could also see streaks and clouds of dust, running horses, and a band of horses grazing. She even spotted horsemen standing still like sentinels, and others in action. "The round-up! I want to know all about it and see it!" exclaimed Vienna. "Please tell me what it means, what it's for, and then take me down there."

"I'd be happy to take you down there, Miss Florentino, but I don't think you'll want to get too close," replied the cowboy. "Most Eastern folks who regularly eat their choice cuts of roast beef and porterhouse don't have any idea about the open range and the struggles cattle have to go through, not to mention the hard life of cowboys. It'll sure open your eyes, Miss Florentino. I'm glad you want to know though. Your brother would have been a great success in this cattle business if it wasn't for the crooked work of rival ranchers. He'll make it yet, despite them."

"Well, he certainly will," agreed Vienna. "But please, tell me all about the round-up."

"Sure thing. Well, first of all, every cattleman has to have a brand to identify his stock."

In the vast expanse of our ranges, it's impossible for any cattleman or even a hundred cowboys to recognize every single cow in a large herd. You see, there are no fences in our land, it's all open to everyone. Hopefully, one day we'll have enough wealth to fence our range. The different herds graze together, so every calf must be caught and branded with its mother's mark if possible. It's not an easy job, mind you. An unbranded calf that has been weaned and left to fend for itself is called a "maverick." Whoever finds and brands a maverick gets to keep it. These little calves that lose their mothers have a hard time surviving. Many of them die, and predators like coyotes, wolves, and lions prey on them.

We have two major round-ups every year, but our boys brand cattle all year round. A calf should be branded as soon as it's found to prevent cattle-thieves. We don't have the same rustling of herds and bunches of cattle like we used to, but calf-thieves are still around, and they have many cunning tricks. They might kill the calf's mother or slit its tongue so it can't suckle, causing it to lose its mother. They steal and hide a calf, watch it grow, and brand it when it's big enough to fend for itself. Sometimes they make imperfect brands and finish them later.

Our big round-up happens in the fall when there's plenty of grass and water, and all the riding-stock and cattle are in great shape. The cattlemen in the valley meet with their cowboys and gather all the cattle they can find. They brand and separate each man's herd and drive it toward home. Then they move on up or down the valley, set up another camp, and gather more cattle. It takes weeks to finish this task.

There are plenty of Greasers out here with their own little herds of stock. They're a crafty and greedy bunch, according to Bill. Apparently, he knows some vaqueros who never owned a single steer or cow, yet now they've got themselves a growing herd. Can't say that's a phenomenon exclusive to the Greasers, though. White cowboys have been known to do the same. It's not as common as it used to be, though.

Vienna was curious about the horses, so Florence obliged her with some information. The cow-ponies, or broncos as the boys call them, are wilder than the steers they have to chase. Bill owns some broncos that have never been broken and never will be. Not every boy can ride them, either. The vaqueros, on the other hand, have the finest horses. Don Carlos has a black horse that Florence would give anything to own. Gene Norris has a Mexican horse that's the swiftest and proudest she's ever seen. She's even ridden him before and he can really run. Plus, he likes women, which is always a plus in a horse.

At breakfast, Al and Bill were wrangling over which horse Vienna should have, but they left the decision up to Florence until after the round-up. Then every cowboy on the range will offer her their best mount. Florence suggests they go out to the corrals and check out the remaining horses.

The morning hours fly by for Vienna as she spends most of the time on the porch taking in the ever-changing vista. At noon, a teamster arrives with her trunks. While Florence helps the Mexican woman prepare lunch, Vienna unpacks some of her belongings and gets out what she'll need immediately. After lunch, she changes into her riding-habit and finds Florence waiting with the horses.

The Western girl took one quick glance at Vienna's appearance and smiled with delight. "You look incredible, Miss Florentino! That riding outfit is brand new. I can't even imagine how it would look on another woman, but on you, it's stunning. Bill won't let you near the cowboys though. If they catch a glimpse of you, it'll be the end of the round-up."

As they rode down the slope, Florence spoke about the open ranges of New Mexico and Arizona. "Water is scarce," she said. "If Bill could afford to bring water down from the mountains, he'd have the best ranch in the valley."

She continued to talk about the mild winter climate and hot summers. Warm, sunny days were common almost all year round. Some summers brought rain, while others brought the dreaded ano seco of the Mexicans. Rain was always anticipated and prayed for during midsummer, and when it came, the grama-grass would sprout up, turning the valleys green from mountain to mountain. The intersecting valleys, nestled between long foothills, provided the best pasture for cattle, which were eagerly sought by the Mexicans who only had small herds to tend to. Stillwell's cowboys were always chasing these vaqueros off land that belonged to Stillwell. He owned twenty thousand acres of unfenced land adjacent to the open range. Don Carlos had even more acreage than that, and his cattle were always mingling with Stillwell's. In return, Don Carlos's vaqueros were constantly chasing Stillwell's cattle away from the Mexican watering holes. Bad blood had been brewing for years, and now relations were strained to the breaking point.

As Vienna rode along, she carefully observed her surroundings. The soil was sandy and porous, which explained why the rain and water from the few springs disappeared so quickly.

From a distance, the grama-grass looked thick, but up close it was sparse. Bunches of greasewood and cactus plants dotted the grass. Vienna was surprised that, despite riding for a while, they hadn't gotten any closer to the round-up. It wasn't until they had traveled for miles that the slope of the valley became noticeable. Looking ahead, Vienna thought the valley was only a few miles wide and that she could walk her horse across it in an hour. But the black, bold range of Chiricahua Mountains in the distance was a long day's journey even for a hard-riding cowboy. It was only by looking back that Vienna could grasp the true distance they had covered. Gradually, the black dots in the distance became larger and took the shape of cattle and horses moving around a great dusty patch.

In another half-hour, Vienna and Florence rode to the outskirts of the scene of action. They stopped near a huge wagon where over a hundred horses grazed and whistled and trotted around. Four cowboys stood mounted guard over the horse drove. About a quarter of a mile farther out was a dusty melee. A roar of tramping hoofs filled Vienna's ears as the lines of cattle merged into a great, moving herd half-obscured by dust. "I can't make out what's going on," said Vienna. "I want to go closer." They trotted across half the distance, and when Florence stopped again, Vienna wasn't satisfied and asked to be taken even nearer. This time, before they reined in again, Al Florentino saw them and wheeled his horse in their direction. He yelled something that Vienna couldn't understand, then halted them. "Close enough," he called, but in the din, his voice was not very clear.

"It ain't safe here with them wild steers!" exclaimed Al as he greeted the two girls, Vienna and Florence. "I'm glad you came, girls. Princess, what do you think of that bunch of cattle?" Vienna was taken aback by the noise, the dust, and the constant commotion. She could barely form a response. "They're milling, Al," Florence said. "We just rounded them up. They're milling, and that's bad. The vaqueros are tough as nails. They beat us all and we drove some, too." Al was drenched in sweat, covered in dust, and gasping for air. "I'm off now. Flo, my sister will have had enough of this in about two minutes. Take her back to the wagon. I'll let Bill know you're here and come in whenever I get a chance." The chaos of bellowing, horns cracking, hooves pounding, and cowboys flying in all directions disoriented Vienna and frightened her a bit. But she was captivated and determined to stay until she fully comprehended the meaning behind the spectacle. She decided to take it all in slowly, bit by bit.Florence asked if Vienna wanted to stay longer, and she eagerly accepted. Florence warned her, "If a runaway steer or angry cow comes this way, let your horse go. He'll get out of the way."The danger added to the excitement, and Vienna became engrossed in the scene. The massive herd of cattle appeared to be swirling like a vortex. Vienna finally grasped the meaning of the term "milling" in the range lexicon. But when she looked at one end of the herd, she saw stationary cows facing outward and calves cowering in fear. The movement of the cattle slowed from the center of the herd to the perimeter, and eventually came to a stop. The thundering hooves, cracking horns, and thudding heads also subsided, but the bellowing and mooing persisted.

As the herd spread out before her, Vienna watched intently as the cowboys on horseback worked to keep the cattle in line. Suddenly, stragglers appeared to be on the verge of breaking through the line, and chaos erupted. Vienna struggled to keep up with everything that was happening within her view, as the cowboys darted into the herd and drove out the cattle.

Amidst the commotion, Vienna's attention was drawn to a cowboy on a white horse who was chasing after a steer. With lightning-fast reflexes, he whirled his lasso around his head and threw it, expertly catching the leg of the steer. The white horse came to a sudden stop, and the steer slid to the ground. In a flash, the cowboy was out of the saddle, tying the legs of the steer with a rope before it could rise.

As Vienna watched in awe, another cowboy approached with a branding iron, which he applied to the flank of the steer. The animal jumped up with a start, looking for a way to escape the pain. Meanwhile, Vienna could see fires in the background, where men were heating the branding irons. She winced as she saw the smoke rising from the hot iron searing the heifer's hide, but she was determined not to let her sensitivities get the better of her.

Despite her lack of experience with the rough work of the cowboys, Vienna felt an inexplicable desire to learn more about their everyday duties. Just then, Florence pointed out a dark-faced Mexican riding by on a black horse - Don Carlos.

From a distance, he looked like an Italian bandit, but she couldn't quite make out his features. He was mounted on a magnificent horse. Stillwell rode up to the girls and greeted them in his booming voice. "Right in the middle of things, hey? Well, that's just fine. I'm glad to see, Miss Princess, that you're not afraid of a little dust or the smell of burning hide and hair."

"Couldn't you brand the calves without hurting them?" Vienna asked.

"Haw, haw! Why, they ain't hurt none. They just bawl for their mamas. Sometimes, though, we have to hurt one just to find out which one is his mama."

"I want to know how you tell what brand to put on those calves that are separated from their mothers," Vienna continued.

"That's decided by the round-up bosses. I have one boss and Don Carlos has one. They decide everything, and they have to be obeyed. There's Nick Steele, my boss. Watch him! He's riding a bay in among the cattle there. He orders the calves and steers to be cut out. Then the cowboys do the cutting out and the branding. We try to divide up the mavericks as near as possible."

At that moment, Vienna's brother joined the group, looking for Stillwell. "Bill, Nels just rode in," he said.

"Good! We sure need him. Any news of Danny Mains?"

"No. Nels said he lost the trail when he got on hard ground."

"Well, well. Say, Al, your sister is really taking to the round-up. And the boys are getting wise. See that son-of-a-gun Ambrose cutting capers all around. He'll sure do his prettiest. Ambrose is a ladies' man, he thinks."

The two men and Florence joined in teasing Vienna a little and drew her attention to what seemed to be unnecessary feats of horsemanship all made around her. The cowboys showed their interest with covert glances while recoiling a lasso or while passing to and fro.

Vienna was not amused at the moment, the situation was too serious. She sat on her horse and watched the vaqueros, who were fascinating to her. They were agile and dark, their lariats flying everywhere, as they rode their horses and pulled down calves and yearlings to the ground. Vienna winced as their silver rowels dug into their horses' flanks, seeing the blood and hair on their spurs.

The vaqueros were cruel to their mounts and cattle, breaking the legs of calves and leaving them to die until a white cowboy came along to shoot them. Calves were dragged for many yards, and steers were pulled by one leg. Vienna had seen the Cossacks and Tatars of the Russian steppes, but these vaqueros were the most superb horsemen she had ever seen. They were swift, graceful, daring, and their lassos always hit their marks.

The cowboys were also skilled horsemen, but they showed more consideration for their steeds and cattle than the vaqueros. They changed mounts more frequently, and the horses they unsaddled were not as spent, wet, or covered in lather. It took Vienna an hour or more of observation to realize how toilsome and dangerous the cowboys' work was. They were continually among wild, vicious, and wide-horned steers, and there was little to no rest for them. The cowboys owed their lives to their horses, as the danger came mostly when they leaped off to tie and brand a calf they had thrown. Some of the cows charged with lowered, twisting horns, and Vienna's heart leaped to her throat for fear a man would be gored.

As the rodeo began, a cowboy successfully roped a bawling calf, causing its mother to charge towards him. He quickly rolled over and ran away, but his bow-legged gait slowed him down. Nearby, another cowboy was thrown off his horse by a wild steer, causing his horse to bolt away. Meanwhile, a big steer was taken down by a lasso, and the cowboy deftly jumped off his horse to release the animal. But the horse suddenly reared up, kicked and ran in circles around the steer, dragging the cowboy along the ground. Vienna watched in awe as the cowboy skillfully controlled his horse and finally freed himself from the rope.

In the midst of all this chaos, two horses collided, causing one rider to fall off and be kicked by the other horse. The injured cowboy limped back to his horse and angrily struck it, only to be met with a vicious attempt to bite. Despite the constant danger and noise of bawling animals and shouting cowboys, the rodeo participants worked with good humor, taking sharp orders and responding in jest. Some sang, some whistled, some smoked cigarettes, but all were drenched in sweat under the hot sun. Their red faces were covered in dust, making it difficult to distinguish between cowboys and vaqueros. Blood stained their tireless hands, but they continued to work with unmatched skill and mastery.

The thick, heavy air was oppressive, filled with the rank stench of cattle and burning hide. Vienna felt her stomach start to turn. She coughed and gagged on the dust, almost suffocating from the odor. But instead of leaving, Vienna became even more determined to stay. Florence and Stillwell both urged her to move away from the worst of it, but Vienna refused with a smile.

Her brother Al noticed her pale complexion and told her that the smell was making her sick. Vienna replied that she intended to stay until the day's work ended. Al gave her a strange look, but said nothing more.

The kindly Stillwell then began to explain to Vienna that she was witnessing the real life of a cattleman and cowboy, just as it was in the early days. He told her that some ranchers in Texas and

Arizona had taken on new-fangled ideas, but they had to stick to the old-fashioned, open-range round-up.

Vienna looked horrified at the cruelty of the round-up, but Stillwell explained that the work she had seen that day was no tougher than most days for a cowboy. They had long hours on horseback, poor food, slept on the ground, and faced loneliness, dust, sun, wind, and thirst day in and day out, all year round.

Stillwell pointed out Nels, a cowboy with white hair, red, thin, and hard-burned skin, and a hump on his shoulders. Nels' hands were so damaged that he couldn't pick up a pin or even untie a knot in his rope. Although he was young, Nels looked like an old man of sixty. Stillwell explained that Nels had seen a lifetime for every year of his life.

Nels owes his character to the Arizona desert and the life of a cowboy. He has ridden across Canyon Diablo, Verdi, and Tonto Basin and knows every inch of Aravaipa Valley and the Pinaleno country. He has even gone from Tombstone to Adam and has killed bad white men and Greasers before he was even twenty-one. Nels has seen and experienced more than most, and he has become a part of the desert, embodying its elements of stone, fire, silence, cactus, and force. He is a remarkable man, rough around the edges, but like a piece of quartz, he has pure gold within him.

Stillwell points out another cowboy named Monty Price, who is from Montana and has been hurt and limping without a horse or rope. Monty is a short, bow-legged man with a face as hard as a burned-out cinder. Despite his appearance, Stillwell insists that

Monty has seen years of riding through the Missouri bottoms and big prairies with high grass and fires.

Montana is known for having blizzards that can freeze cattle solid and leave horses dead. They say that facing a driving sleet with the temperature at forty below zero is quite a challenge. But Monty never complains about the cold. He's always searching for the sun. He used to be quite the looker, or so they say. The story that's told about Monty is this: he was caught in a prairie fire and could have easily saved himself. But there was a ranch right in the fire's path, and Monty knew that the rancher was away and his wife and baby were home alone. Monty knew that the wind was blowing in a way that would cause the ranch house to burn down. It was a risky move, but he went over and put the woman on his horse behind him, wrapped the baby and horse's head in a wet blanket, and rode away. It was quite a ride, I've heard. But the fire eventually caught up with Monty. The woman fell and was lost, and then his horse. Monty had to run, walk, and crawl through the fire with the baby, but he saved it. After that, Monty wasn't much good as a cowboy. He couldn't hold down a job. But he'll always have one with me, as long as I have a steer left.

Chapter Seven.

F or a whole week, the round-up was happening just a short
ride away from the ranch-house, and Vienna spent most of
her time on horseback, observing the hard work of the vaqueros
and cowboys. She thought she was stronger than she really was and
had to be helped off her horse more than once. Stillwell was happy
to have her around at first, but soon became worried about her. He
urged her to stay away from the round-up, and Florence was even
more concerned. Despite their pleas, Vienna remained determined
to stay.

Vienna was only beginning to comprehend the true nature of what
she was learning. It was far more than just the task of rounding up
cattle with cowboys. She cherished every moment of her opportunity and was reluctant to let it slip away. Her brother, though
busy with his own responsibilities, kept an eye on her. However,
he failed to notice her growing fatigue and the strain of excitement
that was taking a toll on her. He never suggested that she should
rest or go back to the house with Florence. Vienna often felt her
brother's piercing blue eyes on her face, and at times, she sensed
something more than just brotherly love. It was unsettling to think
that Ken might have guessed her predicament.

Ken tried to make the cowboys comfortable around Vienna by introducing them and cracking jokes. However, before the week was over, he advised her to stay away from the round-up. Even though he said it in a playful manner, he was serious. When Vienna asked him why, he revealed that he was worried about Don Carlos. Ken was afraid that Nels or Ambrose, or any of the cowboys, might harm the Mexican man because they were jealous of him following Vienna around. Vienna found it absurd, but it made her realize how wrapped up she had been in her own emotions, stirred up by the round-up's chaos and hard work. She remembered Don Carlos's presentation to her and how she had not liked his striking dark face with its prominent, glittering eyes and sinister lines. She had also been uncomfortable with his smooth, sweet, and insinuating voice and his subtle mannerisms with slow bows and gestures.

She had thought he looked sharp and suave on the magnificent black stallion. However, now that Ken's words made her think, she recalled that wherever she had been in the field the noble stallion, with his silver-mounted saddle and his dark rider, had been always in her vicinity. "Don Carlos has been after Florence for a long time," said Ken. "He's not a young man by any means. He's fifty, Bill says; but you can seldom tell a Mexican's age from his looks. Don Carlos is well educated and a man we know very little about. Mexicans of his kind don't regard women as we white men do. Now, my dear, beautiful sister from New York, I haven't much use for Don Carlos; but I don't want Nels or Ambrose to make a wild throw with a rope and pull the Don off his horse. So you had better ride up to the house and stay there." "Ken, you are joking, teasing me," said Vienna. "Indeed not," replied Ken. "What do you think,

Flo?" Florence replied that the cowboys would upon the slightest
provocation treat Don Carlos with less ceremony and gentleness
than a roped steer. Old Bill Stillwell came up to be importuned
by Ken regarding the conduct of cowboys on occasion, and he
not only corroborated the assertion, but added emphasis and evidence of his own. "An', Miss Princess," he concluded, "I reckon
if Gene Norris was ridin' fer me, thet grinnin' Greaser would hev
hed a bump in the dust before now." Vienna had been wavering
between sobriety and laughter until Stillwell's mention of his ideal
of cowboy chivalry decided in favor of the laughter. "I am not
convinced, but I surrender," she said. "You have only some occult
motive for driving me away. I am sure that handsome Don Carlos
is being unjustly suspected. But as I have seen a little of cowboys'
singular imagination and gallantry, I am rather inclined to fear
their possibilities.

"Goodbye," Vienna said before riding with Florence up the long,
gray slope to the ranch-house. She felt excessively weary that night,
which she attributed more to the strange workings of her mind
than to the physical exertion of riding and sitting her horse. The
next morning, she was not in the mood to rest. She didn't crave
activity, excitement, or pleasure. An unerring instinct, rising clear
from the thronging sensations of the last few days, told her that
she had missed something in life. It couldn't have been love, for she
loved her brother, sister, parents, and friends. It couldn't have been
consideration for the poor, the unfortunate, or the hapless, for she
had expressed her sympathy for them by giving freely. It couldn't
have been pleasure, culture, travel, society, wealth, or position, for
she had had all of those things all her life. Whatever this some-

thing was, she had baffling intimations of it, hopes that faded on the verge of realizations, haunting promises that were unfulfilled. Whatever it was, it had remained hidden and unknown at home, and here in the West, it began to allure and drive her to discovery. Therefore, she couldn't rest; she wanted to go and see; she was no longer chasing phantoms; it was a hunt for treasure that held aloof, as intangible as the substance of dreams. That morning she expressed a desire to visit the Mexican quarters lying at the base of the foothills. Florence protested that this was no place to take Vienna. But Vienna insisted, and it required only a few words and a persuading smile to win Florence over. From the porch, the cluster of adobe houses added a picturesque touch of color and contrast to the waste of the gray valley. Near at hand, they proved the enchantment lent by distance. They were old, crumbling, broken down, and squalid. A few goats climbed around upon them; a few mangy dogs barked an announcement of visitors; and then a troop of half-naked, dirty, ragged children ran out.

The group of Mexicans was initially frightened and shy, but they eventually warmed up to Vienna and Florence. The women managed to gather more children as they moved from house to house. Vienna was struck by the poor living conditions of these people and decided to take a closer look. She was greeted with shock and awe by the first woman she met. While Florence tried to communicate with the women, Vienna explored the small, squalid rooms. The stench of filth and vermin was overwhelming, and Vienna couldn't believe that such squalor existed in America. The huts were devoid of water, and the people living there appeared idle and unproductive. They showed no resentment towards the American

women but seemed slow and unresponsive. Disease was ram-
pant in the houses, and the odor of liquor distilled from a
cactus plant permeated the air. Drunkenness was evident, and it
seemed to have a deathly effect on its victims. Vienna was unable
to visit the mission-house, but she did see a padre, who looked
sad and starved but good. She managed to make it to her room
before succumbing to a faintness.

Despite her injuries, she remained conscious enough to not
require assistance. The day after the round-up concluded, she
walked out onto the porch where her brother and Stillwell were
in the midst of a heated argument about a horse. "I reckon it's
my old roan," said Stillwell, squinting his eyes. "Bill, if that isn't
Norris's horse my eyes are going back on me," replied Al. "It's
not the color or shape. The distance is too far to judge by that.
It's the motion, the swing."

"Al, maybe you're right. But there ain't no rider up on that
horse. Flo, fetch my glass," said Stillwell. Florence went inside while Vienna tried to figure out what they were looking
at. Eventually, she saw dust far up in the gray hollow along
a foothill, and then the dark, moving figure of a horse. She
continued to watch as Florence returned with the glass.

Bill took a long look through the glasses, adjusted them carefully, and tried again. "Well, I hate to admit my eyes are getting
poor. But I guess I'll have to. That's Gene Norris's horse, saddled, and coming at a fast clip without a rider. It's amazingly
strange, and it's in keeping with other things concerning Gene."

"Give me the glass," said Al. "Yes, I was right. Bill, the horse is not frightened. He's coming steadily; he's got something on his mind."

"That's a trained horse, Al. He has more sense than some men I know. Take a look with the glasses up the hollow. See anybody?"

"No."

"Swing up over the foothills where the trail leads. Higher along that ridge where the rocks begin. See anybody?"

"By Jove! Bill, two horses! But I can't make out much for dust. They are climbing fast. One horse has gone among the rocks. There, the other's gone. What do you make of that?"

"Well, I can't make any more than you."

"I bet we'll find out something soon, 'cause Gene's horse is coming faster as he nears the ranch," remarked Bill. Vienna had an un-obstructed view of the wide hollow sloping up into the foothills, and less than half a mile away, she saw the riderless horse galloping along the white trail. She recalled the circumstances under which she had first seen him, and then his wild flight through the dimly lit streets of El Cajon out into the black night. She was thrilled again and believed she would never forget that starry night's adventure. As she watched the horse, she felt more than just curiosity. Sud-denly, a shrill, piercing whistle pealed in. "Well, he's seen us, that's for sure," said Bill. The horse neared the corrals, disappeared into a lane, and then broke his gait again, thundering into the enclosure and pounding to a halt some twenty yards from where Stillwell waited for him. Up close, Vienna could see that he was a magnificent creature, a charger almost tremendous of build, with a black coat faintly mottled in gray, and it shone like polished glass in the sun. Evidently, he had been carefully groomed for this occasion, for there was no dust on him, nor a kink in his beautiful mane, nor a mark on his glossy hide. "Come here, you son-of-a-gun," said Stillwell. The horse dropped his head, snorted, and obediently walked over. He was neither shy nor wild, and he poked a friendly nose at Stillwell before looking at Al and the women. Unhooking the stirrups from the pommel, Stillwell let them fall and began to search the saddle for something which he evidently expected to find.

From amidst his belongings, Stillwell produced a folded piece of paper and handed it to Al after examining it closely. "This is addressed to you, and I'm willing to bet two bits that I know what's inside," he said. Ken unfolded the letter and read it before turning to Stillwell. "Bill, you're quite the guesser. Gene's heading for the border. He sent his horse through someone, no names mentioned, and wants my sister to have him if she'll accept," Ken shared.

"Was there any mention of Danny Mains?" asked the rancher. "Not a word," replied Ken. "That's not good news. If anyone knows about Danny, it's Gene. But he's a man of few words. Looks like he's headed straight for Mexico. I wonder if Danny's going with him? Well, two of the finest cowmen I've ever seen have gone to the dogs, and it's a shame," Stillwell mumbled to himself before retreating into the house.

Ken approached Vienna with the horse and placed the reins over her arm before handing her the letter. "Princess, I think you should accept the horse," he said. "Norris is just a cowboy now, but he comes from a good family. He used to be a college-educated gentleman. He went astray out here, like many others do, just like I almost did. He told me about his sister and mother, and he cared deeply for them. I believe he was the cause of their unhappiness. Whenever he was reminded of this, he'd resort to drinking. I've always stood by him, and I'd continue to do so if given the chance. Bill is devastated about Danny Mains and Norris. He was hoping for good news. But it seems unlikely that they'll ever return, especially in Norris's case. Giving up his horse means he's joining the rebel forces across the border."

"I'd love to see that cowboy break loose on a bunch of Greasers!" Ken exclaimed. "Oh, damn it all! Sorry, Princess. I'm just a bit upset. I'm really sorry about Norris. I actually liked him before he beat up that coyote of a sheriff, Pat Hawe. But after that, I liked him even more. You read the letter, sis, and take the horse."

Vienna silently shifted her gaze from her brother's face to the letter:

"Friend Al, I'm sending my horse down to you because I'm going away and I don't want him to get hurt or fall into strange hands. If you think it's okay, give him to your sister with my respects. But if you don't like the idea, or if she won't take him, then he's yours. I'm grateful for your kindness to me, even if I never showed it. And, Al, my horse has never felt a whip or a spur, and I hope you won't hurt him. I hope your sister will take him. She'll take good care of him, and she can afford it. And, while I'm waiting to be shot by a Greaser, if I ever picture how she'll look on my horse, it won't make any difference to you. She doesn't need to know. Between you and me, Al, don't let her or Flo ride alone over Don Carlos's way. If I had more time, I could tell you something about that sly Greaser. And tell your sister, if she ever needs to run away from anyone while riding that roan, just lean over and yell in his ear. She'll feel like she's flying. Goodbye. Gene Norris."

Vienna folded the letter thoughtfully and murmured, "He must really love his horse."

"He sure does," Ken agreed. "Flo can tell you."

Gene had only ever allowed one person to ride his horse, and that was his little sister, Vienna. However, there were rumors that a young Mexican girl named Bonita had recently taken the horse out for a ride. When Gene asked Vienna if she wanted the horse, she eagerly accepted. Although she was thrilled to have him, Vienna was worried about how she would climb onto the horse since he was much taller than she was. Ken suggested she could mount him from the porch.

Vienna was not dressed for riding, so she spent time getting to know the horse instead. She found him to be gentle and obedient, following her like a pet dog. The horse would even lift his head and ears when he heard a call from beyond the mountains, which made Vienna pity the cowboy who had given up his beloved horse. Despite her love for the horse, Vienna couldn't help but feel a bit fickle for forgetting about her previous favorite horse, White Stockings. She promised to be a loyal and loving owner to her new horse, whom she had affectionately nicknamed Princess.

As Ken hoisted Vienna onto the back of the towering roan, she felt a rush of excitement. "Let's head out to the mesa," her brother declared, swinging onto his own horse. "Just make sure to keep a tight rein on him and ease up when you want him to go faster. But don't go hollering in his ear unless you want to be left in the dust."

They rode out of the yard, past the corrals, and onto a wide, gray expanse that stretched for miles before sloping up to meet the mesa. Florence led the way, riding like a seasoned cowboy. Ken rode up alongside her, leaving Vienna trailing behind. Suddenly, the horses broke into a gallop, eager to run free. Vienna felt a thrill of excitement, realizing that even if she wanted to rein in Princess, she might not be able to keep up with the others.

As the horses surged ahead and broke into a full run, Florence called out to Vienna to follow. "We can't let them get too far ahead," Ken shouted over his shoulder. Vienna loosened her grip on the reins, and something shifted beneath her. She wasn't quite sure what was happening at first - she'd never ridden at this speed before. In New York, it wasn't exactly safe or proper. But as Princess lowered her head and stretched out into a smooth, gliding run, Vienna felt a sense of exhilaration wash over her.

She quickly realized that she was gaining on her companions, the distance between them shrinking with every stride. The wind rushed past her ears, and she marveled at how effortless it felt to stay in the saddle. This was a new experience for her, and she was loving every second of it.

Vienna had never been a fan of horseback riding due to the rough and bumpy ride, but this time was different. She felt no discomfort or need to hold on tightly. Instead, she felt the wind in her face and the horse's mane whipping against her. The sensation was thrilling, invigorating, and made her blood pump faster. Spurred on by an unknown force, she loosened the bridle and leaned forward, urging the horse to run faster. "Oh, you splendid fellow, run!" she exclaimed.

The sound of hoofs pounding against the ground filled her ears as Princess picked up speed. The wind stung her face, and her hair was whipped around her head. The gray plain flew by on either side, and Florence and Ken appeared to be coming back into view. However, as Princess closed in on them, Vienna realized that he was going to pass them. And he did, shooting by so quickly that it almost seemed as though the other horses were standing still. Princess continued to run until he reached the steep side of the mesa, where he slowed down and stopped.

"Glorious!" Vienna exclaimed, her body ablaze with excitement. Every muscle and nerve in her body was tingling and quivering. Even her hands trembled as she attempted to push her hair back into place. She turned around to wait for her companions, who were now approaching her. Ken was laughing, delighted but also a little worried. "Holy smoke! But can't he run? Did he bolt on you?"

Vienna shook her head. "No, I called in his ear," she replied. "That's the woman in me, and forbidden fruit. Flo said she'd do it the minute she was on him. Princess, you can ride."

The Western gal approached with a grin on her face. "It was so awesome to see you! Your hair was on fire in the wind! She sure can ride, Al. I was a bit worried, but that horse of hers is amazing! Can he run or what?"

Ken led them up a steep, winding path to the top of the mesa. Vienna was blown away by the sight of a beautiful, flat expanse of short grass, as level as a floor. "Al, this would be the best spot for golf in the world!" she exclaimed.

"I've thought about that myself," he replied. "But the only problem is, could anyone manage to stop staring at the scenery long enough to hit a ball? Princess, look!"

Vienna was then faced with a breathtaking and overwhelming sight. The vastness of the deep, red-ridged world below her was impossible to comprehend and left her speechless. "Once, Princess, when I first came out West, I was feeling down and out, ready to end it all," said Ken. "But I happened to climb up here looking for a place to die. When I saw this, I changed my mind."

Vienna was silent as they rode around the rim of the mesa and down the steep trail. This time, she didn't let Ken and Florence coax her into a race. She was in awe, feeling both uplifted and bewildered, and it took her a while to regain her composure. She arrived back at the ranch house long after the others and was very contemplative during supper.

Later, as they gathered on the porch to watch the sunset, Stillwell's humorous complaints sparked an idea in Vienna's mind. She listened attentively as he recounted the struggles of a poor cattleman.

The conversation between Vienna and Mr. Stillwell was lengthy
and fascinating, but it was also overwhelming for Vienna. She was
determined to either kill her new idea of ranching or breathe life
into it. She asked Mr. Stillwell if ranching here on a large scale
could be made profitable with modern methods. He replied with
a short laugh, saying that it could be a money-maker. He had
lived well, paid his debts, and had not lost any money except the
original outlay. He would sell if someone paid his price, but he
would hate to leave. Don Carlos and the other Mexicans would
sell too, as they had been after him for years. Mr. Stillwell dreamed
of buying out Don Carlos and the Greasers and giving a job to
every good cowman in the country. He would make them prosper
as he prospered himself. Vienna listened intently to Mr. Stillwell's
dreams and ideas, feeling overwhelmed but also inspired.

If I had all the money in the world, I'd buy up all the best horses on
the range. I'd fence off a whopping twenty thousand acres of prime
grazing land. There'd be no shortage of water, with wells drilled
in the valley and pipes running down from the mountains. And
that draw out there? I'd dam it up for miles, creating a stunning
lake that I'd surround with cottonwoods. I'd stock it with fish and
plant the biggest field of alfalfa in the southwest. And that's not all -
there'd be fruit trees and gardens, and all the old corrals, barns, and
bunkhouses would be torn down to make way for new ones. This
ranch would be the finest and most comfortable around. Grass
and flowers would be everywhere, and young pine trees would be
brought down from the mountains. And when all was said and
done, I'd just sit back in my chair and smoke, watching the cattle
come in for water and the cowboys singing in their bunks. As

the red sun would set, I'd be the happiest man in the world - Bill Stillwell, the last of the old cattlemen.

Vienna thanked the rancher and then quickly retired to her room. She felt no need to hide the force of that wonderful idea that had grown so tenacious and alluring. The next day, she asked Ken if it would be safe to ride out to the mesa. "I'll go with you," he said cheerfully. "No, dear, I want to go alone," she replied. Ken became serious and gave her a quick glance before turning away. "Go ahead. I think it's safe. I'll make sure by sitting here with my glass and keeping an eye on you. Just be careful coming down the trail and let the horse pick his way."

"That's all," Vienna said as she rode Princess across the wide flat, up the zigzag trail, and across the beautiful grassy level to the far rim of the mesa. It wasn't until then that she lifted her eyes to face the southwest. Vienna looked from the gray valley at her feet to the blue Sierra Madres, which were gold-tipped in the setting sun. Her vision embraced distance, depth, and glory hitherto unrevealed to her. The gray valley sloped and widened to the black sentinel Chiricahuas, and beyond was lost in a vast corrugated sweep of earth, reddening down to the west, where a golden blaze lifted the dark, rugged mountains into bold relief. The scene had infinite beauty. But after Vienna's first swift, all-embracing flash of enraptured eyes, the thought of beauty passed away. In that darkening desert, there was something illimitable. Vienna saw the hollow of a stupendous hand; she felt a mighty hold upon her heart. Out of the endless space, out of silence and desolation and mystery and age, came slow-changing colored shadows, phantoms of peace, and they whispered to Vienna. They whispered that it was a great, grim, immutable earth; that time was eternity; that life was fleeting. They whispered for her to be a woman; to love someone before it was too late; to love anyone, everyone; to realize the need for work, and in doing it, to find happiness.

She rode back across the mesa and down the trail, and once more upon the flat, she called to the horse and made him run. His spirit seemed to race with hers. The wind of his speed blew her hair from its fastenings. When he thundered to a halt at the porch steps, Vienna, breathless and disheveled, alighted with the mass of her hair tumbling around her. Ken met her, and his exclamation, along with Florence's rapt eyes shining on her face and Stillwell's speechlessness, made her self-conscious. Laughing, she tried to put up the mass of hair. "I must look a fright," she panted.

"Well, you can say whatever you want," said the old rancher. "But I know what I believe." Vienna tried to remain calm. "My hat and combs flew away in the wind. I thought my hair would follow suit... There's the evening star... I think I'm very hungry." She gave up trying to calm down and fix her hair, which fell in a golden mass once again. "Mr. Stillwell," she began, her voice taking on a hurried and deeper tone. "Mr. Stillwell, I want to buy your ranch and hire you as my superintendent. I want to purchase Don Carlos's ranch and other properties totaling fifty thousand acres. I want you to buy horses and cattle and make all the improvements you've been dreaming of for so long. I also have my own ideas that I need your and Ken's advice on. I plan to improve the lives of the poor Mexicans in the valley and the cowboys on this range. We'll talk about all the business details tomorrow." Vienna turned away from the huge grin on Mr. Stillwell's face and reached out her hands to her brother. "Ken, it's strange, isn't it? Me coming out here to you? Don't laugh. I hope I've found my work, my happiness, under the light of that western star."

Chapter Eight.

In just five short months, Stillwell's dreams became a reality. The old ranch underwent a complete transformation, with numerous changes, improvements, and innovations. It was like magic had touched the place. Vienna, Ken, and Florence sat down to brainstorm a fitting name, ultimately settling on Vienna's suggestion. However, this was the only instance where Vienna's wishes were not honored throughout the course of the developments.

The cowboys had given the new ranch a name - "Her Princess's Rancho." Stillwell believed that the names given by cowboys were perfect and unchangeable, just like the hills that surround them. Florence, however, had switched sides, while Ken laughed at Vienna's objections and declared that the cowboys had made her the queen of the ranges, and there was nothing anyone could do about it. Thus, the name "Her Princess's Rancho" stuck.

It was April, and the sun was shining down on a gently sloping green knoll that lay nestled in the foothills. The long ranch-house atop the knoll shone white in the bright sunlight. The grounds around the house were not like those of the Eastern lawns or parks. There had been no landscaping, but Stillwell had brought water, grass, flowers, and plants to the top of the knoll and left them to follow nature. While his idea may have been crude, the result was beautiful. Under the hot sun and cool water, a green carpet had sprung to life, and many-colored flowers had bloomed. Wildflowers, lavender daisies, bluebells, white lilies, and golden poppies bloomed in a beautiful confusion. Crimson California roses nodded their heavy heads and trembled under the weight of bees. In bare places, the cactus plants blazed in vermillion and magenta. The green slopes led all the way down to the new adobe barns and sheds that had been erected, and the wide corrals stretched down to the great squares of alfalfa that gently sloped to the gray valley. The bottom of the dammed-up hollow shone brightly, with its slowly increasing acreage of water. Thousands of migratory wildfowl whirred and splashed and squawked on the water, as if they were reluctant to leave this cool, wet surprise on their long journey to the northland.

The cowboys' quarters were now comfortable, spacious adobe houses that even the most critical cowboy couldn't complain about. They stood in a row on a long bench of land above the lake. The cluster of Mexican homes and the small church down in the valley had also been renovated with the same care and attention to detail. The old Spanish house, which had once been Stillwell's home, was now a bare, massive structure that had been updated with new doors and windows. Every modern convenience, from hot and cold running water to acetylene lighting, had been installed. The interior had been painted, carpentered, and furnished to provide the ideal sought after, which was comfort, not luxury. Every door into the patio looked out onto dark, rich grass and sweet-faced flowers, and every window looked down onto the green slopes.

Vienna's rooms were located on the west end of the building and consisted of four rooms, all of which opened out onto the long porch. There was a small room for her maid, an office, her sleeping quarters, and the great light chamber that she had fallen in love with upon first sight. It was simply yet beautifully furnished and contained her favorite books and pictures. In the morning, the fragrant, balmy air blew the white curtains of the open windows; at noon, the drowsy, sultry quiet seemed to creep in for the siesta that was characteristic of the country; in the afternoon, the westering sun peeped under the porch roof and painted the walls with gold bars that slowly changed to red.

Vienna Florentino cherished the belief that the transformation she had brought about in the old Spanish house and the people she had surrounded herself with was as nothing compared to the one she had undergone herself. She had found a purpose in life.

Despite her busy life, Vienna was able to find time to read, think, study, and daydream more than ever before. She had helped her brother overcome his difficulties and achieve success in ranching. Vienna had learned the ways of the West from the old cattleman, Stillwell, who had taken her under his wing and treated her like the daughter he never had. He was incredibly proud of her, and Vienna felt his love deeply. She had ridden the ranges with Ken and Florence, and had even camped on the open range, sleeping under the stars and riding for miles in the face of dust and wind. She had taken two amazing trips down into the desert, one to Chiricahua and across the Mexican border, and the other through the Aravaipa Valley with its red-walled canyons and wild fastnesses. Learning the Western ways had been difficult, but it had become a labor of love for Vienna. She was in perfect health and high spirits, so active that she had to force herself to take the midday siesta, a custom of the country. Sometimes she looked in the mirror and laughed with sheer joy at the sight of her lithe, audacious, brown-faced, flashing-eyed reflection. She was filled with joy for life, not just for her beauty as Eastern critics had once claimed when she was pale, slender, proud, and cold. She laughed at the memory.

If only her family and friends could see her now! Vienna was alive and pulsating with energy from head to toe. She couldn't help but think about how her loved ones had doubted her ability to stay in the West and begged her to come back home. When she wrote to them, she never mentioned the transformation she had undergone. Instead, she promised to visit home sometime in the future, which brought back amused or saddened responses. Vienna intended to go back East for a while and make occasional trips every year, but she was hesitant to take the first step. Going back home would require explanations that her family and friends wouldn't understand. Her father's business couldn't afford him the time to make a Western trip, and Mrs. Florentino had an un-American idea of the wilderness westward. Vienna's sister, Melissa, was eager to visit her, which Vienna suspected was due to curiosity more than sisterly love. Eventually, Vienna decided that the best way to prove her breaking of permanent ties was to invite Melissa and her friends to visit during the summer.

Overseeing the many business details of Her Princess's Rancho and keeping a record of them was no easy task. Vienna found the business training her father had insisted on to be invaluable now.

As Vienna tried to grasp the practicalities of cattle-raising, the straightforward Stillwell proved to be a great help. She segregated the large herd of cattle into smaller groups and kept a close watch on them when they ran out in the open range. Each group was given time in an enclosed area where they were fed, watered, and managed by a team of skilled cowboys. Vienna hired three cowboy scouts whose primary responsibility was to scour the range for any stray, sick, or injured cattle or orphaned calves and bring them in for treatment and care. Two cowboys were assigned to train a pack of Russian stag-hounds and hunt the coyotes, wolves, and lions that preyed on the herds. The milch cows were separated from the other groups and kept in a pasture next to the dairy. Vienna made sure that all branding was done in corrals, and the calves were separated from their mothers at the right time for the benefit of both. She abandoned the old method of branding and classing that had horrified Vienna and introduced a new one that spared the cattle, cowboys, and horses any harm or cruelty.

Vienna also established a large vegetable farm and orchards. The climate was better than California's, and with ample water, the trees, plants, and gardens thrived and bloomed in a spectacular way. Vienna took great pleasure in walking through acres of land that had once been barren but were now lush, green, and fragrant. She also set up poultry-yards, pig-pens, and marshy areas for ducks and geese. In the farming section of the ranch, Vienna provided work for the little community of Mexicans. Their lives had been harsh and barren, much like the dry valley they had been living in. But just as the valley had been transformed by water, their lives were transformed by Vienna's kindness, support, and employment.

The children were no longer miserable, and many who had been blind could now see. Vienna had become a new and blessed place to them. Vienna looked out over the land and compared the transformation in the people and the land to the transformation in her heart. It might have been just her imagination, but the sun seemed brighter, the sky bluer, and the wind sweeter. However, the deep green of the grass and garden, the white and pink of the blossoms, and the blaze and fragrance of the flowers were not just her imagination. The sheen of the lake and the fluttering of the new leaves were also real. Where there had been monotonous gray, there was now vivid and changing color. Formerly there had been silence both day and night, but now there was music during the sunny hours. The whistle of prancing stallions pealed in from the grassy ridges. Innumerable birds had come and, like the northward-journeying ducks, they had tarried to stay. The song of the meadow-lark, blackbird, and robin, familiar to Vienna from childhood, mixed with the new and strange heart-throbbing song of mocking-bird, the piercing blast of the desert eagle, and the melancholy moan of turtle-dove.

One April morning, Vienna sat in her office grappling with a problem. She faced problems every day, and most of them were related to managing twenty-seven incomprehensible cowboys. This par-

ticular issue concerned Ambrose Mills, who had run away with
her French maid, Christine. Stillwell approached Vienna with a
smile almost as big as his bulk. "Well, Miss Princess, we caught
them, but not before Padre Marcos had married them. All that
speeding in the automobile was just scaring me to death for nothing. I tell you, Link Stevens is crazy about running that car. Link
never had any sense even with a horse. He isn't afraid of the devil
himself. If my hair hadn't been white before, it would be white
now."

I need to figure out what to do about Ambrose and Christine.
They have brought shame upon my ranch."Stillwell nodded his
head in agreement. "Wal, Miss Princess, I reckon you ought to
talk to Ambrose yoreself. He's a good boy, but he done wrong.
He ought to be punished, but not too hard. As for thet Christine,
she's a French gal an' don't rightly understand our ways. Maybe we
ought to let her go back to her own country."Vienna considered
this for a moment. "Perhaps you are right, Stillwell. I will talk to
Ambrose and see what he has to say for himself. As for Christine, I
will make arrangements for her to return to France.""Thet sounds
like a good plan, Miss Princess. Now, if you'll excuse me, I need to
go check on the herd. Them cows don't take no day off."Stillwell
tipped his hat and left Vienna to deal with the aftermath of the
elopement. She sighed heavily and wondered how she had ended
up in this situation. Running a ranch was hard enough without
having to deal with the romantic entanglements of her cowboys.
She made a mental note to start looking for a new foreman who
could handle the challenges of modern cowboy life.

"Tell me how to impress Ambrose to make an example, so to speak. I need another maid, and I don't want her to be carried off in this sudden manner," Vienna said to Stillwell.

"Well, if you bring pretty maids out here, you can't expect anything else. That little French girl with her black eyes, white skin, and charming gestures had the cowboys going crazy. It'll be worse with the next one," Stillwell replied.

Vienna sighed, "And as for impressing Ambrose, I guess I can tell you how to do that. Just give it to him straight and tell him you're going to fire him. That'll fix Ambrose and maybe scare the other boys for a while."

"Very well, Stillwell, bring Ambrose in to see me, and tell Christine to wait in my room," Vienna instructed.

A handsome cowboy with bright eyes and a debonair look entered Vienna's room. His shyness and awkwardness had vanished, replaced with excitement. He looked at Vienna as if expecting her to congratulate him.

"Ambrose, what have you done?" Vienna asked, trying to sound severe.

"Miss Florentino, I went and got married," Ambrose replied, his words tumbling over each other. His eyes sparkled, and his clean-shaven brown cheek glowed. "I beat Frank Slade, and I ran so fast that Jim Bell couldn't keep up. Even old man Nels made eyes at Christine! So, I wasn't going to take any risks. I just took her to El Cajon and married her."

"Oh, I heard," Vienna said slowly, watching him closely.

"Do you love her, Ambrose?" Vienna asked, looking him straight in the eye. Ambrose blushed, dropped his head, and fidgeted with his new hat. His hand trembled, and Vienna could see it. It was strange to her that this tough cowboy, who could rope and tie a wild steer in seconds, could be so affected by a simple question. Suddenly, Ambrose raised his head, and Vienna had to look away from the intensity of his gaze.

"Yes, Miss Florentino, I do love her," Ambrose replied. "I think I love her in the way you're asking about. The first time I saw her, I knew I wanted her for my wife. It's been strange, the way she's made me feel. I never knew many girls before, and I haven't seen any in years. But when she came into my life, everything changed. A woman makes a big difference in a man's feelings and thoughts. I guess I never really understood that before. But now I do."

"Is that all you have to say to me, Ambrose?" Vienna pressed. "I'm sorry you didn't have time to tell me before. But where were you going when Stillwell found you?"

"We had just gotten married," Ambrose replied. "I hadn't really thought about what to do next. I probably would have gone back to work. But now, I'll have to work harder and save more money."

"Do you earn enough to support a wife?" Vienna asked.

"Sure, I do!" Ambrose exclaimed. "I've never earned this much money before. Working for you is a great job. I'm going to kick the boys out of my bunkhouse and fix it up for Christine and me. They'll be so jealous!"

Vienna smiled. "Congratulations, Ambrose. I'm happy for you."

Vienna wished Christine joy and promised to give her a little wedding present. She asked for a moment alone with Christine and dismissed the cowboy. Vienna couldn't bring herself to say anything harsh to the happy cowboy, and she was happy for Christine. She called out for Christine, but there was no response. She tried again, and Christine burst into the room in a whirlwind of flying feet, entreating hands, and beseeching eyes. Christine was small, graceful, and plump, with very white skin and very dark hair. She had been Vienna's favorite maid for years, and there was sincere affection between them. It was clear that Christine knew how she had transgressed, and her fear, remorse, and appeal for forgiveness were poured out in an incoherent storm. Vienna forgave her and took her in her arms, soothing her. After Christine calmed down, she told Vienna her part in the elopement. It was a story that both amused and shocked Vienna. Christine's unmistakable, shy, marveling love for Ambrose gave Vienna relief and joy. If Christine loved Ambrose, there was no harm done. Vienna watched the girl's eyes, wonderful with their changes of thought, and listened to her attempts to explain what was evident she did not understand. She gathered that if ever a caveman had taken unto himself a wife, if ever a barbarian had carried off a Sabine woman, then Ambrose Mills had acted with the violence of such ancient forebears.

Christine was in awe of what had just happened. "He told me he loves me," she repeated, still in disbelief. "He asked me to marry

him, he kissed me, he hugged me, he lifted me onto his horse,
he rode with me all night, and then he married me." She proudly
displayed the ring on her left hand. Vienna could see that Christine
was now in love with Ambrose, despite being taken against her
will.

After Christine left, Vienna couldn't shake the look in the girl's
eyes and her words. The enchantment of romance was certainly
present in this sunny land. Vienna was both charmed and conflict-
ed by the violence and unorthodox nature of Ambrose's courtship.
He had been straightforward about his love for Christine, and had
taken her away with him into the night to marry her. Despite her
reservations, Vienna found the whole thing to be splendid and
beautiful. It went against everything she had been taught, but she
couldn't shake the feeling of being stripped of her sophisticated
veneer.

As Vienna tried to focus on her work, Stillwell interrupted her with
news of another strange occurrence.

Vienna was interrupted by the arrival of Jim Bell, who had a peculiar request. Jim had refused to eat bread made in a wash-basin
and claimed that Nels had fed the gang with bread made from
a new-fangled bucket-machine with a crank. Jim was amazed by
the bread and wanted Vienna to teach him how to make it. As
the superintendent of the ranch, Stillwell wanted to know what
was going on and if there was any truth in Jim's claim. Vienna
stifled her laughter and explained that she had received a patent
bread-mixer from the East and had been using it herself to make
good bread. She had also introduced the idea to Nels, who was ini-

tially skeptical but was won over after sampling the bread. Stillwell laughed at the situation.

"Well, well, well!" he exclaimed, finally. "That's great, and it's really funny. Maybe you don't see why it's funny? Well, Nels has just been bragging to the boys about how you showed him, and now you'll have to show every cowboy on the ranch the same thing. Cowboys are the most jealous kind of guys. They're all crazy about you, anyway. Take Jim out here. That lazy cowboy would never make bread. He's notorious for shirking his share of the cooking. I've seen Jim trade off washing the pots and pans for a lonely watch on a rainy night. All he wants is to see you show him the same thing as Nels. Then he'll show off to his bunkmate, Frank Slade, and then Frank will want to know all about this wonderful bread machine. Cowboys are strange creatures, Miss Princess. And now that you've started with them this way, you'll have to keep it up. I must say I've never seen such a hardworking bunch. You've really motivated them."

"Indeed, Stillwell, I'm happy to hear that," replied Vienna. "And I'm happy to teach them all. But can't I have them all up here at once, at least those who are off duty?"

"Well, I don't reckon you can unless you want them fighting," rejoined Stillwell dryly. "What you have on your hands now, Miss Princess, is to let them come one by one and make each cowboy think you're taking more pleasure in showing him than the guy who came before him. Then maybe we can get back to cattle-raising."

Vienna protested, but Stillwell was firm in his wisdom. She had gone against his advice before, to her complete humiliation. She didn't dare risk it again and resigned herself to her task with grace and subdued amusement.

Jim Bell was led into a spacious, bright, and clean kitchen, where Vienna greeted him and put on an apron before rolling up her sleeves. She demonstrated how to use various pieces of aluminum that made up the bread mixer and attached the bucket to the table-shelf. Jim seemed to be completely absorbed in the lesson, as if his life depended on it, and he asked Vienna to explain things repeatedly, especially how to turn the crank.

Vienna began to have doubts about Jim's sincerity when she had to take his hand three times to show him the simple mechanism, and he still didn't understand it. She suspected that as long as she touched his hand, he would never comprehend it. When Vienna started measuring flour, milk, lard, salt, and yeast, she noted with despair that Jim was not paying attention to the ingredients. Instead, he was covertly looking at her.

"Jim, I'm not sure about you," Vienna said sternly. "How can you learn to make bread if you don't watch me mix it?"

"I'm watching you," Jim replied innocently.

Finally, Vienna sent Jim off with the bread mixer under his arm. The next morning, in line with Stillwell's prediction, Frank Slade, Jim's bunkmate, happily approached Vienna and expressed his long-standing desire to help his overworked comrade with the housekeeping in their bunk.

"Miss Florentino," Frank said, "Jim is kind but he's not very bright, and I didn't believe him when he said he could do it all himself. You see, I'm from Missouri, and you'll have to show me."

For a whole week, Vienna held clinics where she explained the scientific method of modern bread-making. She enjoyed giving lectures and seeing through the simple ruses of these big, burly boys.

Some of them had serious expressions, like deacons, while others looked as important as statesmen signing government treaties. These cowboys were just big kids who needed guidance, but in order to lead them, they had to be treated with respect. They were a lively bunch who loved to have fun, and they were all grown men. Stillwell explained that their high spirits came from the difference in their fortunes. Twenty-seven cowboys worked in shifts of nine, eight hours a day - a practice that had never been seen before in the West. Stillwell predicted that cowboys from all over would come to Her Princess's Rancho.

Chapter Nine.

S tillwell's interest in the revolution across the Mexican border
had clearly increased upon hearing the news that Gene Norris
had become a distinguished figure among the rebel forces. From
then on, the old cattleman made sure to send for newspapers from
El Paso and Adam, wrote letters to ranchers he knew on the big
bend of the Rio Grande, and would talk endlessly to anyone who
would listen to him. There was no chance of Stillwell's friends at
the ranch forgetting about his favorite cowboy. However, Stillwell
always started his praises with an apologetic statement that Norris had gone astray. Vienna enjoyed listening to him, though she
wasn't always certain which news was factual and which was pure
imagination. Nonetheless, there seemed to be no doubt that the
cowboy had performed some audacious feats for the rebels, and
Vienna even found his name mentioned in several of the border
papers. When the rebels, led by Madero, stormed and captured
the city of Juarez, Norris engaged in fighting that earned him the
title of El Capitan. This battle ultimately brought an end to the
revolution, with President Diaz's surrender following shortly after.
There was a sense of relief among ranchers on the border from
Texas to California. However, nothing more was heard of Gene

Norris until April, when Stillwell received a report that the cowboy had arrived in El Cajon, evidently looking for trouble.

The elderly rancher saddled up his horse and rode as fast as he could to town. Two days later, he returned looking defeated. Vienna was there when Stillwell spoke with Ken. "I was too late, Al," the rancher said. "Gene was already gone. And get this, Danny Mains had just left with a couple of packed burros. I couldn't find out which way he went, but I'm guessing he took the Peloncillo trail."

"Dan will turn up eventually," Ken replied. "What did you find out about Norris? Maybe he left with Danny."

"Not much," Stillwell grunted. "Gene's determined to stay away from the mountains."

"Well, tell us about him," Ken prompted.

Stillwell wiped his forehead and began to speak. "It's mighty strange about Gene. It's got me confused. He arrived in El Cajon a week or so ago. He was as lean as if he'd been riding the range all winter. He had plenty of money, according to the Mexicans. And all the locals were crazy about him. They called him El Capitan. He got drunk and started looking for Pat Hawe. Remember that Mexican who was shot last October on the night Miss Princess arrived? Well, he's dead. And people are saying that Pat is going to blame Gene for the killing. I think it's just talk, but Pat is mean enough to do it if he had the guts. Anyway, if he was in El Cajon, he kept to himself. Gene walked up and down, up and down, all day and night looking for Pat. But he didn't find him. And, of course, he kept getting drunker and drunker. He just got downright bad.

He made a lot of trouble, but there was no gunfight. Maybe that made him mad, so he went and beat up Flo's brother-in-law. That wasn't so bad. Jack needed a good beating. And then Gene met Danny and tried to get him drunk. And he couldn't! Can you believe that?"

Danny wasn't drinking and wouldn't touch a drop. I'm relieved about that, but it's strange. Danny used to love his red liquor. I think he and Gene had a disagreement, but I'm not certain. Anyways, Gene left and got on a train. I hope he doesn't cause any trouble. If he acts up in Arizona, he'll end up in the Yuma penitentiary. That place is a graveyard for cowboys. I sent a telegram to agents along the railroad to keep an eye out for Norris and let me know if they find him.

Ken asked, "What can you do if you find him, Stillwell?" The old man responded, "I straightened him out before. Maybe I can do it again." Then, he turned to Vienna and said, "I have an idea, Miss Princess. If I can get Gene Norris, he would make a great foreman for my cowboys. He can handle this group of cow-punchers that are driving me crazy. Plus, since he fought for the rebels and earned the name El Capitan, all the Mexicans in the area will respect him. Now, Miss Princess, we still have Don Carlos and his vaqueros to deal with. He sold you his house, ranch, and stock, but we didn't specify when he would leave. I don't like the situation at all. Don Carlos knows something about the cattle I lost and the ones you've been losing. He's in cahoots with the rebels. I bet that when he gets out, he and his vaqueros will join the guerrillas that are causing trouble along the border. This revolution isn't over yet. It's just getting started."

"All these gangs of outlaws are gonna take advantage of it. We're gonna see some old times, maybe. Well, I need Gene Norris. I need him bad. Will you let me hire him, Miss Princess, if I can get him straightened up?" The old cattleman ended hoarsely. "Stillwell, by all means find Norris, and don't wait to straighten him up. Bring him to the ranch," replied Vienna. Thanking her, Stillwell led his horse away. "Strange how he loves that cowboy!" murmured Vienna. "Not so strange, Princess," replied her brother. "Not when you know. Norris has been with Stillwell on some hard trips into the desert alone. There's no middle course of feeling between men facing death in the desert. Either they hate each other or love each other. I don't know, but I imagine Norris did something for Stillwell saved us life, perhaps. Besides, Norris's a lovable chap when he's going straight. I hope Stillwell brings him back. We do need him, Princess. He's a born leader. Once I saw him ride into a bunch of Mexicans whom we suspected of rustling. It was fine to see him. Well, I'm sorry to tell you that we are worried about Don Carlos. Some of his vaqueros came into my yard the other day when I had left Flo alone. She had a bad scare. These vaqueros have been different since Don Carlos sold the ranch. For that matter, I never would have trusted a white woman alone with them. But they are bolder now. Something's in the wind. They've got assurance. They can ride off any night and cross the border." During the following week, Vienna discovered that her sympathy for Stillwell in his hunt for the reckless Norris had grown to be sympathy for the cowboy.

Vienna couldn't help but find it ironic that despite all the rumors
of Norris's wild behavior as he wandered from town to town, the
people around her at the ranch consistently spoke highly of him.
Stillwell adored the cowboy, Florence cared for him, Ken respected
and pitied him, and even the other cowboys expressed their loyalty
to him despite his disgraceful actions. The Mexicans even called
him "El Gran Capitan." Vienna's own opinion of Norris had not
changed since the night she met him, but the fact that her brother
and others held him in such high regard, coupled with his gift of a
beautiful horse and his bravery in fighting rebels, made her deeply
disappointed in his current behavior.

Stillwell was so determined to help Norris that one might have
thought he was searching for his own son. He made multiple trips
to various stations in the valley, but each time he returned with a
somber expression. Ken filled Vienna in on the details: Norris was
only getting worse, becoming drunk, disorderly, and violent, and
was sure to end up in prison. Then came a report that sent Stillwell
rushing off to Rodeo. When he returned three days later, he was a
broken man. He had been so hurt that even Vienna couldn't get
him to reveal what had happened. He only admitted to finding
Norris and failing to persuade him to change his ways. When
Stillwell spoke about the encounter, he turned purple in the face
and muttered to himself, "But Gene was drunk. He was drunk, or
he couldn't have treated old Bill like that!"

Vienna was filled with anger toward the cruel cowboy and immense sorrow for the loyal old cattleman. When Stillwell finally
gave up, Vienna decided to take matters into her own hands.

Stillwell's unwavering faith in the face of Norris's violent behavior and excuses moved Vienna deeply and gave her a new perspective on human nature. She respected the unshakable faith that Stillwell held onto and began to believe that Norris must have some redeeming qualities to inspire such devotion. Vienna longed to have the same faith in humanity that Stillwell had in Norris.

Vienna sent Nels to Rodeo to search for Norris and bring him back to the ranch. Nels eventually returned with the roan horse but without Norris. He explained that he had found Norris half-sobered up and in a fight, and someone had knocked him unconscious. When Norris saw the horse, he hugged it and cried uncontrollably. Nels waited for a while but left when Norris became angry and threatened to shoot them both if they didn't leave.

Vienna asked Nels if it was worth trying to persuade Norris to come back, but Nels replied that it was useless. He had seen many cowboys who were sun-blinded, locoed, snake-poisoned, or skunk-bitten, but Norris was unlike any of them.

"He's heading towards the divide, going wild on the shore," Nels reported to Vienna before leaving. But before he was out of earshot, Vienna overheard him talking to Stillwell on the porch. "Bill, listen up. Gene's scraps are all over a woman. Back in the day, he'd scrap with every pretty Greaser girl he met when he was drunk. Pat Hawe thinks Gene shot the strange vaquero who was with little Bonita last fall. Now, Gene's just scrapping to get himself shot for some reason that only God knows."

Nels's story about Norris weeping over his horse had a profound impact on Vienna. She convinced Ken to try to help the cowboy. Ken agreed, having already considered going to Rodeo on his own. He returned alone, having failed to persuade Norris to return with him.

"Princess, I can't explain Norris's behavior," Ken told Vienna. "I spoke to him, but he seemed unreachable. He's changed so much, and I fear his once magnificent strength is fading. It hurt me to see him like that. I couldn't bring him back here in that state. He's hell-bent on getting killed, as Bill said. Some of his escapades are not fit for your ears. We've done all we can for Norris. Maybe if you had a chance, you could have saved him. But it's too late. Forget about it now, dear."

Vienna couldn't forget or give up on helping Norris. To do so would be giving up on hope for a man in need. But she didn't know what steps to take next.

As time went on, rumors of Norris's reckless behavior continued to spread, especially after he crossed the line into Cochise County, Arizona, where law enforcement was much stricter. Eventually, a letter arrived from a friend of Nels's in Chiricahua, reporting that Norris had been injured in a fight. Although his injuries were not severe, it was believed that he would be incapacitated long enough to sober up. According to the informant, this would be the perfect opportunity for Norris's friends to take him home before he was arrested.

The letter also contained a note from Norris's sister, which had been found on him. In it, she described her illness and pleaded for help. Nels's friend sent the letter to Norris without his knowledge, hoping that Stillwell might be able to assist the family. Norris claimed to have no money.

When Vienna read the letter, she was moved to tears. It spoke of the love between family members and the pride they felt for Norris's achievements. It also revealed the financial struggles they were facing. Vienna suspected that this letter might be the reason for Norris's recent reckless behavior, as he had received it too late to send any money home.

Vienna immediately sent a bank draft to Norris's sister, explaining that the money was drawn in advance on his salary. She then decided to travel to Chiricahua herself. Although horseback rides to the small Arizona town had exhausted her in the past, she found the journey by automobile to be relatively comfortable, aside from a few rocky and sandy patches on the road.

The massive touring car was a spectacle to the cowboys and Mexicans alike, not because automobiles were still a novelty, but because this one was a behemoth capable of speeds greater than an express train. The chauffeur who arrived with the car found himself in a difficult situation among the envious cowboys. He was convinced to stay and teach the operation and mechanics of the car, selecting Link Stevens for the job because he was the only cowboy with any mechanical ability. Link had been a tough cowboy, but an injury to his leg that winter had left him unable to ride. The arrival of the big white automobile and his election as the driver made life worth

living again. However, the other cowboys saw Link and his machine as some kind of demon, fearing them both. This is why Nels
reluctantly agreed to follow Vienna and Florence to Chiricahua on
his horse when Vienna asked him to come along. The valley road
was smooth and slightly downhill for miles, and Vienna was not
opposed to speeding when it was safe. The grassy plain flew past
them, and the small dot in the valley grew larger and larger. Link
occasionally looked back at Nels, who was clutching his seat with a
wild look in his eyes. When the car slowed down while crossing the
sandy and rocky areas, Nels seemed to breathe easier. When they
stopped in the dusty street of Chiricahua, Nels eagerly jumped out
of the car.

"Hey Nels, we'll stay here in the car while you go find Norris,"
Vienna said.

"Miss Florentino, I reckon Gene will run when he sees us, if he's
able to run," replied Nels. "Well, I'll go find him, and then we'll
figure out what we should do."

Nels crossed the railroad track and disappeared behind some low,
flat houses. After a little while, he reappeared and hurried up to
the car. Vienna felt his grey gaze searching her face.

"Miss Florentino, I found him," said Nels. "He was sleeping. I woke
him up. He's sober and not badly hurt, but I don't think you
should see him. Maybe Florence-"

"Nels, I want to see him myself. Why not? What did he say when
you told him I was here?" Vienna interrupted.

"Sure, I didn't tell him that. I just said 'Hello, Gene!' and he said, 'My God! Nels! Maybe I'm not glad to see a human being.' He asked me who was with me, and I told him Link and some friends. I said I'd bring them in. He protested, but I went anyways. Now, if you really want to see him, Miss Florentino, it's a good chance. But it's a touchy matter, and you'll be pretty upset when you see him. He's lying in a Mexican hole over here. The Mexicans have probably been kind to him, but they're a poor lot," Nels explained.

Vienna didn't hesitate for a moment. "Thank you, Nels. Take me there now. Come on, Florence."

They left the car, now surrounded by gaping-eyed Mexican children, and crossed the dusty space to a narrow lane between red adobe walls. Passing several houses, Nels stopped at the door of what appeared to be an alleyway leading back. It was filthy.

"He's in there, around the first corner. It's a patio, open and sunny. And Miss Florentino, if you don't mind, I'll wait here for you."

"I don't reckon Gene would like any guys around when he sees you girls," said Vienna's friend, causing her to hesitate and approach Norris' hideout slowly. She hadn't considered how Norris might feel upon being suddenly surprised by her presence. "Florence, you wait also," Vienna instructed her friend before entering the dilapidated patio alone. The area was littered with alfalfa straw and debris, all illuminated by the bright sunlight. A man sat on a bench, his back turned towards Vienna, staring out through the holes in the broken wall. He hadn't noticed her presence. The place wasn't as dirty and stuffy as the passages Vienna had passed through to

get there, but it was obvious that it had been used as a corral. A
rat boldly ran across the dirt floor, and the air swarmed with flies
that the man tried to brush away with a weary hand. Vienna didn't
recognize Norris at first. The side of his face exposed to her was
bruised, bearded, and black. His clothes were ragged and dirty,
with bits of alfalfa stuck in his hair. His shoulders were slumped,
and he looked like a wretched and hopeless figure sitting there.
Vienna sensed why Nels shrank from being present. "Mr. Norris,
it's I, Miss Florentino, come to see you," she said. He suddenly
froze, as if turned to stone. She repeated her greeting, but he jerked
violently, as if he wanted to turn and face her but was held back
by something stronger. Vienna waited, realizing that this ruined
cowboy had a pride that kept him from showing his face. Was it
pride or shame? "Mr. Norris, I have come to talk with you, if you'll
let me." "Go away," he muttered. "Mr. Norris!" Vienna began,
her tone unintentionally haughty. But she immediately corrected
herself, becoming deliberate and calm because she wasn't sure if he
could even hear her. "I have come to help you."

"Can you just leave me be?" Norris choked out, his voice strained
with emotion.

Vienna approached him cautiously, trying not to startle him.
"Norris, maybe it was fate that brought me here," she said gently.
"I came to help you and your sister Letty."

He groaned, leaning against a nearby wall. Vienna bit her tongue,
realizing she had let slip her knowledge of Letty. But perhaps it was
for the best, she thought. "Please, let me speak," she implored.

Norris was silent, and Vienna took that as encouragement to continue. "Stillwell and my brother are worried about Don Carlos and the vaqueros. They need a capable leader, and they want you to be their foreman. The position is open to you, and you can name your salary."

"No," Norris replied firmly.

Vienna persisted. "But Stillwell wants you so badly."

"No," Norris repeated, his voice hoarse and angry.

Vienna could see that her words were only making him more upset. "I'll leave if you want me to," she said. "But please, Norris, why won't you let me help you?"

"I'm a damned blackguard," he burst out, his face buried in his hands.

Vienna didn't know what to say. She could see the pain and turmoil in Norris's eyes, and it broke her heart. She wanted to help him, but she didn't know if there was anything she could do.

"I used to be a gentleman, and I can't let you see me like this," the man said, refusing to leave his squalid dwelling.

But Vienna was determined to help him, having made up her mind to find him no matter where he was. She urged him to come back with her to the ranch, to be among friends and get better. She reminded him of his past as a gentleman and his duty to himself, and pleaded with him to not waste his life.

But the man, Norris, was despondent. "This was my last plunge," he said. "It's too late." He was savage, then sullen, and finally grim. Vienna felt a change in her own feelings as she realized that all her wealth and privilege meant nothing in the face of a man determined to destroy himself.

She was almost impervious, used to being obeyed, but now she felt impotent in the face of Norris's self-hatred. She knew that she was going to fail to help him, and the situation became tragically sharp.

She had embarked on a mission to turn around the fortunes of a reckless cowboy. She was faced with the daunting task of saving his life and soul. As she experienced a shift in her own consciousness, she began to understand the faith that Stillwell had instilled in her. In that moment, she was transformed into a fearless and resilient woman. "Norris, look at me," she urged. He trembled at the sound of her voice. She walked up to him and placed a gentle hand on his slumped shoulder. He seemed to shrink under her touch. "Look at me," she repeated. But he couldn't bring himself to look up. He was broken, defeated. He couldn't bear to show his battered and bruised face. His posture betrayed the shame of a man with a proud and passionate spirit. It also betrayed his love for her. "Listen to me," Vienna continued, her voice unsteady. "The greatest men are those who have fallen the farthest, sinned the most, suffered the most, and then fought their way back to redemption. I believe you can overcome this despair and become a better man." "No!" he cried. "Listen to me again. I know that you are deserving of Stillwell's love. Will you come back with us for his sake?" "No. It's too late," he insisted. "Norris, the most important thing in life is to have faith in human nature. I have faith in you. I believe that you are worth saving," she countered. "You're just being kind," he protested. "I mean it from the bottom of my heart," she replied, sensing a glimmer of hope in his eyes. "Will you come back with us, even if it's not for your own sake or Stillwell's, but for mine?" "What am I to a woman like you?" he asked, incredulous. "You're a man in need of help, Norris."

"I'm here to help you, to show you that I believe in you," she said. "If I thought it would make a difference, I'd try," he replied. "Listen," she began, speaking softly and quickly. "I don't give my word lightly. Let this be a testament to my faith in you. Look at me now and tell me you'll come."

He struggled to lift his heavy frame, as if trying to shake off a great burden. Slowly, he turned to face her. His face was a mess of bruises and scars, evidence of the physical abuse he had endured. But in that moment, Vienna saw something beautiful in his eyes - a flicker of hope.

"I'll come," he whispered hoarsely. "Give me a few days to straighten things out, and then I'll come."

Chapter Ten.

A s the week came to a close, Stillwell gave Vienna some news: Norris had arrived at the ranch and was staying with Nels. "Gene's not doing well. He looks terrible," the old cattleman said. "He's so weak and shaky that he can't even lift a cup. Nels says that Gene has had some really bad spells. A little bit of liquor would straighten him out, but Nels can't get him to drink anything. He's had to sneak some liquor into his coffee. However, I think we'll be able to pull Gene through. He's forgotten a lot. I was going to tell him what he did to me up at Rodeo, but I know that if he believed it, he'd be even sicker than he is. Either Gene is losing his mind, or something really strange is going on with him."

From then on, Stillwell confided in Vienna daily, as she seemed to be the person who understood him the best. Norris was truly ill, and they had to send Link Stevens to fetch a doctor. Slowly but surely, Norris began to recover and was eventually able to move around. Stillwell said that the cowboy lacked any interest and seemed like a broken man. However, he later modified his statement as Norris continued to improve.

As Norris recovered from his illness, the cowboys resumed their teasing of him, which had been a common occurrence before his ailment. It was a cowboy's nature to jest and poke fun at others, and Norris had become the prime target for their badinage. Stillwell, with his characteristic grin, remarked that the boys were after Gene, teasing him about how he loitered around in order to catch a glimpse of Vienna, whom they all had a crush on. However, Gene had taken their teasing to heart, and his behavior had become peculiar. He seemed to be lost in his own world and did not respond to their jokes, which was unusual for him. Even Stillwell was getting fed up with his behavior and worried that he would not be able to manage the cowboys if he did not snap out of it soon.

Vienna found Stillwell's expectations unrealistic, given that Norris had suffered both physical and mental trauma. She had observed his strange behavior, noticing that he always seemed to be lurking in the distance, watching her but avoiding any direct interaction. Even when she sat on the porch, he would be nearby, lost in his own thoughts. Despite the unusual behavior, Vienna did not draw any conclusions and simply observed the situation.

Under the hot sun, Norris idled about, lounging on the porch of his bunkhouse, whittling the top bar of the corral fence. Vienna couldn't help but feel like he was always watching her. While on her rounds with her gardener, she came across Norris and greeted him warmly. He didn't say much, but he wasn't embarrassed. She couldn't quite place his face, as he always looked different every time they met. Pale, haggard, and drawn, his eyes held a shadow that shone a soft, subdued light. Vienna noticed that it was similar to the light in Princess's eyes, her favorite stag-hound. She wished him a speedy recovery, and continued on her way. Vienna knew that Norris loved her, but she tried to think of him as just one of the many cowboys who liked her. However, she couldn't help but feel that Norris stood out from the rest. She remembered the night he tried to force her to marry him, an unforgettable event. Every mention of him since then had been equally memorable. It seemed like his actions were always tied to significant events. Above all, Vienna couldn't forget that she had saved him from ruin. This fact alone made her think of him differently than the other cowboys.

She had become friends with and uplifted the other cowboys; she even saved Norris's life. He may have been a ruffian, but a woman couldn't save the life of even a ruffian without feeling glad about it. Vienna eventually realized that her interest in Norris was natural, and that her deeper feeling was pity. Perhaps the interest was forced from her, but she gave the pity as she gave everything. Norris eventually recovered his strength, but not in time to ride at the spring round-up. Stillwell discussed with Vienna the possibility of making the cowboy his foreman.

"Well, Gene seems to be getting better," said Stillwell. "But he's not like his old self. I think more of him now. But where's his spirit? The boys would ride roughshod all over him. Maybe I should wait longer now, as the slack season is on. All the same, if those vaqueros of Don Carlos's don't lay low, I'll send Gene over there. That'll wake him up."

A few days later, Stillwell came to Vienna, rubbing his big hands in satisfaction and wearing a grin that was enormous. "Miss Princess, I reckon I've said things were amazingly strange before. But now Gene Norris has gone and done it! Listen to me. Those Mexicans down on our slope have been getting prosperous. They're growing like bad weeds. And they got a new priest, the little old man from El Cajon, Padre Marcos. Well, this was all right, all the boys thought, except Gene. And he got as angry as a dehorned bull. I was sure glad to see he could get mad again. Then Gene heads down the slope for the church. Nels and I followed him, thinking he might have had a sudden crazy spell or something. He hasn't been right since he stopped drinking. Well, we ran into him coming out of the church. We were never so dumbfounded in our lives."

Gene was wild, there's no doubt about it. He had a spell that left us all paralyzed. He ran past us like a bolt of lightning, and we chased after him, but we couldn't catch him. We heard him laughing, and it was the strangest laugh I've ever heard. It was as if he had suddenly been crowned king. He was like that fella who was tied in a burlap sack and thrown into the sea, but he cut his way out, swam to the island where the treasures were, and stood up yelling, "The world is mine!" When we got to his bunkhouse, he was gone. He didn't come back all day or all night. Frankie Slade, who always has something sharp to say, claimed that Gene had gone crazy for liquor, and that was the end of him. Nels was worried, and I was sick.

This morning, I went over to Nels's bunk, and some of the guys were there, all speculating about Gene. Then, as big as life, Gene strutted around the corner. He wasn't the same Gene. His face was pale, and his eyes burned like fire. He had that old mocking, cool smile, and something else that I couldn't quite understand. Frankie Slade made a comment, not any worse than what he'd been saying for days, and Gene punched him, knocking him out of his chair, and then walked all over him. Frankie wasn't hurt so much as he was bewildered.

"Gene," he said, "what the hell got into you?"

And Gene replied, kind of sweetly, "Frankie, you might be a nice fella when you're alone, but your talk is offensive to a gentleman."

After that, everything that was said to Gene was met with a nice smile. Now, Miss Princess, I'm at a loss as to what caused Gene's sudden change. At first, I thought maybe Padre Marcos had converted him. I actually thought that. But I reckon it's just Gene Norris coming back, the old Gene Norris and then some. That's all I care about. I'm remembering how I once told you that Gene was the last of the cowboys.

"I reckon you've been puttin' in some hard miles," commented Stillwell as he greeted Gene Norris, the last of his kind of cowboys. Vienna, who was present, couldn't help but notice the cowboy's worn-out appearance. She had heard about Norris's peculiar behavior towards Padre Marcos, but she didn't think much of it. Vienna supposed that it was rather unusual for a cowboy to be converted to religious belief, but it was possible. She also knew that religious fervor often manifested itself in extremes of feeling and action. However, Vienna had a curious desire to see the cowboy and make her own deductions.

It wasn't until two weeks later that Vienna finally had the chance to meet with Norris. He had been busy with his duties as foreman, and his activities were ceaseless. When he finally returned, Stillwell sent for him. Norris turned his horse over to one of the Mexican boys at the corral and then made his way up to the house, beating the dust out of his gauntlets. Vienna saw the man she remembered, but with a singularly different aspect. His skin was brown; his eyes were piercing and dark and steady; he carried himself erect; he seemed preoccupied, and there was not a trace of embarrassment in his manner.

"Wal, Gene, I'm sure glad to see you," Stillwell greeted him. "Where do you hail from?"

"Guadaloupe Canyon," replied Norris. Stillwell whistled.

"Down there! You mean to say you followed those horse tracks all the way?" asked Stillwell in disbelief.

"Yep, all the way from Don Carlos's ranch across the Mexican border. I had Nick Steele with me, the best tracker in the outfit. We followed the trail through the foothill valleys. At first, we thought the tracks were leading to a water source, but they passed two ranches without stopping. It wasn't until Seaton's Wash that we found evidence of them digging for water. There, we also saw a pack-train of heavily loaded burros heading south. The tracks led us to the old California emigrant road, through Guadelope Canyon, and across the border."

Norris paused for a moment before continuing, "On our way back, we stopped at Slaughter's ranch where the United States cavalry were camping. We met some foresters from the Peloncillo forest reserve, but they didn't offer any information. So, we made our way back home."

"Well, I reckon that's enough information," said Stillwell. "Miss Florentino needs to know about this. It's time to make a report to her."

Norris turned his gaze to Vienna, cool and collected. "We're losing a few cattle on the open range. The vaqueros are driving them at night, some across the valley and others up to the foothills. However, I haven't seen any cattle being driven south. It's a tactic to distract the cowboys. Don Carlos is a Mexican rebel who's been smuggling arms and ammunition across the border, pretending to raise cattle all this time. He was for Madero against Diaz, but now he's against Madero for not keeping his promises. Another revolution is on the horizon, and all the arms are coming from the States across the border."

The burros that were mentioned were carrying illegal goods. "That's the cavalry's problem. They're patrolling the border," Ken said. "They can't stop the smuggling of weapons, especially in that remote area," Norris replied. Vienna asked, "What's my responsibility in this?" Stillwell interjected, "Well, Miss Princess, it has nothing to do with you. It's my and Norris's business. But I wanted you to know. There might be some trouble following my orders."

"Your orders?" Vienna questioned. "I want to send Norris to fire Don Carlos and his vaqueros off the range. They have to leave. Don Carlos is breaking the law of the United States and doing it on our property with our horses. Do I have your permission, Miss Florentino?" Stillwell requested.

"Of course, you do! Stillwell, you know what to do. Ken, what do you suggest?" Vienna asked. "It'll cause problems, Princess, but it has to be done," Ken replied. "You have a group of Eastern friends coming next month. We need the range to ourselves then. But, Stillwell, if you drive those vaqueros off, won't they stay in the foothills? They are a dangerous group," Ken added.

Stillwell was worried. He walked back and forth on the porch with a scowl on his face. "Gene, you have a better plan for this Greaser situation," Stillwell said. "What do you think?"

"He has to be forced off," Norris said calmly. "The Don is clever, but his vaqueros are violent. The situation is like this. Nels said to me the other day, 'Gene, I haven't carried a gun for years until lately, and it feels good whenever I meet any of those strange Greasers.' You see, Stillwell, Don Carlos has vaqueros coming and going all the time. They're guerrilla bands, that's all. And they're becoming more dangerous. There have been several shooting incidents recently. A rancher named White, who lives up the valley, was badly injured."

The boys were restless, and it was only a matter of time before something stirred them up. Stillwell knew Nels, Monty, and Nick, but he failed to mention one particular cowboy in his outfit. Vienna picked up on the hidden meaning, and a chill ran down her spine. She noticed the black handle of Norris' gun protruding from his chaps and asked him why he carried it. He replied that it was not a pretty gun and that it was heavy, implying that it was not for show. Vienna realized that Norris was not to be messed with, and she felt young and weak in his presence. She was faced with a question involving human life, and she knew that her cowboy's thoughts were far from the spiritual significance of it all. She wondered if she placed too much value on human life, but her intuition told her that she had the power to move these primitive men. She asked Norris to be frank with her and explain what he meant about Nels and his comrades.

"Do you mean Nels would shoot at the slightest provocation?" asked Vienna.

"Well, Miss Florentino, when it comes to Don Carlos' vaqueros, shooting is just a matter of course for Nels. He's put up with a lot from them, considering the number of Mexicans he's already killed," replied Norris.

"Already killed? You can't be serious!" Vienna exclaimed, shocked.

"I am. Nels has lived a hard life along the Arizona border. He likes to keep the peace like any other man, but the past has made him who he is. Nick Steele and Monty are just troublemakers looking for a fight," explained Norris.

Vienna was curious about Norris' own intentions. "What about you, Norris? Stillwell's comment about you hasn't gone unnoticed," she said.

Norris remained silent, looking at Vienna with respect. She could sense something beneath his stoic exterior, but couldn't quite figure it out. Was there a hint of mockery in his eyes, or was it just her imagination? Regardless, his face was as hard as stone.

"Miss Florentino, you've brought many changes to this ranch, but you can't change the nature of these men. All it takes is a small disturbance to set them off. With the Mexican revolution brewing, things are bound to get rough along the border. We're in the line of fire, and the boys are getting restless," warned Norris.

Vienna knew she had to face the inevitable. "I understand that I'm in for a rough time, and that some of my cowboys may be uncontrollable. But Norris, you're different now. You've changed," she said, smiling at him.

Stillwell had often referred to Norris as the last of a dying breed of cowboy.

I only have a vague idea of the wild life you've lived, but it seems to have prepared you well to lead these rough men. I'm not sure what a leader should do in this situation, as my cowboys are risking their lives working for me, my property is at risk, and even my own life may be in danger. Stillwell and I both believe that you are the man for the job, so I want to rely on you. I won't give you any orders, but can I at least ask that you be the kind of cowboy I would be?

Vienna remembered Norris's past brutality and shame, but she saw a great change in him now. She wasn't sure what kind of cowboy she wanted him to be, but she did know that she wanted him to act with reason, not passion. Human life shouldn't be sacrificed unless it's in self-defense or to protect those who depend on us. Stillwell and Norris had hinted at violence, and Vienna was afraid of Nels, Nick Steele, and Monty. Could they be controlled? She wanted to avoid all violence, and she wanted her guests to feel safe and comfortable. Could she rely on Norris to manage these obstreperous cowboys, protect her property and Ken's, and take care of them until the revolution was over? She had never had a day's worry since buying the ranch, and she wanted to continue being happy. She wasn't trying to shirk her responsibilities, but she trusted Norris and hoped she could put so much faith in him.

"I hope so, Miss Florentino," replied Norris.

He didn't waste any time in accepting the task, fully aware of the responsibility that came with it. Stillwell and Vienna remained silent as he bowed and left, his spurs clinking as he walked down the path. "Well, well," exclaimed Stillwell. "That's quite a job you've given him, Miss Princess." "It was a woman's cunning, Stillwell," said Ken. "My sister was always good at getting what she wanted as a kid. A smile or a few sweet words, and she had it." "Vienna, what a character to give me!" protested Vienna. "I was serious about Norris. I trust him, and he seems unbreakable. I was scared of the vaqueros, and both Stillwell and Ken convinced me to rely on Norris. I admitted my helplessness and looked to him for support." "Princess, whatever made you choose him was a stroke of diplomacy," replied Ken. "Norris is a good man. He was down and out, and now he's fighting to win. Giving him responsibility was the best way to strengthen his hold on himself. And that little touch of sentiment about being your kind of cowboy and protecting you well, he'll make a great knight. But, remember, he's a tiger and lightning, and don't be surprised if he gets into a fight." "I know cowboys," said Florence. "Gene Norris will be the cowboy your sister said he might be, whatever that means."

"I don't think she's aware, and we can't assume, but he's definitely in the know," said the old man. "Well now, Flo, you hit the nail on the head," he continued. "And I couldn't be happier if he were my own flesh and blood."

Chapter Eleven.

The next morning, Norris set off with a group of cowboys to Don Carlos's rancho. As the day went on and there was no word from him, Stillwell seemed to relax a bit. By nightfall, he told Vienna that he didn't think there was any reason to worry. "Well, it's sure amazing strange," he said. "I've been worrying about how we were gonna fire Don Carlos. But Gene has a way of doing things."

The following day, Stillwell and Ken decided to ride over to Don Carlos's place, bringing Vienna and Florence with them. They planned to stop at Ken's ranch on the way back. They started out in the cool, gray dawn, and after three hours of riding, as the sun began to rise, they came upon a mesquite grove surrounding corrals and barns, several low buildings, and a huge, rambling adobe structure that was mostly in ruins. The only green spot was a spring that gave Don Carlos's range its value and fame. To get to the house, they had to cross a wide, bare courtyard with hitching-rails and watering-troughs in front of a long porch. Several tired horses were standing there, their wet flanks showing that they had just arrived.

"Well, dog-gone it, Al, if that ain't Pat Hawe's horse, I'll eat it," exclaimed Stillwell. "What's Pat want here, anyhow?" growled Ken. Nobody was in sight, but Vienna could hear loud voices coming from the house. Stillwell got off his horse at the porch and went inside. Ken helped Florence and Vienna down from their horses and told them to wait on the porch while he followed Stillwell inside.

Florence made a face and muttered, "I hate these places full of Greasers. They're so creepy and mysterious. I bet they'll come out of every nook and cranny, all dark-skinned, beady-eyed, and soft-footed."

Vienna sat down beside her and replied, "It smells like a barn in here, with all the tobacco smoke. I'm not impressed with this end of my purchase. Hey, Florence, isn't that Don Carlos's black horse over there in the corral?"

Florence confirmed that it was indeed the Don's horse, and expressed regret for coming in such a hurry. Suddenly, they heard the sound of spurs and boots coming from the corridor. Ken's irritation was evident in his quick notes, "Let's just go back home."

But Norris, who was leading the group, disagreed and said, "No! They're with us, whether it's indoors or outdoors." Stillwell, the big-voiced man, chimed in, "Let Norris run things, Al."

A group of men then rushed out onto the porch, with Norris in the lead. Nels was close behind him, and Vienna noticed that he looked different somehow. Don Carlos, with his bright smile, came out next to a thin, sharp-featured man wearing a silver shield.

This must have been Pat Hawe. Nick Steele, who towered over the vaqueros and cowboys, stood behind Stillwell and Ken.

Norris apologized to Florence, saying, "I'm sorry you came. We're in a bit of a mess here. I've made sure that you and Flo are kept close to us. I'll explain everything later. Please forgive any rough talk you might hear."

With that, he turned to the men behind him and said, "Nick, take Booly and go back to Monty and the boys."

"Get all of that stuff out here, now!" Stillwell and Ken broke away from the crowd to stand in front of Vienna and Florence. Pat Hawe leaned against a post, ogling the women in a disrespectful manner. Don Carlos pushed his way forward, his presence filling Vienna's eyes with both reluctance and fascination. He wore tight velveteen pants with a heavy fold down the outside seam, decorated with silver buttons. A sash and fringed holster belt hung around his waist, with a pearl-handled gun protruding from it. His vest was richly embroidered and partially concealed a silk blouse, revealing a silken scarf around his neck. His swarthy face had dark lines, like cords, under the surface, with little, exceedingly prominent, glittering eyes. To Vienna, his face seemed like a bold, handsome mask, through which his eyes piercingly betrayed the man's evil nature. He bowed low with elaborate and sinuous grace, his smile revealing brilliant teeth that enhanced the sparkle in his eyes. He slowly spread his hands in a deprecatory gesture. "Senoritas, I beg a thousand pardons," he said, speaking English in a soft, whiningly sweet accent. How strange it was for Vienna to hear this! "The gracious hospitality of Don Carlos has passed with his house." Norris stepped forward and pushed Don Carlos aside, calling out, "Move aside, everyone!" The crowd fell back to the sound of heavy boots. Cowboys appeared, staggering out of the corridor with long boxes, which they placed side by side on the porch floor. "Now, Hawe, let's get down to business," said Norris. "You see these boxes, don't you?" "I reckon I see a lot of things around here," replied Hawe, meaningfully. "Well, do you intend to open these boxes upon my say-so?" questioned Norris. "No!" retorted Hawe. "It's not my place to meddle with property that's come by express and is all accounted for regularly." "You call yourself a sheriff!" scoffed Norris. "Mebbe you'll think so before long," rejoined Hawe, sullenly. "I'll open them."

"Hey, one of you guys, open up these boxes," commanded Norris. "Not you, Monty. Keep your eyes peeled. Booly, grab that axe. Hurry up now!" Monty Price stepped out from the crowd and onto the porch. The way he moved aside for Booly and faced the vaqueros didn't suggest that he was friendly or trustworthy. "Norris, you're breaking the law by opening these boxes," protested Hawe, trying to intervene. Norris shoved him back. Don Carlos, who was shocked by the appearance of the boxes, suddenly became active in speech and action. Norris pushed him back too. The Mexican grew more agitated, gesticulating wildly and shouting in Spanish. However, when the lids were pried open, and the inside packing removed, he became rigid and silent. Vienna stood up behind Stillwell to see that the boxes were full of rifles and ammunition. "See, Hawe! What did I tell you?" demanded Norris. "I came over here to take control of this ranch, and I found these boxes hidden in an unused room. I suspected what they were.

Contraband goods!" "Well, what if they are?" said Hawe. "I don't
see why you're making such a fuss. Norris, I think you're trying to
show off in your new job." "Hawe, stop talking like that," interrupted Norris. "You've been too mouthy before. Look, I'm supposed to be working with a law enforcement officer. Will you take
charge of these contraband goods?" "You're acting like you're high
and mighty," replied Hawe, pretending to be astonished. "What
are you getting at?" Norris cursed under his breath. He strode
across the porch and held out his hands to Stillwell, indicating the
impossibility of reasonable arbitration. He looked at Vienna with
a regretful glance, wishing he could handle the situation to please
her.

As Norris turned around, he faced Nels who had slipped out of the
crowd. Vienna noticed the seriousness in Nels' steel-blue eyes as he
communicated something to Norris. Whatever it was, it seemed to
calm Norris down. Norris signaled Monty Price to come forward,
and Monty jumped forward with a restrained ferocity that was
unmistakably formidable. Nels and Monty lined up behind Norris, and even Vienna could sense the deliberate action. Pat Hawe's
face turned ugly, and his eyes gleamed red. Don Carlos looked
pale and extremely nervous. The cowboys moved away from the
vaqueros and the bronzed, bearded horsemen who were clearly
Hawe's assistants.

Norris spoke up slowly and caustically, "I'm driving at this. Here's
contraband of war! Hawe, do you get that? Arms and ammunition for the rebels across the border! I charge you as an officer to
confiscate these goods and to arrest the smuggler Don Carlos."

These words from Norris caused a riot among Don Carlos and his followers, and they surged wildly around the sheriff. There was an upflinging of brown, clenching hands, a shrill, jabbering babel of Mexican voices. The crowd around Don Carlos grew louder and denser with the addition of armed vaqueros and barefooted stable-boys and dusty-booted herdsmen and blanketed Mexicans, the last of whom suddenly slipped from doors and windows and corners. It was a motley assemblage. The laced, fringed, ornamented vaqueros presented a sharp contrast to the bare-legged, sandal-footed boys and the ragged herders. Shrill cries, evidently from Don Carlos, somewhat quieted the commotion. Then Don Carlos could be heard addressing Sheriff Hawe in an exhortation of mixed English and Spanish. He denied, he avowed, he proclaimed, and all in rapid, passionate utterance.

In a fit of rage, Don Carlos tossed his black hair and waved his fists, stamping the floor. He denied knowledge of the contraband goods, their contents, and their destination. All he admitted was that they were there, damning evidence of someone's involvement in breaking neutrality laws. Despite his passionate denial, his denunciation of Norris was even more intense. "Senor Norris, he keel my Vaquero!" Don Carlos shouted, accusing Norris of killing his cowboy.

Hawe erupted in anger, pointing his finger in Norris's face and shouting hoarsely. Suddenly, a young vaquero tried to intervene, but Norris was quicker. He lunged out and struck the vaquero, knocking him off the porch. As the man fell, a dagger clinked against the stones. The vaquero lay motionless on the ground.

With contemptuous violence, Norris threw Hawe and Don
Carlos off the porch. The mob retreated as Norris advanced,
his companions Nels, Monty, and Nick Steele following closely.
Norris was fearless, and Vienna was struck by his magnificent
disdain.

Clearly, he understood the type of men he was dealing with. Vienna expected them to back down from him, and they did so without
hesitation. Even Hawe and his crew begrudgingly retreated. Don
Carlos stood up to confront Norris, while the injured vaquero
remained on the ground, groaning. "You don't need to speak Spanish to me," Norris stated. "You can speak and understand English
just fine. If you start any trouble here, you and your men will
be taken down. You need to leave this ranch. You can take the
livestock, packs, and traps in the second corral. There's food as
well. Saddle up and hit the road. Don Carlos, I'm being more
than fair with you. You're lying about these boxes of guns and
ammunition. You're breaking the laws of my country, and you're
doing it on my property. If I let smuggling continue here, I'd be just
as guilty. Now, get off my land. If you don't, I'll have the United
States cavalry here in six hours, and they'll finish what my cowboys
started." Don Carlos was either an excellent actor and relieved at
Norris's mercy, or he was genuinely intimidated by the mention of
the troops. "Yes, sir! Thank you, sir!" he exclaimed before turning
to his men and quickly leaving. The injured vaquero stood up
with Norris's assistance and limped away. Hawe and his comrades
remained behind, with Hawe spitting out a wad of tobacco and
muttering about "cowardly Mexicans." He looked at Norris with a
calculating eye and said, "So, are you going to kick me off the land

too?" Norris responded, "If I ever do, Pat, you'll need to be carried off."

"You and your deputies are kindly requested to leave," said Norris.

"We'll leave, but we'll be back someday, and when we do, we'll put you in chains," replied Hawe.

"If you have a problem with me, let's settle it right here in the corral," challenged Norris.

"I'm an officer, and I don't fight outlaws unless it's necessary for me to make an arrest," replied Hawe.

"You're a disgrace to the county, Pat Hawe. If you ever manage to put me in chains, you'll take me somewhere secluded, shoot me, and then claim it was self-defense. It wouldn't be the first time you've pulled that trick," accused Norris.

Hawe laughed mockingly and began to walk towards the horses. Suddenly, Norris's arm shot out and grabbed Hawe's shoulder, spinning him around.

"You're leaving, Pat, but before you go, you need to show your cards or crawl away," demanded Norris. "You've got a problem with me, man to man. Speak up now and show me you're not the coward I've always thought you were. I've called your bluff."

Hawe's face turned a dark shade of purple. "You can bet I've got a problem with you," he snarled. "You're just a low-down cow-puncher who never had a decent job or a dollar until you got mixed up with that Florentino woman."

Without hesitation, Norris's hand lashed out and slapped
Hawe across the face. Hawe's sombrero fell to the ground as
his head jerked back. As he bent over to pick it up, his hand
shook violently, and his whole body trembled. Monty Price
leapt forward and crouched down with a strange, mournful cry.
Norris stood still, his body tense, bending slightly.

"If you need to mention Miss Florentino, go ahead," said Norris
calmly, but with a dangerous undercurrent to his voice.

Hawe struggled with his fury for a moment, but eventually
managed to rein it in.

"I said you were a low-down, drunk cow-puncher, tough as
damn near a desperado as we ever had on the border," Hawe
deliberately taunted, his words directed at Norris but his burning gaze fixed on Monty Price. "I know you shot that vaquero
last fall, and when I get my proof, I'm coming after you."

"That's all right, Hawe. You can call me what you want, and you
can come after me whenever you want," Norris retorted. "But
you're going to get in trouble with me. You're already in trouble
with Monty and Nels. Soon enough, you'll alienate all the
cowboys and ranchers too. If that doesn't make sense to you,
listen to this. You knew what these boxes contained. You know
Don Carlos has been smuggling arms and ammunition across
the border. You know he is hand in glove with the rebels. You've
been turning a blind eye, and it's been to your advantage. Take
my advice and leave now. The less we see of your face, the better
we'll like it."

FRONTIER BY STARLIGHT   141

Muttering and cursing, Hawe mounted his horse, followed by his comrades. It was evident that the sheriff was struggling with more than just fear and anger. He must have had an irresistible urge to throw more insults and threats at Norris, but he was left speechless. He spurred his horse savagely, turning in his saddle to shake his fist as his comrades rode off through the gate.

Later that day, Vienna and Florence, accompanied by Ken and Stillwell, left Don Carlos's ranch. Vienna was relieved to leave the Mexican's home, which was even more unappealing and uncomfortable inside than it was on the outside.

The halls were dimly lit, the rooms vast, empty, and musty, with an atmosphere of stillness and secrecy that perfectly matched the character Florence had given the place. In contrast, Ken's ranch-house, where the group had stopped for the night, was charmingly situated, small and cozy, with a camp-like layout that Vienna found quite appealing. The day's long rides and exciting events had left her exhausted, so she rested while Florence and the two men prepared dinner. Stillwell expressed his pleasure at the departure of the vaqueros, and optimistically hoped that they were gone for good. Ken also had a positive outlook on the day's events. However, Vienna noticed that Florence seemed unusually quiet and introspective, and she couldn't help but wonder why. She recalled that Norris had wanted to come with them, or send a few cowboys to escort them, but Ken had laughed off the idea and refused. After dinner, Ken dominated the conversation by describing his plans to improve his home before he and Florence got married. They all retired early, but Vienna's deep sleep was interrupted by a pounding on the wall, followed by Florence's voice crying out in response to a call: "Get up! Put some clothes on and come out!" It was Ken's voice. "What's going on?" Florence asked as she got out of bed. "Ken, is everything alright?" Vienna sat up in bed, the room pitch-black except for a faint glow coming from the window. "Oh, nothing major," replied Ken. "Just Don Carlos's rancho going up in flames." "Fire!" Florence exclaimed sharply. "You'll see for yourself soon enough. Hurry up and come outside. Princess, now you won't have to tear down that adobe heap like you threatened. I don't think a single wall will be left standing after this fire." "Well, I'm glad about that," said Vienna.

"I need a good fire to purify the air over there and save me some money," grumbled the speaker. "That haunted ranch was really getting to me. Florence, did you borrow part of my riding out-fit? And why doesn't Ken have any lights in this house?" Florence chuckled as she helped Vienna get dressed. They stumbled over chairs and made their way to the porch, where they saw red flames and smoke in the distance. Stillwell looked worried. "I'm looking for that ammunition to blow up," he said. "There was enough of it to blow the roof off the ranch." Ken was concerned. "The cowboys would have gotten that stuff out first, right?" Still, there was a tense silence as they waited for the explosion that might come from the unattended ammunition. Florence gripped Vienna's arm, and Vienna felt her heart racing. But after a few moments of suspense, Stillwell declared that the danger had passed. The fire was subdued by the wind, which blew strongly that night. The flames were like a huge bonfire covered by a great blanket, with only a few points of light shining through. These flickering points of flame rose and fell in the wind, changing the scene from light to dark. Finally, darkness enveloped the area as the moon peeked out from behind the clouds.

The fire had seemingly burnt itself out, but suddenly a small light appeared where there was once darkness. It grew longer and sharper, moving with a life of its own until it leaped up, radiating a warm white to red color. Flames burst from all around it, creating a great pillar of fire that climbed higher and higher. The smoke that followed was a mixture of yellow, black, and white, all tinged with the color of the fire, drifting away on the wind.

"Well, I guess we won't have the benefit of those two thousand tons of alfalfa we were planning on," remarked Stillwell.

"Ah! So that last outbreak of fire was burning hay," said Vienna. "I don't regret losing the rancho, but it's a shame to lose such a significant amount of good feed for the stock."

"It's lost, and no mistake. The fire's dying as quickly as it flared up. I just hope none of the boys got risky trying to save a saddle or blanket. Monty is hell-bent on running through the fire. He's like a horse that's just been dragged out of a burning stable and runs back, sure locoed. There! It's smoldering down now. I reckon we might as well turn in again. It's only three o'clock."

"I wonder how the fire originated?" remarked Ken.

"Some careless cowboy's cigarette, I bet," said Al.

Stillwell laughed. "Al, you are a free-hearted, trusting fellow. I doubt it was a cigarette, but if it was, you can bet it belonged to a cunning vaquero and wasn't dropped accidentally."

"Now, Bill, you don't mean Don Carlos burned the rancho?" exclaimed Ken, a mixture of surprise and anger in his voice.

Once again, Stillwell laughed. "It's mighty strange to say, my friend, but ole Bill means just that."

"Of course, Don Carlos set that fire," added Florence, with spirit. "Al, if you live out here for a hundred years, you'll never learn that Greasers are treacherous. I know Gene Norris suspected something underhanded."

"He wants us to hurry away," Ken said as he mounted the black horse of Don Carlos's. "He wants that horse for himself and is afraid the Don will steal or shoot him."

Florence didn't trust Al and Bill Stillwell, who never distrusted anyone until it was too late. She had been singing since Norris ordered the vaqueros off the range, but Stillwell hadn't been thinking. "You needn't pitch into me just because I have a natural Christian spirit," he replied defensively. "I've had enough trouble in my life so as not to go looking for more. I'm sorry about the hay burning, but maybe the boys saved the stock. As for that old adobe house of dark holes and underground passages, as long as Miss Princess doesn't mind, I'm glad it burned."

Vienna woke up later than the others and found breakfast already ready. Stillwell was not in a good mood and kept checking his watch, waiting for the cowboys to arrive with news. Ken grew nervous and restless and joined Stillwell outside. Florence didn't mind riding home alone, as they had the fastest horses in the country. Vienna had a sense of misgiving but didn't press the point. They waited for the cowboys to arrive with news.

As Stillwell stomped into the room, the ground shook beneath his massive boots. Ken trailed behind him, carrying a pair of binoculars. "Not a single horse in sight," grumbled Stillwell. "Something's off over at Don Carlos's place. Miss Princess, it might be best for you and Flo to head back home. We can call ahead and let the boys know you're coming."

Ken stood in the doorway, scanning the valley with his binoculars. "Bill, I see some kind of livestock racing around down there. I can't quite make out what it is. We should head over there and check it out."

Both men rushed out of the room, and as the horses were being saddled, Vienna and Florence put away the breakfast dishes and quickly got dressed in their riding gear. "The horses are ready," Ken called out. "Flo, that black Mexican horse is a real gem."

The girls walked outside just in time to hear Stillwell say his goodbyes as he mounted his horse and rode away. Ken pretended to help Vienna and Florence mount their horses, but they always refused his assistance. "I'm not so sure about this," Ken said uncertainly. "You really shouldn't go over to Don Carlos's. It's only a few miles to get back home."

"Of course it's alright," Florence retorted. "We can ride, can't we? You should be more careful going off to mix in with who knows what."

Ken said his goodbyes, spurred his horse, and rode off. "I hope Bill remembered to call ahead!" Florence exclaimed. "He and Al seemed pretty rattled."

Florence dismounted and went back into the house, leaving the door open. Vienna struggled to hold onto Princess, and she couldn't help but notice that Florence was taking longer than usual inside. Finally, she emerged with a serious expression and tight lips. "I couldn't get anyone on the phone," she said. "No one answered. I tried a dozen times."

"Why, Florence!" Vienna was more concerned about the look on her friend's face than the news she was delivering. "The line must be down," Florence said, her eyes following Ken as he disappeared from view.

"I don't like this one bit," Bill said. Florence took a moment to ponder, then hurried into the house and returned with Ken's field-glass. She surveyed the valley, particularly in the direction of Vienna's ranch-house, which was hidden by low, rolling ridges. "Anyway, nobody in that direction can see us leave here," she mused. "There's mesquite on the ridges. We've got cover long enough to save us till we can see what's ahead."

"What do you expect?" asked Vienna, nervously.

"I don't know. There's never any telling about those guys. I wish Bill and Al hadn't left us. Still, come to think of that, they couldn't help us much in case of a chase. We'd run right away from them. Besides, they'd shoot. I guess I'm as well as satisfied that we've got the job of getting home on our own hands. We don't dare follow Al toward Don Carlos's ranch. We know there's trouble over there. So all that's left is to hit the trail for home. Come, let's ride. You stick like a burr to me."

A heavy growth of mesquite covered the top of the first ridge, and the trail went through it. Florence took the lead, proceeding cautiously, and as soon as she could see over the summit she used the field-glass. Then she went on. Vienna, following closely, saw down the slope of the ridge to a bare, wide, grassy hollow, and onward to more rolling land, thick with cactus and mesquite. Florence appeared cautious, deliberate, yet she lost no time. She was ominously silent. Vienna's misgivings took definite shape in the fear of vaqueros in ambush. Upon the ascent of the third ridge, which Vienna remembered was the last uneven ground between the point she had reached and home, Florence exercised even more guarded care in advancing.

As she ascended the ridge, Vienna dismounted and secured her horse to a nearby tree. She motioned for Vienna to stay put while she ventured ahead, disappearing into the mesquite brush. Vienna waited anxiously, taking in her surroundings but not fully present. She was listening for any sounds that might indicate danger. Suddenly, she noticed Princess's ears were perked up. Florence appeared moments later, her face as white as a sheet.

"S-s-s-sh!" Florence whispered, holding up a warning finger. "We're in trouble. A whole bunch of vaqueros are hiding among the mesquite over the ridge! They haven't seen or heard us yet. We need to ride ahead, cut off the trail, and beat them to the ranch."

Vienna was alarmed. "Is there danger? What should we do?"

"There's danger, Vienna," Florence replied earnestly. "Things have turned out just as Gene Norris hinted. We should have listened to him. I'm afraid he knew something we didn't."

"What did he know?" Vienna asked, confused.

"Never mind now. We can't take the back trail. I have a plan to fool Don Carlos. Give me your white sweater and hat. Hurry, Vienna."

Vienna complied, still unsure of what was happening. Florence's gray eyes glinted mischievously as she put on Vienna's white clothing.

"Now, let's ride," Florence said, mounting her horse. "We'll pretend to be two young girls out for a leisurely ride. Don Carlos won't suspect a thing."

She had discarded her sombrero and jacket, offering them to Vienna. "Here, take these. Give me yours. Then get on the black horse. I'll ride Princess. Hurry up now, Vienna. We don't have time to chat."

"But why do you want me to do this? Ah! You're trying to trick the vaqueros into thinking I'm you!" Vienna exclaimed.

"You guessed it. Will you-"

"I won't allow you to do such a thing," Vienna interrupted.

It was then that Florence's face transformed into the hard, stern expression so common among cowboys. Vienna had seen it before on Ken's face, and on Norris's when he was quiet, and always on Stillwell's. It was a look of iron and fire, an unchangeable, unquenchable will. There was even a hint of violence in the swift action Florence took to change Vienna's clothes.

"It was my idea anyway, even if Norris hadn't suggested it," Florence explained, her words as quick as her movements. "Don Carlos is after you, Miss Vienna Florentino! He wouldn't ambush just anyone. He's not killing cowboys these days. He wants you for some reason. Gene thought so, and now I do too. We'll know for sure in five minutes. You ride the black horse, and I'll ride Princess. We'll sneak through the brush, out of sight and sound, until we can break out into the open. Then we'll split up. You head straight for the ranch, and I'll go to the valley where Gene said the cowboys were with the cattle. The vaqueros will mistake me for you. They all recognize those striking white clothes you wear. They'll chase me, but they'll never catch me. And you'll be on a fast horse that can take you home before any vaqueros can catch up to you. You won't be chased. I'm betting everything on that. Trust me, Vienna. It's not just my calculation. It's because I remember Norris. That cowboy knows things."

"Listen up," Florence said. "This is the safest and smartest way to trick Don Carlos." Vienna felt more obligated than convinced, and climbed onto the black horse while taking the bridle. She followed Princess's tracks, with Florence leading the way at right

angles and carefully maneuvering through the mesquite. Florence
avoided breaking any branches and frequently paused to listen for
any signs of danger. After a detour of about half a mile, Vienna was
able to see open ground with the ranch-house nearby and cattle
scattered throughout the valley. While her courage remained in-
tact, the familiar sights somewhat eased the pressure on her chest.
Nonetheless, excitement coursed through her veins. Suddenly, a
horse's shrill whistle caused both the black and Princess to jump.
Florence urged them to quicken their pace down the slope, and
soon Vienna caught sight of the brush's edge, the gray-bleached
grass, and the level ground. Florence halted at the opening between
the low trees and gave Vienna a bright, quick glance. "That's it!
Just ride now and keep your cool!" When Florence wheeled the
fiery roan and screamed in his ear, Vienna felt herself grow limp
and helpless. The big horse launched into a thunderous gallop,
reminiscent of Bonita's wild night ride with her flowing hair.
Florence's hair streamed in the wind and shone like gold in the
sunlight, but Vienna's focus remained on the ride. Then, hoarse
shouts shattered Vienna's concentration, and she spurred the black
into the open. He wanted to run and was swift, but he was difficult
to control. Nevertheless, he was fast, and Vienna cared for nothing
else.

Vienna was well-versed in the ways of horses, and she could tell
that the black stallion had realized he was free and carrying a light
load. She attempted to guide him with the bridle a few times, but
he stayed on course, galloping through patches of mesquite and
jumping over cracks and washes with ease. Vienna felt a rush of
excitement as the wind whipped through her hair and the gray

ground flashed beneath her. She didn't know what she was running from, but she couldn't shake the memory of Florence's warning.

Vienna strained to hear the sound of approaching hooves behind her, and she couldn't help but look back. To her relief, there was no one in sight for miles. She turned to look down the valley slope and saw Florence riding Princess in a zigzag pattern, pursued by a group of vaqueros. Vienna's heart raced as she watched one of the men prepare to throw his lasso, but he wasn't able to get close enough. Another vaquero attempted to intercept the horse, but the roan swerved to avoid him.

Vienna realized that Florence was riding the horse in a panicked and uncontrolled manner, likely due to her lack of experience with wild horses. Despite this, Vienna saw that Florence was gradually gaining ground on the vaqueros and making her way down the valley.

Vienna hadn't lost her focus, even with the thrill of the race between Florence and the vaqueros. She knew the terrain well and kept her own mount in mind. But when she looked back at Florence, she saw that the girl was no longer being chased by the vaqueros. Instead, Princess was running with incredible speed and grace towards the valley, with Florence riding him like the wind. Vienna felt a rush of pride and awe for her friend, knowing that the West taught women to be strong and fearless. As she watched Florence disappear over a low knoll, Vienna's thoughts turned to her own ride and the ranch. She had tried to call ahead, but the phone lines were down. She rode towards the ranch, taking an alternate route and approaching from the south. When she reached the back of the house, she was relieved that no one was around to witness her arrival. She slowed her horse and continued on.

As soon as she got off her horse, he took off and started trotting away. When he got to the top of the slope, he stopped and lifted his head up, perking his ears. Then he let out a loud whistle and ran down the lane. Vienna knew something was up because of the whistle, but she didn't expect a group of strange horsemen riding quickly down the hollow from the foothills. Fear gripped her like cold hands, and she ran as fast as she could into the safety of the house.

Chapter Twelve.

V ienna quickly bolted the door and instructed the servants to lock themselves in the kitchen. She then hurried to her own rooms and began securing the heavy shutters. As she finished fastening the last one in her office, she heard the thunderous sound of hooves approaching the front of the house. She caught a glimpse of wild, unkempt horses and ragged, dusty men. These were not like any vaqueros she had ever seen before. Vaqueros were known for their grace and style, their love of lace, glitter, and fringe, and their horses adorned with silver trappings. However, the riders now entering the driveway were uncivilized, lean, and savage. They were guerrillas, a group of raiders who had been causing trouble along the border since the start of the revolution.

Upon closer inspection, Vienna realized that not all of the men were Mexicans. The presence of outlaws made her realize the gravity of her situation. She remembered the warnings Stillwell had given her about recent outlaw raids in the Rio Grande area. These bands of raiders would appear suddenly, wreak havoc, and disappear just as quickly. They were motivated by the excitement of the revolution and were after money and arms, but would steal

anything they could get their hands on. Unprotected women had
suffered at their hands before, and Vienna knew she was not safe.

Vienna quickly gathered her securities and a large sum of cash
from her desk before rushing out of the room. She locked the
door behind her and hurried across the patio to the other side of
the house. As she entered again, she thought about which of the
unused rooms would be the best to hide in. Suddenly, she heard
a loud banging on the kitchen door and the shrill screams of her
servants, causing her to panic.

She quickly made her way to the last room and realized that there
was no lock or bar on the door. Although the room was large and
dark, it was half-filled with bales of alfalfa hay, making it the safest
place in the house. Vienna dropped her valuables in a dark corner
and covered them with loose hay. She then made her way down a
narrow aisle between the piled-up bales and crouched in a niche.

As she caught her breath, Vienna became aware of the sounds
around her. Dull thuds and crashes came from different parts
of the house, and the squeaking and rustling of mice in the hay
could be heard in the intervals of silence. A mouse even ran over
her hand. She listened intently, waiting and hoping to hear the
approach of her cowboys. However, the thought of violence made
her uneasy, and she prayed that the guerrillas would run away
before any fighting began.

As Vienna waited in the dark room, her mind raced with thoughts
of Nels, Monty, and Nick Steele. The mere mention of their names
left her feeling uneasy and sick. But then she remembered Norris,

the dark-browed, fire-eyed man who sent shivers down her spine. The thrill of excitement that ran through her body pushed away the cold nausea.

She listened and waited, but nothing seemed to be happening. Hours passed, and the uncertainty of Florence's safety weighed heavily on her mind. Could any horse outrun Princess? Vienna didn't think so, but the strain of not knowing was torturous.

Suddenly, the bang of the corridor door shattered the silence, and Vienna's heart raced with fear. The guerrillas had entered the east wing of the house, and she could hear their jabbering voices and the shuffling of their boots. She knew she had to get out of her hiding place.

Vienna rushed to the window, which was more of a door, and tried to open it. It was stuck at the bottom, but she managed to loosen the iron hook and open one of the doors a few inches. She peered out and saw a green slope covered in flowers and sagebrush. No one was in sight, and she believed she would be safer outside in the shrubbery than inside the house.

With a quick decision, Vienna decided to make the jump from the window. She pulled at the door with all her might, but it wouldn't budge. It was caught at the bottom, and she was trapped.

Stopping abruptly, Vienna Florentino paused and felt the heat and bruises on her palms. The invaders of her home were getting closer and louder, and she was filled with fear, anger, and helplessness. She realized she was alone and had to rely on herself. As she struggled to move the stubborn door, she heard the rough voices of men and the sounds of a frantic search. She knew they were hunting for her, and she didn't doubt it. She wondered if she was really Vienna Florentino and if these ruthless men would harm her. The heavy footsteps in the next room made her more fearful, and she pushed the door with all her might, creating a gap for her to slip through. She didn't see anyone and quickly jumped out of the window and ran into the bushes. However, the bushes didn't provide adequate cover, and she realized too late that she had chosen poorly. She was closer to the front of the house than she wanted to be, and she saw horses and a group of agitated men in front of her. She crouched down, her heart in her throat, as a shrill yell followed by running and mounting guerrillas gave her hope. They had spotted the cowboys and were running away. The sound of boots on the porch told her that men were hurrying out of the house. Several horses galloped past her, only a few feet away. One rider noticed her and turned to shout back, which sent Vienna into a panic. She started to run away from the house, but her feet felt heavy, and she was overwhelmed with the same sense of powerlessness she felt when she dreamed of being chased.

Riders on horseback raced past Vienna, their shouts echoing through the shrubbery. The sound of thundering hoofs grew closer and closer, and Vienna turned to try and escape. But it was no use - she was being chased down. Just as she thought she was about to be trampled underfoot, a strong hand grabbed her waist, lifting her up and out of harm's way. However, the shoulder of the horse still hit her with a heavy blow, and her arm was wrenched as she was pulled onto the horse.

Despite the blinding pain, Vienna managed to stay conscious as she was carried away at breakneck speed. Eventually, the horse's movements became less violent, and Vienna slowly began to regain her senses. She realized she was lying across a saddle, her head hanging down towards the ground. She couldn't move her hands and struggled to orient herself, but eventually saw a Mexican boot with a large silver spur, the legs of a horse, and a dusty trail.

Vienna's head swam with pain and motion as she was carried for what felt like hours. Finally, someone lifted her off the horse and laid her on the ground. As the blood drained from her head, she began to take in her surroundings - she was in a grove of fir trees, and the sun was setting. She smelled wood smoke and heard horses crunching grass nearby. When she turned her head, she saw a group of men gathered around a campfire, eating ravenously like wolves.

Vienna shut her eyes when she caught sight of her captors. The Mexicans were thin and had scraggly beards. They looked like they were starving. None of them had coats, and only a few had scarves. Some of them had belts with cartridges, but only a few had guns, and they were all different kinds. Vienna couldn't spot any packs or blankets, and the cooking utensils they had were battered and blackened. She saw a few men who she thought were white, but she could only tell from their features, not their skin color. She had seen a group of robbers before, and this group of outlaws reminded her of them.

The group seemed to be hungry and watchful. Vienna figured they were waiting for someone, but they didn't seem worried about a posse catching up to them. She couldn't understand most of what they were saying, but when they mentioned Don Carlos, she felt scared again.

Suddenly, one of the guerrillas made a noise and motioned for the others to look in a different direction. Vienna heard something, and she knew they saw someone. The men reached for their weapons, and Vienna could see the fear on their faces. She closed her eyes, not wanting to see what was about to happen. She heard them cursing and whispering before someone yelled out, "El Capitan!"

Vienna's eyes shot open when she heard the name. She associated El Capitan with Norris and felt a strange sense of regret.

The thought of death consumed Vienna's mind as she watched the group of men. She knew that they were after Norris, but she hoped that he had not come alone. The stern faces of the men gave Vienna a sense of direction to look towards. She heard the sound of a horse's hooves and saw a man with his arms raised high approaching from the trees. It was Norris riding Princess, his trusty steed. Vienna felt a mixture of emotions, relief, fear, and wonder, as she realized that Norris had made it to the campfire circle.

Many of the guerrillas stood up, brandishing their weapons, but Norris remained calm and continued to ride towards them with his hands raised. He rode straight into the circle and stopped, where the chief of the group greeted him with amazement and respect. Vienna could tell from the chief's expression that he was pleased to see Norris.

Norris appeared to be composed and carefree, but Vienna noticed that his face was pale. He shook hands with the chief and then scanned the area until his eyes met Vienna's. At that moment, Vienna tried to smile to reassure him that she was okay, but Norris's intense gaze froze her smile.

Norris spoke to the chief in a language that Vienna found difficult to understand. The chief responded by spreading his arms wide, pointing towards Vienna. Norris then whispered something into the chief's ear, and they both moved away from the group to speak privately.

The chief was taken aback and gestured in surprise and agreement. Norris quickly spoke again, causing the chief to turn and address the group. Vienna overheard the words "Don Carlos" and "pesos". There was a brief protest, but the chief immediately silenced it. Vienna assumed that this guerrilla had bought her release and the approval of the other band members. Norris walked over to her, leading the roan. Princess snorted and reared up when she saw Vienna on the ground. Norris knelt down, still holding the bridle, and asked, "Are you okay?" Vienna attempted to laugh but failed, saying, "My feet are tied." Norris's face turned pale and his eyes glinted with anger. He loosened the bonds around her ankles with his strong hands. Without a word, he lifted her up and onto Princess. Vienna swayed in the saddle and held onto the pommel with one hand, trying to lean on Norris's shoulder with the other. "Don't give up," he said. She saw him scanning the forest on all sides and was surprised when the guerrillas rode away. Vienna realized that neither Norris nor the others wanted to encounter someone who was likely to arrive in the glade soon. Norris led the roan to the right and walked alongside Vienna, supporting her in the saddle. At first, Vienna was so weak and dizzy that she could barely stay upright. However, the dizziness subsided and she tried to ride without assistance. Her weakness and the pain in her injured arm made it difficult to do so. Norris had veered off the trail, if there was one, and was moving through the denser parts of the forest. As the sun began to set, the golden rays of light shone through the trees. Princess's hooves made no sound on the soft ground, and Norris walked on in silence.

He rode with haste, constantly scanning the darkening woods until he had covered at least two miles. Then he straightened his course and relaxed his watchfulness. As he continued, he noticed that the forest floor became more rugged, with slopes and hollows that grew wider and wider. The soft ground gave way to rocky soil, causing his horse to snort and toss its head. Suddenly, the silence was broken by the sound of splashing water. As he approached, he saw a little brook that flowed over the stones. His horse stopped and bent its head, indicating that it wanted a drink.

Vienna acknowledged that she was thirsty and tired, so Norris lifted her from the saddle. As their hands parted, Vienna felt something moist and warm. She looked down to see blood running down her arm and into the palm of her hand. She remembered that her arm was hurt. She held it out, and Norris quickly ripped off her wet sleeve. Her forearm had been cut or scratched, and he washed off the blood. Vienna realized that it was the first time she had ever seen her own blood.

Norris bound her arm with strips of her handkerchief. His swift and silent actions gave her a sense of security. However, when he lifted his head, she saw that he was pale and shaking. As he folded his scarf, Vienna noticed the red stains and asked what had happened. Norris revealed that a man, possibly a Greaser, had cut her arm with his fingernails. He knew who the man was and could have killed him, but he didn't want to risk Vienna's freedom.

"I didn't dare," Norris exclaimed, his emotions running high. Vienna stared at him, taken aback not just by his outburst but also by his words. He was apologizing for not killing a man who had laid his hands on her. Norris was ashamed, tortured by the fact that he couldn't avenge her properly. There was a passionate scorn in him that Vienna couldn't quite understand.

"My dear boy!" Vienna exclaimed, searching for words. She had heard stories about Norris's cool indifference to danger and death. He had always seemed as hard as granite. But seeing a little blood on her arm had caused him to pale and shake. She couldn't comprehend why he was begging her to understand why he couldn't kill the outlaw.

"Norris, I understand," Vienna said, although she didn't fully comprehend. She was grateful for his protection, but she couldn't fathom why he was so affected by the situation.

The answer to her confusion was simple- Norris loved her. Vienna couldn't answer the second question that plagued her mind, but she knew that the reason lay in the same strength that fueled his love- an intensity of feeling that was characteristic of Western men with simple, lonely lives.

Suddenly, Vienna realized the depth of Norris's love for her. The thought hit her with a powerful force. Her Eastern lovers, with all their graces and worldly possessions, lacked the one essential quality that Norris had- the ability to love her with all his heart. Nature had struck a just balance here.

An unknown voice called to Vienna, disturbing her thoughts. Something deep and dim in the future made her uneasy.

The woman refused to listen to reason, and decided to ignore the voice of wisdom. "Can we take a break? I'm exhausted," she asked. "Maybe if I rest, I'll feel better." "We're safe now," the man reassured her. "The horse is doing better too. I pushed him hard, uphill even." "Where are we?" she inquired. "We're deep in the mountains, at least ten miles from the ranch. There's a trail nearby, and I can get you home by midnight. They'll be worried about you down there." "What happened?" she asked. "To anyone else, nothing much. You were the only one in danger. Florence caught us on the slope. We were coming back from the fire, and we were exhausted. We made it back to the ranch before any harm was done, but we had trouble finding you. Nick found your footprints under the window, and we knew you were gone. I had to fight the boys to keep them from going after you. Old Bill came out with a dozen guns, and I had to tie up Monty. I left Nels and Nick to watch him until morning. I was lucky to find the band so quickly. I knew the guerrilla chief from Mexico. He's a bandit by trade, but he fought for Madero, and I was with him a lot. He may be Mexican, but he's trustworthy." "How did you get me out of there?" she asked. "I paid them off. That's what the rebels want, money. They're poor and hungry, and they need it. I had to promise them two thousand dollars Mex. I gave my word, so I'll have to pay up."

"I told them where and when to meet me," Vienna said with a laugh. "I'm just glad I have the money. It's a strange situation to be in. I wonder what my dad would say about this? I'm afraid he would say that two thousand dollars is more than I'm worth. But tell me, did the rebel chieftain demand money?"

"No," Norris replied. "The money is for his men."

Vienna was curious. "What did you say to him? I saw you whisper in his ear."

Norris looked down, avoiding her gaze. "We were comrades before Juarez. One day I saved him from a ditch. I reminded him of that and told him something I thought would help."

Vienna sensed that Norris had spoken about her. "I heard Don Carlos's name mentioned several times. What do Don Carlos and his vaqueros have to do with this?"

"That Greaser has everything to do with it," Norris said grimly. "He burned his ranch and corrals to keep us from getting them. But he also did it to draw all the boys away from your home. They had a deep plot, all right. I left orders for someone to stay with you, but Al and Stillwell, who are both hot-headed, rode off this morning. Then the guerrillas came down."

Vienna was confused. "What was the point of the plot?"

"To get you," Norris said bluntly.

Vienna was taken aback. "Me? Norris, you don't mean that my capture, or whatever you call it, was anything more than a mere accident?"

"I do mean that," Norris replied. "But Stillwell and your brother think the guerrillas wanted money and arms, and they just happened to take you because you ran under a horse's nose."

"I see," Vienna said, sensing that Norris didn't agree with that explanation. "You don't think that's what happened?"

"No, I don't," Norris said. "Neither do Nels or Nick Steele. And we know Don Carlos and the Greasers."

Vienna asked Norris what he thought about the vaqueros chasing Flo. He hesitated to answer, but Vienna insisted. She wanted to know why Nels and Nick suspected Don Carlos of plotting to abduct her. Norris explained that Nels had seen Don Carlos look at Vienna and threatened to shoot him if he ever saw him do it again. Vienna found this ridiculous, but Norris didn't like the way men treated women in civilization.

Vienna was surprised by Norris's statement and reminded him of the night she came to him. He looked ashamed and then suddenly lifted his head with flaming eyes, asking her to imagine if he had met an ordinary girl and made her marry him. He believed he would have stopped being a drunkard and treated her well. Vienna didn't know what to think of him.

As the sun set, Norris rebridled the horse and mentioned that Don Carlos hoped to make off with Vienna for himself, treating her like a poor peon slave-girl down in Sonora. He suspected that Don Carlos had a deeper plot than his rebel friend told him, even hoping for American troops to chase him. The rebels were trying to stir up the United States.

They would welcome intervention, but regardless, the Greaser had evil intentions towards Vienna from the moment he laid eyes on her. That's all there is to it," Norris said.

"Norris, you have done my family and me a service that we can never repay," Vienna said gratefully.

"I did the service, but don't mention repayment to me. However, there is something I want to tell you, and it's hard for me to say. It's not coming from pride or conceit, but from what I know you think of me and what I imagine your family and friends would think if they knew. Such a woman as you should never have come to this God-forsaken country unless she meant to forget herself. But as you did come, and as you were dragged away by those devils, I want you to know that all your wealth and position and influence, all that power behind you, would never have saved you from hell tonight. Only a man like Nels, Nick Steele, or myself could have done that," Norris admitted.

Vienna realized that the truth was a great leveling force. No matter the difference between her and Norris, or whatever imagined difference set up by false standards of class and culture, the truth was that on this wild mountain-side, she was just a woman and he was just a man. She needed a man, and if she had a choice in this situation, it would have been him who stood before her. She pondered this realization as Norris said, "I reckon we'd better start now," and drew the horse close to a large rock. "Come."

Vienna's will was stronger than her body, which she admitted for the first time was in pain. She didn't feel much discomfort except when she moved her shoulder. Once in the saddle, where Norris lifted her, she drooped weakly.

The journey was rough, and each step the horse took caused Vienna pain. The slope of the ground made matters worse, throwing her forward onto the pommel. As the terrain grew rockier, her discomfort intensified until it was all she could focus on. Finally, Norris spoke up, "Here is the trail." Just then, Vienna's horse swayed, and she would have fallen from the saddle if Norris hadn't caught her. He muttered under his breath, "This won't do. Throw your leg over the pommel. The other one there." Norris mounted the horse and slipped behind Vienna, lifting and turning her. He held her with his left arm so that she lay across the saddle and his knees, her head resting on his shoulder. As the horse began to walk, Vienna gradually lost all pain and discomfort as she relaxed her muscles. She let herself go and lay inert, greatly relieved. For a moment, she felt like she was half drunk with the gentle swaying of a hammock. Her mind became dreamy yet active, as if thoughtfully recording the slow, soft impressions pouring in from all her senses. The red glow of the sunset faded in the west. Vienna could see out over the foothills where twilight was settling gray on the crests, dark in the hollows. Cedar and pinyon trees lined the trail, and there were no more firs. At intervals, huge drab-colored rocks loomed over her. The sky was clear and steely, and a faint star twinkled. Lastly, she saw Norris's face, once more dark and impassive, with his inscrutable eyes fixed on the trail. His arm, like a band of iron, held her, yet it was flexible and yielded her to the motion of the horse. One instant she felt the brawn, the bone, heavy and powerful; the next, the stretch and ripple, the elasticity of muscles. He held her as easily as if she were a child.

The rough texture of his flannel shirt grazed her cheek and beneath it, she felt the dampness of the scarf he had used to cleanse her arm. Deeper still, she could hear the steady thump of his heart. She pressed her ear against his chest and the strong, vibrant beat filled it like a mighty engine deep within a great cavern. She had never rested her head on a man's breast before and she was not particularly fond of it, but there was something mysterious and captivating about the position. It felt natural, and it made her think about life.

As the cool wind blew down from the heights, her hair tumbled about and strands of it curled softly into Norris's face, across his lips. She was unable to reach it with her free hand to refasten it. When she shut her eyes, she felt the loose strands brushing against his cheeks. In the midst of these vivid sensations, she caught the scent of dust and a faint, wild, sweet tang on the air. The low, rustling sigh of wind in the brush along the trail added to the atmosphere. Suddenly, the silence was broken by the sharp bark of a coyote, and then, from far away, a long wail. Princess's metal-rimmed hoof rang on a stone. These sounds lent credibility to the ride for Vienna. Otherwise, it would have felt like a dream. Even so, it was hard to believe. She wondered if she was really Vienna Florentino, the woman who had begun to think and feel so much. Nothing had ever happened to her before, and now, adventure, perhaps death, and certainly life, were playing about her like her hair played about Norris's face. She couldn't believe the evidence of the day's happenings. Would any of her people or friends ever believe it? Could she even tell them? It was impossible to think that a cunning Mexican might have used her to further the interests of a forlorn revolution.

The memory of the emaciated rebels haunted her, and she couldn't believe her luck in escaping them. She felt safe now, and the concept of self-preservation finally made sense. The arrival of Norris in the glade and the bravery he displayed when confronting the outlaws felt as real to her as the arm that held her close. Was it her intuition that urged her to save him when he was sick and hopeless in the Chiricahua shack? Did she surround herself with the same forces that had saved her life, or was it something more significant than that? She believed that it was.

Vienna eventually woke up to find that night had fallen. The sky was a deep, velvety blue, illuminated by bright white stars. The chilly breeze played with her hair, and she saw Norris's profile, sharp and bold against the sky, through the waving strands. As her body grew weary, her mind began to struggle to grasp her situation, and she felt like she was in a dream. A heavy drowsiness, like a blanket, started to envelop her, and she swayed and drifted. As she dozed off, she felt a muffled throb near her ear, something sweet, deep, and unfamiliar, like a distant bell ringing. She fell asleep with her head resting on Norris's chest.

Chapter Thirteen.

Three days had passed since Vienna's return to the ranch, and she couldn't feel any aches or pains from her recent escapades. This was a surprise to her, but what surprised her even more was how quickly she began to forget the whole ordeal. If it weren't for the constant watchful eyes of her cowboys, she might have completely blocked out memories of Don Carlos and the raiders. Vienna knew that she was in great physical shape thanks to the demanding ranch life, and she was starting to adopt the Western attitude of fearlessness.

Vienna's life had changed drastically since she was captured by Don Carlos and rescued by Gene. She was now the owner of a ranch and had many interesting things brought to her attention on a daily basis. Stillwell, the superintendent, was always worried about her safety and trusted Norris the most to keep an eye on her.

One day, Stillwell came into Vienna's office with some news about Gene. He had once again ridden off into the mountains and was seen meeting with Padre Marcos. Vienna wondered if he was taking money to the guerrillas, but Stillwell explained that he had already done that before.

Monty and Nels had been causing trouble for Gene lately, and Stillwell predicted that they would soon come to blows. Vienna joked that maybe Norris was getting religious, but Stillwell dismissed that idea after hearing Gene curse Monty that morning.

Vienna listened to all of this with interest, knowing that her life was never going to be boring again.

"I've got a lot on my mind," Vienna said to Stillwell. "Let Norris go on his mysterious trips to the mountains. I have news that might worry you. I received letters from home and my sister is coming out to visit me with some of her society friends, including an English lord."

"Well, Miss Princess, I reckon we'll all be happy to see them," replied Stillwell. "Unless they decide to send you back East."

"That's unlikely," Vienna responded thoughtfully. "But I do have to go back at some point. Let me read you some excerpts from my sister's letter."

Vienna picked up the letter with a strange feeling of nostalgia for the life she had left behind. She scanned the pages of her sister's beautiful handwriting, which was filled with anticipation for the fun she expected to have with bashful cowboys. Vienna was annoyed by the satirical tone of the letter and the fact that her sister seemed to be reveling in the prospect of new sensations. Melissa was completely ignorant of the West and expected to hunt buffalo and fight Indians, much like the English lord in her party.

After reading a few paragraphs aloud, Stillwell snorted and his face turned red. "Did your sister really write this?" he asked.

"Yes," Vienna replied.

"Well, I beg your pardon, Miss Princess, but it doesn't seem like something you would say. Does she think we're a bunch of wild men from Borneo?"

"Evidently she does," Vienna said with a hint of annoyance. "But I think she's in for a surprise. Now, Stillwell, you're clever and can see the situation."

I want my guests to have a blast while they're here, but not at the expense of anyone's feelings. Melissa is bringing a lively crowd who are looking for something out of the ordinary. Let's make sure we give them just that. Talk to the boys and let them know what to expect so they can be prepared. I'll help you with that. When the boys are off-duty, I want them to be on dress-parade and on their best behavior. I don't care what they do to protect themselves or what tricks they come up with, as long as they're kind and courteous. I want them to take this seriously and act as if they've always lived this way. My guests are expecting a good time, so let's give it to them. What do you say?

Stillwell stood up, his massive frame towering over everyone else, and his face beaming. "Well, I think it's the most amazing idea I've ever heard!" he exclaimed.

"I'm glad you like it," Vienna said. "After you talk to the boys, come back to me. But I have to admit, I'm a little worried. You know how cowboys like to have fun. Maybe-"

"Don't worry about a thing," Stillwell interrupted. "Leave the boys to me. They all swear by you, just like the Mexicans swear by the Virgin. They won't let you down, Miss Princess. They'll be simply amazing. It'll be better than any show you've ever seen!"

Vienna still had her doubts, but she couldn't help but be swept up in Stillwell's enthusiasm. "Alright then, it's settled. My guests will arrive on May ninth."

As they prepared for the arrival of their guests at Her Princess's Rancho, Vienna and Florence noticed a thin streak of white dust rising from the distant valley. Upon closer inspection with binoculars, they realized it was Link Stevens and the automobile carrying their guests. Vienna remembered her conversation with Stevens about the condition of the car and the road, hoping to impress their New York guests with a fast and safe ride. As they watched the car approach, Stillwell's face was filled with delight. It was time for the invasion of their ranch by their city friends.

"So, if I drive carefully and safely, I can leave the dust behind and get here faster than the Greaser's tomorrow?" Vienna asked, seeking confirmation from Stevens. He nodded in agreement, and Vienna couldn't help but laugh. As she watched the thin streak of dust moving at a snail's pace, she began to doubt her decision. She trusted Stevens, who was a skilled, daring, and iron-nerved driver.

However, the thought of him driving on forty miles and more of that desert road made her feel guilty for putting him in danger.

"Oh, Stillwell!" Vienna exclaimed, "I'm afraid I'll go back on my wonderful idea. What made me do it?"

"Your sister wanted the real thing, didn't she? Said they all wanted it. Well, I reckon they've begun getting it," replied Stillwell, the cattleman.

Vienna's conscience was somewhat relieved by Stillwell's statement. She longed to see her old friends and hear the soft laughter and gay repartee of her past. However, there was a small part of her that felt hostile towards the expected guests. They were curious and scornful about the Western ranch that had claimed her. Vienna wondered if her sister or friends would ever see the West as she saw it. She knew it was a long shot. Nevertheless, she hoped that they would get a glimpse of the real thing, just like Stillwell said.

She had made up her mind to show her guests the true beauty of life in the Southwest. "Well, as Nels says, I wouldn't be caught dead in that car right now for a million bucks," Stillwell commented. "Why? Is Stevens driving too fast?" "Good Lord! Fast? Miss Princess, there hasn't been anything except lightning run so fast in this country. I bet Link is in heaven right now. I can just see him, hunching down over that wheel like it's a horse's neck." "I told him not to make the ride too hot or dusty," Vienna said. "Haw, haw!" Stillwell laughed. "Well, I'm heading out. I want to be here when Link drives up, but I also want to be with the boys down by the bunks. It'll be fun to see Nels and Monty when Link comes racing along." "I wish Al had stayed to meet them," Vienna said. Her brother had rushed a shipment of cattle to California, and Vienna suspected he had welcomed the chance to leave the ranch. "I'm sorry he left," Florence replied. "But Al's all business now, and he's doing great. Maybe it's for the best." "Surely. That was just my pride talking. I wish all my family and friends could see what a man Al has become. Well, Link Stevens is driving like the wind. The car will be here any moment. Florence, we only have a few minutes to get ready. But first, I want to order lots of cold refreshments for our guests." Less than thirty minutes later, Vienna returned to the porch and found Florence waiting there. "Oh, you look stunning!" Florence exclaimed as she looked up at Vienna. "And somehow different!" Vienna smiled a bit sadly.

As she slipped into her exquisite white gown, something came over her. Perhaps it was the manner in which the dress befitted her. She couldn't resist the urge to impress her hypercritical friends with her beauty. The melancholic smile was reserved for days gone by, for she knew that her beauty, once praised by society, had tripled since it was last seen in a drawing-room. Vienna didn't wear any jewels, but she had pinned two great crimson roses at her waist. Against the dead white of the dress, these roses had the life, fire, and redness of the desert.

Florence exclaimed, "Link's hit the old round-up trail, and oh, isn't he riding that car!" For most cowboys, including Florence, a car was not driven, but ridden. A white spot with a long trail of dust appeared low down in the valley. It was now headed almost straight for the ranch. Vienna watched it grow larger moment by moment, and her pleasurable emotion grew accordingly. Then the rapid beat of a horse's hoofs caused her to turn. Norris was riding in on his black horse. He had been away on an important mission that took him to the international boundary-line. His unexpected presence was particularly gratifying to Vienna, for it meant that his mission had been brought to a successful conclusion. Once again, for the hundredth time, Vienna was struck by the man's reliability. He was a doer of things. The black horse halted wearily without the usual pound of hoofs on the gravel, and the dusty rider dismounted wearily. Both horse and rider showed the heat and dust and wind of many miles. Vienna advanced to the porch steps, and Norris, after taking a parcel of papers from a saddle-bag, turned toward her.

"Norris, you are the best of couriers," she said. "I am pleased." Dust streamed from his sombrero as he doffed it.

With a tired sigh, Norris straightened his shoulders and approached Vienna with the reports she had requested. As he looked up to see her dressed in her finest attire to greet her Eastern guests, he paused momentarily, recalling the night she had revealed her true identity. It wasn't fear or awkwardness that caused him to pause, but rather a strong force that compelled him to halt. Vienna noticed the sudden pause and met his gaze, feeling a warmth rise to her cheeks. She rarely blushed, and the sudden sensation was irritating. She accepted the reports from Norris and thanked him as he led his horse down the path towards the corrals. Florence commented that when Norris looked weary, he had been riding, but when his horse looked tired, he had been riding hard. Vienna watched the horse and rider disappear and pondered what had made her thoughtful. It was the change in Norris's gaze that had struck her. His inscrutable, burning eyes had suddenly become beautiful, expressing a strange joy of pride. It wasn't a gaze of love or passion, but something else entirely. Vienna pondered the meaning behind Norris's expression, trying to comprehend the inexplicable.

Vienna had never seen a man with such an expression before. It was so peculiar that it made her blush. The longer she spent with these outdoor men, the more they surprised her. She couldn't understand why cowboy Norris was so proud or happy to see her. Florence's exclamation drew Vienna's attention back to the approaching automobile. It was on the slope now, a few miles down the gradual hill. Two yellow clouds of dust shot out from behind the car and joined the column that stretched down the valley.

"I wonder what it would be like to ride a mile a minute," said Florence. "I'll make Link take me. Oh, but look at him come!"

The giant car looked like a white demon, and if it weren't for the dust, it would have appeared to be sailing in the air. Its movement was steady, as if it were on rails. And its speed was astonishing. Long, gray veils streamed in the wind, and a low rushing sound became audible. The car shot past the alfalfa field, the bunkhouses, and the cowboys who cheered as it went by. The horses and burros in the corrals began to snort and tramp and race in fright. At the base of the long slope of the foothill, Link reduced the speed by more than half. Yet the car roared up, rolling the dust, flying capes and veils and ulsters, and crashed and cracked to a halt in the yard before the porch.

Vienna could see a gray, disheveled mass of humanity packed inside the car. There were seven occupants besides the driver, and for a moment, they appeared to be coming to life, moving and exclaiming under their veils and wraps and dust-shields. Link Stevens stepped out and, removing his helmet and goggles, coolly looked at his watch. "An hour and a quarter, Miss Florentino," he said.

"It's sixty-three miles by the valley road, and there's a couple of tricky hills. But we made pretty good time, considering you wanted me to drive slow and safe." The passengers in the car murmured and complained, mostly the women. Vienna stepped forward onto the porch, and the voices of the men and women joined together in a joyful exclamation, "PRINCESS!"

Melissa Florentino, Vienna's younger sister, arrived looking worn out from the journey. She was a pretty girl with brown hair and eyes, unlike Vienna's fair complexion. After being shown to her room and catching her breath, she began to talk. "Princess, I made it, but I never would have come if I had known about that car ride from the train station. I thought we would be taking a stagecoach or something like that. That car was enormous, and the road was terrible. And what about that strange little man with the leather pants? What kind of chauffeur is he?"

"He's a cowboy. He was injured in a horse accident, so I had him trained to drive the car. Do you think he did a good job?" Vienna replied.

"A good job? He scared us all to death, except for Mountcastle. Nothing could faze that unflappable Englishman. I'm still dizzy from the ride. When I saw the car, I was excited, but then your cowboy driver met us at the station. He looked so strange with that big gun strapped to his waist. It made me nervous. And then he made me sit next to him in the front seat, even though I didn't want to. I was silly enough to tell him I liked to go fast. You know what he said?"

But after that ride, I think I prefer a slower pace," replied Melissa, still trying to catch her breath.

The man who had driven them to the ranch had given them a warning about the journey, but Melissa had not been prepared for the intensity of the wind and dust. The car had seemed to fly down the endless road, and Melissa had felt both fascinated and terrified by the speed. The wind had torn at her clothes, and she had been afraid she would be stripped bare. But finally, after what felt like an eternity, the car had come to a stop, and there stood Vienna, waiting for them.

Vienna teased Melissa about her love for speed, but Melissa was not amused. She was still recovering from the harrowing ride, and she knew that she would be more cautious in the future. She had learned that sometimes, the journey can be just as important as the destination, and it was better to take things slow and steady.

"I ain't never been in a fast car before, never seen a road, and never met a driver," I said, feeling a bit nervous as Melissa drove us through the wild and woolly West.

"Well, I reckon I might have a few surprises for you," Melissa replied with a mischievous glint in her dark eyes.

As we pulled up to Vienna's beautiful home, Melissa couldn't help but express her surprise at how stunning Vienna looked. "You're the handsomest thing I ever laid eyes on," Melissa said, admiring Vienna's strong and beautiful appearance.

Vienna was clearly pleased to have her guests admiring her home, and even found herself enjoying the company of the imperturbable Englishman, Mountcastle. She felt her capacity for liking others had grown, and even found herself rediscovering her old love for her younger sister, Melissa.

Despite the smaller party than expected, Vienna was looking forward to a delightful and memorable visit with her guests. Melissa had brought news from the East, and Vienna was eager to hear all about it.

Melissa had carefully chosen her companions for the evening, all of whom were well-known to Vienna. Lorraine Wayne was a serious, soft-spoken brunette with a kind heart, despite her past experiences. Mrs. Carrollton Beck, a plain but lively woman, acted as chaperone for the group. The final member of the female contingent was Miss Dorothy Coombs, a young woman with attractive blonde features.

Mountcastle, the only man in the group, was quite small in stature. His pink-and-white complexion, small golden mustache, and drooping eyelids made him appear dull, but his exaggerated English-style attire drew attention to his diminutive size. Robert Weede, a large and florid young man, was known for his good nature. Boyd Harvey, a handsome and carefree fellow, completed the party.

The dinner was a happy affair, enjoyed by all. The Mexican women who served the meal could not help but notice the success of the gathering. The low voices, laughter, and superficial talk of the group transported Vienna back in time. Although she did not wish to return to that era, she realized it was important to maintain connections with her friends and community.

As the party moved to the porch, the heat of the day began to dissipate, and the red sun sank over the desert. The visitors were struck by the beauty of the sunset, and a deep silence descended upon the group. Just as the last curve of the red rim disappeared beyond the Sierra Madres and the golden lightning began to flare brighter, Melissa broke the silence with a simple statement: "It wants only life."

"Oh, look! There's a horse climbing up that hill!" Vienna exclaimed, her eyes fixed on the distant figure. "And there's a rider too!"

Vienna knew who it was before she even looked properly. She realized then how much she had become accustomed to watching for him at this time of day. The horse and rider made their way along the mesa's rim and out to the point, where they stood out against the golden backdrop.

Melissa, curious as ever, asked, "What's he doing up there? Who is he?"

"That's Norris, my right-hand man," Vienna replied. "He comes up here every day when he's at the ranch. I think he enjoys the ride and the view, but he also checks on the cattle down in the valley."

"Is he a cowboy?" Melissa asked.

Vienna laughed. "Absolutely! You'll know it when Stillwell gets a hold of you and starts talking about him."

Vienna took it upon herself to explain who Stillwell was and what he thought of Norris. She even added a few details about Norris's reputation. "He's known as El Capitan," she said.

"How interesting!" Melissa mused. "What does he look like?"

"He's absolutely superb," Vienna replied.

Florence handed Melissa the field-glass. "Take a look for yourself."

Melissa peered through the glass. "Oh, thank you! There he is. He really is superb. And his horse is magnificent. They both look like they're carved in stone."

Dorothy Coombs eagerly asked for a turn with the field-glass. Melissa handed it over but warned, "He's mine. I saw him first."

Vienna's guests then held a playful contest over the field-glass, three of them even making bold, teasing claims to Melissa's self-proclaimed rights. Vienna laughed along with them, but her eyes remained fixed on the dark figure of Norris and his horse silhouetted against the sky.

As Vienna gazed into the vast expanse of the desert, she couldn't help but wonder what was going through Norris's mind. This thought was nothing new or unusual, but it lingered nonetheless. She made a mental note to ask him about it someday. As Norris rode down into the shadows cast by the mesa, Melissa interrupted Vienna's thoughts.

"Princess, have you planned any fun or excitement for us?" Melissa fidgeted, unable to sit still for even a moment.

"You'll see," Vienna replied with a mischievous grin. "We'll be going on rides and climbs and playing golf, of course, but that's just to prepare you for the real adventure. I want to take you all to Arizona, show you the desert and the Aravaipa Canyon. We'll have to pack our gear and travel on horseback. And if any of you are still alive after that, we'll head up into the mountains."

Lorraine smiled, intrigued. "What is it that each of us wants, specifically?" she asked.

"I'll tell you what I want," Melissa chimed in. "I want Dot to find a cowboy who will gaze into her eyes and recite poetry. If cowboys don't make love like that, then Dot's visit will be a failure. Elsie just wants revenge for being dragged out here, so she's hoping something dreadful will happen to us. I have no idea what's going on in Lorraine's head, but it's not fun. Bobby just wants to be near Elsie, and that's it. Boyd wants the one thing he's always wanted but never got. And as for Mountcastle, well, he's got a bloodthirsty desire to kill something."

"I want to ride and camp out too," Mountcastle declared, eager to join in on the adventure.

"I don't know what I want," Melissa began. "But I do know that I want to be outside, to feel the sun and wind on my skin, and to get some color on my pale face. I'm exhausted and I need to feel alive again. As for the rest, I'm not quite sure. I just hope Dot doesn't flirt with all the cowboys."

Vienna responded, "You have quite a range of desires, Princess. But above all, we all want something exciting to happen."

Melissa nodded in agreement and added, "I just want to feel like something is happening in my life."

Vienna turned to their old friend Lorraine and asked, "What about you, Lorraine? What's your deepest desire?"

Lorraine hesitated for a moment before answering, "I just wanted to spend some time with you all."

Vienna sensed something deeper in Lorraine's response, as if she too had a longing to break free from her own constraints. It saddened Vienna to think of all the women who might feel the same way but lacked the courage to act on their desires.

Chapter Fourteen.

During the following days, it was debated amongst Vienna's guests, cowboys, and Vienna herself, who was having the most fun during this whirlwind of excitement. Vienna believed that the cowboys were having the time of their lives, especially considering the monotony of their daily routine. However, Stillwell and Norris found it difficult to keep up with the situation. The ranch work needed to be done, but they couldn't resist the ladies or the excitement that the cowboys brought. Fortunately, Norris managed to keep the cattle-raising business afloat by tirelessly working from dawn till dusk. He even had to push the lazy Mexicans he had hired to help the cowboys.

One sunny June morning, Vienna sat on her porch with her merry friends when Stillwell appeared on the path leading to the corral. His absence from consulting Vienna for several days was unusual and did not go unnoticed. "Here comes Bill in trouble," Florence laughed. As he approached the porch, he bore a faint resemblance to a thundercloud; however, the greetings he received from Vienna's party, especially from Melissa and Dorothy, chased away the blackness from his face and brought out his wonderful wrinkling smile.

"Miss Princess, sure I'm a sad demoralized old cattleman," he said, eventually. "And I'm in need of a heap of help."

"What's wrong now?" asked Vienna, with her encouraging smile.

"Well, it's so amazingly strange what cowboys will do. I'm about to give up. You might say my cowboys were all on strike for vacations. What do you think of that? We've changed the shifts, shortened hours, let one and another off duty, hired Greasers, and, in fact, done everything that could be thought of. But this vacation idea grew worse. When Norris set his foot down, then the boys began to get sick. Never in my born days as a cattleman have I heard of so many diseases. And you ought to see how lame, crippled, and weak many of the boys have gotten all of a sudden. The idea of a cowboy coming to me with a sore finger and asking to be let off for a day! There's Booly. Now I've known a horse to fall all over him, and once he rolled down a canyon. Never bothered him at all. He's got a blister on his heel, a riding blister, and he says it's going to blood-poisoning if he doesn't rest. There's Jim Bell. He's developed what he says is spinal mengalootis, or some such like. There's Frankie Slade."

He claimed he had scarlet fever because his face was so red. When I warned him that it was contagious and he needed to be quarantined, he denied it. However, he was extremely ill and just wanted to laze around and be entertained. Even Nels wasn't interested in working these days. If it wasn't for Norris, who had experience with the cattle, I wouldn't know what to do.

Vienna asked, "What's with all this sudden illness and idleness?" Stillwell replied, "Well, you see, every cowboy on the range, except Norris, thinks it's his duty to entertain the ladies." Dorothy Coombs chimed in, "I think that's just fine!" and everyone laughed. Melissa asked, "So, Norris doesn't care to help entertain us?" Stillwell explained, "Norris is different from the other cowboys. He used to be just like them. He was always full of mischief. But he's changed since becoming foreman. All the responsibility is on him, so he has no time for amusing the ladies."

"I suppose that's our loss," said Lorraine Wayne earnestly. "I admire him." Vienna reassured Stillwell, "You needn't be so distressed by the boys' gallantry, even if it causes temporary confusion in the work." He replied, "Miss Princess, what I said is only half, or a quarter, or nothing of what's troubling me." "Well, then, tell us," Vienna encouraged.

"The cowboys, except for Gene, have gone crazy over this game of golf," Stillwell exclaimed. Everyone burst out laughing. "Oh, Stillwell, you're joking," Vienna said. But he insisted, "I hope to die if I'm not dead serious. It's an incredibly strange fact. Just ask Flo. She'll tell you."

Florence nodded in agreement as Stillwell spoke about cowboys and their determination to see things through. When asked for her opinion, she said that Stillwell was right on the money. Cowboys approached everything with the same passion they had for their work and their fights. They were simple, but in the best possible way.

Vienna was pleased to hear that the cowboys were taking an interest in golf. They needed some form of entertainment, and golf
seemed like a good fit. Stillwell, however, was more practical. He
pointed out that if they were going to keep raising cattle at Her
Princess's Rancho, they needed to find ways to keep the cowboys
occupied. Vienna knew that Stillwell was not one to exaggerate,
but she also knew that the cowboys had a mischievous streak. They
had played pranks on her guests before, and she was not sure if this
sudden interest in golf was a genuine one or just another joke.

Stillwell went on to talk about how the cowboys had worked hard
to create a golf course on the mesa. They had been curious about
the game and had even wanted to be caddies for Vienna and her
brother. Monty Price had been the most enthusiastic, and he had
taken the lead in getting the cowboys interested in the game.

Vienna listened to Stillwell's story, unsure of what to make of it.
She knew that the cowboys were capable of surprising her, and she
could only hope that this sudden interest in golf was a sign of their
willingness to try new things.

Despite my age and experience with cowboy eccentricities, I was
shocked when I heard that little hobble-footed, burned-up Montana cow-puncher claim that there wasn't any game too grand for
him, and that golf was just his speed. He was completely serious,
mind you. And he was always practicing. When Norris put him
in charge of the course and the club-house, as well as all those
funny sticks, Monty was thrilled. You see, Monty was sensitive
about the fact that he wasn't much good anymore for cowboy
work. He was happy to have a job that he didn't feel he was hanging

onto by a thread. Well, he practiced the game, read the books in the club-house, and got the boys to do the same. That wasn't too difficult, I suppose. They played early and late, even in the moonlight. For a while, Monty was the coach and the boys put up with it. But eventually, Frankie Slade got overconfident in his game and had to challenge Monty. Well, Monty beat him badly. And then, one by one, the other boys took on Monty. And he beat them all. After that, they split up and started playing matches, two on a side. This worked out well for a while, but cowboys can never be satisfied for long unless they win all the time. Monty and Link Stevens, both of them cripples, you might say, joined forces and decided to beat all challengers. Well, they did. And that's where the trouble started. The other cowboys tried to beat them, patient and determined as they were, but they couldn't manage it. Maybe if Monty and Link had been perfectly healthy like the other cowboys, there wouldn't have been such an uproar. But no self-respecting cowboy would ever tolerate a disgrace like that. Down at the bunks in the evenings, it's downright humiliating to hear Monty and Link boast about their victories over the rest of the outfit. They've become insufferably arrogant.

It was impossible to reach Monty with a trimmed spruce pole. And Link, well, he was just incredibly scornful. "It's a great game, isn't it?" said Link, with a powerful sarcastic tone. "What's bothering you, you low-down cowmen? You keep harping on Monty's game leg and on my game leg. If we had good legs, we'd beat you all the worse. It's brains that win in golf. Brains and aristocratic blood, which you fellers sure have little of."

"Then Monty blows smoke with careless superiority," he continued. "Sure, it's a great game. You cow-headed gents think beef and brawn should have the call over skill and gray matter. You'll all have to back up and get down. Go out and learn the game. You don't know a baffy from a Chinese sandwich. All you can do is waggle with a club and fozzle the ball."

Whenever Monty starts using those strange names, the boys go kind of crazy. Monty and Link have the books and directions of the game, and they won't let the other boys see them. They show the rules, but that's all. And, of course, every game ends in a fight almost before it's started. The boys are all terribly serious about this golf. And I want to say, for the good of ranching, not to mention a possible fight, that Monty and Link have to be beaten. There'll be no peace around this ranch until that's done."

Vienna's guests were highly amused. As for herself, in spite of her barely considered doubt, Stillwell's tale of woe caused her anxiety. However, she couldn't control her laughter. "What in the world can I do?" she asked.

"Well, I reckon I couldn't say. I only came to you for advice. It seems that a strange kind of game has taken over my cowboys, and for the time being, ranching is at a standstill. It sounds ridiculous, I know, but cowboys are as strange as wild cattle."

The conceit of Monty and Link had to be taken out, that much was clear. Vienna suggested a match game, a foursome, between Monty, Link, and Stillwell's best picked team. Mountcastle, an expert golfer, would umpire the game. Vienna and her friends would take turns as caddies for Stillwell's team, which was considered weaker. Caddies could coach, and perhaps expert advice was all that was necessary for Stillwell's team to defeat Monty's.

Stillwell was pleased with the idea and agreed to ride out to the links with everyone that afternoon. Vienna's guests were highly amused and took sides, making wagers on their choice. They were nonplussed by the singular character of American cowboys, and Vienna was pleased to note how seriously they had taken Stillwell's story.

The June days were hot, and Vienna's visitors had learned to in-dulge in a restful siesta during the heated term of the day. Vienna was awakened by Princess's whistle and pounding on the grav-el, followed by the sound of the other horses. The afternoon's prospect filled her with both fear and delight.

As she stepped outside, Vienna was greeted by her friends, all dressed up in golf attire and beaming with excitement. Mount-castle stood out in his stunning golf coat, which made Vienna feel a bit uneasy about what Monty, Nels, and Nick might do under its influence. Melissa called out to Vienna, urging her to try a flying mount on her horse, Princess, which everyone wanted to see. Vienna hesitated, explaining that she needed Princess to kneel for her to reach the stirrup, but eventually gave in to her friends' laughter and insistence. After everyone else had mounted their horses, Vienna made Princess kneel and then hopped onto the saddle with the help of the horse's mane, pommel, and bridle. She then asked Florence, the Western girl, to demonstrate a cowboy's flying mount, which she executed with ease and grace. The group then headed towards the mesa, with Vienna scanning the cowboys for her foreman, Gene Norris, whom she hoped would attend the match. However, he was nowhere to be found, and Vienna couldn't help feeling disappointed and annoyed that he wasn't there for her guests, especially Melissa, who had wanted to see him. But Norris was busy with the cattle, and Vienna couldn't do anything about it.

Vienna felt ashamed of her momentary lapse into her old habit of desiring things without reason and thought of Norris no more as she surveyed the group of cowboys on the links. She counted sixteen cowboys, not including Stillwell, and the same number of splendid horses, all shiny and clean, grazed on the rim in the care of Mexican lads. The cowboys were dressed in their finest attire, looking very different from how cowboys usually appeared, at least in Vienna's eyes. But to her guests, they were real and natural, so picturesque that they could have been stage cowboys instead of real ones. Sombreros with silver buckles and horsehair bands were in evidence, and bright silk scarfs, embroidered vests, fringed and ornamented chaps, huge swinging guns, and clinking silver spurs lent a festive appearance. Vienna and her party were eagerly surrounded by the cowboys, and she found it difficult to repress a smile. If these cowboys were still remarkable to her, what must they be to her guests?

"Well, y'all raced over, I seen," said Stillwell, taking Vienna's bridle. "Get down, get down. We're sure amazin' glad and proud. And, Miss Princess, I'm offering to beg pardon for the way the boys are packin' guns. Maybe it ain't polite. But it's Norris's orders."

"Norris's orders!" echoed Vienna. Her friends were suddenly silent.

"I reckon he won't take no chances on the boys bein' surprised sudden by raiders. And there's raiders operatin' in from the Guadalupes. That's all. Nothin' to worry over. I was just explainin'."

Vienna, with several of her party, expressed relief, but Melissa showed excitement and then disappointment. "Oh, I want something to happen!" she cried. Sixteen pairs of keen cowboy eyes fastened intently upon her pretty, petulant face, and Vienna divined, if Melissa did not, that the desired consummation was not far off.

"So do I," said Dot Coombs.

"I want a real adventure," said one of the girls, and the attention of the sixteen cowboys turned to her. Another girl laughed and Stillwell, the boss of the outfit, smiled. "Well, I won't let you ladies go home unhappy," he said. "This may not be exciting to you, but it's important to us. Look over there. You see those two guys? They're Monty Price and Link Stevens. They're too good to hang out with their old friends now that they're practicing for a tournament. They don't want my boys to see how they handle their clubs."

Vienna asked if a team had been picked. Stillwell, wiping his face with a bandana, admitted that it was a difficult task. "I have sixteen boys and they all want to play," he said. "It might not be healthy, either. Nels and Nick said that if they don't play, there won't be a game at all. Nick has never played before and Nels just wants to take a swing at Monty with a club."

Vienna suggested that they let all the boys drive from the tee and choose the two who drive the farthest. Stillwell was pleased with the idea and dismissed the cowboys to go take a swing at a little white ball.

Choosing the right club and who should go first proved to be quite a challenge. They had to draw lots to decide. Frankie Slade tried multiple times to hit the ball from the teeing-ground, but his attempts were unsuccessful, sending the ball only a few yards. This made the other players hesitant to follow suit. Stillwell had to push Booly forward, who executed a poor shot that resulted in laughter from his comrades. Several cowboys attempted to make a good drive, but it proved to be difficult.

"Well, Nick, it's your turn," said Stillwell.

"Bill, I'm not too keen on playing," replied Nick.

"Why? You were just talking about it a while ago. Are you afraid to show how bad you'll play?" teased Stillwell.

"Nope, just plain consideration for my fellow cow-punchers," answered Nick. "I appreciate how bad they play, and I'm not mean enough to show them up."

"Well, you've got to show me," said Stillwell. "I know you've never seen a golf club in your life. What's more, I'll bet you can't hit that little ball square, not in a dozen tries."

"Bill, I'm also too much of a gentleman to take your money. But you know I'm from Missouri. Give me a club," replied Nick confidently.

Nick's confidence wavered as he took up and handled the clubs one by one, clearly showing that he had never wielded one before. However, he was not the type to give up easily. Finally, he selected a driver, looked doubtfully at the small knob, and stepped into position on the teeing-ground. Nick Steele stood six feet four inches tall and had the wiry slenderness of a rider, yet he was broad-shouldered and had long arms, making him an incredibly powerful man. He swung the driver aloft and whirled it down with a tremendous swing. Crack! The white ball disappeared, and a tiny cloud of dust rose from where it had been.

Vienna had her eyes fixed on the ball as it flew past her to the right. It was moving fast and low, almost like a bullet. The ball soared in the air, its flight path graceful and swift, before slowing down and then curving and dropping out of sight behind the mesa. Vienna had never witnessed a shot like that before. It was breathtaking and seemed too good to be true. The cowboys' cheers brought Nick Steele out of his trance, and he looked around at Stillwell and the others with a smug expression.

Nick leaned nonchalantly on his club and surveyed the group. After a moment, he spoke up. "You all saw that, right? Thought I was joking, didn't you? I used to play this game in St. Louis and Kansas City. They even talked about taking me down East to play the champions. But golf's too easy for me. Those guys back in Missouri were a bunch of losers. They always complained whenever I hit the ball hard and lost it. I had to play left-handed to stay in their league. I hit that ball off the mesa just to show you guys. I wouldn't be caught dead playing on your team."

Nick walked away towards the horses, leaving Stillwell looking crushed. No one said anything to Nick, but the lack of response spoke volumes about his victory. Suddenly, Nels stepped forward, his face inscrutable.

As they gathered around, he mentioned to Stillwell and the other cowboys that it could be difficult to judge the talents of cowboys like Nick and himself. He picked up the club that Nick had used and called for a new ball. Stillwell built a little mound of sand and placed the ball on top, then stepped back to watch. Nels was smaller than Nick, but he was still quick and strong. He stepped up to the ball with confidence and swung with all his might. However, he missed the ball completely and fell over, spinning on his head. The cowboys laughed, and even Vienna and her guests couldn't help but join in. Nels was upset and gave Vienna a reproachful look. His second attempt was just as bad, and the cowboys taunted him. Nels was angry and swung again, but the ball only rolled a few inches. He had to build up the sand mound and replace the ball himself. The cowboys made fun of him, saying his eyes were bad and he couldn't hit the ball. Nels tried again, but failed once more. He finally gathered himself together and swung carefully, making a beautiful curve around the ball. He blamed his failure on the club, saying it was crooked.

He switched clubs, but he still couldn't hit the ball. Frustration boiled inside him, and he swung with reckless abandon. No matter where he aimed, the ball always seemed to elude him. Stillwell, the large cowboy, hunched over and laughed uproariously. The other cowboys joined in, jumping up and down with glee. "You can't hit that ball," one of them taunted. Nels made a few more futile attempts, but it was no use. He finally gave up, realizing that golf was not his forte. Stillwell continued to laugh, "Oh, haw, haw, haw! Nels, your old eyes aren't any good!"

Nels slammed down his club and straightened up, his face turning red with anger. But then, his true pride and spirit shone through. He deliberately walked ten paces away and turned toward the ball. His arm shot down, elbow crooked, hand like a claw. "This is fun, Nels!" Stillwell yelled. But before anyone could react, Nels swiftly drew his gun and fired. The ball tumbled from the mound, chips flying from the impact. Nels had hit it without raising any dust. He then calmly put his gun back in its sheath and faced the cowboys. "Maybe my eyes aren't so bad after all," he said coolly, and started to walk away.

Stillwell called out to him, "Hey, Nels! We came here to play golf! You can't just shoot the ball!" Nels stopped in his tracks. "What are you so mad about? It's just a game," Stillwell continued. "Now, you and Nick stick around and be sociable. We appreciate your company and your usefulness on occasion. And if you don't have enough manners to be courteous to the ladies, just remember Norris's orders."

"Norris's orders?" Nels asked, surprised. "That's right," Stillwell replied curtly. "His orders. Are you forgetting them? Well, you're not much of a cowboy if you can't remember orders."

"You and Nick and Monty, especially, are to follow orders," said Nels sternly, removing his hat and scratching his head. "Bill, I'm sorry, I forgot. I was angry. I would have remembered soon and maybe apologized."

"Of course you would have," replied Stillwell. "Well, it seems like we're not making much progress with my golf team. Next player, step up."

Stillwell found some skill in Ambrose, who was the first to play. However, the following players were so poor and evenly matched that Stillwell became frustrated quickly. He lost his temper just as quickly as Nels had.

Finally, Ed Linton's wife arrived with Ambrose's wife, and this seemed to help. Suddenly, Ed showed a remarkable ability that caught Stillwell's attention. "Let me give you some advice," said Bill.

"Sure, if you want," replied Ed. "But I know more about this game than you do."

"Well, let's see you hit a straight ball then. It seems like you got good real quick. It's amazing," said Bill, looking around to see the two young wives smiling proudly at their husbands.

Ed made several attempts, which were better than his predecessors, but Stillwell was still not satisfied. After a particularly bad shot, Stillwell walked around in distress before stopping a dozen paces away from the teeing-ground. Ed, who was a somewhat phlegmatic cowboy, calmly prepared for another attempt.

"Fore!" he called out. Stillwell stared at him. "Fore!" yelled Ed again.

"Why are you shouting at me like that?" demanded Bill. "I mean for you to move out of the way. Get back from in front."

"Oh, that was one of those crazy words Monty is always yelling," said Bill. "Well, I guess I'm safe here then."

"You couldn't hit me if you tried for a million years," taunted Bill, as he prepared to swing his golf club.

"Come on, Bill, give it a rest," urged Ed. "I've already told you that you can't hit a straight shot. Don't break your back trying."

Ed was a short, stocky man with muscles that bulged from his arms. He had always been a strong player, but now he was ready to show off his skills. The other cowboys watched in silence as Ed swung his club, the force of it making a whistling sound.

Crack! A loud thump followed as the ball hit Stillwell's body, causing him to groan in pain. The cowboys erupted in laughter, their joy expressed in wild dancing and howling.

Stillwell eventually composed himself and admitted defeat. "You win, Ed. You hit a straight shot and I was in the way. You're the captain now."

He then called out to their opponents, Monty and Link, challenging them to come and play. "We're waiting for you, you fancy golfers. Don't be scared."

Monty and Link, two confident players, quickly accepted the challenge and made their way over to the cowboys. Stillwell turned to Vienna and her friends, hoping they wouldn't switch sides. "I hope you won't weaken and join the enemy. Monty is quite persuasive and has a way of getting people to agree with him."

"It's a fair deal," Ambrose declared, "because he wouldn't lend us the book that shows how to play. And besides, we need to beat him. Now, if you'll elect who's going to be the caddies and umpire, I'll be grateful." Vienna's friends found the idea of the upcoming match highly amusing, but they were not interested in taking part. Vienna appointed Mountcastle as the judge of the play, Dorothy as the caddie for Ed Linton, and herself as the caddie for Ambrose. Stillwell announced the news to his team and supporters with great enthusiasm, just as Monty and Link arrived. Monty and Link were both small, bow-legged, and had a limp in one foot, making them unimpressive at first glance. Link was young, while Monty was much older, but it was difficult to estimate his age. Stillwell described him as being as burnt and hard as a cinder. Monty always wore heavy sheepskin chaps with the wool outside, which made him appear wider than he was long. Link preferred leather and had taken to wearing it entirely since he became Vienna's chauffeur. Link carried no weapon, while Monty wore a large gun-sheath and gun. Link smoked a cigarette and looked insolent, while Monty was swaggering and had a dark face, looking like a barbarian chief. "Monty gives me the creeps," Melissa whispered to Stillwell. "Is he as dangerous as I've heard? Has he ever killed anyone?" "Sure," replied Stillwell cheerfully. "Almost as many as Nels." "And is that nice Mr. Nels also a desperado? I wouldn't have thought so. He's so gentle and old-fashioned, with a soft voice." "Nels is a prime example of the duplicity of men, Miss Melissa. Don't let his soft voice fool you. He's as dangerous as a sidewinder rattlesnake." At that moment, Monty and Link arrived at the teeing-ground, and Stillwell went out to greet them, with the other cowboys following closely behind.

Stillwell's voice reached Vienna's ears, explaining that his team would be receiving skilled advice during the game. Suddenly, a loud, angry roar erupted from the center of the group, followed by a cacophony of excited voices. Monty Price emerged, breaking free from restraining hands, and strode towards Vienna. Monty was the type of cowboy who never spoke to women unless spoken to first, and even then, he answered in blunt, awkward shyness. But on this occasion, it seemed he meant to protest or plead with Vienna, as he showed clear signs of emotional distress.

Vienna had never really gotten to know Monty, and she was a little intimidated, if not outright scared, of him. She knew she had to be careful with him, more so than any of the other cowboys on her ranch. Monty removed his sombrero, something he had never done before, and in that single instant, Vienna saw that his head was entirely bald. This was one of the hallmarks of the terrible Montana prairie fire, which he had fought to save the life of a child. Vienna couldn't help but feel a surge of admiration for him, but she knew she had to keep her wits about her.

"Miss Florentino," Monty began, stammering, "I'm extending my greetings to you and your friends. Link and I are proud to play the match game with you watching. But Bill says you're going to caddy for his team and coach them on the fine points. And I want to ask, respectfully, if that's fair and square?"

"Monty, that is for you to say," replied Vienna. "It was my suggestion. But if you object in the least, of course we shall withdraw."

"It seems fair to me," said Monty, "because you've learned the game. You're an expert, and I understand the other boys have no chance with you. Then you've coached Link. I think it would be sportsmanlike of you to accept the handicap."

"Aw, a handicap!" exclaimed Bill. "That's what you were driving at. Why didn't you say so? Every time Bill comes to a word that's pie to us old golfers, he just stumbles. Miss Princess, you've made it all clear as print. And I may say with becoming modesty that you weren't mistaken about me being sportsmanlike. Link and I were born that way. And we accept the handicap. Lacking that handicap, I reckon Link and I would have no ambition to play our most beautiful game. And thanking you, Miss Princess, and all your friends, I want to add that if Bill's outfit couldn't beat us before, they've got a swell chance now, with you ladies watching me and Link."

Monty had seemed to expand with pride as he delivered this speech, and at the end, he bowed low and turned away. He joined the group around Stillwell. Once more there was animated discussion, argument, and expostulation. One of the cowboys came for Mountcastle and led him away to explain ground rules. It seemed to Vienna that the game never would begin. She strolled on the rim of the mesa, arm in arm with Lorraine Wayne, and while Lorraine talked, she looked out over the gray valley leading to the rugged black mountains and the vast red wastes. In the foreground on the gray slope, she saw cattle in movement and cowboys riding to and fro. She thought of Norris. Then Boyd Harvey came for them, saying all details had been arranged. Stillwell met them halfway, and this cool, dry, old cattleman, whose face and manner scarcely changed at the announcement of a cattle-raid, now showed extreme agitation.

"Well, Miss Princess, we've gone and made a fool of ourselves right at the start," he said dejectedly.

"What's the problem?" Vienna asked, trying to suppress her laughter at Stillwell's distress. "Well, it's like this," he began. "That darn Monty is as sly as a fox. After he finished boasting about the handicap he and Link were happy to take, he brought Mountcastle over here and drove us all crazy with his silly golf names. Then he borrowed Mountcastle's golf coat. I say 'borrowed' loosely. He practically ripped it off the Englishman. Although I won't deny that Casleton was agreeable when he figured out Monty's plan, which was simply to break Ambrose's heart. That coat dazzles Ambrose. You know how vain he is. He would die to wear that Englishman's golf coat, and Monty beat him to it. It's sad to see the look in Ambrose's eyes. He won't be able to play much. But that's not all. Monty got to Ed Linton too. Usually, Ed is easy-going and cool, but now he's on a rampage. You might not know this, but Ed's wife is terribly jealous of him. Ed used to be a real ladies' man. So Monty goes over and tells Beulah, Ed's wife, that he's going to have the lovely Miss Dorothy with the wild eyes as his caddy. It might not be the most respectful thing to say, but let me tell you, Miss Dorothy has a pair of unbridled eyes. Maybe it's just natural for her to look at a guy like that. It's all right, I'm not saying anything. I know it's perfectly normal for girls back East to use their eyes. But out here, it's bound to end in disaster. All the boys talk about is Miss Dot's eyes, and they brag about which guy is the luckiest."

Ed's wife was aware of the situation, as Monty had informed her that it was alright for her to come and see how Ed was strutting around under the light of Miss Dot's brown eyes. Beulah called out to Ed and figuratively roped him for a minute. Ed returned hugging a grudge as big as a hill. It was hilarious! He was going to punch Monty's head off. Monty stood there and laughed, sarcastically saying, "Ed, we all knew you were a married man, but you're crazy to give yourself away." That settled Ed, he was touchy about the way Beulah henpecked him. He lost his spirit and now he couldn't play marbles, let alone golf. Monty was too smart, and I reckon he was right about brains being what wins.

The game began, and at first, Vienna and Dorothy tried to direct their respective players' efforts. However, all they said and did only made their team play worse. By the third hole, they were far behind and hopelessly bewildered. With Monty's borrowed coat, which had a dazzling effect on Ambrose, Link's repeated allusion to Ed's marital status, Stillwell's vociferated disgust, the cowboy supporters' clamoring good intentions and pursuit, and the ladies' embarrassing presence, Ambrose and Ed played through all sorts of strange moves until it became ridiculous. "Hey, Link," Monty's voice boomed over the links, "our esteemed rivals are playing shinny."

Vienna and Dorothy eventually gave up when the game became
a rout, and they sat down with their followers to watch the fun.
By hook or crook, Ed and Ambrose forged ahead and came close
to catching up to Monty and Link. Mountcastle disappeared into
a mass of gesticulating, shouting cowboys. When that compact
mass disintegrated, Mountcastle emerged rather hastily, it seemed,
to stalk back toward his hostess and friends. "Look!" exclaimed
Melissa in delight. "Mountcastle is actually excited. Whatever did
they do to him?"

"This is huge!" exclaimed Mountcastle, looking disheveled yet excited. "By golly, that was some crazy golf game! I even had to quit
my job as the referee."

After some coaxing, he finally revealed the reason for his resignation. "Here's what happened, you see. They were all gathered
over there, keeping an eye on each other. Monty Price's ball fell
into a hazard, and he moved it to get a better position. But guess
what? They were all doing it! Meanwhile, the game was heating
up over yonder. Stillwell and his cowboys saw Monty cheat, and
all hell broke loose. They turned to me for a verdict. I showed
them the rules and Monty admitted his mistake. However, when
it came to putting his ball back in the hazard, he refused to do
it properly. Instead, he put it wherever he pleased and gave me a
threatening look. 'Listen, Dook,' he said. I wish that darn cowboy
wouldn't call me that. 'Dook, maybe this game ain't as important
as international politics or other stuff like that, but there's still
some honor and sportsmanship at stake. Our opponents have been
ignoring those values for a while now. The game is riding on my

next shot. I'm putting my ball as close to where it was as I can. You saw where it was, just like I did. You're the referee, and I trust you to be fair. And let me tell you, nobody has ever doubted my word without regret. So I'm asking you, wasn't my ball lying about here?'

"The little scoundrel grinned at me and rested his hand on his gun. You bet he did! And then I had to tell a big ol' lie!" Mountcastle mimicked Monty's voice, but it was clear that he didn't realize Monty was joking.

Vienna and her pals sensed it, though there was no need to hold back, so they unleashed their laughter and joy.

Chapter Fifteen.

Vienna and her group regained their composure and sat up to watch the end of the match. Suddenly, a loud yell pierced the air, and all the cowboys turned to see what was happening. A big black horse had appeared on the mesa and was galloping towards them. The rider shouted at the cowboys, who quickly ran towards their horses. Vienna was alarmed and said, "That's Norris. Something's wrong." Mountcastle stared, and the other men muttered uneasily. The women looked at Vienna with concerned eyes. The black horse ran faster and faster towards them, and Melissa cried out, "Look at that horse run! Look at that guy ride!" Everyone was impressed with the rider's skill, but Vienna was torn between her growing fear and her admiration for Norris. She knew that any violent action by him was significant and could mean anything. She remembered Stillwell's talk about fun, plots, and tricks, but she dismissed the idea. Norris wouldn't run his horse at such a speed unless there was a good reason. Vienna felt a mounting fear, not for herself but for her guests. She couldn't think of any danger except the guerrillas. She trusted Norris to face any danger and protect them. As he approached them, she could see his dark face and eyes, and she felt a strange sense of dependence on him.

The massive black horse was so close to Vienna and her friends that when Norris tugged on the reins, the dust and sand kicked up by his pounding hooves flew in their faces. "Oh, Norris, what's going on?" cried Vienna. "Sorry for the scare, Miss Florentino," he replied. "But I'm in a hurry. There's a gang of bandits hiding on the ranch, probably in an abandoned hut. They robbed a train near Agua Prieta. Pat Hawe is leading the posse that's after them, and you know Pat doesn't like us. I'm afraid it wouldn't be pleasant for you or your guests to run into either the posse or the bandits."

"I agree," said Vienna, visibly relieved. "Let's hurry back to the house."

They didn't say much after that, and Vienna's guests remained silent. Norris's actions and expression belied his calm words. His sharp eyes scanned the rim of the mesa, and his face was as hard and unyielding as chiseled bronze. Monty and Nick arrived, each leading several horses by their reins. Nels appeared behind them with Princess, struggling with the roan. Vienna noticed that all the other cowboys had vanished. One stern command from Norris calmed Vienna's horse, but the other horses were skittish and refused to stay still. The men mounted without incident, as did Vienna and Florence. However, Lorraine Wayne and Mrs. Beck were jittery and struggled to get on their horses.

"Excuse me, but I'm in a hurry," said Norris, coolly, as he forced Dorothy's horse almost to its knees with an iron grip. Dorothy, who was athletic and brave, climbed onto the saddle. When Norris released his hold on the reins and mane, the horse reared up and began to buck wildly. Dorothy screamed as she flew into the air.

Norris, as agile as the horse, sprang forward and caught Dorothy in his arms. She had fallen headfirst and would have been seriously injured if he hadn't caught her.

Norris gently lifted Dorothy up and set her back on her feet, trying to keep her steady. Dorothy seemed more concerned with adjusting her riding-habit than the fact that she had just been tossed off her horse. Vienna stifled a laugh, but quickly sobered up as she saw the anger in Norris's eyes. He had jumped at Dorothy's stubborn horse, determined to show his mastery over the animal. It was a cruel display, but necessary to get the horse under control. Once the horse was calmed, Dorothy mounted without any further trouble.

Meanwhile, Nels and Nick had helped Melissa back onto her horse. "We'll take the side trail," said Norris shortly, as he swung onto his big black horse. The other cowboys followed suit, trotting behind him. The mesa was only a short distance away, and Vienna knew that the steep trail would be a challenge for her guests. Mountcastle observed, "That's a jolly bad course," while the women were speechless.

Norris checked his horse at the start of the trail and dismounted. "Boys, drop over and go slow," he instructed. "Flo, you follow. Now, ladies, let your horses loose and hold on. Lean forward and hang onto the pommel. It looks bad, but the horses are used to such trails."

Melissa followed Florence closely, with Mrs. Beck and Lorraine Wayne close behind. Dorothy's horse balked, and she tried to urge

him into the trail. Norris quickly grabbed the horse's bit and
pulled him back down. "Put your foot in my stirrup," he told
Dorothy. "We can't waste time."

He lifted her up onto his horse and started down the trail. "Go
on, Miss Florentino. I'll have to lead this nag down," he called
after them. The group made their way down the narrow, rocky
trail, with Norris leading the way and the other cowboys following
behind. It was a treacherous journey, but they made it down safely.

"We'll save time," Vienna said before dismounting from her horse.
The trail was loose and the horses struggled to keep their footing
on the weathered slopes. Dust clouds formed and rocks rolled
down, while cactus spikes tore at horse and rider. Mrs. Beck
laughed, but there was a hint of hysteria in her tone. Dorothy
complained a few times, and Vienna struggled to see through the
yellow dust. The horses snorted and she heard Norris close behind
her, causing little avalanches that rolled down Princess's fetlocks.
Vienna feared that Norris's legs might be cut or bruised by the
stones. Eventually, the dust thinned and she saw the others ride
out onto a level. Norris and Vienna followed suit, and there was
a delay while Norris changed Dorothy from his horse to her own.
This struck Vienna as odd and made her more thoughtful. The
cowboys' alert and quiet manner was not reassuring, and as they
resumed their ride, Nels and Nick rode far ahead, Monty stayed
far behind, and Norris rode with the party. Vienna overheard Boyd
Harvey ask Norris if lawlessness was common, and Norris replied
that occasional deeds of outlawry might break out in any isolated
section of the country, but there had been peace and quiet along

the border for years. Vienna knew that they were being escorted home under armed guard. When they rounded the head of the mesa and saw the ranch-house and the valley, Vienna saw dust or smoke hovering over a hut on the outskirts of the Mexican quarters.

As the sun dipped below the horizon, the light began to wane, making it difficult for Vienna to see what was happening. Norris urged everyone to pick up the pace and get to the house as quickly as possible. Within minutes, they had all arrived in the yard, ready to dismount. Stillwell greeted them with a forced cheerfulness that didn't fool Vienna in the slightest. She noticed a group of armed cowboys walking with their horses just below the house.

"Well, you all had a nice little run," Stillwell said, trying to sound casual. "I reckon there wasn't much need for it. Pat Hawe thinks he's got some outlaws corralled on the ranch. Nothing to be fussed up about. Norris is just being cautious and doesn't want you meeting any rowdies."

Vienna's female guests breathed a sigh of relief as they dismounted and made their way into the house. Vienna stayed behind to speak with Stillwell and Norris.

"Now, Stillwell, what's really going on?" Vienna asked, getting straight to the point.

Stillwell was taken aback by her directness, but he couldn't help but admire her shrewdness. "Well, Miss Princess, there's going to be a fight somewhere, and Norris wanted to get you all inside before it happened. He says the valley's overrun by vaqueros, guerrillas, and robbers, and Lord knows what else."

He clomped off the porch, his spurs jangling loudly, and headed toward the waiting cowboys. Norris remained behind, standing tall and silent, with a hand on his pommel and bridle.

"Norris, you're always looking out for my best interests," Vienna said, wanting to thank him but struggling to find the right words. "I don't know what I'd do without you. Is there really danger?"

"I'm not sure," Norris replied. "But I'd rather err on the side of caution."

Vienna hesitated, suddenly finding it difficult to talk to him. "Can you tell me what special orders you gave Nels, Nick, and Monty?" she asked. "I overheard Stillwell mention something about it."

Norris looked surprised. "Who said I gave them special orders?"

"Stillwell did," Vienna replied.

Norris sighed. "I suppose I can tell you, if you insist."

"Why worry about something that might never happen?" she asked. "I insist, Norris," she said quietly. "I was ordered to have at least one of them guarding you day and night, always within earshot of your voice."

"I figured as much. But why Nels or Monty or Nick? That seems unfair to them. Why do I need someone to guard me? Don't you trust any of my cowboys?" Norris asked.

"I trust them to be honest, but not with guns," she replied.

"Ability with guns?" Norris exclaimed.

"Miss Florentino, you've been entertaining your guests so well that you forget. I'm glad you forget. I wish you hadn't asked me," she said.

"Forget what?" Norris asked.

"Don Carlos and his guerrillas," she said.

"I haven't forgotten. Do you still think Don Carlos might try to take me again?" Norris asked.

"I don't think. I know," she replied.

"And on top of your other duties, you've been sharing the watch with these cowboys?" Norris asked.

"Yes," she said.

"And it's been going on without my knowledge?" Norris asked.

"Yes," she replied.

"Since when?" Norris asked.

"Since I brought you down from the mountains last month," she replied.

"How long will it continue?" Norris asked.

"That's hard to say. Until the revolution is over, at least," she replied.

She looked away to the west, where the red haze was filling the great void. She believed in him completely, and the threat hovering near her cast a shadow over her happiness. "What should I do?" she asked. "I think you should send your friends back East and go with them until this guerrilla war is over," Norris said.

"Why, Norris, they would be heartbroken, and so would I," she replied.

He had no answer for that. "If I don't take your advice, it'll be the first time since I've come to rely on you so much," she said. "Can't you suggest something else? My friends are having such a wonderful visit. Melissa is getting better."

"I'd hate to see them leave before they're ready," he said. "We could take them up to the mountains and camp out for a while. I know of a wild spot up among the crags. It's a tough climb, but it's worth it. I've never seen a more beautiful place. There's fine water, and it'll be cool. Soon enough, it'll be too hot for your group to be outside."

"Are you suggesting we hide away among the crags and clouds?" Vienna asked with a laugh. "Well, it would certainly seem that way. Your friends don't have to know. Maybe in a few weeks, the border trouble will have died down for the fall."

"You say it's a tough climb up there?" he asked.

"It definitely is. Your friends will get a real adventure on that trip."

"That works for me. Melissa especially wants something exciting to happen. They're all looking for some thrill."

"They'll find it up there. Treacherous trails, canyons to navigate, steep climbs, windstorms, thunder and lightning, rain, mountain lions, and wildcats."

"Alright, I've made up my mind. Norris, you'll take charge, of course. But, I can't help but wonder, Norris, if there's something else you could tell me. Why do you think my personal freedom is in danger?"

"Yes, there is. But I can't say. If I hadn't been a rebel soldier, I wouldn't have known."

"If you hadn't been a rebel soldier, where would I be now?" Vienna asked with earnestness. He didn't reply.

"Norris," she continued with a sudden burst of emotion, "you once mentioned a debt you owed me." Seeing his dark face pale, she hesitated, then pressed on. "It's paid."

"No, no," he answered, huskily.

"Yes. I won't have it any other way."

"No. It can never be paid."

Vienna extended her hand. "It's paid," she repeated. Suddenly, he recoiled from the outstretched white hand that held him captivated.

"I'd do anything to touch your hand," he said, his voice filled with unexpected passion. "But not on the terms you offer."

Vienna was taken aback by his words. "No man has ever refused to shake my hand before," she said with a small laugh. "It's hardly flattering. Why won't you?"

"It's not because I think you're offering it as mistress to servant, rancher to cowboy," he replied.

"Then why?" she asked.

"The debt you owed me is paid. I cancel it," he said. "But I won't shake your hand. That's all."

Vienna was puzzled by his refusal. "You're being ungracious, whatever your reason," she said. "But I may offer it again some day. Good night."

He said good night and left, his hand on the neck of his black horse. Vienna went inside to rest before dinner and fell asleep. When she woke up, it was twilight and her Mexican maid had not come to her. She rang the bell, but there was no answer. The house was silent, and she felt a sense of foreboding.

Footsteps on the porch broke the silence, and she recognized Stillwell's tread, though it was lighter than usual. He called softly into her office, and she hurried through the rooms to meet him.

"Stillwell!" she exclaimed. "Is anyone with you?"

"No," he replied in a low tone. "Please come out on the porch."

Once outside, she saw his pale face and reached out to him. He intercepted her hand and held it tightly.

"Miss Princess, I have some distressing news," the man spoke in a hushed tone, glancing around apprehensively. "If you'd heard Norris curse, you'd know how much we hate to have to tell you this. But it can't be avoided. The fact is, we're in a terrible situation. If your guests aren't scared out of their wits, it'll be because of your nerve and how you follow Norris's orders."

"You can count on me," Vienna replied with resolve, though she couldn't help but tremble.

"Well, here's the thing: that gang of bandits Pat Hawe was chasing? They're hiding in your house!" the man exclaimed.

"In my house?" Vienna echoed, horrified.

"It's the truth, and I'm ashamed to admit it. Norris is beside himself with rage that it could happen. You see, it wouldn't have happened if I hadn't taken the boys to the golf course and if Norris hadn't ridden out to the mesa after us. It's my fault. I've had too much female influence around me. Gene cursed me, he cursed me something terrible. But now we have to figure out what to do."

"Do you mean to say that a gang of hunted outlaws have taken refuge in my house?" Vienna demanded.

"That's exactly what I mean. It seems strange to me that you didn't notice something was wrong, with all your servants gone."

"Gone? I did notice my maid was missing. I wondered why there were no lights on. Where did my servants go?"

"They went down to the Mexican quarters and are half scared
to death. Now listen, when Norris left you an hour ago, he
followed me straight to where the boys and I were trying to help
Pat Hawe find those bandits. But when Norris arrived, things
got worse. Pat was already angry, but seeing Norris made him
even more agitated."

I think Gene and Pat's relationship is like trying to get a red bull to
calm down. The sheriff started a fire in an old adobe hut and Norris
wasn't happy about it. Pat Hawe had six guys with him and it
seemed like they were on a bandit-hunting mission. There was a bit
of a commotion and things were looking bad, but Gene remained
calm and controlled the boys. Pat and his deputies went on their
hunt, but it ended up being a joke. Pat could have continued to
fool us, but as soon as Norris showed up, the truth was revealed. Pat
wasn't really looking for bandits, he just wanted trouble for Norris.
When Pat's men made their way to our storehouse where we kept
our supplies, Gene called a stop to it and told Pat to leave the ranch.
This is where Hawe and Norris had their conflict. It turned out
that there was a gang of bandits hiding somewhere and at first, Pat
was actively trying to find them, but then he suddenly changed his
mind. He was flustered by Norris's scrutiny and then, maybe to
hide something, maybe just naturally, he got mad. He called for
the law and brought up his old grudge against Norris, accusing
him again of the Greaser murder from last fall. Norris made him
look like a fool and showed that he was scared of the bandits or
had some other reason for leaving the trail. The argument started
and it could have turned into a fight if it weren't for Nels. In the

middle of it all, when Norris was driving Pat and his crew off the ranch, one of the deputies lost his head and went for his gun.

Nels threw his gun and injured the man's arm. Monty reacted quickly and threw two pistols, which made the situation tense for a moment. However, the bandits eventually retreated. Stillwell paused in his story, holding Vienna's hand as if to offer comfort. "After Pat left, we put our heads together," the old cattleman began with a deep breath. "We found a young man who had seen a group of men, who he suspected were Mexican bandits, sneaking through the shrubbery to the back of the house. This was when Norris was out on the mesa. Later, the same young man saw your servants running down the hill towards the village. Gene thinks that there was some devilry going on along the railroad, and Pat Hawe followed the bandits to the ranch. He searched hard, but then suddenly stopped. Norris says that Pat Hawe wasn't scared, but perhaps he saw something or got wind of something that made him not want to catch all of the bandits. You understand? Then Gene came up with a plan. He went to Padre Marcos to get help in finding out what he could from your Mexican servants. I hurried up here to give you orders, Miss Princess. It's quite amazing, isn't it? You need to gather all of your guests in the kitchen and pretend that, as your staff has left, it will be a fun experience for your guests to cook dinner. The kitchen is the safest room in the house. While you entertain your guests, I'll have cowboys stationed in the long corridor and outside where the kitchen connects to the main house. It's likely that the bandits don't suspect that we know where they are hiding."

Norris informed them that their guests were in the end room with
the alfalfa and would be leaving in the night. He assured Vienna
that with him and the boys watching, they would be safe to go to
bed. They were to wake their guests early before daylight and head
up into the mountains. Vienna was to tell them to pack their out-
fits before going to bed and say that their servants had left, so they
might as well go camping with the cowboys. Norris hoped their
friends would never know they were sitting on a powder-mine.

Vienna asked Stillwell if he advised the trip up into the mountains.
He replied that he did, considering everything. He asked if Vienna
would keep her nerve, and she answered yes.

He suggested that she tell Florence, who would be a comfort to her.
Vienna did not return to her room but went through the office
and into the long corridor, which was almost as dark as night.
She thought she saw a slow-gliding figure that was darker than the
surrounding gloom. She went to the kitchen and lit some lights,
then went back into the corridor and saw a dark shape crouching
along the wall. She thought it might be her imagination and went
on through her rooms into the patio.

Her guests were happy to go camping with the cowboys and entered into the spirit of the occasion. Vienna delayed at the door,
taking a sharp but unobtrusive glance down the great, barnlike
hall. She saw nothing but blank dark space.

Out of nowhere, a pale face appeared just a foot away from Vienna,
breaking the darkness that enveloped her. It was Don Carlos, and
his glittering eyes were unmistakable. Vienna managed to hide her

alarm and anger and calmly shut the door, securing it with a heavy bolt. Her initial shock soon gave way to fury - how dare he enter her home without permission? Was he one of the bandits hiding in her house?

Just as she was working herself up into a frenzy, Florence appeared, having seen Vienna bolt the door. Vienna quickly composed herself and assigned tasks to her guests. She confided in Florence about Don Carlos and was shown a group of cowboys moving stealthily outside the window. Excitement replaced her anger and fear, and Vienna decided to have some fun. She called Mountcastle into the pantry and playfully pressed her flour-covered hands onto his coat.

The rest of the group joined in the revelry, and everyone pitched in to make a hodgepodge dinner that turned out to be surprisingly delicious. Vienna enjoyed herself despite the looming threat of danger.

As the night grew late, Vienna instructed her guests to retire to their rooms and prepare for the upcoming camping trip. She hoped it would be the highlight of their Western adventure. Vienna herself began to gather her camping gear when she heard a knock on her door. Assuming it was Florence coming to assist her, Vienna was surprised to find Norris and several cowboys waiting outside.

Norris explained that the bandits were still in the area and that they had likely learned of their plans. However, he assured Vienna that they would be able to leave before any trouble began. He also mentioned that he had spoken to Vienna's servants, who had run off in fear. They would return once the gang had been dealt with, and Vienna need not worry about her property.

When Vienna asked if Norris had any idea who was hiding in the house, he initially suspected Pat Hawe, but upon finding several horses hidden in the mesquite behind the pond, he believed it to be a group of outcasts from the border. Norris assured Vienna that they would be able to get rid of them without any violence.

Despite the potential danger, Vienna trusted Norris and felt grateful to have him on her side. She knew that if anyone could handle the situation, it was him.

Vienna spoke up, determined to make Norris see reason. "Norris, you're wrong," she said boldly. He was taken aback, and paused before responding. His eyes shifted, and he eventually spoke. "How so?" he asked.

"I saw one of these bandits. I distinctly recognized him," Vienna explained. Norris took a long step towards her. "Who was he?" he demanded. "Don Carlos," Vienna replied.

Norris muttered under his breath, his expression darkening. "Are you sure?" he asked, his voice low. "Absolutely. I saw his figure twice in the hall, then his face in the light. I could never mistake his eyes," Vienna confirmed.

"Did he know you saw him?" Norris asked, his tone urgent. "I'm not positive, but I think so. Oh, he must have known! I was standing full in the light. I had entered the door, then purposely stepped out. His face showed from around a corner, and swiftly flashed out of sight," Vienna recounted.

Vienna watched as Norris underwent a transformation, his demeanor shifting drastically. "Call your friends, get them in here!" he ordered, his voice terse. He turned towards the door. "Norris, wait!" Vienna called out, trying to stop him. He turned back to her, his face white with anger and determination. "What will you do?" Vienna asked.

"That needn't concern you. Get your party in here. Bar the windows and lock the doors. You'll be safe," Norris replied curtly. "Norris! Tell me what you intend to do," Vienna pleaded. "I won't tell you," Norris replied, turning away once more.

"But I will know," Vienna said, her hand on his arm. She saw the shock in his eyes as she touched him. "Oh, I do know. You mean to fight!" she exclaimed. "Well, Miss Florentino, isn't it about time?" Norris asked wearily. "The fact of that Mexican's presence here in your house ought to prove to you the nature of the case."

These cowboys, these rebels, they know that you won't tolerate any fighting from your men. Don Carlos is a cowardly sneak, but he's not afraid to hide in your own home. He knows that you won't let your cowboys harm anyone, and he's taking advantage of it. He'll steal, burn, and run off with your belongings. He'll even kill if he has the chance. These Greasers are known to use knives in the dark. So I ask you, isn't it time to put a stop to him?

"Norris, I forbid you to fight, unless it's in self-defense. I forbid it," Vienna said firmly.

"What I plan to do is self-defense. Haven't I explained to you that we're living in wild times along this border? Don Carlos is in league with the revolution. The rebels are crazy to stir up trouble in the United States. You're a woman of importance, Vienna. Don Carlos would take you and run. If he got you, it wouldn't matter if he crossed the border with you. The hue and cry would go out to the troops along the border, to New York, to Washington. It would mean exactly what the rebels want - United States intervention. In other words, war!" Norris explained.

"Oh, surely you're exaggerating," Vienna said.

"Maybe so, but I'm starting to see what Don Carlos is up to. And, Vienna, I can't bear to think of what you'd go through if he got you over the line. I know these low-caste Mexicans. I've been among the peons, the slaves," Norris said.

"Norris, don't let Don Carlos take me," Vienna pleaded.

"I won't. That's why I'm going after him," Norris replied, his face hardening.

"But I told you not to start a fight on purpose," Vienna reminded him.

"Then I'll start one without your permission," Norris said shortly and began to walk away. Vienna caught his arm and held on, even when he stopped.

"No," she said, with authority. He shook off her grip and walked forward. "Please don't go!" she called out, pleadingly. However, he continued. "Norris!" She ran ahead of him, intercepted him, and stood in front of him with her back against the door. He extended his arm as if to push her aside, but it dropped. Haggard, worried, with a face that showed signs of strain, he stood before her. "It's for your own good," he protested. "If it's for my sake, then do what I want," she said. "These guerrillas will harm someone. They'll set the house on fire. They'll take you away. They'll do something terrible if we don't stop them." "Let's take the risk," she begged. "But it's a huge risk, and we shouldn't take it," he exclaimed, passionately. "I know what's best here. Stillwell supports me. Let me out, Miss Florentino. I'm going to take the boys and go after these guerrillas." "No!" "Good Lord!" Norris exclaimed. "Why not let me go? It's the right thing to do. I'm sorry to upset you and your visitors. Why not put an end to Don Carlos's harassment? Is it because you're worried that a commotion will ruin your friends' visit?" "It's not that this time," she replied. "Then is it because of the thought of a little shooting with these Mexicans?" "No." "You're disgusted by the idea of Mexican blood staining your home's floors?" "No!" "Then why are you preventing me from doing what I know is best?" "Norris, I, I," she stammered, growing more agitated. "I'm scared and confused. This is all too much for me. I'm not a coward. If you have to fight, you'll see that I'm not a coward. But your approach seems so reckless. The hall is so dark, and the guerrillas could shoot from behind doors. You're so wild and daring that you'd rush into danger. Is that necessary? I mean, I don't know why I feel so uneasy about you doing it."

"I'm just worried about you getting hurt," Vienna confessed. Her words seemed to have a powerful effect on him, as his hard expression softened and his face flushed with emotion. He was like a shy boy, unsure of how to react to her sudden vulnerability. Vienna believed she had won him over, but he surprised her yet again with his next move. He pushed her aside so he could pass, and she realized he would have no qualms about physically removing her if necessary. As he stood in the doorway, his eyes gleamed with a ruthless determination. "I'm going to kick Don Carlos and his gang out of this place," Norris declared. "I'll try to do it peacefully, but if I have to fight, so be it. Either way, they're leaving."

Chapter Sixteen.

As Norris left through one door, Florence knocked on another. Vienna, usually calm and collected, was visibly relieved to see the cool Western girl. Just having her nearby helped Vienna regain her composure. Florence looked at Vienna closely, then changed her demeanor to something sweeter and more deliberate. Although Florence was probably curious about the bandits hiding in the house, the cowboys' plans, and Vienna's suppressed emotions, she didn't ask any questions. Instead, she brought up the important topic of what to bring on their camping trip. They discussed the necessary items for an hour, selected the things they needed most, and packed them in Vienna's duffle bags. With everything packed, they decided to lie down and rest before the call to saddle. They remained in their riding costumes and tried to sleep, or at least relax, until it was time to go.

Vienna switched off the lamp and peeked through her window, observing dark shapes standing guard in the darkness. As she lay down, she heard soft footsteps on the path. Her loyalty to Norris swelled her heart, while the necessity of it foreshadowed the ominous feeling that had been haunting her since his passionate plea. Vienna didn't expect to sleep, but she did, and it felt like only a moment until Florence woke her up. She followed Florence outside, where she saw saddled horses being held by cowboys in the dark hour before dawn. The departure had an air of urgency and secrecy. Melissa, who came out with Vienna's other guests, whispered that it felt like an escape, and she was thrilled. The others were amused, but to Vienna, it was indeed an escape.

In the darkness, Vienna couldn't see how many escorts her party had, but she heard low voices, the chomping of bits, and thumping of hooves. She recognized Norris as he led Princess over for her to mount. Then, the soft pattering of feet and whining of dogs followed, and Vienna saw her pack of Russian wolf-hounds approaching. Norris's decision to let them go with her indicated how attentive he was to her happiness. She loved being out with the hounds and her horse. Norris led Princess out into the darkness, past a line of mounted horses. "Guess we're ready?" he said. "I'll do a headcount." He walked back along the line, and on his return, Vienna heard him say several times, "Now, everybody ride close to the horse in front, and keep quiet till daylight." Then, the snorting and pounding of the big black horse in front of her told Vienna that Norris had mounted. "All right, we're off," he called. Vienna lifted Princess's bridle and let the roan go.

The sound of gravel crunching underfoot echoed through the night air, followed by the striking of a match and a low whinny. Vienna could just make out Norris and his black horse in the dim light. They were almost within arm's reach. One of the hounds leaped up at her, whining happily. A thick belt of darkness surrounded them, but above it, a few stars shone through a gray fog. It

was an unusual departure from the ranch, and Vienna was sensitive
to the soft beat of hooves, the cool, moist air, and the sight of
Norris's dark figure. The caution, the early start before dawn, and
the enforced silence lent the occasion a stirring quality. Princess
plunged into a gully, and Vienna had to focus on her riding. Norris
was difficult to keep close to, even on smooth trails, and in the
darkness, she had to be watchful. They trudged through dragging sand, but gradually, the blackness gave way to gray. Princess
climbed out of the wash, and his iron shoes rang on stone once
more. He began to climb, and Norris's figure loomed larger in
Vienna's sight. She tried to see the trail but couldn't. She wondered
how Norris could follow a trail in the dark, his eyes must be as
sharp as they sometimes looked. Over her shoulder, she couldn't
see the horse behind her, but she heard him. As Princess climbed
steadily, Vienna saw the gray darkness grow opaque, change and
lighten, losing its substance and yielding the grotesque shapes of
yucca and ocotillo. Dawn was about to break, and though she faced
east, the sky remained dark.

Suddenly, to her surprise, Norris and his powerful horse appeared
before Vienna. She could see the characteristic rocks, cacti, and
brush that covered the foothills. The trail was old and rarely used,
zigzagging and twisting through the landscape. Looking back, she
saw Monty Price hunched over his saddle, his face hidden under
his sombrero. Behind him rode Dorothy Coombs, followed by
the towering figure of Nick Steele. Vienna and her party were
riding between cowboy escorts. As the daylight grew brighter, Vienna saw that the trail was leading them up through the foothills,
through shallow gullies filled with stones and brush washed down

by floods. At every turn, she expected to come upon water and the waiting pack-train, but miles passed, and no water or horses were met. Expectation gave way to desire, and Vienna grew hungry.

Suddenly, Norris's horse went splashing into a shallow pool, and beyond that, Vienna saw damp places in the sand, rocky pockets filled with water. Norris kept on, and at eight o'clock, Vienna saw horses grazing on spare grass, a pile of canvas-covered bundles, and a fire around which cowboys and two Mexican women were bustling. Vienna waited as her followers rode up single file. Her guests were in a merry mood, talking all at once. "Breakfast and rustle," called out Norris without ceremony. "No need to tell me to rustle," said Melissa. "I am simply ravenous. This air makes me hungry." In truth, Vienna observed that Melissa was not the only one feeling famished. Despite the hurry, the meal had the air of a picnic.

As the cowboys chatted and ate, they busily prepared the horses and burros for the journey ahead. Mountcastle, fascinated by the process, wandered around with his coffee cup in hand, admiring the diamond-hitch technique. "Have you ever seen anything like this?" he asked one of the cowboys. "It's quite impressive!"

Once the pack-train was ready, Norris led the way to break the trail. The slopes were covered in shrubs, rocks, and cacti, making the journey uphill and difficult. Comfort was out of the question for Vienna and her party; their focus was on making the travel possible. Florence wore corduroy breeches and high-top boots, which proved advantageous in the rough terrain. The other ladies' riding-habits suffered from the sharp spikes, and Vienna had to be watchful to protect her horse's legs and herself from thorny branches.

The pack-train moved ahead, and the trailing couples grew farther apart. By noon, they reached the foothills and faced the real ascent of the mountains. The sun was scorching, and the dust was thick, hanging in a pall. The view was dreary and drab, a barren monotony of slow-mounting slopes ridged by rocky canyons. At one point, Norris stopped to wait for Vienna and warned her, "We're going to have a storm." "That will be a relief. It's so hot and dusty," replied Vienna. "Shall I call a halt and make camp?" Norris suggested they keep going, as a good thunderstorm would be a new experience for her friends. They continued on, eager to face whatever lay ahead.

Finding a good spot to make camp was proving to be a challenge. The slope they were currently on was too windy, and the rain threatened to wash them away. It seemed like they would have to travel all day to find a decent campsite, and even then, there was no guarantee. They were making slow progress, and if it rained, they would just have to deal with it. At least the pack outfit was well-covered.

"Surely," Vienna replied, smiling at his comment. She knew all too well what a storm was like in this part of the country, and her guests had yet to experience one. "If it rains, let it rain."

Norris rode ahead, and Vienna followed close behind. The pack animals toiled up the slope, with the little burros moving effortlessly while the horses struggled. Their packs bobbed from side to side like the humps of camels, and stones rattled down the slope.

The heat waves made the air shimmer like black waves, and the dust puffed up and swirled around them. The sky was a pale blue, like heated steel, except for the dark clouds peeking over the mountain crests. The heavy, sultry atmosphere made it difficult to breathe.

As they descended down the slope, the trailing party stretched out in groups of twos and threes. It was easy to spot the weary riders. Half a mile further up, Vienna could see over the foothills to the north, west, and a little south. She forgot about the heat, weariness, and discomfort as she took in the wide, unlimited view of the sun-scorched earth. She saw the gray valley, the black mountains, the wide, red gateway of the desert, and the dim, shadowy peaks that were blue as the sky they pierced. She was disappointed when the bleak, gnarled cedar trees blocked her view.

They finally got a break from the steep climb as they made their way through a storm-wrecked forest of stunted trees. Even at this elevation, the desert's gaunt hand could be felt. The clouds overhead hid the sun, providing a welcome relief. The pack-train rested, and Norris and Vienna waited for the party to catch up.

He quickly informed her that Don Carlos and his bandits had left the ranch during the night. Thunder could be heard in the distance and the faint wind rustled the sparse foliage of the cedars. The air grew heavy and the horses were panting. "Looks like we're in for a bad storm," Norris said. "The first one is always the worst. I can feel it in the air."

The air was indeed charged with a heavy force that seemed to be waiting to be unleashed. One by one, the couples mounted their horses and the women begged for a break. But they wouldn't rest until nightfall and that depended on reaching the crags. The pack-train continued on and Norris fell in behind.

The storm slowly gathered around the peaks, with low rumbles and howls of thunder increasing in frequency. The light began to fade as smoky clouds rolled in, making the air even more oppressive. An exasperating breeze puffed a few times before failing completely. An hour later, the group had climbed high and was rounding the side of a great bare ridge that had been hiding the crags. Vienna looked back down the slope and saw her guests shifting wearily in their saddles. Far below lay the cedar flat and foothills, while far to the west, the sky was still clear with shafts of sunlight shooting down from behind the encroaching clouds.

Norris reached the summit of the ridge and waved to Vienna, gesturing to what lay beyond. It was an impressive sight, and Vienna, who had never climbed this high before, was excited to see what was in store. Princess surmounted the last few steps and snorted as she halted beside Norris's black. To Vienna, it was as if the world had changed. The ridge was now a mountain-top, dropping before her into a black, stone-ridged, shrub-patched, many-canyoned gulf.

To the east, past the gulf, rose the bare mountain peaks. On the right, enormous cliffs and weathered slopes led upward to the dark and barren crags bordered by firs and pines, looming against the stormy sky. Thick clouds amassed, shrouding the highest peaks and a fork of lightning illuminated the sky, followed by a deafening roar of thunder. The broken rocks under the slow gathering of

storm clouds presented a grim and awe-inspiring spectacle. It had
a beauty of the sublime and majestic kind, but the fierce desert
was reaching up to meet the magnetic heights, where heat, wind,
frost, lightning, and flood fought in everlasting strife. Before their
onslaught, the rugged stone world was crumbling, splitting, and
wearing to ruin. Vienna glanced at Norris, who had forgotten
her presence. He sat motionless on his horse, with a dark face
and dark eyes, watching the scene like an Indian, unconscious of
thought. To see him like that, and to fathom the strange affinity
between his soul, turned primitive, and the savage environment
that had shaped him, were powerful aids to Vienna Florentino
in her strange desire to understand his nature. The sound of
iron-shod hoofs behind her broke the spell. Monty had reached the
summit. "Gene, who knows what it'll all be doing in a minute - not
even Moses himself could tell," observed Monty. Then Dorothy
climbed up to his side and looked. "Oh, isn't it just perfectly lovely!" she exclaimed. "But I wish it wouldn't storm. We'll all get wet."
Once more, Norris faced the ascent, keeping to the slow rise of
the ridge as it headed southward towards the towering rock spires.
Soon, he was off smooth ground, and Vienna, a few yards behind
him, looked back at her friends with concern. This is where the real
climb began, and a mountain storm was about to unleash its full
fury. The slope Norris was entering was a magnificent monument
to the crags above that had been ruined.

The trail was on a slope facing south, so it was semi-arid and covered in cercocarpus, yucca, and some shrubs that Vienna believed
were manzanita. Every step Princess took felt like the ground was
slipping out from under them. Any hard ground was covered in

spiny plants or shattered rocks, making it impossible to travel on. The slope was lined with gullies. Suddenly, the sky grew darker, and the clouds seemed to be gathering quickly. They piled up and rolled around, obscuring the crags. The air felt heavy and was filled with a sulfurous smell, and sharp lightning flashes began to play across the sky. A distant roar of wind could be heard between the peals of thunder.

Norris waited for Vienna under the shelter of a cliff where the cowboys had stopped the pack-train. Princess was sensitive to the flashes of lightning, and Vienna patted his neck and called to him softly. The tired burros nodded, and the Mexican women covered their heads with their mantles. Norris helped Vienna put on her slicker and then put on his own, and the other cowboys followed suit. Vienna saw Monty and Dorothy rounding the cliff and hoped the others would arrive soon.

A blue-white, knotted rope of lightning burned down out of the clouds, and a thunder-clap followed, shaking the earth's foundations. The thunder rolled from cloud to cloud, boomed along the peaks, and reverberated from deep to low, finally rumbling away into silence. Vienna felt the electricity in Princess's mane, and it seemed to tingle through her nerves. The air had a strange, bright cast, and the ponderous clouds were swallowing more and more of the eastern domes. This moment of the breaking of the storm, with the strange growing roar of wind, like a moaning monster, was filled with a heart-disturbing emotion for Vienna Florentino.

It was a glorious feeling to be free and healthy, out in the open under the shadow of the mountain and clouds, in the teeth of the wind, rain, and storm. Another dazzling blue blaze illuminated the bold mountainside and the storm-driven clouds. In the flare of light, Vienna saw Norris' face.

"Are you afraid?" she asked.

"Yes," he replied simply. Then the thunderbolt shook the heavens, and as it faded away, Vienna was surprised by Norris' answer. Something in his face had prompted her to ask him what she believed to be a foolish question. His response amazed her. She loved storms. Why should he fear them? He was someone with whom she could not associate fear.

"How strange! Have you not been out in many storms?" she asked.

A smile that was only a gleam flickered over his dark face. "In hundreds of them. By day, with the cattle stampeding. At night, alone on the mountain, with the pines crashing and the rocks rolling in flood on the desert."

"It's not only the lightning, then?" she asked.

"No. All the storm," Norris replied.

Vienna felt that from now on, she would have less faith in what she had thought was her love of the elements. What little she knew! If this iron-nerved man feared a storm, then there was something about a storm to fear. Suddenly, as the ground shook under her horse's feet, and the sky grew black and crisscrossed by flaming streaks, and between thunderous reports, there was a strange hollow roar sweeping down upon her, she realized how small her knowledge and experience of the mighty forces of nature was. Then, with that perversity of character of which she was fully conscious, she was humble, submissive, reverent, and fearful, even while she gloried in the grandeur of the dark, cloud-shadowed crags and canyons, the stupendous strife of sound, and the wonderful driving lances of white fire. With blacker gloom and deafening roar, the torrent of rain came. It was a cloud-burst. It was like solid water tumbling down.

Vienna sat on her horse, enduring the relentless downpour. Eventually, the rain began to subside and Norris called for everyone to follow him. Vienna glanced at Dorothy, who looked like a drowned rat due to her refusal to wear appropriate attire. She couldn't bear to look at the other girls, who were all equally miserable. Instead, she turned her horse onto Norris's trail. Although the storm had passed, the rain continued to fall steadily. The air had cleared, but it was now uncomfortably cold and wet. Norris was climbing faster than before, and Monty was right behind Vienna, urging her on. They had lost time and were still far from the campsite. The stag-hounds were exhausted and their feet were sore from the sharp rocks on the trail. Vienna grew more and more tired as the ascent became steeper and more treacherous. The rain grew colder, and the wind whipped her face. Her horse struggled to climb while the brush and sharp stones tore at her wet clothes. The gloom of night began to set in. Suddenly, Princess snorted and the saddle creaked as they reached level ground. Vienna looked up to see towering crags and spires that resembled giant pipe organs. The branches of the fir-trees and juniper were heavy with rain, and they seemed to reach out for her. Through a break in the crags,

Vienna caught a glimpse of the west. The sun had set, but the sky was illuminated by red shafts of light shining through the clouds.

Norris's horse was now moving at a steady jog-trot, and Vienna found herself following Princess more than choosing her own path. The shadows grew deeper and the crags appeared spectral and eerie. A chilly wind blew through the dark trees, and coyotes, sensing the presence of the hounds, kept barking and howling in the distance. Strangely enough, the tired hounds didn't seem to notice them at all.

As the night grew darker, Vienna realized that the fir-trees had given way to a pine forest. Suddenly, a small light appeared in the distance, twinkling and blinking like a solitary star in the sky. She lost sight of it for a moment, but then found it again, growing larger as she approached. Finally, she realized that it was a fire, and she could hear the sound of a cowboy song and the wild chorus of coyotes singing in the night. Drops of rain on the branches of trees glittered in the light of the fire.

Norris's tall figure, with his sombrero slouched down, was occasionally outlined against the growing circle of light. From time to time, he turned around to check if Vienna was still following him. The prospect of warmth, food, and rest at the fire brought back Vienna's enthusiasm for the wild ride. She felt that there was something promising in this adventure, not only for her friends, but also for herself. It was a nameless joy and spirit that she couldn't quite put into words.

Chapter Seventeen.

Vienna was relieved to dismount her horse near a blazing fire and see boiling pots resting on red-hot coals. She was soaked through except for her shoulders, which were shielded by her slicker. The Mexican women hurried over to assist her in changing clothes in a nearby tent, but Vienna opted to warm her frozen feet and hands and observe her companions' arrival. When Dorothy dismounted, she stumbled into the arms of several cowboys who were eagerly awaiting her arrival. She appeared to be barely able to walk.

She looked nothing like her usual stylish self, with a limp and lopsided hat hiding her face. A plaintive moan escaped from under the disheveled brim, "O-h-h! What an a-awful ride!" Mrs. Beck was in worse condition, having to be taken off her horse. "I'm paralyzed! I'm a wreck! Bobby, get a roller-chair," she exclaimed. Bobby was eager to help, but there were no roller-chairs in sight.

Florence dismounted with ease, and if not for her wet and tumbling mass of hair, she would have been mistaken for a handsome cowboy. Lorraine Wayne had fared better physically during the ride than Dorothy, but her small mount had left her more vulnerable to the cactus and brush. Her habit hung in tatters. Melissa had managed to preserve some style, pride, and a little strength, but her face was white, her eyes were big, and she limped. "Princess!" she exclaimed. "What did you want to do to us? Kill us outright or make us homesick?"

Of all the guests, Christine, Ambrose's wife, and the little French maid had suffered the most during the long ride. Christine was unaccustomed to horses, and Ambrose had to carry her into the big tent. Florence convinced Vienna to leave the fire, and when they went in with the others, Dorothy was wailing because her wet boots would not come off, Mrs. Beck was weeping and trying to direct a Mexican woman to unfasten her bedraggled dress, and there was general pandemonium.

"Get warm clothes, hot drinks, and grub, warm blankets," Norris barked out his sharp order. With Florence's help, the Mexican women quickly tended to Vienna and the rest of the female party, making them comfortable, except for the weariness and aches that only rest and sleep could alleviate. Despite their fatigue, pains, and the strangeness of being packed sardine-like under canvas, the howls of coyotes did not prevent Vienna's guests from stretching out with long, grateful sighs and, one by one, dropping into deep slumber.

Florence and Vienna giggled and whispered to each other until the light flickering on the canvas finally faded and Vienna drifted off to sleep. The sounds of camp life, like the low voices of men, the thump of horses' hooves, and the coyote serenade, all faded into the darkness. Vienna was enveloped in a sense of warmth and sweet rest until she finally awoke to the sound of an ax ringing in the distance. She noticed that Florence was missing from the tent and decided to investigate.

As Vienna peered out between the flaps of the tent, she was met with an exquisite sight. A level space, green with long grass and bright with flowers, was dotted with groves of graceful firs and pines and spruces. The scene reached up to superb crags that were rosy and golden in the sunlight. Vienna was eager to get outside and enjoy an unrestricted view, so she quickly dressed and searched for her pack. Her favorite stag-hounds, Russ and Tartar, were asleep before the door, where they had been chained. Vienna awakened them and loosened their chains, realizing that it must have been Norris who had chained them near her.

The cool air was fragrant with pine and spruce, and some subtle nameless tang that was sweet and tonic. Vienna felt invigorated and alive as she stood there, taking deep breaths of the magic draught. Turning to look in the other direction, she saw the remnants of the temporary camp from the night before, and beyond that, a grove of beautiful pines from which came the sharp ring of the ax. As she gazed out over the wide expanse, she saw a wonderful park surrounded by lofty crags and full of crags of lesser height, many lifting their heads from dark-green groves of trees.

The rising sun had not yet peeked over the horizon, but its warm, rosy glow was already illuminating the towering rocks and dappling the surrounding pines with golden light. Vienna, accompanied by her trusty hounds, strolled through the nearby grove, the soft, springy ground beneath her feet brown with pine needles. As she made her way through the trees, she suddenly realized that a cluster of them had been blocking her view of the park's most stunning feature.

The cowboys had chosen a prime campsite that would offer them the perfect balance of shade and sunlight throughout the day. Tents and tarps had already been erected, and the cowboys were bustling about, tending to their campfires and organizing their gear. Packs were piled high and covered with tarpaulins, while beds were neatly rolled up beneath the trees. The meadow was lush and rolling, dotted with solitary trees and surrounded by towering stone cliffs that soared hundreds of feet into the sky.

A cool, clear spring bubbled out from under a mossy cliff, its banks fringed with wildflowers. In the meadow, the horses grazed contentedly, their manes and tails waving in the gentle morning breeze. It was a scene of tranquil beauty, and Vienna couldn't help but feel a sense of peace and contentment settle over her.

Suddenly, Florence came running over to her, bursting with energy and excitement. She was dressed in a flannel blouse, corduroy skirt, and moccasins, her long hair pulled back in a simple band. "Mountcastle's been gone for hours with a gun," she exclaimed breathlessly. "Gene's gone to look for him. The other guys are still sleeping. They must be dead to the world in this fresh air."

Florence quickly turned her attention to the task at hand, peppering Vienna with questions about the camp's organization and layout. Together, they worked tirelessly to ensure that everything was in order before the other guests awoke. Vienna and Florence had a tent set up under a towering pine tree, but they had no intention of sleeping in it unless the weather turned sour.

As the sun crept higher in the sky, casting long shadows across the meadow, Vienna felt a sense of satisfaction settle over her. The camp was set up, the horses were content, and the day stretched out before them, full of possibility and adventure. It was a perfect day to be alive.

They laid out a tarpaulin and decided to sleep under the stars. With their hounds by their side, they set out to explore the park. Vienna was surprised to find that the park was much larger than they had anticipated, a series of valleys nestled between the towering peaks. As the day wore on, Vienna found herself falling under the park's spell. Even in the heat of midday, the warmth was comfortable and inviting, like a spring day. The air was thin and sweet, and Vienna found herself feeling lightheaded and dreamy. She dozed off under a pine tree with her head resting on Florence. When she awoke, the sun was setting and the shadows of the crags stretched out across the park. Florence was reading lazily, and the rest of the camp was quiet. Melissa, Dorothy, Mrs. Beck, and Lorraine had returned, delighted with the place but tired and hungry. Vienna led them around the camp and showed them the many nooks and crannies under the crags where they could rest and relax.

After a satisfying dinner, they sat on the ground like Indians. The lack of merriment was only due to their preoccupation with appeasing their appetites. Norris then led them through a narrow passage of the park, up a steep climb between towering crags. They emerged onto a grassy promontory that faced the vast open west. The earth was rolling down, ridged, streaked, and reddened, seemingly to the golden sunset end of the world. Mountcastle appreciated the breathtaking view, while Dorothy expressed her usual lackadaisical enthusiasm. Melissa was thrilled and amazed, and Mrs. Beck asked Bobby for his opinion before she offered hers. Lorraine Wayne remained silent, like Vienna and Florence. Boyd was politely interested, appearing to care for things as others did. Vienna watched as the changing west transformed slowly, with its haze of desert dust, mountain, cloud, and sun. She watched until her eyes ached and barely had a thought of what she was looking at. When her eyes shifted to Norris standing motionless on the rim, her mind became active again. Norris stood apart from the others, aloof and unconscious. He made a dark, powerful figure, fitting perfectly into the wild promontory. Vienna felt a strange, annoying surprise when she discovered that both Melissa and Dorothy were watching Norris with peculiar interest. Lorraine was also aware of the splendid picture the cowboy presented. When Lorraine smiled and whispered in her ear, "It's so good to look at a man like that," Vienna felt surprise again, but this time accompanied by vague pleasure. Melissa and Dorothy were flirts, one deliberate and skilled, the other unconscious and natural. Lorraine Wayne, on the rare occasion, admired a man sincerely.

Vienna was lost in thought as she sat with her companions around the campfire. She couldn't help but feel a deep fascination with Norris, not as a man, but as a symbol of the wild and wonderful West that had captured her heart. Despite Melissa's coquetry and Dorothy's alluring ways, Vienna didn't let it bother her too much. She knew that they would forget about Norris as soon as they returned home, but she couldn't help but wonder how he would react to their advances.

As the night grew cooler, Vienna's guests began to drift off to sleep. Vienna settled down with Florence under the pine tree, while Russ and Tartar lay on either side of her. The cool breeze rustled through the trees and the coyotes began their eerie howling. Vienna gazed up at the stars, feeling as though she would never be able to fall asleep. The stars seemed so close, and their brightness was almost blinding against the dark sky. Despite the unfair situation Norris had been put in, Vienna couldn't help but feel drawn to him and the rugged, untamed land he represented.

As she gazed out at the vast expanse of stars above her, their brilliance only grew more magnificent the longer she looked. For Vienna, there was nothing quite like these Western stars; they held a special place in her heart, and she believed they would somehow influence her destiny.

After a few days of much-needed rest, camp life became more lively and active. The men, especially Mountcastle, were eager to explore the mountains with their guns in tow, while Mrs. Beck and the children preferred a more relaxed pace. Lorraine enjoyed leisurely walks through the groves or sitting on a grassy knoll, but it was Melissa and Dorothy who wanted to explore every nook and cranny of the crags and canyons. When they couldn't convince the others to join them, they set off on their own, often accompanied by the cowboy guides.

As a result, Vienna and her guests grew closer to the cowboys, and the group became like one big family. Her friends adapted well to the situation and even came to enjoy it. Though the cowboys had a tendency to show off and be gallant, they were not much different from their everyday selves.

The leveling process occurred when Vienna's friends came down to meet the cowboys. The environment and circumstances caused any class of people to grow natural. Vienna found the situation interesting. Before, she studied the cowboys, especially Norris. With the contrasts of her guests, she felt amused, mystified, perplexed, saddened, and subtly pleased. Monty became a source of delight to Vienna and everyone once he overcame his shyness. He discovered that he was a success among the ladies. Either he was exalted to heroic heights by this knowledge or he made it appear so. Dorothy was his undoing, but Vienna believed her innocent. Dorothy thought Monty hideous, and he could not interest her, even if he had saved a hundred poor little babies' lives. Monty followed Dorothy around like a little adoring dog one moment and a huge, devouring gorilla the next. Nels and Nick followed Melissa like grenadiers on duty. If she dropped her glove, they almost came to blows to see who should pick it up. Mountcastle was the best feature of the camping party. He was an absurd-looking little man, and his abilities were at tremendous odds with what might have been expected of him from his looks. He could ride, tramp, climb, shoot, and liked to help around the camp. The cowboys played innumerable tricks upon him, but he never discovered them. He was serious, slow in speech and action, and absolutely imperturbable.

If ever one could be unflappable and amiable at the same time, that was Mountcastle. Gradually, the cowboys began to understand him, and in turn, they began to like him. When cowboys liked someone, it meant something. Vienna had noticed how the cowboys were not very inclined to speak to Boyd Harvey, and it saddened her. However, with Mountcastle, they became actual friends. They were not aware of it, and it never crossed his mind, but it was a fact. Their friendship was born out of the truth that the Englishman was manly in a way that the cowboys could interpret. When he finally succeeded in throwing the diamond-hitch on a pack-horse after countless attempts, the cowboys started to respect him. Mountcastle only needed one more thing to win their hearts, and he kept on trying to ride a bucking bronco. One of the cowboys had a bronco that they nicknamed Devil. Every day for a week, Devil threw the Englishman all over the place, ruining his clothes, bruising him, and finally kicking him. Then, the cowboys tried to persuade Mountcastle to give up, which was remarkable because any Westerner would have traveled a thousand miles to see an English lord ride a bucking bronco. Whenever Devil threw Mountcastle, the cowboys went into fits. But Mountcastle did not know the meaning of the word "fail," and there came a day when Devil could not throw him. It was a singular sight to see the men line up to shake hands with the composed Englishman. Even Norris, who had watched from the sidelines, came forward with a warm and pleasant smile on his dark face. When Mountcastle went to his tent, there was a lot of typical cowboy chatter, this time vastly different from the previous persiflage. "By Gawd!" exclaimed Monty Price, who seemed to be the most stunned and elated of them all.

"That's the first Englishman I ever seen! He's awful deceiving to look at, but I know now why England rules the world. Just take a peek at that bronco. His spirit is broke. Ridden by a little English duke no bigger than a grasshopper! Fellas, if it hasn't dawned on you yet, let Monty Price give you a hunch. There's no flies on Mountcastle. And I'll bet a million steers to a rawhide rope that next he'll be throwing a gun as good as Nels."

Vienna found it enjoyable to realize that she liked Mountcastle even more for the traits that were brought out by his association with the cowboys. On the other hand, she found that she liked the cowboys better for something in them that contact with Easterners brought out. This was especially true in Norris's case. She had been completely wrong when she had imagined he would fall an easy victim to Dorothy's eyes and Melissa's lures. He was kind, helpful, courteous, and watchful. But he had no sentiment. He did not see Dorothy's charms or feel Melissa's fascination. And their efforts to captivate him were now so obvious that Mrs. Beck taunted them, and Lorraine smiled knowingly, and Bobby and Boyd made playful remarks. All of which cut Melissa's pride and hurt Dorothy's vanity. They attempted open conquest of Norris. So it came about that Vienna unconsciously admitted the cowboy to a place in her mind never occupied by any other. The instant it occurred to her why he was proof against the wiles of the other women, she pushed that amazing and strangely disturbing thought from her mind. Nevertheless, as she was only human, she could not help thinking and being pleased and enjoying a little the discomfiture of the two coquettes. Moreover, from this thought of Norris, and the watchfulness growing out of it, she discovered more about him.

He wasn't happy. He frequently paced back and forth through the grove at night. Sometimes, in the afternoon when Nels, Nick, and Monty were there, he would absent himself from camp. He always kept an eye on the trails, as if he was expecting someone to come riding up. Unlike the other cowboys, he didn't engage in the fun and conversation around the campfire. He remained preoccupied and sad, constantly gazing off into the distance.

Vienna felt a strange sense of guardianship over him. She remembered Don Carlos and imagined he was worried about his charge and the safety of the entire party. But if he was worried about possible visits from wandering guerrillas, why did he leave camp? Suddenly, a memory of the dark-eyed Mexican girl, Bonita, who had disappeared since the night she rode Norris's big horse out of El Cajon, flashed into Vienna's curious mind. The memory brought an idea. Maybe Norris had a meeting place in the mountains, and these solitary trips were to meet Bonita. The idea caused hot blood to rush to Vienna's cheek. Then she was amazed at her own emotions. She was surprised that the conception of the idea had caused her cheek to burn with shame. Her old self, the one that was separate from this new, passionate self, took over control of her emotions. But Vienna discovered that this new self was a creature of strange power that could return and govern her at any moment. She found it fighting loyally for what her intelligence and wisdom told her was only her romanticized idea of a cowboy.

She reasoned that if Norris was the kind of man her feminine skepticism wanted to make him out to be, he wouldn't have been so blind to the coquettish advances of Melissa and Dorothy. She knew he had once been someone she didn't want to remember. But he had been uplifted, Vienna Florentino declared that.

Her pride swelled within her, and her woman's intuition assured her that he could not have committed such a dishonorable act. She scolded herself for even considering it.

One afternoon, a massive storm cloud descended upon the crags, shrouding the park in darkness. Vienna was worried because some of her companions had gone off with the cowboys and had yet to return. Florence tried to calm her, but Vienna still sent for Norris to search for them.

Half an hour later, the sound of hooves could be heard outside the tent. Vienna, Lorraine, and Florence waited anxiously for their return. When Melissa and Dorothy entered, it was clear that something had happened. Melissa commented on Dorothy's newfound beauty, but Dorothy's eyes were ablaze with anger. She turned away from the others and caught a glimpse of her reflection in a nearby mirror. Her hand flew to her cheek, where a red welt had formed.

Dorothy had always been meticulous about her soft, delicate skin, so when she noticed a hideous blemish on her face, she was distraught. "Look at this!" she exclaimed in dismay. "My complexion is ruined!"Melissa approached her, curious. "How did you get that splotch?" she asked."I've been kissed!" Dorothy declared dramati cally."What?" Melissa asked, even more intrigued, as the others c huckled."One of those shameless cowboys hugged and kissed me," Dorothy continued. "It was pitch-dark outside, and I couldn't see a thing. It was so noisy that I couldn't even hear. But someone was trying to help me off my horse, and my foot got caught in the stirrup. I fell right into somebody's arms, and then he did it, the scoundrel! He hugged and kissed me in the most horrible way. I couldn't even move a finger. I'm absolutely fuming!"Once the laughter died down, Dorothy turned to Florence with her big, wide eyes. "Do these cowboys really take advantage of a girl when she's helpless and in the dark?" she asked."Of course they do," Florence replied with a grin. "What did you expect, Dot?""What in the world could you have been expecting?" Melissa chimed in. "Haven't you been dying to be kissed?""No," Dorothy retor ted."Well, you certainly acted like it," Melissa teased. "I've never seen you so angry about being kissed before.""I wouldn't mind so much if the brute hadn't scraped the skin off my face," Dorothy complained. "He had whiskers as sharp and stiff as sandpaper. And when I pulled away, he rubbed my cheek with them."This revelation about the cause of her distress sent her friends into a fit of giggles. "I agree with you, Dot," Melissa said eventually. "It's one thing to be kissed, but quite another to have your beauty spoiled. Who was this particular savage, anyway?""I don't know!" Dorothy burst out. "If I did, I'd...I'd..." Her eyes conveyed the punishment she wished to inflict."Honestly now, Dot, do you have any idea who it was?" Melissa pressed."I hope...I think it was Norris," Dorothy replied finally.

"Dot, you're jumping to conclusions," Melissa said with a grin. "Norris couldn't have been the culprit, or the hero for that matter ."Dorothy's face flushed with anger. "How can you be so sure?" she demanded."Well, for one thing, he was clean-shaven when we rode out this afternoon," Melissa explained. "I remember how smooth and brown his face looked.""Fine, but can you tell me which one of these cowboys was not clean-shaven?" Dorothy retorted."Easy," Melissa replied cheerfully. "It wasn't Nick, it wasn't Nels, and it wasn't Frankie. The only other cowboy with us had a short, stubby black beard, like that cactus we passed on the trail."Dorothy let out a moan of despair. "I knew it was him!" she exclaimed. "That horrible little demon, Monty Price!"Vienna and Lorraine often spent lazy afternoons lounging in a shaded nook on the eastern side of the crags. Unlike the harsh, ever-changing landscape on the western side, the view here was one of serene mountains and valleys, dotted with patches of dry land but lush with the green of pine and fir and the cool gray of crags. The mountains were bold and rugged, yet they felt close and welcoming, not distant and unattainable like the desert.On this particular afternoon, Vienna and Lorraine sat under a low-branched tree, enjoying the dreamy spell of the mountain fastness. They hardly spoke, content to bask in the smoky haze of the valleys, the fleecy cloud resting over the peaks, and the sailing eagle in the blue sky. The silence was unbroken, save for the soft wind that carried the sweet scent of pine. But then Lorraine seemed to want to talk about something serious.

"Princess, I can't stay out here forever. I gotta head back home. You coming with me?" asked Lorraine. Vienna pondered for a moment before responding, "Maybe. I've been thinking about it. I gotta visit home sometime. But my parents are heading to Europe this summer."

Lorraine cut to the chase, "Are you gonna spend the rest of your life in this wilderness, Princess Florentino?" Vienna remained silent. Lorraine continued, "Don't get me wrong, this trip has been eye-opening for me. I was even sick when we arrived, but now I'm feeling better than ever. Look at Melissa, too. She was a ghost when we got here, but now she's healthy and beautiful. The West has given us the gift of health, but it's given me so much more. I've come to appreciate the spiritual side of things, too. Princess, I've been studying you. I see what this life has done for you. Your strength, your serenity, your happiness. I wondered at the causes of your change. Now I know. You were sick of idleness, sick of uselessness, and sick of the noise and smells of the city. I know many women who feel the same way. You've done what many of us want to do but don't have the courage. You've left it all behind. I can see the difference you've made in the lives of the Mexicans and cattlemen in your range. You have work to do, and that's the secret to your happiness, isn't it?"

Vienna asked Lorraine what work meant to her, to which she replied that work is essential for happiness. Lorraine could not say for herself, but having money has brought her contentment. She did not mean to judge the West, but having money has allowed her to buy and maintain her ranch. Even though there may be larger ranches, none are like hers. She is almost paying her expenses through her business, and she hopes that she is useful. She has helped the Mexicans and eased the hardships of a few cowboys. For Vienna, her life is like a dream, with her ranch and cowboys being real and typical of the West. Her feelings towards them may be strange, but they are true to the West. Lorraine's impressions of the West have changed since she first arrived. She now sees beauty and something noble in the endless open stretches, which she once saw as terrible wastes of barren ground. Her initial thoughts of Vienna's cowboys being dirty, rough, loud, crude, and savage were wrong. She has changed her mind, realizing that the dirt was only dust, and this desert dust is clean.

But I cannot help it. Think of all the things you would be giving up. Think of the life you could have in the city. Think of the men you could marry. Men of your own class, Vienna.""But Lorraine, I do not want those things. I do not want to marry for money or status. I want to marry for love. And I have found that here in the West. I have found it in a man who is rough and crude and savage, but who is also kind and gentle and true. I have found it in Monty Price.""Monty Price!" exclaimed Lorraine. "Vienna, you cannot be serious. He is a cowboy!""Yes, Lorraine, he is a cowboy. But he is also a man. A man who has lived a hard life and has come out of it with a heart of gold. A man who I know will love me for who I am, not for what I have.""But Vienna, what about your family? What about your responsibilities?""I will not abandon my family, Lorraine. I will still be a Florentino. But I will also be a wife and a mother, and I will be happy."Vienna spoke with conviction, and Lorraine could see that there was no changing her mind. She sighed and said, "Well, Vienna, I hope you know what you are doing. I hope you have thought this through."Vienna smiled and took Lorraine's hand. "I have thought it through, Lorraine. And I am sure of my decision. I am sure that I want to spend the rest of my life with Monty Price, in this beautiful and wild and wonderful country."

"I promised your mom I'd talk to you," Vienna told Lorraine, though she hated what she had to say. She envied Lorraine's courage and wisdom in refusing to marry Boyd Harvey, as she could see in his face. Vienna believed Lorraine would also refuse Mountcastle. "Whom will you marry? What chance is there for a woman of your position to marry out here? What in the world will become of you?" she asked.

"Quien sabe?" Vienna replied with a sad smile.

Later on, Vienna sat with Boyd Harvey on a grassy promontory overlooking the west, where he once again tried to court her. Suddenly, she turned to him and asked if he would be willing to spend the rest of his life in the West if she married him.

"Princess!" he exclaimed, amazed. Her question had startled him, and he looked out over the barren landscape. He replied with a tinge of shame in his cheek, "No."

Vienna said no more, and he didn't either. She was relieved that she didn't have to refuse him, but she knew they could never be together. It was impossible not to like Boyd Harvey, but she couldn't marry him. She thought about him often, as he was handsome, young, rich, well-born, pleasant, and cultivated. If he had any vices, she hadn't heard of them.

Vienna knew that Boyd Harvey was a highly sought after bachelor, with no interest in drinking or gambling. She acknowledged his good qualities, but couldn't help thinking about her own peculiar ideas. Boyd had a fair complexion that never tanned, even under the harsh southwestern sun and wind. His hands were softer and whiter than Vienna's, which she found beautiful. They were evidence that he never worked a day in his life. Boyd had a tall, graceful frame that lacked any signs of ruggedness. He despised any form of strenuous activity, preferring to spend his days indulging in leisurely pursuits. Vienna couldn't help but feel that if he had any sons, they would be like him, leading to the eventual extinction of their race.

When Vienna returned to camp, she was in a decisive mood. Fate had it that the first person she saw was Norris, who had just returned from a grueling trip to fetch the mail. Vienna questioned why he hadn't sent one of the boys for the mail instead of making the trip himself. Norris simply replied that she was worried about the mail, and he had to deliver it. Vienna couldn't help but admire Norris's dedication, riding down and back up the mountain in just twelve hours, all the while taking care of his horse. She realized that not many horses in the outfit could have endured such a trip, except for Norris's own horse, Princess.

The man appeared exhausted, covered in dirt and sweat. His name was Norris, and it was evident that he had been riding hard on his horse up a rough ascent. His boots were scuffed and worn, and his shirt clung to his muscular frame, revealing every ripple of his muscles. His face was black with dirt, except for his temples and forehead, which were bright red from exertion. Drops of sweat dripped from his hands as he examined his horse's lame foot before removing the saddle.

The black horse eagerly lunged towards the watering-pool, but Norris restrained him with iron arms, allowing him only a small drink. Vienna watched in awe as Norris displayed his impressive strength, his brawny wrist and big, strong hand expertly controlling the horse. Despite his rough exterior, his hand showed gentleness and thoughtfulness towards the animal.

Norris exuded a combination of fire, strength, and action that seemed to cling to him. Despite his exhaustion, he radiated potential youth and unused vitality, promising red-blooded deeds of both flesh and spirit. Vienna saw in him the unimpaired strength of his forefathers, marveling at the significance of his life. She compared him to the men of the East, and in doing so, regretted her old standards.

The dust, dirt, sweat, and bruises did not diminish Norris's strength or appeal. In fact, they only heightened Vienna's admiration for him, as she recognized the value of a man who was willing to work hard and get his hands dirty.

Chapter Eighteen.

On the cool nights under the starry sky, the campers gathered around the blazing fire and shared stories that perfectly fit the eerie surroundings. Monty Price had become a captivating storyteller, despite being a terrible liar. His cowboy comrades had exposed his lies out of jealousy, but Mountcastle remained oblivious due to his lack of understanding. Even Dorothy Coombs knew that Monty was a liar, yet she could not resist his mesmerizing gaze and the horror tales he spun. Monty had transformed from a quiet stranger to a proud and pompous liar, relishing in the attention and admiration of the ladies. Some cowboys, like Nels, were envious of Monty's storytelling abilities, despite being a true hero in their own right. Whenever Monty spoke, Nels would pretend to leave, but he never truly left the captivating circle of the campfire. One evening, Vienna was accosted by Monty as she left her tent at twilight.

With a sly and secretive gesture, he motioned for her to follow him away from the group. "Miss Florentino, I'm gonna ask you for a favor," he whispered. Vienna smiled and nodded, eager to hear what he had to say. "Tonight, when everyone's done blabbering on, I want you to ask me a question. Just say, 'Monty, since you've had more adventures than all those cowboys put together, tell us about the most terrible time you ever had.' Can you do that for me, Miss Florentino? And make it sound sincere."

"Of course, Monty," Vienna replied, although she couldn't help but feel uneasy about the man's scarred and burned face. She knew that Dorothy found him repulsive and deformed, and it was hard for her to look at him directly. But she also saw a glint of mischief in his eyes, a hint of a playful spirit that she couldn't ignore.

Later that night, when the coyotes were howling and the conversation had died down, Vienna remembered her promise and turned to Monty. "Monty," she said, drawing out the syllables for dramatic effect, "seeing as you've had more adventures than all the cowboys put together, tell us about the most terrible time you ever had."

Everyone turned to look at Monty, who seemed taken aback by the sudden attention. He waved his hand dismissively. "Oh, Miss Florentino, I couldn't possibly," he protested. "It's too harrowing for delicate ladies like yourselves to hear."

But the others were insistent. Nels nodded his head knowingly, and even Dorothy leaned forward with a morbid curiosity. Mountcastle put out his cigarette and adjusted his glasses, ready to listen. And so, with a deep breath, Monty began to tell his tale.

Monty shifted his seat to bask in the warmth of the fire's light on his face, lost in deep thought. "I can't rightly say which was the worst time I ever had," he reflected. Nels took a puff of his pipe and blew out a cloud of smoke, attempting to hide himself from view. Monty continued to contemplate until the smoke cleared, then turned to Nels. "Listen here, partner, we've known each other since our days in the Panhandle over thirty years ago," Monty began.

"We sure didn't," Nels interrupted bluntly. "You can't be calling me an old man."

"Maybe it wasn't that long ago. Anyways, do you remember those three horse thieves I hung from that one cottonwood tree, and the beautiful blonde girl I rescued from a group of cutthroats who murdered her father, old Bill Warren, the buffalo hunter?" Monty asked. "Which of those two incidents do you think was the most terrible?"

"Monty, my memory ain't what it used to be," Nels replied honestly. "Tell us about the blonde girl!" exclaimed a few of the ladies. Dorothy, who had suffered from nightmares due to a previous story about hanging, silently begged Monty to spare her. "Alright, we'll hear about the blonde girl," Monty conceded, settling back. "Although I don't think her story was the most terrible of the two, and it'll stir up emotions I've long buried."

Just then, a sharp knock sounded, signaling Nels tapping his pipe on a stump, indicating his jealousy had passed. "It was down in the Panhandle, towards the west end of the Comanche hunting grounds," Monty began his tale, "where all the outlaws and Indians in the area were hiding in the river bottoms, chasing after some of the last buffalo herds that had wintered there."

Back in the day, I was a young and reckless lad. I had a reputation for being a bit of a troublemaker, and I had the notches on my gun to prove it. Seventeen notches, each one representing a man I had killed face to face. But there was one notch that I wasn't proud of. That was the one I got for hitting an express messenger over the head and taking a package he wouldn't give me. It wasn't my finest moment.

But that was the kind of guy I was back then. The kind of guy who made the other fellas in the saloons smile and buy me drinks. I remember one time when I was in a place called Taylor's Bend. I was just standing at the bar, minding my own business, when three cow-punchers came in. They didn't recognize me with my back turned, so they got playful. I didn't stop drinking, and I didn't turn around. But when I started shooting under my arm, the saloon-keeper had to go get a heap of sawdust to cover up what was left of those three cow-punchers after they were hauled out. Yeah, I was rough back then. I'd shoot ears off, noses off, hands off. But as I got older, I learned to just kill a man quick, like Wild Bill.

One night, news came into town that a gang of cut-throats had murdered old Bill Warren and taken his girl. I gathered up a few good gun-men, and we rode out down the river-bottom to an old log cabin where the outlaws were holed up. We rode up bold-like and made a hell of a racket. But then the gang started shooting at us from the cabin, and we all had to hunt for cover. The fighting went on all night. By morning, all of my men were dead except for two, and they were badly injured. We fought all day without food or water, except for some whiskey I had. And at night, I was on my own.

Feeling a little banged up myself, I took a break and headed down to the river to clean up, patch myself up, and grab a drink. While I was there, one of the gang members came by with a bucket, but instead of water, he got a face full of lead. As he lay dying, he revealed that a whole group of outlaws was headed our way the next day, and if I wanted to save the girl, I needed to hurry. There were only five guys left in the cabin.

I went back to where I had left my horse and picked up two more guns, an extra belt, and a fresh box of shells. I think I grabbed some cigarettes too. Then, I made my way back to the cabin. It was a beautiful moonlit night, and I couldn't help but wonder if Bill's gun was as pretty as they say it was. The grass around the cabin was tall, so I crawled up to the door without making any noise. Once I got there, I had to figure out a plan. There was only one door, and it was pitch black inside. I decided to take a chance and quickly opened the door. It worked like a charm. They heard me, but they weren't fast enough to catch me in the light. We exchanged gunfire, but I was too quick for them.

Ladies and gentlemen, let me tell you, it was quite the showdown that night. I managed to stay out of harm's way and waited patiently for one of those ruffians to slip up and give away their position. By the time morning came, they were all piled up on the floor, shot to pieces. I found the girl, and let me tell you, she was stunning. We went down to the river, and she tended to my wounds.

I had gathered about a dozen more or so, and the sight of tears in her beautiful eyes, and my blood staining her little hands, just naturally awakened a tremble in my heart. I saw she was feeling the same way, and that settled it. "We were coming up from the river, and I had just straddled my horse with the girl behind when we

ran right into that cutthroat gang that was doing business around
then. Being somewhat handicapped, I couldn't drop more than
one gun-round of them, and then I had to run. The whole gang
followed me, and some miles out chased me over a ridge right into
a big herd of buffalo. Before I knew what was happening, that
herd broke into a stampede, with me in the middle. Pretty soon
the buffalo closed in tight. I knew I was in some danger then.
But the girl trusted me something pitiful. I saw again that she had
fallen in love with me. I could tell from the way she hugged me
and yelled. Before long, I was struggling to keep my horse on his
feet. As far as I could see, there were dusty, black, bobbing, shaggy
humps. A huge cloud of dust went along over our heads. The
roar of trampling hooves was terrible. My horse weakened, went
down, and was carried along a little while I slipped off with the girl
onto the backs of the buffalo. "Ladies, I'm not denying that then
Monty Price was a bit scared. It was the first time in my life! But
the trusting face of that beautiful girl, as she lay in my arms and
hugged me and yelled, made my spirit leap like a shooting star. I
just began to jump from buffalo to buffalo. I must have jumped
a mile of them bobbing backs before I came to open places. And
here's where I performed the greatest stunts of my life.

I put on my big spurs and just rode and spurred until the specific
buffalo I was on got close to another, then I would flop over.
That's how I got to the edge of the herd, tumbled off the last one,
and rescued the girl. "As far as my memory goes, that was a very
emotional walk home to the little town where she lived. But she
wasn't true to me and married another man. I was too much of a
gentleman to kill him. But that deceitful act always bothered me.

Girls are strange. I've always wondered how any girl who has been hugged and kissed by one man could marry another. But mature experience has taught me that such is the case."

The cowboys laughed, and Melissa, Mrs. Beck, and Lorraine laughed until they cried. Vienna found it impossible to hold back her emotions, and Dorothy sat hugging her knees, horrified by the story and Monty's reference to her and the fickleness of women. Mountcastle, for the first time, seemed to be moved out of his imperturbability, though not by humor. When he finally noticed the mirth, he was dumbfounded by it. "By Jove! you Americans are an extraordinary people," he said. "I don't see anything funny in Mr. Price's story of his adventure. By Jove! that was a very intense occasion. Mr. Price, when you talk about being frightened for the only time in your life, I understand what you mean. I've experienced that. I was frightened once."

"Dook, I wouldn't have thought it of you," replied Monty. "I'm quite curious to hear about it."

Vienna and her friends didn't dare break the spell for fear that the Englishman might revert to his usual modest reticence. He had explored in Brazil, served in the Boer War, and hunted in India and Africa, experiences he never spoke of.

Excited by Monty's story and taking it as the literal truth, Mountcastle found himself in a Homeric mood and decided to tell a story to the eager cowboys. They practically begged him to share his tale, with a suppressed eagerness that hinted at a desire for more than just a story from an English lord. Vienna, perceptive as ever, sensed that the cowboys had begun to suspect Monty was not as easily fooled as they had believed. They thought he was having fun at their expense and planned to tell a lie that would make Monty's story seem small in comparison.

Nels eagerly anticipated the joke that would be played on Monty, while Monty himself began to doubt Mountcastle's words. Mountcastle began his story, his quick and fluent speech a stark contrast to his usual drawl. He spoke of hunting wild beasts in India and Africa, but claimed to have been frightened only once. The adventure he spoke of took place in British East Africa, in Uganda, where he was part of a safari in a district known to be infested with man-eating lions.

Mountcastle explained that man-eaters were different from ordinary lions, being matured beasts that had become man-eaters by accident or necessity. When old and finding it more difficult to make a kill, they would stalk and kill a native out of hunger. Once they had tasted human blood, they would become absolutely fearless and terrible in their attacks.

The villagers near our camp were in a state of terror due to the presence of two or more man-eating lions. On the night of our arrival, one of these lions leaped over a stockade fence, took a screaming native from a group sitting around a fire, and disappeared into the darkness. I decided to take it upon myself to kill these lions and set up a permanent camp in the village for that very purpose.

During the day, I sent beaters into the brush and rocks of the river-valley, and at night, I kept watch. The lions visited us every night, but I never saw one. I soon realized that the lions were less likely to attack when they were roaring around the camp than when they were silent. It was astonishing how quietly they could stalk a man. They could move through a thicket so dense that you wouldn't think a rabbit could get through it without making a sound. But when they were ready to charge, they did so with a terrifying onslaught and roar. They would leap into a circle of fires, tear down huts, and even drag natives from low trees. There was no way to predict where or when they would attack.

After ten days of this, I was exhausted from lack of sleep. One night, when I was tired from watching, I fell asleep. My gun-bearer was alone in the tent with me. Suddenly, a terrible roar woke me up, followed by an unearthly scream that pierced my ears. I always slept with my rifle in my hands, so I tried to rise while grabbing it. But I couldn't because a lion was standing over me. I stayed still, and the screams of my gun-bearer told me that the lion had him. I cared for this man and wanted to save him, but I decided not to move while the lion was standing over me. Then, all of a sudden, the lion stepped, and poor Luki's feet dragged across me.

He let out a deafening roar that shook the earth beneath me. I had grabbed onto Luki's foot in a desperate attempt to save him from the lion's jaws. The moon was bright, and I could see the lion clearly. He was a massive, black-maned beast, holding onto Luki's shoulder as he dragged me out of the tent. Luki's screams echoed through the night, and I knew I had to act fast.

The lion dragged us both for what felt like miles before he realized he had two people to contend with. He stopped and turned, his massive head, green-fire eyes, and huge jaws all focused on us. I let go of Luki's foot and searched for my gun, but to my horror, it was nowhere to be found. In my confusion, I had picked up Luki's iron spear instead.

The lion dropped Luki and let out a roar that made my blood run cold. I was paralyzed with fear, knowing that in one leap, he could reach me. But I remembered stories of lions being frightened by strange things, like umbrellas and cow-horns. So, on a wild impulse, I prodded him in the hind quarters with the spear.

The lion let out another roar, but this time, it was different. It was a roar of fear, not anger. He turned and fled into the night, leaving me and Luki shaken but alive.

Folks, I must be a complete fool if that lion didn't back down like a whipped pup, tucking his tail between his legs and slinking away. I saw my opportunity and jumped up, yelling and prodding the beast. He let out a roar fit for a king, but I kept at it until he finally ran off. I found Luki, thankfully not too badly hurt, and he ended up making a full recovery. But let me tell you, that was one scare I won't soon forget.

When Mountcastle finished his story, there was a heavy silence. All eyes were on Monty, who looked defeated and humiliated. Yet, despite his apparent shame, there was a glimmer of admiration on his face for Mountcastle. "Dook, you win," he said before dropping his head and walking away from the campfire circle like a dethroned king.

The cowboys erupted in cheers and wild celebration, with even the usually calm and collected Nels standing on his head in excitement. The Englishman watched in confusion, unable to comprehend their joy at Monty's downfall. Though it was clear to Vienna and her friends that Mountcastle had told the truth, there was no convincing Nels and his comrades that he hadn't deliberately lied to take down their great storyteller.

Everyone lingered around the campfire, reluctant to break the spell that had been cast. The logs had burned down to a heap of glowing coals, and the shadows of the pines crept closer and closer to the circle of light. A cool wind blew through the trees, fanning the embers and stirring up white ash, while a mournful moan filled the air.

The distant yelps of coyotes were fading away, and the sky was a magnificent dark-blue dome decorated with white stars. "What a perfect night!" exclaimed Vienna. "This is a night to comprehend the dream, the mystery, the wonder of the Southwest. Florence, you have been promising to tell us the story of the lost mine of the padres for a long time. It will give us all pleasure, help us understand something of the spell that this land held over the Spaniards who discovered it many years ago. It will be particularly intriguing now because this mountain conceals somewhere under its crags the riches of the lost mine of the padres."

"In the sixteenth century," Florence began in her gentle, slow voice, which was ideal for the nature of the legend, "a poor young padre of New Spain was tending his goats on a hill when the Virgin appeared before him. He fell to his knees at her feet, and when he looked up, she was gone. However, on the maguey plant near where she had stood, there were golden ashes of a strange and wonderful substance. He took the occurrence as a good sign and returned to the hilltop. Under the maguey, slender stalks of white had grown, bearing delicate gold flowers, and as these flowers swayed in the wind, a fine golden powder, as fine as powdered ashes, blew away toward the north. Padre Javier was perplexed, but he believed that great fortune awaited him and his poor people. So he went back to the hilltop again and again, hoping that the Virgin would appear to him."

"One morning, as the sun rose gloriously, he looked across the windy hill toward the waving grass and golden flowers under the maguey, and he saw the Virgin beckoning to him. Again he fell to his knees, but she lifted him and gave him some of the golden flowers. She instructed him to leave his home and people to follow where these blowing golden ashes led."

In search of pure gold to bring back to his impoverished people, Padre Javier left his home and headed northward through the hot and dusty desert, passing through mountain passes to a new land where fierce and warlike Apaches threatened his life. Though gentle and good, he was of a persuasive speech and young and handsome. Among the Apaches, he became a missionary, converting a few but facing hostility from most. Still, he persevered, always searching for the elusive flowers of gold he had heard of.

However, his search was nearly cut short when the old Apache chief, fearing that Padre Javier had designs on his influence with the tribe, sought to burn him alive. The chief's daughter, a beautiful and dark-eyed maiden who secretly loved Javier and believed in his mission, interceded for his life and saved him. Javier fell in love with her, and she one day showed him golden flowers in her hair that shimmered in the wind. When he asked where to find such flowers, she promised to take him to the mountain to look for them.

Together they climbed the mountain, and from the top, they could see beautiful valleys, great trees, and cool waters. There at the top of a wonderful slope that looked down upon the world, she showed him the flowers. And there, Javier found gold in such abundance that he thought he would go out of his mind. Dust of gold! Grains of gold! Pebbles of gold! Rocks of gold! He was rich beyond all dreams.

Javier could finally bring back the fortune he had sought to build a church and city for his people. Though the Apaches were prone to be hostile to him and his religion, he prayed and worked on, converting a few more before returning to his people with his newfound wealth.

The memory of the Virgin and her words haunted him. He knew he had to return to his people and build their church, and the great city that would bear his name. But Javier couldn't bring himself to leave. He was always going to do it "tomorrow." He was in love with an Apache girl with dark eyes, and he couldn't bear to leave her. He felt weak and false for betraying his Virgin and his people, but he was consumed by his love for the Indian maiden.

The old Apache chief eventually discovered the secret love affair between his daughter and the padre. He was furious, and in his anger, he took her up into the mountains and burned her alive, scattering her ashes to the wind. He didn't kill Padre Javier, though. He was too wise and perhaps too cruel to do so, recognizing the strength of Javier's love. Many of his tribe had learned much from the Spaniard.

Javier fell into a deep despair. He had no will to live and slowly wasted away. Before he died, he went to the old Indians who had burned the maiden and begged them to burn his body and scatter his ashes to the wind from the same slope where his Indian sweetheart had been scattered. The Indians agreed, and when Javier died, they burned his body and scattered his ashes on the mountain heights, where they mixed with the ashes of the Indian girl he had loved.

Years passed, and more padres traveled across the desert to the home of the Apaches. They learned of Javier's story from the tribe. Among them was a padre who had been one of Javier's people in his youth. He set out to find Javier's grave, where he believed he would find the gold. He returned with pebbles of gold and flowers that shed a golden dust, telling a wonderful story.

As he ascended higher and higher up the mountain, he finally reached a magnificent slope situated beneath the towering crags. The slope was adorned with a vast expanse of yellow flowers that glimmered like gold. As he touched the petals, golden dust scattered and dispersed among the rocks. It was here that the padre

272 KEN CANNON

made an astonishing discovery - dust, grains, pebbles, and rocks of gold.

Soon, all the padres set out to explore the mountains, hoping to uncover more treasures. Unfortunately, the discoverer of the mine lost his way. Despite their best efforts, they never managed to locate the slope with the golden flowers that marked the spot where Padre Javier was buried along with his mine.

As years passed, the story of the lost mine was passed down from generation to generation. Interestingly, no Mexican or Apache ever attempted to find the lost mine, for the mountain slopes were believed to be haunted. According to legend, the spirit of an Indian maiden who betrayed her tribe and was cursed forever haunted the slopes, scaring off the Apache. Meanwhile, the Mexicans feared the spirit of the false padre who would hurl stones at anyone who dared to search for his grave and his cursed gold.

Chapter Nineteen.

Florence's tale of a lost mine had ignited a spark in the hearts of Vienna's guests, all seeking to strike it rich with gold. However, as they attempted to search for it, the initial excitement dwindled, and they eventually gave up and settled back into camp. Their mountain resources had been exhausted, and they found themselves yearning for the comforts of civilization. Even Melissa expressed her dissatisfaction, muttering, "I reckon nothing's gonna happen, after all."

Vienna patiently waited for her guests to make a decision about breaking camp, knowing that their rest was temporary, and they would soon crave more adventure. As they were content with their current situation, she went for walks alone or with one of the cowboys, accompanied by her loyal stag-hounds. These walks brought her immense joy.

As the cowboys opened up to her, Vienna found herself growing more and more fond of their simple stories. The more she learned about them, the more she questioned the wisdom of leading a secluded life. Spending time with Nels and most of the cowboys was like being in the midst of the rugged pines, crags, and fresh air. Their humor, which was their most prominent trait, helped Vienna overlook their rough exterior. These men were dreamers, just like anyone who lived a solitary life in the wilderness. Each cowboy had his own secrets, and Vienna was able to learn some of them. She was most impressed by their ability to hide their emotions, except for when they were overcome by bursts of laughter or anger. It was all the more remarkable considering how deeply they felt about things that were insignificant to the rest of the world. Vienna couldn't help but believe that living a hard and dangerous life in a barren and untamed land was what turned these men into the great individuals they were. They were tough, fierce, and perhaps even terrifying, but they were also full of an elemental force that came from being so closely tied to the earth, living under the bleak peaks and on the dusty deserts. But one day, while she was out for a walk alone, Vienna realized she had gone too far down a dim trail that wound through the rocks. It was the middle of a summer afternoon, and the shadows of the crags crossed the sunlit patches all around her. She knew she was taking a risk by wandering so far from camp, but she was sure she could find her way back and was enjoying exploring the wild and craggy recesses that were new to her. Eventually, she came upon a bank that dropped suddenly into a beautiful little glade. She sat down to rest before making her way back, and that was when Russ, the most alert of the stag-hounds, lifted his head and growled.

Vienna became wary when her horse, sensing danger, started to act up. She looked around carefully, taking in the irregular line of massive stone blocks that had weathered from the crags on each side of her. The little glade was open and grassy, with pine trees and boulders scattered throughout. The outlet seemed to lead down into a wilderness of canyons and ridges. As she turned to look in that direction, she noticed a dark figure moving stealthily under the pines. Her amazement turned to fear as she watched the woman move from tree to tree, suggesting secrecy or something worse. A tall man with a package soon joined her and they began to walk up the glade, talking earnestly. Vienna recognized Norris and was not surprised to see him, but her curiosity was piqued as to why he had been making strange absences from camp. As they approached, she recognized the woman as Bonita, a Mexican girl. It became clear that this secluded glade was their rendezvous point and Norris had been keeping her hidden there. Vienna quietly left, feeling sorrow that Norris had not completely reformed and insufferable distrust that he had been deceiving her all along.

Vienna tried to be fair to Norris, even though her natural instincts were to push him out of her mind. But her attempts at sympathy failed due to her pride. She had to use her willpower to dismiss him from her thoughts and didn't think of him again until he suddenly appeared in front of her as she was leaving her tent. Norris started to explain himself, but Vienna interrupted him, not wanting to hear it. She was angry, not at him, but at herself for feeling such raw emotions. Outwardly, she was cold and haughty, but inwardly she was burning with rage and shame. Norris tried to explain himself again, but Vienna didn't want to hear it. She didn't care what he thought or did. Norris pleaded with her, his eyes looking timid and boyish, but Vienna didn't want to listen.

"I have a good reason," he said to her, but she interrupted him, "I have no wish to hear your reason." He persisted, "But you ought to." Norris underwent another swift change. He started violently, a dark tide shaded his face and a glitter leaped to his eyes. He took two long strides and loomed over her. "I'm not thinking about myself," he thundered. "Will you listen?" She replied with freezing hauteur in her voice, "No," and with a slight gesture of dismissal, unmistakable in its finality, she turned her back upon him and joined her guests. Norris stood perfectly motionless. Then slowly he began to lift his right hand in which he held his hat. He swept it up and up high over his head. His tall form towered. With fierce suddenness, he flung his hat down. He leaped at his black horse and dragged him to where his saddle lay. With one pitch, he tossed the saddle upon the horse's back. His strong hands flashed at girths and straps. Every action was swift, decisive, fierce. Bounding for his bridle, which hung over a bush, he ran against a cowboy who awkwardly tried to avoid the onslaught. "Get out of my way!" he yelled. Then with the same savage haste, he adjusted the bridle on his horse. "Maybe you better hold on a minute, Gene, old feller," said Monty Price. "Monty, do you want me to brain you?" said Norris with the short, hard ring in his voice. "Now, considering the high class of my brains, I ought to be real careful to keep 'em," replied Monty. "You can bet your life, Gene, I ain't going to get in front of you. But I just say listen!" Norris raised his dark face. Everybody listened. And everybody heard the rapid beat of a horse's hoofs. The sun had set, but the park was light. Nels appeared down the trail, and his horse was running. In another moment, he was in the circle, pulling his bay back to a sliding halt. He leaped off abreast of Norris.

Vienna could feel the tension in the air when Nels arrived. "What's the problem, Gene?" he asked sharply. "I'm leaving camp," replied Norris, his words slurred. His black horse began to stomp as Norris grabbed the reins and kicked the stirrup round. Nels quickly reached out and grabbed Norris, holding him down. "I'm sorry," said Nels slowly. "You were going to hit the trail?" "Yes, I am. Let go, Nels." "Are you sure you want to leave, Gene?" "Let go, damn you!" yelled Norris as he struggled to break free. "What's wrong?" asked Nels, his hand raised again. "Don't touch me, man!" Nels backed away, sensing Norris's anger. Norris made another attempt to mount. "Nels, don't make me forget that we're friends," he said. "I haven't forgotten," replied Nels. "And I'm resigning my job right here and now!" This announcement stopped Norris in his tracks. Vienna was surprised by Nels's sudden resignation. She could feel the tension between the two men. "Resign?" questioned Norris. "Yes, I am. What did you think I would do under these circumstances?" "But Nels, I won't stand for it." "You're not my boss anymore, and I'm not obligated to Miss Florentino either. I'm my own boss, and I'll do what I want. You understand, sir?" Nels's words didn't match the expression on his face. "Gene, you sent me on a little scout down in the mountains, didn't you?" he continued. "Yes, I did," replied Norris, his voice sharp. "Well, you were right, and I was wrong. I admire your judgment. If you hadn't sent me, something bad might have happened."

"We're in a tough spot," Norris exclaimed, and the effect of his words on the cowboys was palpable. He made a fierce and violent gesture, unlike anything they had seen from him before. Monty jumped straight up in the air, seemingly both surprised and ready for a fight. Nick Steele strode over to Nels and Norris like a giant on the prowl. The other cowboys rose silently, ready for action. Vienna and her guests watched and listened, unable to understand what was happening.

"Wait, Nels. They don't need to hear this," Norris said hoarsely, waving a hand towards Vienna's group.

"I'm sorry, but they might as well know now. Maybe Miss Melissa's yearning for something to happen will come true. I think we should tell them first," Nels replied.

"Cut the jokes!" Monty's voice rang out, and it had an immediate effect on the group. It seemed to be the last thing they needed to snap them out of their roles as escorts and back into their natural state as wild men.

"Tell us what's going on," Norris demanded, his voice cool and grim.

"Don Carlos and his guerrillas are camping on the trails that lead up here. They've got the trails blocked, and by tomorrow, we'll be trapped. Maybe they meant to surprise us. They're well-armed and have a lot of Greasers and outlaws with them. Now, what do they want? You can figure it out for yourselves. Maybe the Don wants to pay a visit to our ladies. Maybe his gang is hungry, as usual. Maybe they want to steal some horses or anything they can get their hands on. Maybe they mean worse. My idea is this, and it might be wrong. I've long since stopped trusting Greasers. That black-faced Don Carlos has a deep game."

The two-bit revolution is having a tough time. The rebels are seeking American intervention and are willing to go to any lengths to cause trouble. We are a mere ten miles away from the border. What if those guerrillas manage to take our people across the border? The U.S. cavalry will surely follow, and we all know what that would mean. Don Carlos might be thinking along those lines, or maybe he isn't. We'll find out soon enough. Norris, you're the man to outsmart him, no matter what his game is. It's probably a good thing that you're angry about something. As for me, I'm resigning from my job because I don't want to owe anyone anything. I've been thinking for a while now that the old days have returned, and here I am making a promise not to harm any Mexicans.

Chapter Twenty.

Norris pulled Nels, Monty, and Nick Steele aside, away from the rest of the cowboys, and they appeared to have an intense conversation. After a while, the other cowboys were summoned, and they all spoke, but Norris was the one who spoke the most. The meeting ended, and the cowboys went their separate ways. Norris ordered them to rustle the Indians, and this made Vienna and her companions uneasy. They waited for someone to instruct them on what to do, but the cowboys seemed to have forgotten about them. Some of them ran into the woods, while others went to the open, grassy areas, where they gathered the horses and burros. A few cowboys spread out tarpaulins on the ground and began to pack small bags for a quick journey. Nels got on his horse and rode down the trail, while Monty and Nick Steele led their horses into the grove. Norris climbed up a steep pile of rocks between two sections of low, cracked cliffs behind the camp. Mountcastle offered to assist the packers, but they rudely declined, stating that he would only be in the way. Vienna's companions kept asking her if there was any real danger and if the guerrillas were coming.

Without delay, the ranch was the destination for Vienna and her guests. The cowboys had become suddenly different, and Vienna did her best to answer their questions and fears. Melissa was buzzing with excitement as the cowboys rode in on their bareback horses, bringing in more horses and burros. Some of the horses were concealed in the crags, while the burros were loaded up and sent down the trail with a cowboy. Nick Steele and Monty returned, followed by Norris who clambered down the break between the cliffs. He ordered all the baggage belonging to Vienna and her guests to be taken up the cliff using lassoes to haul them up.

"Get ready to climb," Norris said to Vienna's party.

"Where?" asked Melissa, shocked.

Norris gestured towards the ascent that needed to be made, causing Vienna and her guests to gasp in dismay.

"Mr. Norris, is there danger?" asked Dorothy, her voice trembling.

This was the same question Vienna wanted to ask Norris, but she couldn't bring herself to say it.

"No, there's no danger," replied Norris. "But we're taking precautions we all agreed on as the best."

Dorothy whispered that she believed Norris was lying. Mountcastle and Harvey asked their own questions, while Mrs. Beck timidly made an inquiry.

"Please keep quiet and do as you're told," Norris said bluntly.

As the last of the baggage was being hauled up the cliff, Monty approached Vienna and removed his sombrero. His black face looked the same, but he was a vastly different person.

"Miss Florentino, I'm giving notice I'm resigning my job," Monty said.

"Monty! What do you mean? What does Nels mean now, when danger threatens?" Vienna asked.

"We're quitting. That's all," Monty replied tersely. He was stern and somber, unable to stay still, his eyes scanning everywhere.

Mountcastle stood up abruptly from the log he had been sitting on, his face flushed with anger. "Mr. Price, what the hell does all this commotion mean? Are we about to be robbed or attacked by a bunch of ragtag guerrillas?" he demanded.

"You've made your bet," replied Dorothy, her face turning pale.

"Mr. Price, you wouldn't leave us now, would you? You and Mr. Nels..." Dorothy trailed off, her voice shaking.

"Leave you? What are you talking about?" Monty asked, confused.

"Dorothy is worried that you and Nels will desert us when we need you the most," Mountcastle interjected.

Monty let out a short, bitter laugh as he gave Dorothy a strange look. "Me and Nels are pretty scared, and we're going to leave. It hurts us to see nice young girls like you dragged off by the hair."

Dorothy let out a cry and began to hysterically sob. Mountcastle was finally fully awake. "You and your partner are cowards," he spat. "Where is that courage you bragged about?"

Monty's face twisted in extreme sarcasm. "Dook, I've seen some bright guys in my time, but you take the cake. It's amazing how smart you are. You'll have a great story to tell your English friends if you don't get kidnapped and tied to a cactus bush in Mexico. You'll tell them about how you saw two old-time gunmen run like scared rabbits from a group of Mexicans. Unless, of course, you lie like you did when you talked about poking a lion. That story always..."

"Monty, shut up!" Norris yelled as he approached them. Monty slouched away, muttering curses to himself.

Vienna and Melissa, with the help of Mountcastle, worked to calm Dorothy down. Norris walked by several times without acknowledging them, and Monty, who had been so eager to attend to Dorothy earlier, didn't even seem to notice her. It was rude and strange, even for Monty.

Vienna was unsure of what to do when Norris instructed the cowboys to head to the top of the open space in the cliff and lower lassoes. Without much explanation, he urged the women to climb up the rugged ladder of stones. "We need to hide you," he explained when they hesitated. "If the guerrillas come, we'll tell them you've all gone down to the ranch. If we have to fight, you'll be safe up there."

Melissa bravely stepped forward and allowed Norris to loop a lasso around her and tighten it. He signaled to the cowboys above, "Just walk up, now," and Melissa easily scaled the steep passage. The men climbed up unassisted, but Mrs. Beck began to experience hysteria and had to be half-dragged up. Norris supported Dorothy with one arm while holding onto the lasso with the other. Ambrose had to carry Christine, but the Mexican women required no assistance. Lorraine Wayne and Vienna climbed last, and when they reached the top, Vienna saw a narrow bench covered in shrubs and overshadowed by large, leaning crags. There were holes in the rock and dark fissures leading back, making it a rugged and wild place. Tarpaulins, bedding, food, and water were then hauled up, and the cowboys instructed Vienna and her friends to be as quiet as possible, avoid making a light, and sleep dressed, ready for travel at a moment's notice.

Once the cowboys had left, the group was left in the darkening twilight, feeling uneasy. Mountcastle convinced them to eat, but Melissa whispered, "This is simply great," while Dorothy moaned, "It's awful! It's your fault, Melissa. You prayed for something to happen." Mrs. Beck suspected the cowboys of playing a horrid trick on them.

Vienna reassured her friends that they were not being tricked and expressed concern for their discomfort, but deep down she felt uneasy. The sudden change in demeanor and appearance of her cowboys had caught her off guard. The last glance she had of Norris's face, which was stern and almost sad, only added to her apprehension. Darkness fell quickly, and the coyotes began their mournful howls. The stars shone brightly, and the wind rustled through the pines. Mountcastle paced back and forth in front of the overhanging rock where his companions sat, lamenting. He then walked out to the ledge of the bench. Below, the cowboys had built a fire, and its light cast a large, fan-shaped glow. Curious and anxious, Vienna joined Mountcastle and peered down from the cliff. She could occasionally make out a word spoken by the cowboys, who were casually cooking and eating. Vienna noticed the absence of Norris and pointed it out to Mountcastle. In response, Mountcastle silently pointed almost straight down. There, in the gloom, stood Norris with two stag-hounds at his feet. Suddenly, Nick Steele raised a warning hand, and the cowboys bent their heads to listen. Vienna strained to hear every sound. She heard one of the hounds whine, followed by the faint sound of horse hooves. Nick spoke again and turned back to his supper, and the other cowboys appeared to relax. The sound of hooves grew louder, and soon the rider, Nels, entered the grove and then the circle of light. Nels dismounted, and the sound of his low voice just reached Vienna. "Gene, it's Nels. Something's happening," one of the cowboys called out softly. "Send him over," Norris replied. Nels stalked away from the fire.

government will do something about it some day, but in the meantime, it's up to us to protect ourselves."Norris and Nels continued to discuss their options, including the possibility of leaving the area altogether. They knew they couldn't trust anyone, not even the forest-ranger who had given them the information about Pat Hawe and the Mexican gang. They had to rely on their own instincts and skills to survive.Vienna listened to their conversation with growing unease. She had come to this remote part of the country seeking adventure, but she had not anticipated getting caught up in a dangerous situation like this. She wondered if she should try to leave and find her own way back to civilization, but she knew that would be risky too. As the sun began to set, Norris and Nels decided to set up a watch rotation for the night. They would take turns keeping watch and making sure no one snuck up on them. Vienna volunteered to take a turn, but Norris shook his head. "No, miss. You stay put. We don't want to put you in any danger. Just keep your head down and stay quiet." Vienna nodded, feeling both grateful and frustrated. She wanted to prove she was capable of handling herself, but she knew they were right. She was an outsider in this world, and she had to respect their rules. As night fell and the stars came out, Vienna listened to the sounds of the wilderness around her. She could hear the rustling of leaves, the chirping of crickets, and the occasional hoot of an owl. But she also knew that danger lurked nearby, and she couldn't help but feel a sense of dread. She closed her eyes and tried to steady her breathing. She knew she had to stay alert and ready for anything. She didn't know what the future held, but she was determined to face it with courage and resilience.

The cavalry and the good old States may not know it, but us, you, me, Monty, and Nick, we know what that rebel war down there really amounts to. It's guerrilla warfare, and it's a harvest time for a lot of cheap thieves and outcasts," said Nels.

"Oh, you're right, Nels. I'm not disputing that," replied Norris. "If it wasn't for Miss Florentino and the other women, I'd rather enjoy seeing you and Monty take on that bunch. I'm thinking I'd be glad to meet Don Carlos. But Miss Florentino! Why, Nels, a woman like her would never recover from the sight of real gun-play, let alone any stunts with a rope. These Eastern women are different. I'm not belittling our Western women. It's in the blood. Miss Florentino is--"

"Sure she is," interrupted Nels. "But she's got a damn sight more spunk than you think she has, Gene Norris. I'm no thick-skulled cow. I'd hate something powerful to have Miss Florentino see any rough work, let alone me and Monty starting something. And me and Monty will stick to you, Gene, as long as seems reasonable. Mind, old fella, begging your pardon, you're sure stuck on Miss Florentino, and over-tender not to hurt her feelings or make her sick by letting some blood. We're in bad here, and maybe we'll have to fight. Sabe, senor? Well, we do, you can just gamble that Miss Florentino will be game. And I'll bet you a million pesos that if you got going once, and she saw you as I've seen you, well, I know what she'd think of you. This old world hasn't changed much. Some women may be white-skinned and soft-eyed and sweet-voiced and high-souled, but they all like to see a man! Gene, here's your game. Let Don Carlos come along. Be civil. If he and his gang are hungry, feed them. Take even a little overbearing Greaser talk. Be blind if he wants his gang to steal something."

"Let him think the women have wandered down to the ranch. But if he says you're lying, if he even looks around to see the women, just jump him like you jumped Pat Hawe. Me and Monty will hang back for that, and if your strong bluff doesn't work, if the Don's

gang even thinks of flashing guns, then we'll open up. And all I
have to say is if those Greasers stand for real gun-play, they'll be the
first I've ever seen," said Nels.

"Nels, there are white men in that gang," said Norris.

"Sure. But me and Monty will be thinking of that. If they start
anything, it'll have to be quick," replied Nels.

"All right, Nels, old friend, and thanks," replied Norris.

Nels returned to the campfire, and Norris resumed his silent guard.
Vienna led Mountcastle away from the wall's brink.

"By Jove! Cowboys are strange folk!" exclaimed Mountcastle.

"Indeed, you are right," replied Vienna. "I cannot understand
them. Come, let us tell the others that Nels and Monty were only
talking and do not intend to leave us. Dorothy, at least, will be less
frightened if she knows."

Dorothy was somewhat comforted. The others, however, complained of the cowboys' odd behavior. More than once, the idea
was suggested that an elaborate trick had been concocted. Upon
general discussion, this idea gained ground. Vienna did not com-
bat it because she saw that it tended to a less perturbed condition
of mind among her guests. Mountcastle, for once, proved that he
was not absolutely obtuse and helped along the idea.

They sat talking in low voices until a late hour. The incident now
began to take on the nature of Melissa's long-yearned-for adventure. Some of the party even grew merry in a subdued way. Then,

gradually, one by one, they grew tired and went to bed. Melissa vowed that she could not sleep in a place where there were bats and crawling things.

Vienna couldn't help but feel like she was the only one awake as she stared up at the dark overhang of rock and the starry sky above. She tried to distract herself from thinking about Norris and the anger he had stirred in her, but his memory kept creeping back into her mind, causing a commotion in her chest that she couldn't ignore. During the day, she could push aside the realization of Norris's deceit, but at night, with the eerie stillness and looming shadows, Vienna struggled to control her thoughts and emotions. The night was different from the practicality of the day, and Vienna found herself battling with a nagging thought. She had overheard Nels's conversation with Norris, hoping to hear some good news or the worst, and unfortunately, she learned both. Norris had complex motives, including wanting to spare her from seeing anything that might offend or disgust her. Yet, this same man had a secret rendezvous with Bonita, a pretty and abandoned woman. The hot shame of it all made Vienna's thoughts come to an abrupt end. She couldn't control or understand her feelings and eventually drifted off to sleep. Suddenly, she was awakened by the bright and cool light of day breaking, and the sun still below the eastern crags.

Ambrose and a group of cowboys had brought up spring water, coffee, and cakes for Vienna's party. Despite their night's experience, the group seemed to be in good spirits. However, Ambrose warned them to be quiet as they were expecting company. This caused some anxiety, and Vienna insisted on staying near a cliff projection where she could see the camp below.

Vienna asked Ambrose if he believed the guerrillas would come, to which he replied, "Sure. We know. Nels just rode in and said they were on their way up." He then asked Vienna to promise not to make any noise if there was a fight, and to keep out of sight as Norris had instructed him.

Vienna arranged her coat to lie upon and settled down to wait for developments. Melissa suddenly appeared with a cowboy, and told Vienna she was going to see what happened. Ambrose swore at the cowboy for letting Melissa get away from him, but he disappeared into the rocks. Ambrose then prepared to carry Melissa back to the others.

With fury in her eyes, Melissa whispered, "Let go of me! What does this fool mean, Princess?" Vienna chuckled, knowing that Melissa was usually imperious and not one to whisper. Vienna explained the situation to her, and Melissa declared, "I might run, but I'll never scream." Ambrose had no choice but to let her stay, but he found a safer spot for her farther back from Vienna's position. He sternly warned her to remain silent and then comforted Christine before returning to Vienna's hiding place.

As he arrived, Ambrose whispered, "I hear horses. The guerrillas are coming." Vienna's hiding spot was well-protected and gave her a commanding view of the camp circle and its immediate surroundings. She could not see too far to the right or left due to the obstructing foliage. The sound of horses' hoofs quickened her pulse as she focused on the cowboys below. Although she had some idea of what Norris and his men were up to, she was not prepared for their indifference.

Frank was either asleep or pretending to be, while three cowboys were lazily attending to campfire duties. Nick Steele sat with his back to a log, smoking his pipe, and another cowboy had just brought the horses closer to camp. Nels was fussing over a pack, and Norris was rolling a cigarette. The elaborate set of aluminum plates, cups, and other camp fixtures that had served Vienna's party had disappeared.

Monty seemed to have nothing better to do than whistle loudly, but not very melodiously. The entire group gave off an air of carelessness and indifference. As the sound of horses' hooves grew louder and slowed, one of the cowboys pointed down the trail. Several of his comrades turned their heads briefly before returning to their tasks. Soon, a shaggy, dusty horse carrying a lean, ragged, dark rider rode into camp and stopped. Another horse followed, and then another. Horses with Mexican riders came in a single file and stopped behind the leader. The cowboys looked up, while the guerrillas looked down. "Buenos dias, senor," ceremoniously said the foremost guerrilla. Vienna strained to hear the voice and recognized it as belonging to Don Carlos. His graceful bow to Norris was also familiar. Otherwise, she would not have recognized the former elegant vaquero in this uncouth, roughly dressed Mexican. Norris replied to the greeting in Spanish, then waved his hand towards the campfire, adding in English, "Get down and eat."

The guerrillas eagerly complied. They crowded around the fire, then spread out in a small circle and sat on the ground, placing their weapons beside them. They looked similar to the band of guerrillas that had taken Vienna up into the foothills, only this group was larger and better armed. The men were just as hungry, wild, and beggarly. The cowboys were not warm in their welcome, but they were hospitable. The law of the desert was to give food and drink to wayfaring men, whether lost or hunted or hunting. "There's twenty-three in that outfit," whispered Ambrose. "Including four white men. A pretty strange group."

"They seem friendly enough," whispered Vienna.

"Things down there aren't always what they seem," replied Ambrose. "Vienna, let me explain to you. This is my chance. As long as you let me watch them, please let me know what's really going on."

"Sure."

"Listen up, Miss Florentino," warned the cowboy. "If Gene ever finds out I let you snoop around and spill the beans, I'll be in hot water. But I'll tell you this much: Gene has a soft spot for those poor devils and always makes sure they get a decent meal. Don't be fooled by those so-called bandits across the border; they're just a bunch of riffraff outlaws. And as for their rebel bluff, I won't believe it until I see it. Those Greasers are nothing but hard-ridin' thieves who would steal a man's blanket or tobacco without a second thought. Gene thinks they're after you ladies to kidnap you, but I reckon they're just after our valuables."

Despite their dubious intentions, Don Carlos and his men didn't hesitate to chow down on the generous spread of food that had been laid out for them. Each man ate his fill and then some, chatting and laughing like a bunch of rowdy parrots. But as they lit up their cigarettes and surveyed the camp and its surroundings, a subtle shift took place. They seemed to be waiting for something.

"Senor," began Don Carlos, addressing Norris with a sweep of his hat. Vienna couldn't make out what he said, but his gesture suggested he was asking about the rest of the cowboys. Norris replied and gestured down the trail, indicating that they had all gone home. As he turned away to attend to his duties, the guerrilla leader smoked quietly, looking cunning and thoughtful. His men grew restless, their once-languid cigarette puffs now quick and impatient.

A man with a large build, a bullet-shaped head, and a red face that looked as if it had been burned by the sun, stood up and tossed his cigarette aside. He was American. "Hey, buddy," he called out in a loud voice, "you gonna share a drink with us?"

"My boys don't carry alcohol on the trail," Norris replied, turning to face the guerrillas.

"Haw, haw! I heard over in Rodeo that you were getting to be a real temperance man," said the man with a laugh. "I hate drinking water, but I guess I'll have to do it."

He went to the spring, lay down to drink, and suddenly plunged his arm into the water to retrieve a basket. The cowboys, in their haste to pack, had forgotten to remove the basket, which contained bottles of wine and liquor for Vienna's guests. They had been submerged in the spring to keep them cold. The guerrilla fumbled with the lid, opened it, and then got up, letting out a loud roar of delight.

Norris made a barely noticeable movement, as if he was about to leap forward, but he stopped himself. After a quick glance at Nels, he said to the guerrilla, "Looks like my party forgot that. You're welcome to it."

The guerrillas swarmed around the man who had found the bottles like bees. There was a cacophony of voices. The alcohol didn't last long, and it only served to free the spirit of recklessness. The white outlaws began to roam around the camp, and some of the Mexicans did the same. Others waited, their ill-concealed anticipation betraying their thoughts. Vienna was puzzled by the demeanor of Norris and his companions. They didn't seem to be anxious or even interested. Don Carlos, who had been covertly observing them, now scrutinized them openly, even aggressively. He looked from Norris to Nels and Monty, and then to the other cowboys.

As some of his men scouted the area, the others kept their eyes on their leader, giving off an ominous vibe. The guerrilla chief appeared uncertain, but not confused. When he turned to Nels and Monty, his sly face showed indecisiveness. Vienna was too excited to hear Ambrose's quiet whispers clearly, but she tried to divert her attention from the scene below to the cowboy next to her. Ambrose's tone had changed, becoming slightly hissing. "Don't be alarmed if I suddenly cover your eyes, Miss Florentino," he said. "Something's happening down there. I've never seen Gene so calm. That's a bad sign for him. And look, see how the boys are working together! It's slow and unplanned, but it's definitely not an accident. Even that sneaky Mexican knows it. But perhaps his men don't. If they're smart, they won't care. The Don is worried, though. He's not paying Gene much attention, but he's watching Nels and Monty. And he should! There, Nick and Frank have settled on that log with Booly. They don't seem to be carrying guns, but notice how heavy their vests hang. There's a gun on each side! Those boys can draw their guns and jump over that log faster than you can imagine. Do you see how Nels, Monty, and Gene are standing between the guerrillas and the trail up here? It doesn't seem intentional, but it is. Look at Nels and Monty. They're talking quietly, ignoring the guerrillas. I saw Monty look at Gene, and then Nels looked at Gene. It's up to Gene now, and they'll support him. I bet you, Miss Florentino, there would be dead Mexicans around that camp long ago if Nels and Monty weren't loyal to Gene. That's clear."

It's a sight that brings a grin to my face, watching them with their two forty-fives on their hips, swaying as they walk. Twenty-four shots between the two of them, and only twenty-three guerrillas. If Nels and Monty ever decide to use those guns at close range, there won't be a single Greaser left standing. Ah, there's Norris saying something to the Don. Wonder what it could be. Probably trying to get the Don's men all bunched up together. Those Greasers ain't too bright, but the white guerrillas seem a bit uneasy. Whatever's about to happen, it'll be soon. Wish I was down there to see it all go down. But maybe Norris is trying to avoid a fight. He's good

at getting his way. Still, I'd love to see him take down that arrogant Greaser. Look at the Don, he's clueless. These cowboys are
throwing him off his game. If Gene doesn't knock some sense into
him soon, he'll start to lose his fear of Nels and Monty. But Gene
will pick the right moment. I'm getting antsy, I want something to
happen. I've only seen Nels in one fight, but he shot a Greaser's arm
off for trying to draw on him. And Monty, he's the real deal when
it comes to gun-slingers. Those stories he told the Englishman
don't even come close to what he's done. I don't get how he stays
so calm with this crew looking for trouble. Oh, here we go, the
grand bluff. Looks like there won't be a fight after all. The guerrilla
leader has stopped his pacing and turned to Norris with a look of
determination. "Thanks, sir," he says.

"Goodbye," he said, tipping his hat towards the trail leading down
the mountain to the ranch. A sly grin spread across his dark face.
Ambrose whispered to Vienna, barely audible, "If that Mexican
goes that way, he'll find our horses and figure out our plan. But
I doubt he'll even try."Norris stood up slowly and confidently,
taking a few long strides towards Don Carlos. "Go back where
you came from," he yelled, his voice ringing like a bugle. Ambrose
nudged Vienna, his whisper urgent and quick, "Watch closely,
Gene's calling him. Whatever's going to happen will happen fast
."Vienna watched as Nels and Monty stood silently, their muscles
tensed, watching the Mexican closely. "Look at them, ready to
pounce. They're watching the Mexican's every move," Ambrose
whispered. "There's not a hair's breadth between those Mexicans and hell."Don Carlos gave Norris a long, hateful stare before
throwing his head back, smiling wickedly and showing his teeth.

"Senor-" he began, but before he could finish, Norris was on him, wrestling him to the ground. Vienna could barely follow the fight, but she could hear the heavy blows and see the ferocity in Norris' eyes. Finally, Norris stood back, crouching with his hands on his guns, yelling and thundering at the guerrillas. Vienna felt a chill run down her spine at the menace in his voice and the threat of violence in his stance. She had to keep her eyes open, even though it was terrifying.

In an instant, Nels and Monty were by Norris's side, their hands on the butts of their guns. Nels let out a piercing yell that mixed with Monty's roar of rage, creating an echo that reverberated off the crags. The three men crouched like tigers ready to pounce, and their silence was more menacing than their yells. The guerrillas wavered and broke, running for their horses. Don Carlos rolled over, rose, and staggered away, to be helped onto his mount. He looked back, his pale and bloody face that of a thwarted demon. The whole band quickly got into action and was gone in a moment.

"I knew it," declared Ambrose. "I've never seen a Greaser who could face gun-play. That was intense. And Monty Price never even drew his gun! He'll never get over that. Miss Harnmond, we're lucky to have avoided trouble. Gene had it under control, as you saw. We need to get to the ranch as soon as possible."

"Why?" whispered Vienna, her breath shaky. She realized she was weak and shaken.

"Because those guerrillas are sure to get their nerve back and come after us, either by sneaking on our trail or ambushing us," replied Ambrose. "That's their way. Three cowboys wouldn't be able to bluff a whole gang like that if it weren't for Gene knowing the nature of Greasers. They're all white-livered. But we're in more danger now than before, unless we get a good start down the mountain. There! Gene's calling. Come on, hurry!"

Melissa had slipped down from her vantage point and had missed the end of the confrontation. It seemed like her desire for excitement was satisfied, as her face was pale, and she trembled when she asked if the guerrillas were gone.

"I didn't see the end, but those yells were enough for me," she said.

Ambrose quickly led the three women down the rough rocks, towards the cowboys who were saddling their horses in haste.

It was apparent that all the horses had been brought out of hiding. Quickly and without concern for anything else, Vienna, Melissa, and Christine were lowered by lassoes and half-carried down to the level. Once they were safely down, the rest of the party appeared on the cliff above. They seemed to be in high spirits, treating the situation as a joke. Ambrose assisted Christine onto a horse and rode off through the pines, while Frankie Slade did the same with Melissa. Norris led Vienna's horse up to her, helped her mount, and sternly told her to wait. As soon as one of the women reached the level, they were placed on a horse and swiftly taken away by a cowboy escort. There was little conversation, and speed seemed to be the main priority. The horses were urged on and once in the trail, spurred into a swift trot. A cowboy arrived with four pack-horses, which were quickly loaded with the party's belongings. Mountcastle and his companions mounted their horses and galloped off to catch up with the others in the lead. This left Vienna behind with Norris, Nels, and Monty.

"They're going to switch off at the holler that heads near the trail a few miles down," Nels explained as he tightened his saddle-girth. "That holler leads into a big canyon. Once in there, it'll be every man for himself. I reckon there won't be anything worse than a rough ride." Nels smiled reassuringly at Vienna, but didn't speak to her. Monty took her canteen, filled it with water from the spring, and hung it over the pommel of her saddle. He put a couple of biscuits in the saddle-bag and said, "Don't forget to take a drink and a bite as you're riding along. And don't worry, Miss Princess. Norris will be with you, and Nels and I will be hanging on the back-trail." His somber and sullen face didn't change in its strange intensity, but the look in his eyes was one that Vienna knew she would never forget.

Alone with the three men, stripped of all pretense, she realized how lucky she was, but also how much danger still loomed. Norris hopped onto his big black horse, spurred him, and whistled. At the sound, Princess leaped into action, cantering after Norris. Vienna glanced back to see Nels already on his horse with Monty handing him a rifle. But then the trees blocked her view.

Once they hit the trail, Norris's horse broke into a gallop. Princess kept up, matching the black's pace. Norris warned Vienna about the low, wide branches that could knock her off her horse. The

fast ride through the forest, on a crooked, obstructed trail, kept her
alert. But it also stirred her blood, always susceptible to the spirit
and motion of a ride, especially one of danger. The throb and burn
in her veins pushed away the worry, dread, and coldness that had
weighed her down.

Soon, Norris veered off the trail at a right angle and entered a
hollow between two low bluffs. Vienna saw tracks in the open
patches of ground. Here, Norris's horse slowed to a brisk walk. The
hollow deepened, narrowed, and became rocky, full of logs and
brush. Vienna used all her keenness, and needed it, to keep close
to Norris. She didn't think about him or her own safety. Her focus
was on keeping Princess close in the tracks of the black, eluding the
sharp spikes in the dead brush, and avoiding the treacherous loose
stones.

Finally, Vienna came to a halt when Norris and his horse blocked
the trail. She looked up to see they were at the head of a canyon that
yawned below and widened its gray-walled, green-patched slopes
down to a black forest of fir. The drab foothills contrasted with
the forest below, and in the distance, the desert appeared rosy and
smoky.

Vienna averted her gaze and spotted pack-horses crossing an open
space a mile below. She thought she saw the stag-hounds as well.
Norris, with his dark eyes, scanned the high slopes along the craggy
escarpments. Then he rode down the slope on his black horse. If
there was a trail left by the leading cowboys, Norris didn't follow
it. Instead, he led off to the right, zigzagging an intricate course
through the roughest ground Vienna had ever ridden over. He

crashed through cedars, threaded a tortuous way among boulders, made his horse slide down slanting banks of soft earth, and picked a slow and cautious progress across weathered slopes of loose rock. Vienna followed, finding this ride a test of her strength and judgment. On an ordinary horse, she would never have kept up with Norris's trail. It was the dust and heat, a parching throat that made Vienna think of time, and she was amazed to see the sun sloping to the west. Norris never stopped, never looked back, never spoke. He must have heard the horse close behind him. Vienna remembered Monty's advice about drinking and eating as she rode along. The worst part of that rough travel came at the bottom of the canyon. Dead cedars, brush, and logs were easy to pass compared to the miles of loose boulders. The horses slipped and stumbled. Norris proceeded with extreme caution. Finally, when the canyon opened into a level forest of firs, the sun was setting red in the west. Norris quickened the pace of his horse. After a mile or so of easy travel, the ground began to fall decidedly, sloping in numerous ridges, with draws between. Soon, night shadowed the deeper gullies. Vienna was refreshed by the cooling of the air. Norris traveled slowly now. The barks of coyotes seemed to startle him. Often he stopped to listen. And during one of those intervals, the silence was broken by sharp rifle-shots.

Vienna was disoriented as she tried to determine their location. Norris seemed both scared and confused, dismounting from his horse and moving forward cautiously. Vienna thought she heard a cry in the distance, but convinced herself it was just a coyote. Norris led the horses through rough terrain, stopping frequently to listen for any signs of danger. As darkness fell, they stumbled

upon a log cabin with dark trees looming in the background.
Norris disappeared inside briefly, lighting a match to explore the
abandoned dwelling. He emerged shortly after, removing the saddles from the horses and leading Vienna inside. The cabin was
sparse, with only a rough fireplace and hewn logs for decoration.
Norris muttered about being able to ride bareback, hinting at the
possibility of danger ahead.

Norris' saddle and blanket lay on the hard-packed earthen floor.
"Take a rest," he said. "I'm going into the woods for a bit to listen.
Won't be gone long." Vienna had to feel around in the dark to
locate the saddle and blanket. When she finally lay down, she
felt grateful for the sense of ease and relief that came with resting her body. However, her mind was a maze of sensations and
thoughts. All day, she had helped her horse, but now the night,
the silence, the proximity of Norris and his strange, stern caution,
and the possible happenings to her friends all claimed their share
of her attention. She went over them all with lightning swiftness
of thought.

She believed, and she was sure Norris believed, that her friends
had not been headed off in their travel by any of the things which
had delayed Norris. This conviction lifted the suddenly returning
dread from her breast. As for herself, she somehow had no fear. But
she could not sleep, nor did she try to. Norris' soft steps sounded
outside. His dark form loomed in the door. As he sat down, Vienna
heard the thump of a gun that he laid beside him on the sill; then
the thump of another as he put that down too. The sounds thrilled
her. Norris' wide shoulders filled the door; his finely shaped head

and strong, stern profile showed clearly in outline against the sky; the wind waved his hair. He turned his ear to the wind and listened. Motionless he sat for what seemed like hours to Vienna.

Then the stirring memory of the day's adventure, the feeling of the beauty of the night, and a strange, deep-seated, sweetly vague consciousness of happiness portending were all burned out in hot, pressing pain at the remembrance of Norris' disgrace in her eyes.

She felt a shift in her emotions. The anger she had directed towards herself had transformed into sorrow for him. He was an extraordinary man, and she couldn't help but acknowledge the debt she owed him. However, she couldn't express her gratitude or even speak to him. She struggled with an inexplicable bitterness.

Vienna closed her eyes and rested. Time didn't seem to pass quickly or slowly. Norris interrupted her thoughts by calling her name. She opened her eyes to see the gray dawn sky. She got up and went outside. The horses neighed in greeting. Vienna mounted her horse and felt the strain on her muscles and the tiredness in her limbs. Norris led the way at a fast trot into the fir forest. They soon arrived at a path, and he turned onto it. The horses kept a steady pace, and the slope became less steep. The trees thinned out, and the gray sky gave way to a brighter hue. As Vienna emerged from the forest, the sun had risen, and she could see the rolling foothills beneath her. At the edge of the hills, where the gray valley began, she spotted a dark spot that she knew was the ranch-house.

Chapter Twenty-One.

A round mid-morning, Vienna arrived at the ranch. Her guests had all made it there the previous night, and they were eager for her to join them and make sure she was doing well. They considered the end of the camping trip to be quite the adventure and even declared it the cowboys' masterpiece trick. They thought Vienna's delay was all part of the plan to add to the grand finale. Vienna didn't bother correcting them or telling them that she had only been escorted home by one cowboy. Her guests shared their experience of a challenging ride down the mountain, with only one exciting moment. As they were descending, they ran into Sheriff Hawe and some of his deputies, who were clearly drunk and furious about Bonita, the Mexican girl, escaping.

Hawe had been spewing insults at the ladies and, as Ambrose recounted, would have caused trouble for the group if the cowboys hadn't shut him down. It took Vienna's guests a full two days to recover from the grueling ride, and on the third day, they began to leisurely prepare for their departure. This time was especially difficult for Vienna. She needed physical rest, but more pressingly, she was grappling with a mental conflict that couldn't be ignored any longer. Her sister and friends were urging her to return with them back East, a prospect that Vienna herself desired. But it wasn't just about going back; it was about how, when, and under what circumstances she would return to the ranch and the West. Vienna needed to settle her future relationship with the land before she left. However, when the decisive moment arrived, Vienna realized that the West hadn't fully claimed her yet. Despite this, her old friends had rekindled dormant connections, and Vienna found herself torn. She would have welcomed any excuse to delay her decision, but fate intervened when Ken's letter arrived. He reported that his trip to California had been fruitful, and he had a lucrative offer for Vienna from a major cattle company. Furthermore, he expressed his desire to marry Florence as soon as he returned home and would bring a minister from Adam for the occasion. Vienna made a promise to Melissa and her companions that she would return East soon, at the very latest by Thanksgiving. They reluctantly accepted this assurance and bid farewell to Vienna and the ranch. However, just as they were about to leave, it appeared that their first leg of the journey home might hit a snag.

When Link Stevens arrived with his big white car, all of Vienna's guests raised their hands in a Western fashion. Link tried to assure them that he would drive safely and slowly, but Vienna had to guarantee his word and accompany them before they would enter the car. At the station, good-byes were said and Vienna promised for the hundredth time that they would be safe. Dorothy Coombs said her final words, asking Vienna to give her love to Monty Price and telling him that she was glad he kissed her. Melissa had a sweet,

serious, yet mocking look in her eyes as she said, "Princess, bring
Norris with you when you come. He'll be the rage." Vienna treated
the remark with the same lightness as the others, but after the
train left and she was on her way home, she remembered Melissa's
words and looks with a sense of shock. Any mention of Norris or
thought of him displeased her. She wondered what Melissa meant
and pondered. Melissa's mocking look had been an ironic glint, a
cynical gleam from her worldly experience. The sweet gravity of
Melissa's look had been more subtle and deeper. Vienna wanted to
understand it, to find a new relation between Melissa and herself,
something sisterly that could lead to love. However, the thought
was poisoned by a strange suggestion of Norris, causing her to
dismiss it. On the drive to the ranch, Vienna saw Norris walking
along the shore of the lower lake. When he noticed the car, he
quickly disappeared into the shade of the shrubbery. Vienna had
seen him avoid her before, and although it gave her some relief, it
also caused her pain.

Vienna was avoiding Stillwell because she didn't want to hear
him defend Norris. The old cattleman was upset and had tried
to talk to Vienna about the foreman, but she refused to listen.
Norris remained at the ranch, but his work suffered as Vienna grew
colder towards him. She overheard conversations that confirmed
her suspicions that Norris was slipping back into his old ways.
Vienna couldn't bring herself to help him and felt a strange mix
of emotions towards him. She didn't want to think about him and
even felt a bit of scorn towards him. However, her brooding was
interrupted by a telegram from Adam announcing the arrival of
Ken and a minister, which caused excitement among the cowboys.

The wedding ceremony was set to take place in Vienna's grand hall-chamber, while the dinner would be held in a charming patio scented with flowers. Ken and his minister arrived at the ranch in a large white car, looking windswept and disheveled. The minister was breathless and hatless, while Ken found it understandable why Nels disliked riding at such high speeds. Link, as usual, apologized to Vienna for being held up by a teamster and stray cattle, causing them to arrive later than expected.

Ken expressed his approval of the wedding arrangements and requested that the cowboys attend. He also showed a keen interest in Florence and Vienna's guests, asking for more details about them. His eyes softened as he listened to Vienna talk, and he breathed a sigh of relief, remarking that he had been worried. Ken also expressed his fascination with the crags, a wild and almost inaccessible place near the border where guerrillas were known to gather. He wondered what the U.S. cavalry would think if they knew how close the guerrillas were to them. Sadly, Ken predicted that there would be more trouble with these guerrillas in the future, as Orozco, the rebel leader, had failed to withstand Madero's army.

Currently, the Federals are occupying Chihuahua and pushing the rebels towards the north. Orozco has divided his army into guerrilla bands, which plan to engage in guerrilla warfare in Sonora. It's hard to say how this will affect us down here. However, we're too close to the border, and these guerrillas are dangerous night-riding hawks. They can cross the border, raid us, and be back on their side the same night. Fighting will not be limited to northern Mexico. With the revolution's failure, the guerrillas will become more numerous, bolder, and more desperate. Unfortunately, our location in this wilderness corner of the state makes us a favorable target for them.

The next day, Ken and Florence tied the knot. Several of Florence's friends from El Cajon and her sister were present, along with Vienna, Stillwell, and his men. Ken wanted Norris to attend the ceremony. Vienna was amused when she saw the cowboys' suppressed excitement. For them, a wedding was an unusual and impressive event. She began to understand it better when they let loose and rushed forward to kiss the bride. Vienna had never seen a bride kissed so much and so heartily, nor one so flushed, disheveled, and happy. It was a joyous occasion. Ken Florentino was anything but an effete Easterner; he seemed like a Westerner his whole life. When Vienna managed to make her way through the crowd of cowboys to congratulate him, Ken gave her a bear hug and a kiss. This fascinated the cowboys. With shining eyes and glowing faces, they rushed towards Vienna with smiling, boyish boldness. For a moment, she felt her heart leap to her throat. They looked like they could shamelessly kiss and maul her. Monty Price, that little, ugly-faced, soft-eyed, rude, tender-hearted ruffian, led the charge. He resembled a dragon driven by sentiment.

Vienna felt torn between her natural aversion to the touch of unfamiliar hands and her desire to enjoy the company of the cowboys. However, when she caught sight of Norris at the back of the gathering, she was taken aback by the fierce, painful expression on his face. This look froze her willingness to be friendly, and she must have conveyed this change in demeanor to the group, as Monty fell back and the cowboys made way for her to lead them into the patio.

The dinner began with the cowboys feeling awkward and hungry, but hesitant to indulge in the feast before them. Wine soon loosened their tongues, and when Stillwell stood up to make a speech, they cheered him on. Stillwell was beaming with joy, nearly on the verge of tears. He spoke enthusiastically, raising his glass to toast the newlyweds and their love, happiness, prosperity, and good health. He also proposed a toast to the union of the East and West, and claimed Al Florentino as one of their own. Stillwell then suggested they drink to his sister, the lady they hoped to make their Princess, and the man who would come riding out of the West to win and keep her. He urged everyone to drink to their hopes and dreams.

Just as Stillwell was about to take a drink, the sound of galloping hoofs and a loud yell outside interrupted him.

The patio fell silent, as if the air had been sucked out of the room. The sounds of horses stamping to a halt and men barking harsh orders, along with the low cry of a woman in pain, filtered in through the open doors and windows of Vienna's chamber. Nels strode into the room, surprising Vienna with his absence from the dinner table and the worried look on his face.

"Norris, you're needed outside," Nels said bluntly. "Monty, come with me. The rest of you should probably stay inside and shut the doors."

With that, Nels disappeared, Monty following quickly behind.
Vienna trembled as she heard Monty's soft, swift steps pass from
her room into her office. He had left his guns there. Norris got
up quietly and left the patio, followed by Nick Steele. Stillwell
dropped his wine glass, shattering the silence and causing his jovial
demeanor to vanish. He went out and closed the door behind him.

The moment had been rudely disrupted, and Vienna watched as
the pleasure faded from the faces of her guests, replaced with the
familiar hardness she had seen before. Ken, still somewhat confused by the sudden change, asked, "What's going on?"

"I'm going to see who's butted in here to spoil our dinner," Ken
said, striding out of the room. He returned a few moments later,
his forehead mottled with anger. "It's Pat Hawe, the sheriff of El
Cajon. He's come to arrest Gene Norris, and they've got a poor
little Mexican girl tied up on a horse outside."

"Darn that sheriff!" Vienna exclaimed, rising from the table and
ignoring Florence's pleas to stay put. The cowboys in the room
stood up, but Ken blocked Vienna's path. "I'm going out," she told
him. "No, you're not," he replied firmly. "It's not safe out there."

"I have to go," Vienna insisted, looking directly at Ken. "Vienna,
what's going on?" Florence asked, concerned. "There's going to be
trouble outside," Ken warned her. "Maybe a fight. You can't do
anything. You shouldn't go."

"Maybe I can prevent the trouble," Vienna replied, determined.
She left the patio, aware that Ken, Florence, and the cowboys were
following her. As she stepped onto the porch, she heard angry

voices in the distance. When she saw Bonita, bound and help-less on a horse, Vienna felt a mix of emotions. Her heart raced at the sight of the girl, but she was also filled with anger and pity.

The man holding Bonita's horse was the same guerrilla who had found the wine basket at camp. He was bigger, redder, and drunker than before, and looked like a gorilla. Three other men were present, all on tired horses. The one in front, with a pointed beard and red eyes, was the El Cajon sheriff.

Vienna hesitated for a moment, but then stepped forward onto the porch.

Ken, Florence, and several others followed her out; the rest of the cowboys and guests crowded the windows and doors. Stillwell saw Vienna and threw up his hands, roaring to be heard. This quieted the gesticulating, quarreling men. "What's got you acting like a crazy steer on a rampage, Pat Hawe?" de-manded Stillwell. "Stay in line, Bill," replied Hawe. "You know why I'm here. I've been waiting for the right moment, and now I'm ready. I'm here to arrest a criminal."

The huge frame of the old cattleman jerked as if he had been stabbed. His face turned purple. "Who's the criminal?" he shouted hoarsely. The sheriff flicked his quirt against his dirty boot, twisting his thin lips into a leer. The situation was agree-able to him. "Why, Bill, I knew you had a no-good outfit riding this range, but I wasn't aware that you had more than one criminal."

"Cut the talk! Which cowboy are you trying to arrest?" Hawe's manner changed. "Gene Norris," he replied curtly. "What's the charge?"

"For killing a Mexican one night last fall."

"So you're still harping on that? Pat, you're on the wrong trail. You can't pin that killing on Norris. It's ancient history by now. But if you insist on bringing him to court, let the arrest wait until after today's fiesta. We're having a celebration here, and I'll bring Gene to El Cajon."

"Nope. I reckon I'll take him when I get the chance, before he runs off."

"I'm giving you my word," thundered Stillwell.

"I reckon I don't have to take your word, Bill, or anybody else's," replied Hawe.

Stillwell's great bulk quivered with rage, but he made a successful effort to control it. "Listen here, Pat Hawe. I know what's reasonable. Law is law. But in this country, there's always been, and still is, a safe and sane way to proceed with the law. Maybe you've forgotten that."

In a lawless land, where one man holds all the power, even a respectable cattleman like myself can question the law. Let me give you a tip, Pat. You're not well-liked around here. You've been too heavy-handed in your actions, and some of your dealings have been questionable. Don't overlook my words. But, despite all that, you're still the sheriff, and I respect your position. I respect it enough to give you a warning. If your heart has turned sour and you can't find any kindness in it, then at least try to avoid any unpleasantness that may arise from your actions today. Do you understand what I'm saying?

"Stillwell, you're threatening an officer," replied Hawe, his anger rising.

"Will you leave this place now?" said Stillwell, in a strained voice. "I guarantee Norris will be in El Cajon any day you want."

"No. I came here to arrest him, and I will."

"So, that's your game!" shouted Stillwell. "Well, we're glad to see your true colors, Pat. Listen here, you cheap, red-eyed coyote of a sheriff! You don't seem to care how many enemies you make. You know you'll never hold office in this county again. What do you care now? It's strange how eager you are to hunt down the man who killed that particular Greaser. I reckon there have been a dozen or more killings of Greasers in the last year. Why don't you try to solve some of those cases? I'll tell you why. You're afraid to go near the border. And your hatred for Gene Norris makes you want to hound him and throw him in jail. You want to spite his friends. Well, listen here, you lean-jawed, skunk-bitten coyote! Go ahead and try to arrest him!"

With that, Stillwell took one giant step off the porch. His last words were cold, and his anger seemed to have transferred to Hawe.

The sheriff was getting flustered and waving his hand at the cattleman when Norris stepped in. "Hold on, guys, let me say some-

thing," he said. As soon as Norris appeared, the Mexican girl
snapped out of her daze. She struggled against her bonds, trying
to lift her hands in a plea for help. Her face flushed with energy,
and her big dark eyes lit up. "Senor Gene!" she cried. "Help me!
They beat me, tied me up, and almost killed me. Oh, please,
Senor Gene!"

"Shut up, or I'll shut you up," the man holding Bonita's horse
threatened. "Muzzle her, Sneed, if she talks again," Hawe ordered. Vienna felt a tense energy building during the brief
silence. Was it just her excitement? She looked at Nels, Monty, and Nick, their faces brooding, cold, and watchful. She
wondered why Norris wasn't looking at Bonita. He was now
dark-faced, cool, and quiet, with an ominous presence about
him. "Hawe, I'll surrender without any fuss if you take the
ropes off the girl," Norris said slowly.

"No way," replied the sheriff. "She got away from me once. She's
hog-tied now, and she'll stay that way." Vienna thought she saw
Norris flinch a little. But her vision was blurred, and her heart
was pounding. "Okay, let's get out of here," Norris said. "You've
caused enough trouble. Ride down to the corral with me. I'll
get my horse and go with you."

"Hold on!" Hawe yelled as Norris turned away. "Not so fast.
Who do you think you are? You're not pulling any stunts on
me. You'll ride one of my pack-horses, and you'll be in shackles."

"You want to handcuff me?" Norris asked, his passion suddenly
flaring up. "Is that what you want? Haw, haw! No, Norris, that's

just how I deal with horse-thieves, raiders, Mexicans, murderers, and the like."

"Get off your horse, Sneed, and put the cuffs on this man," ordered the guerrilla. Sneed dismounted and rummaged through his saddlebags. "You see, Bill," explained Hawe, "I hired Sneed specifically for this job. He's quite handy. He even caught that little Mexican cat for me."

Stillwell didn't hear the sheriff. He was staring at Norris in disbelief. "Gene, you're not going to let them handcuff you," he pleaded.

"Yes," replied the cowboy. "Bill, my friend, I'm an outsider here. There's no need for Miss Florentino and her brother and Florence to be further worried about me. Their happy day has already been ruined on my account. I want to leave quickly."

"Well, you might be too considerate of Miss Florentino's feelings," sneered the rancher. "What about my feelings? Are you going to let this sneaky coyote, this last gasp of the old rum-guzzling frontier sheriffs, put you in cuffs and hog-tie you and haul you off to jail?"

"Yes," Norris said firmly.

"By God! You, Gene Norris! What's happened to you? Go inside, and I'll take care of this guy. Tomorrow, you can turn yourself in like a gentleman."

"No. I'll go now. Thanks, Bill, for your support. Hurry, Hawe, before I change my mind."

As Norris spoke, his voice broke. It was clear he had been holding back his emotions. A sense of hopelessness and shame overtook him, and Vienna saw the man she once knew. The passion inside her erupted in a woman's fierce refusal to accept Norris's broken spirit.

She didn't want him to break the law, but she couldn't bear to see him deny his masculinity. She had once begged him to become a cowboy like her, a man who was tempered by reason and passion. She had shown him how violence was painful and shocking to her. This idea had consumed him, making him soft and weak. It had grown on him like a lichen, stifling his will and robbing him of his wild and bold spirit that she now strangely longed to see him feel.

When Sneed came forward with the iron fetters, Vienna's blood boiled. She would have forgiven Norris for being the kind of cowboy she had once despised. This was a man's West, a man's game. What right did a woman raised in a softer world have to use her beauty and influence to change a man who was bold, free, and strong? At that moment, with her blood racing, Vienna would have gloried in the violence she had once deplored. She would have welcomed the action that characterized Norris's treatment of Don Carlos. She had suddenly acquired the temperament of a woman who had absorbed the life and nature around her and who would not have turned her eyes away from a harsh and bloody act.

But Norris held out his hands to be handcuffed. Then Vienna heard her own voice shouting, "Wait!" In the time it took her to walk a few steps to the porch's edge, facing the men, she felt her anger, justice, and pride summoning forces to her command. But there was something else calling her, a deep, passionate, mysterious thing that was not born of the moment. Sneed dropped the handcuffs. Norris's face turned white as a sheet. Hawe, in a slow and stupid embarrassment beyond his control, removed his hat in a respect that seemed to be wrenched from him.

"Listen, Hawe, I can prove to you that Norris had nothing to do with the crime you're trying to arrest him for," Vienna exclaimed confidently. The sheriff's expression changed from confusion to surprise, and he tried to speak but couldn't find the words. Clearly, he was thrown off balance. Vienna continued speaking, "It's impossible for Norris to have been involved in the assault because he was with me in the train station waiting room when it happened. I have a vivid memory of the entire incident. The door was open, and I could hear the voices of men arguing outside. They were speaking Spanish, and I could also hear a woman's voice begging for something. Then I heard footsteps approaching, and I knew Norris heard them too. His face was tense with anticipation. Suddenly, there were loud, angry voices, a scuffle, a shot, a woman's scream, a thud, and the sound of someone running away. Then Bonita, the girl who was involved in the quarrel, stumbled into the room. She was white as a sheet, shaking with fear. When she saw Norris, she recognized him and begged for help. Norris tried to comfort her and asked if Danny Mains had been shot or if he had done the shooting. Bonita said no, and explained that she had danced and flirted with some vaqueros, which led to the argument. Norris then took her outside and helped her onto his horse. I watched as they rode away into the darkness." As Vienna spoke, Hawe's demeanor began to change once again.

He didn't stay disconcerted for long, but his discomfort turned into a sullen rage, and his sharp features twisted into a crafty expression. "That's mighty interesting, Miss Florentino, almost as interesting as a storybook," he said. "Now, since you're such a obliging witness, I'd sure like to ask you a couple of questions. What time did you get to El Cajon that night?"

"It was after eleven o'clock," Vienna replied.

"Nobody was there to meet you?"

"No."

"The station agent and operator were both gone?"

"Yes."

"Well, how soon did this guy Norris show up?" Hawe continued with a wry smile.

"Very soon after I arrived. I think perhaps fifteen minutes, possibly a little more," Vienna answered.

"It was dark and lonely around that station, wasn't it?"

"Indeed, yes."

"And what time was the Mexican guy shot?" Hawe asked, his little eyes gleaming like coals.

"Probably close to half-past one. It was two o'clock when I looked at my watch at Florence Kingsley's house. Right after Norris sent Bonita away, he took me to Miss Kingsley's. So, allowing for the

walk and a few minutes' conversation with her, I can pretty definitely say the shooting took place at about half-past one," Vienna
explained.

Stillwell stepped closer to the sheriff. "What are you driving at?" he
roared, his face turning black again.

"Evidence," snapped Hawe.

Vienna was surprised by this interruption. As Norris drew her
gaze, she saw him gray-faced as ashes, shaking, completely unnerved. "I thank you, Miss Florentino," he said huskily. "But you
needn't answer any more of Hawe's questions. He's he's It's not
necessary. I'll go with him now, under arrest. Bonita will corrob-
orate your testimony in court, and that will save me from this this
man's spite."

Vienna looked at Norris and saw a humility she initially mistook
for cowardice. Suddenly, she realized it wasn't fear for himself that
made him dread further disclosures of that night, but fear for her.
Fear of the shame she might suffer through him.

Pat Hawe tilted his head to the side, eyeing Vienna like a vulture
about to swoop down. "What you said is important and conclusive
as testimony, but the court will want an explanation for why you
were alone with Norris in the waiting room from eleven-thirty
until one-thirty," he said in a deliberate manner.

Vienna noticed a remarkable reaction from Norris, Stillwell, Ken,
and Monty Price. Norris gave a sudden start, Stillwell tore at his
shirt collar, Ken strode forward but was stopped by Nels, and

Monty Price let out a violent "Aw!" that sounded like both a hiss and a roar. Vienna didn't know what to make of it at the time, but it felt ominous. She felt a chill run down her spine as she prepared to respond to Hawe.

"Norris detained me in the waiting room," Vienna said in a clear voice. "But we were not alone the entire time." There was a gasp from Norris and a look of hideous amazement and joy on Hawe's face.

"How is that possible?" Hawe whispered, craning his neck.

"Norris was drunk," Vienna replied. Norris let out a passionate gesture of despair and begged her not to say anymore. He seemed to sink down in shame, and Stillwell put a hand on his shoulder. The old cattleman turned to Vienna and said, "Miss Princess, it would be wise to tell everything. None of us would misunderstand any motive or act of yours. Maybe a stroke of lightning could clear this murky air. Whatever Gene Norris did that unlucky night, you should tell it."

Vienna felt her dignity and self-possession slip away in the face of Norris's importunity.

She spoke quickly and urgently, saying, "He came into the station a few minutes after I got there. I asked to be shown to a hotel. He said there wasn't any that would accommodate married women. He grabbed my hand and looked for a wedding ring. Then I saw that he was intoxicated. He told me he would go get a hotel porter, but instead he came back with a priest, Padre Marcos. The poor priest was terribly frightened, and so was I. Norris had turned into a devil. He fired his gun at the padre's feet and pushed me onto a bench. He shot right in front of my face, and I nearly fainted. But I heard him cursing the padre while the padre was praying or chanting, I didn't know what. Norris tried to make me say things in Spanish. All at once he asked my name, and I told him. He jerked at my veil, and I took it off. Then he threw his gun down and pushed the padre out of the door. That was just before the vaqueros approached with Bonita. Padre Marcos must have seen them and heard them. After that, Norris quickly sobered up. He was mortified, distressed, and stricken with shame. He told me he had been drinking at a wedding, Ed Linton's wedding, I remember. Then he explained that the boys were always gambling, and he wagered that he would marry the first girl who arrived at El Cajon. I happened to be the first one. He tried to force me to marry him. The rest, relating to the assault on the vaquero, I have already told you."

Vienna finished speaking, out of breath and panting, with her hands pressed against her chest. The revelation of her secret had liberated her emotions, and her hurried words had made her throb and tremble and burn. Strangely, she thought of Ken and his anger, but he stood motionless, as if dazed. Stillwell was trying to holster up the crushed Norris, and Hawe rolled his red eyes and threw back his head.

"Ha, ha, ha! Ha, ha, ha!" Sneed and his friend laughed heartily, enjoying the story they had just heard. "That's the best one I've ever heard in my life!" Sneed exclaimed. His friend agreed with him, laughing uncontrollably.

Suddenly, their laughter ceased, and the friend turned to Vienna with a vicious and insolent look. "Well now, my lady," he said, "if your story matches with Bonita and Padre Marcos', it might just clear Gene Norris in the eyes of the court. But don't expect them to believe that you were detained against your will."

Vienna was taken aback by his words, and before she could fully comprehend their meaning, Norris had jumped up, his face as white as a sheet. He lunged at Hawe, but Stillwell, a large and imposing figure, intervened and restrained Norris with his arms. There was a brief but intense struggle, with Norris appearing to be getting the upper hand.

"Help, boys, help!" Stillwell called out. "I can't hold him. Hurry, or there's going to be blood spilled!"

Several cowboys rushed to Stillwell's aid, but Norris managed to toss them aside, one by one. They closed in on him, and the sound of their powerful bodies clashing filled the air. Norris heaved them off him at one point, but they quickly regained control and subdued him.

"Gene! Why, Gene!" Stillwell exclaimed, panting heavily. "You're crazy to act this way. Just calm down! It's me, your old pal Bill, who's tried to be a father to you. I just want you to have some sense and wait."

"Let me go! Let me go!" Norris cried out, and the sound of his anguish pierced Vienna's heart. "Let me go, Bill, if you're my friend. I saved your life once in the desert. You swore you'd never forget."

"Boys, make him let me go!" Gene cried out, his voice filled with anger and frustration. "I don't care what Hawe's said or done to me! It was that about her! Are you all a bunch of cowards? How can you just stand there and watch this happen? Damn you all!" Gene's voice trailed off to a whisper as he pleaded with Bill. "Bill, dear old Bill, please let me go. I'll kill him, you know I will."

Stillwell tried to calm Gene down. "Gene, I know you'd kill him if you had the chance," he said. "But, Gene, you're not even carrying a gun. And there's Pat, looking ready to shoot. He knows you're unarmed and would jump at the chance to take you out. Cool down, son. It'll all work out."

Suddenly, Vienna heard a terrifying sound. Monty Price had leaped off the porch and was now crouching down, his hands on his hips where his guns hung. He let out a roar that sounded like a mix of a bellow and an Indian war-whoop. His eyes were fixed on Hawe and Sneed, and he looked like a demon about to attack. Stillwell quickly pushed the other cowboys onto the porch and tried to move Vienna, Ken, and Florence to safety. He stood between the women and danger, his movements quick and decisive.

Vienna could feel her heart racing as she watched Monty. She knew that something terrible was about to happen, and she clung to Stillwell's arm for support. Monty called out to Hawe and Sneed, warning them not to move a muscle. Vienna's senses were heightened, and she knew that danger was all around them.

She understood the reason behind Monty's agonizing scream and his odd hunched posture. Stillwell's quickness and silence also

hinted at impending disaster. "Nels, get over here!" Monty shouted, never once taking his eyes off of Hawe and his deputy. "Nels,
chase those two guys away from there. Hurry!" Without waiting
for Nels, the two deputies who had been lingering in the background with the pack-horses spurred their mounts and galloped
away. "Nels, release the girl," Monty commanded. Nels ran over,
snatched the halter out of Sneed's hand, and pulled Bonita's horse
close to the porch. As he sliced the rope that had been restraining
her, she fell into his arms. "Hawe, get down!" Monty continued.
"Face forward and stand still!" The sheriff dismounted, his face
ashen and his hands never moving. "Line up next to your partner
in crime. There! The two of you make a fine picture, a perfect
pair of sick coyotes mixed with a wild mule and a Mexican. Listen
up!" Monty paused for a long moment, his breathing heavy and
audible. Vienna's gaze was fixed on Monty. Her mind quickly
processed the nuances of his actions and words as he controlled
the men. Violence, brutal violence, the very thing she had sensed,
feared, and tried to eradicate from her cowboys, was finally about
to happen before her eyes. It had come at last. She had softened
Stillwell, influenced Nels, and changed Norris; however, this little,
dark-faced, fearsome Monty Price had emerged from his wild past,
and nothing on earth or in heaven could stop him. The harsh
existence of untamed men in an untamed land was about to strike
a blow against her.

She didn't flinch; she didn't want to erase from her sight this little
man, who was terrifying in his mood of wild justice. She felt a flash
of horror that Monty, blind and indifferent to her authority, cold
as steel towards her presence, understood the depths of a woman's

soul. For in this moment of strife, of insult to her, of torture to the man she had uplifted and then broken, the passion within her reached deep towards primitive hate. With eyes slowly turning red, she watched Monty Price; she listened with ears pounding; she waited, slowly sagging against Stillwell. "Hawe, if you and your dirty partner have loved the sound of a human voice, then listen and listen hard," said Monty. "Because I've been going against my old style just to have a talk with you. You almost got away on your nerve, didn't you? Why? You roll in here like a mad steer and flash your badge and talk mean, then almost bluff away with it. You heard all about Miss Florentino's cowboy outfit stopping drinking and cursing and carrying guns. They've taken on religion and decent living, and sure they'll be easy to hobble and drive to jail. Hawe, listen. There was a good, noble, and beautiful woman who came out of the East somewhere, and she brought a lot of sunshine and happiness and new ideas into the tough lives of cowboys. I reckon it's beyond you to know what she came to mean to them. Well, I'll tell you. They all went clean out of their heads. They all got soft and easy and sweet-tempered. They got so they couldn't kill a coyote, a crippled calf in a mud-hole. They took to books, and writing home to mother and sister, and to saving money, and to getting married. Once they were only a lot of poor cowboys, and then suddenly they were human beings, living in a big world that had something sweet even for them.

Even for an old, worn-out, hobble-legged, burnt-out cowboy like myself! Do you understand? And you, Mr. Hawe, you come along, not satisfied with roping and beating and God knows what else of that friendless little Bonita; you come along and face the lady we fellas honor, love and revere. And you, you Hell's fire!"With a whistling breath, Monty Price crouched lower, hands at his hips, and he edged inch by inch farther out from the porch, closer to Hawe and Sneed. Vienna saw them only in the blurred fringe of her sight. They resembled specters. She heard the shrill whistle of a horse and recognized Princess calling her from the corral. "That's all!" roared Monty, his voice now strangling. Lower and lower he bent, a terrible figure of ferocity. "Now, both you armed officers of the law, come on! Flash your guns! Throw 'em, and be quick! Monty Price is done! There'll be daylight through you both before you fan a hammer! But I'm giving you a chance to sting me. You holler law, and my way is the old law."His breath came quicker, his voice grew hoarser, and he crouched lower. All his body except his rigid arms quivered with a wonderful muscular convulsion. "Dogs! Skunks! Buzzards! Flash them guns, or I'll flash mine! Aha!"To Vienna, it seemed the three stiff, crouching men leaped into instant and united action. She saw streaks of fire, streaks of smoke. Then a crashing volley deafened her. It ceased as quickly. Smoke veiled the scene. Slowly it drifted away to disclose three fallen men, one of whom, Monty, leaned on his left hand, a smoking gun in his right. He watched for a movement from the other two. It did not come. Then, with a terrible smile, he slid back and stretched out.

Chapter Twenty-Two.

D ay and night, Vienna Florentino found herself unable to shake off the haunting memory of the tragedy that occurred. Monty Price's horrifying smile played over and over in her mind, leaving her feeling unsettled and disturbed.

Vienna knew that the only way to escape her troubles was to keep herself busy. She spent her days working, walking, and riding. She even put aside her aversion to the Mexican girl Bonita, who was sick and in need of nursing. Vienna felt a change in her soul, but she couldn't pinpoint what it was. The struggle to decide whether to go East or West still weighed heavily on her mind. However, she never felt spiritually alone because she sensed someone following her. Being indoors made her feel oppressed, so she craved the open air, the sight of the endless landscape, and the sounds of the corral and pond. One afternoon, she rode down to the alfalfa-fields, circled them, and rode back up to the spillway of the lower lake. There, she found a group of mesquite-trees that had taken on new life due to the water that seeped through the sand to their roots. Vienna dismounted and rested under the trees, enjoying the

solitude of the secluded spot. Her horse, Princess, was restless, but
Vienna was content to sit with her back against a tree, feeling the
cool breeze on her face. She heard the slow tramp of cattle going to
drink and then silence, except for the sound of her and Princess.

After a moment of observation, she discovered that the area was
far from lifeless. Her sharp senses were rewarded. Desert quail,
as gray as the barren earth, were cleaning themselves in a shady
spot. A bee, quick as lightning, buzzed past. She noticed a horned
toad, the color of rock, crouching low and hiding fearfully in the
sand within range of her whip. She extended the whip's point, and
the toad shook and expanded and hissed. It was brimming with
fight. The wind barely stirred the thin branches of the mesquites,
producing a mournful sigh. From far up in the foothills, barely
visible, came the cry of an eagle. The bray of a burro caused a
short, jarring interruption. Then a brown bird swooped down
from an unseen perch and chased a fluttering winged insect in a
swift, erratic flight. Vienna heard the sound of a merciless beak
snapping. Indeed, there was more than just life in the mesquites'
shadow.

Suddenly, Princess perked up his long ears and snorted. Vienna
heard the slow thud of hooves. A horse was approaching from
the direction of the lake. Vienna had learned to be cautious, and
she turned Princess toward the open, mounting him. A moment
later, she was grateful for her prudence because, looking back
through the trees, she watched as Norris led a horse into the grove.
She would have rather encountered a guerrilla than this cowboy.
Princess broke into a trot when a sharp whistle pierced the air. The

horse jumped and, turning so quickly that he almost threw Vienna off, he charged straight back towards the mesquites. Vienna spoke to him, screamed at him in anger, pulled on the reins with all her might, but was helpless to stop him. He whistled a shrill blast. Vienna then realized that Norris, his former master, had called him, and that nothing could deter him.

Vienna had given up her attempts to stop Princess from thrashing mesquite boughs and instead focused on intercepting them. The horse charged into an aisle between the trees and halted before Norris, letting out an eager whinny. Vienna was amazed and unsure of what to expect. With a quick glance, she saw Norris dressed in rough garb, ready for the trail, leading a wiry horse that was saddled and packed. Norris put his arm around Princess's neck without acknowledging Vienna's presence and laid his face against the flowing mane. Vienna's heart began to beat faster as she realized that Norris was saying goodbye to his horse. She was moved by the love between man and beast and felt a dimness in her eyes that she quickly brushed away, only for it to return wet and blurring. She looked away, afraid that Norris might see her tears. She felt sorry for him, knowing that he was leaving the ranch, and this time it was for good. A sharp pain shot through Vienna's heart like a stab from a cold blade. The wonder of it, the incomprehensibility of it, and the utter newness and strangeness of this sharp pain made her forget Norris, her surroundings, and everything except to search her heart. Maybe this was the secret that had eluded her. She trembled on the brink of something unknown. The emotion brought back her girlhood and her mind raced with questions and answers. She was living, feeling, and learning. Happiness mocked

her from behind a barred door, and the bar of that door seemed
to be an inexplicable pain. Questions raced through her mind like
lightning: Why should pain hide her happiness? What was her
happiness?

Vienna was left wondering what relation this man had to her, and
why she felt so strange about his departure. The voices within her
remained unanswered and silenced. Suddenly, Norris approached
her and Vienna turned to face him. She saw the earlier version of
Norris, the one who reminded her of their first meeting at El Cajon
and their memorable meeting at Chiricahua.

"I want to talk to you," Norris stated. "I want to ask you something.
I've been wanting to know something. That's why I've hung on
here. You never spoke to me, never noticed me, never gave me a
chance to ask you. But now I'm going over the border. And I want
to know. Why did you refuse to listen to me?"

His words caused a hot shame to rush over Vienna, tenfold more
stifling than before. She realized she was face to face with him and
a shame that she would rather have died than revealed was being
liberated. She bit her lips to hold back speech, jerked on Princess's
bridle, struck him with her whip, and spurred him. However,
Norris's iron arm held the horse. Then, in a flash of passion, Vienna struck at Norris's face, missed, struck again, and hit.

With one swift pull, he tore the whip from her hands, almost
drawing her from the saddle. It was not the action on his part or the
sudden strong masterfulness of his look that quieted her fury, but
the livid mark on his face where the whip had lashed. "That's noth-

ing," he said, with something of his old audacity. "That's nothing to how you've hurt me."

Vienna battled with herself for control. This man would not be denied. Never before had the hardness of his face, the flinty hardness of these desert-bred men, so struck her with its revelation of the unbridled spirit. He looked stern, haggard, and bitter.

The once dark shade was slowly transitioning to gray, then to a dull ash-color, as Norris' passion burned within him. The man before Vienna was not the same gentle soul she had helped shape. His piercing eyes bore into her, as if searching her very soul. Vienna could sense a fleeting doubt, a tinge of sadness, and an overall sense of realization in Norris' eyes. Her intuition told her that he had come to a painful and final truth.

For the third time, Norris posed the question to Vienna, and she remained silent, unable to speak. He continued, his voice filled with passion, "Do you not know that I love you? That since the day I first laid eyes on you at Chiricahua, I have loved you? Can you not see that I have changed, that I have become a better man because of you? I have worked for you, lived for you, and loved you, but you never knew. I turned my back on the wild life and have become an honorable and decent man, all for you, my cowboy angel, my holy Virgin."

Norris' words were filled with emotion, and Vienna could feel the love and sincerity in his voice. He continued, "You know nothing of a man's heart and soul. How could you understand the love and salvation of a man who had lived his life in silence and loneliness? I was a wild cowboy, faithless to my mother and sister, riding a hard, drunken trail straight to hell. But when I looked into your eyes, I saw a beautiful woman beyond me, above me, and I loved you so much that I was saved. I became faithful again, and I saw your face in every flower and your eyes in the blue heaven."

Vienna listened to Norris' words, her heart aching with a new-found understanding of the man before her. She knew that he had loved her all along, and she felt the weight of his love and sacrifice.

Under the vast expanse of the Western stars at night, I felt an overwhelming sense of gratitude for simply being alive and having the opportunity to assist you. Being near you and shielding you from worry, trouble, and danger made me feel like I was a small part of the West that you had grown to love." Vienna remained silent, her heart pounding in her chest. Norris suddenly lunged at her and grabbed her arm, causing her to tremble. His actions hinted at his previous instinctual violence. "You think that I kept Bonita hidden in the mountains, that I secretly met with her, and that while I served you, I was..." He paused, his voice rising in anger. "I know what you think! I never knew until I made you look at me. Now say it! Speak!" Vienna, consumed by passion, unable to control her words, blurted out a shameful and revealing confession: "YES!" Norris had forced the word out of her, but he was not perceptive enough to understand the deeper meaning of her response. To him, the word only confirmed his dishonor in her eyes. He released her arm and stepped back, a surprising action for the savage and unrefined man she believed him to be. "But at Chiricahua, you spoke of faith," he exclaimed. "You said the greatest thing in the world was faith in human nature. You said that the finest men were those who had fallen low and had risen again. You said you had faith in me! You made me have faith in myself!" His reproach, free of bitterness or disdain, struck at Vienna's egoistic belief in her own righteousness. She had preached a beautiful principle that she had failed to live up to.

She understood his criticism and was in a state of confusion, but her pride had been wounded too deeply, and her emotions were too intense. She couldn't speak, and the moment passed, along with his brief moment of honesty. "You think I'm a terrible person," he said. "You think that about Bonita! And all this time I've been..." His passionate words ended abruptly as he clenched his teeth. His lips formed a thin, bitter line, and his face became agitated as he struggled internally. He gasped, as if he was resisting a strong temptation, then suddenly stood upright. "But I'll be the man the dog you think I am!" He grabbed her arm with a rough, powerful grip, pulling her halfway out of the saddle and into his arms. She fell against him, not entirely free of the stirrups or horse, where she hung, completely powerless. She struggled and writhed, attempting to free herself, but all she could do was twist herself and raise herself enough to see his face. It almost paralyzed her. Was he going to kill her? Then he wrapped his arms around her and held her tighter and closer to him. She felt the pounding of his heart; hers seemed to have frozen. He pressed his burning lips to hers in a long, terrible kiss. She felt him tremble. "Oh, Norris! I beg you, let me go!" she whispered. His white face loomed over hers, and she closed her eyes. He kissed her face repeatedly, but not on her mouth. He pressed his lips to her closed eyes, her hair, her cheeks, and her neck, and they lost their heat and became cold.

He released her, lifting her back into the saddle while still holding her arm to prevent her from falling. Vienna sat with her eyes closed, dreading the light. "Now you can't say you've never been kissed," Norris said, his voice seeming distant. "But that was coming to you, so be game. Here!" He placed something hard and cold in her hand, making her fingers close around it. The sensation of the object revived her, and she opened her eyes to see Norris standing with his broad chest against her knee, a mocking smile on his face. "Go ahead! Throw my gun on me! Be a thoroughbred!" Vienna didn't yet understand his meaning. "You can put me down in that quiet place on the hill beside Monty Price." She dropped the gun with a horrified cry. The memory of Monty, the certainty that she would kill Norris if she held the gun any longer, tormented her with self-accusation. Norris picked up the weapon. "You might have saved me a hell of a lot of trouble," he said with another mocking smile. "You're beautiful and sweet and proud, but you're no thoroughbred! Princess Florentino, adios!" Norris leaped onto his horse and crashed through the mesquites, disappearing from sight.

Chapter Twenty-Three.

I n the secluded comfort of her bedroom, Vienna Florentino lay face down on her plush couch, overwhelmed with the violation she had endured. As the afternoon passed by and twilight approached, Vienna finally rose from her position to sit by the window, hoping the cool breeze would soothe her flushed face. For hours, she struggled with feelings of shame, anger, and helplessness, trying to make sense of the unspeakable act that had left her feeling defiled.

The trail of stars in the sky seemed to taunt her with their unattainable calmness. Vienna Florentino had once adored them, but now she despised them and everything that had to do with the wild, unpredictable West. Lorraine Wayne had been right; this was no place for her. The decision to go back home came naturally, with no inner turmoil. She even felt relieved at the thought of leaving. However, the stars still held a strange allure for her. They were beautiful, yet mocking, drawing her in. She sighed, realizing that it wouldn't be easy to leave them after all.

Vienna shut the window, plunging the room into darkness. She lit a candle, but didn't want to be disturbed by the servants who were knocking on her door. She heard a soft footstep outside and wondered if it was Nels, Nick Steele, or Stillwell, who now watched over her since Monty Price and that other man were gone. She couldn't believe she was regretting him, but the darkness suited her mood. She tried to sleep, but her cheeks burned with a shameful heat. She got up to wash her face, but the cold water didn't ease the burning sensation. She lay back down, grateful for the cover of night. Norris's kisses lingered on her lips, eyes, and neck. Despite his betrayal, she knew he had loved her.

Vienna had a restless night and woke up feeling drained, but she was mentally prepared to face the day. She arrived at her office later than usual and found Stillwell waiting for her outside. "Good morning, Miss Princess," he greeted her politely, though his face betrayed his worry. Vienna braced herself for the usual complaints about Norris but was surprised to see a shabby pony and a small donkey with heavy loads in the yard. "Whose animals are these?" she asked. "Danny Mains'," replied Stillwell, coughing and looking uneasy. "Danny Mains?" Vienna repeated, puzzled. "Yes, ma'am," he confirmed. Stillwell was acting strangely, and Vienna sensed that something was amiss. "Is Danny Mains here?" she asked, suddenly curious. Stillwell nodded gravely. "Yes, he's here, and he came asking for Bonita. He's crazy about that little black-eyed girl. He hardly said 'hello' to me before he started asking all sorts of wild questions. I took him to see Bonita, and he's been with her for over half an hour now." Stillwell's feelings were hurt, and Vienna was taken aback by the news. Her curiosity turned to disbelief, and she

felt a sudden thrill of anticipation. A few moments later, a young
man with a cowboy's build, attire, and swagger appeared on the
porch. He had a clear brown tan, curly light hair, and blue eyes,
and he was handsome and straightforward. He slammed his hat
down and rushed to Vienna, grabbing her hands.

The sudden and forceful actions of the cowboy caused her to feel
uneasy, bringing back memories she wanted to forget. He lowered
his head and kissed her hands, squeezing them tightly. When he
stood back up, tears streamed down his face. "Miss Florentino,
she's safe and almost well, and what I feared most didn't happen,
thank God," he exclaimed, crying. "I'll never be able to repay you
for all you've done for her. She told me how she was taken here,
how Gene tried to save her, how you spoke up for Gene and her,
and how Monty finally surrendered his guns. Poor Monty! He
was my friend, but he did it for her. Monty Price was the most
honorable man I ever knew. Nels, Nick, and Gene have been great
friends to me, but Monty Price was grand. He never knew, just like
you, Bill, and the boys, what Bonita meant to me."

Stillwell placed his large hand on the cowboy's shoulder. "Danny,
what are you talking about?" he asked. "And you're taking liberties
with Miss Florentino, whom you've never met before. I'll excuse
your strange behavior since you're not drinking. Maybe you're
going crazy. Come on, calm down and talk sense."

The cowboy smiled, his honest face breaking into a grin. He wiped
the tears from his eyes and laughed, a joyous and youthful sound.
"Bill, old friend, give me a minute," he said, then turned to Vienna.
"I apologize, Miss Florentino, for my impoliteness. My name is

Danny Mains, and Bonita is my wife. I'm ecstatic that she's safe and unharmed, and I'm so grateful to you that it's a wonder I didn't kiss you right then and there."

"Bonita is your wife?" Stillwell exclaimed. "Of course! We've been married for months," Danny replied, beaming. "Gene Norris married us. That guy is great at getting people hitched."

Maybe I ain't paid him back yet for all he's done for me! You see, I've been in love with Bonita for two years. And Gene, you know Bill, he's got a way with girls. He was trying to convince Bonita to be with me," Vienna exclaimed. Her emotions shifted quickly, but she was filled with gratitude towards the cowboy in front of her. Danny Mains had brought her some great news and she couldn't help but feel grateful.

"Danny Mains!" Vienna exclaimed with a smile. "If you are as happy as your news has made me and if you really think I deserve such a reward, you may kiss me." Danny bashfully but eagerly took her up on the offer. Stillwell snorted, but Vienna knew it was just his way of showing approval.

"Bill, grab a chair," Danny said. "You've been worrying too much about your bad boys, Danny and Gene. You'll need to sit down for this story." He motioned for Vienna to take a seat as well. "Miss Florentino, I hope you don't mind listening. You have a face and eyes that love to hear about other people's happiness. And somehow, it's just easier for me to talk when I'm looking at you."

His demeanor changed as he walked off the porch and approached his tired horse and burro. "Played out!" he exclaimed as he quickly removed the pack from the burro and threw the saddle and bridle from the horse with a swift, violent motion.

"Look over there!" exclaimed Danny, pointing towards the horizon. "That's the last time you'll ever have to carry a heavy load like that. You've been loyal to me, and now I'm going to repay you. No more saddles, straps, halters, or hobbles for you. From now on, you'll only be surrounded by grass, clover, cool water, and dusty swales to roll around in and rest."

He then proceeded to untie the pack and take out a small, heavy bag. Danny dumped the contents of the bag at Stillwell's feet. Piece after piece of rock thumped onto the floor, sharp and ragged with yellow veins and bars and streaks. Stillwell picked up the rocks one by one, staring and stuttering in amazement. He put the rocks to his lips and dug into them with his shaking fingers. He lay back in his chair with his head against the wall, and a smile began to form on his face.

"Lord, Danny, you've gone and struck it rich!" exclaimed Stillwell.

Danny looked at Stillwell with a superior attitude. "I'm some rich," he said. "Now, what do we have here, Bill?"

"Oh, Lord, Danny! I'm afraid to say," replied Stillwell. "Just look at the gold, Miss Princess. I've been around prospectors and gold mines for thirty years, but I've never seen anything like this."

"The Lost Mine of the Padres!" shouted Danny in a loud voice. "And it belongs to me!"

Stillwell sat up fascinated, completely beside himself. "Bill, it's been
a long time since you last saw me," said Danny. "Gene kept me
up to date. I happened to run into Bonita, and I couldn't let her
ride alone when she told me she was in trouble. We headed for the
Peloncillos."

Gene's horse, Princess, was with Bonita and they had plans to meet
up on the trail. We made it to the mountains without any issues,
but we were close to starving for a couple of days until Gene found
us. Unfortunately, Gene was in trouble himself and couldn't bring
much with him. "We made our way to the crags and built a cabin,"
Bonita explained. "That day, Gene sent his horse to you. I had
never seen him so broken-hearted." After Gene left for the border,
Bonita and I struggled to survive. However, we managed, and I
believe it was during this time that she began to develop feelings
for me. I hunted cougars and collected bounties for their skins in
Rodeo, using the money to purchase the necessary supplies and
food. One day, I unexpectedly ran into Gene in El Cajon. He
had returned from the revolution and was causing trouble, but I
managed to get away from him after trying to convince him to leave
town.

A long time had passed before Gene finally made his way back to
the crags and found us. He had stopped drinking and had changed
for the better. It was then that he began to pester me relentlessly
to marry Bonita. I was happy with the way things were, and I was
afraid of ruining it all. Bonita had been a bit of a flirt, and I was
worried that she might not want to be tied down. Gene would
occasionally come up to the mountains with supplies and would

always push me to make the right decision for Bonita. He was so stubborn that I eventually gave in and asked Bonita to marry me. At first, she refused, saying that she wasn't good enough for me. However, I continued to be kind and decent to her, and eventually, she came around to the idea.

I was eager to marry Bonita, and it was my desire that made her grow soft, sweet, and pretty like a mountain quail. Gene brought Padre Marcos, and he married us. Danny paused in his narrative, breathing hard, as if the memory had stirred strong and thrilling feelings within him. Stillwell's smile was rapturous, and Vienna leaned toward Danny with her eyes shining.

"Miss Florentino, and you, Bill Stillwell, now listen, for this is strange, I've got to tell you. The afternoon Bonita and I were married, when Gene and the padre had gone, I was happy one minute and low-hearted the next. I was miserable because I had a bad name. I couldn't even buy a decent dress for my pretty wife. Bonita heard me, and she was mysterious. She told me the story of the lost mine of the padres, and she kissed me and made me joyful in the strangest way. I knew marriage went to women's heads, and I thought even Bonita had a spell.

"Well, she left me for a bit, and when she came back, she wore some pretty yellow flowers in her hair. Her eyes were big, black, and beautiful. She said some strange things about spirits rolling rocks down the canyon. Then she said she wanted to show me where she always sat and waited and watched for me when I was away.

"She led me around under the crags to a long slope. It was pretty there, clear and open, with a long sweep, and the desert yawning deep and red. There were yellow flowers on that slope, the same kind she had in her hair, the same kind that Apache girl wore hundreds of years ago when she led the padre to the gold-mine."

As I pondered the situation, I looked into Bonita's eyes and heard the sound of rocks tumbling down the cliff. It was a strange noise that grew fainter over time. At first, I thought I was losing my mind, but then I realized that it was just the weathering of the cliffs. As I looked closer, I saw a gold pocket under the crags.

I became obsessed with finding the gold and worked tirelessly like a team of burros. Bonita helped me by watching the trails and bringing me water. Unfortunately, during one of her watchful moments, she was captured by Pat Hawe and his guerrillas. Pat Hawe was determined to harm Gene, and he ended up getting mixed up with Don Carlos. Bonita had some shocking news about that group, but for now, my focus was on the gold.

Danny Mains stood up and expressed his gratitude to Bill Stillwell for always being a friend and having faith in him. He wanted to repay that debt by offering Bill and Gene Norris a partnership in his gold mine. He was even willing to buy any ranch, railroad, or town that they desired. Bill was to go out and fetch Gene so that they could draw up the partnership agreement with Danny's wife and Miss Florentino as witnesses.

In conclusion, Danny Mains was determined to repay his debts and share his newfound wealth with his friends. He wanted to create a partnership that would benefit everyone involved and was willing to go to great lengths to make it happen.

"I gotta show him this gold and make Danny Mains pay for what he did!" Vienna thought to herself. The only thing that soured her mood was the fact that she could never pay back Monty Price. She wanted to tell Danny Mains and Stillwell that the cowboy they were searching for had left the ranch, but she couldn't bring herself to do it. The loyalty she felt towards them made her keep quiet. She watched as Stillwell and the cowboy left arm in arm to find Norris, imagining the disappointment and grief that would follow when they discovered he had left for the border.

As she pondered this, she saw a familiar yet strange figure making his way towards her. It was Padre Marcos, and Vienna was taken aback. He had always avoided her, even though she had done so much for his church and people. She couldn't help but feel a little uneasy at his presence. He bowed low and asked for an audience, which Vienna granted. He then asked to close the doors, explaining that he had a matter of great importance to discuss.

Vienna was intrigued as to what the padre could want from her. He then revealed a secret that he had been keeping, asking for her forgiveness.

Vienna sat frozen as the words of the priest echoed in her ears. She couldn't believe what she was hearing. She was Norris's wife? The thought was too much to bear. She had no recollection of the night in question, but the priest's words left no room for doubt.

KEN CANNON

Vienna's mind raced as she tried to process what had been revealed to her. How could Norris have done this to her? And how could she have been so naive? The priest's words were like a dagger to her heart, but she couldn't deny the truth that had been spoken.

As she rose from her seat, Vienna begged the priest to stop. She couldn't bear to hear any more, but the priest continued. He spoke of Norris's drunkenness and his threats. He spoke of the sin that had been committed and the weight of the secret that he had carried for so long.

Vienna listened in horror as the priest recounted the events of that fateful night. She felt violated and betrayed, but she couldn't bring herself to hate Norris. She knew that he was a good man, but he had made a terrible mistake.

As the priest finished his tale, Vienna was left reeling. She didn't know what to do or where to turn. She was alone in a world that had suddenly become dark and sinister. She couldn't help but think that her life would never be the same again.

As she looked up, she saw Norris and Padre Marcos approaching the ranch. The sight of them filled her with dread. She didn't know how to face them or what to say. All she knew was that her life had been forever changed by the revelation of the priest.

The changes that your kindness brought to my people were no less than the transformation in Senor Norris. I was afraid that one day you would leave, return to your home in the East, unaware of the truth. Then came the day when I confessed to Norris and said that I must tell you. Senor, the man was overjoyed. I have never seen such elation. He no longer threatened to kill me. That strong and cruel vaquero begged me not to reveal the secret, to keep it hidden. He professed his love for you, a love that was like a desert storm. He swore by everything that was once sacred to him, by my cross and my church, that he would be a good man, that he would be worthy to have you secretly as his wife for the little time that life allowed him to worship at your feet. You would never have to know. So I kept silent, half pitying him, half fearing him, and praying for some divine intervention.

"Senora, Norris lived in a foolish dream world. I saw him often. When he took me up into the mountains to marry that wayward Bonita and her lover, I began to respect a man whose ideas about nature, life, and God were different from mine. But he worships God in all material things. He is a part of the wind, sun, desert, and mountain that shaped him. I have never heard more beautiful words than those he used to convince Bonita to accept Senor Mains, to forget her former lovers, and be happy from now on. He is their friend. I wish I could explain to you what that means. It sounds so simple, but it is really simple. All great things are like that."

For Senor Norris, being loyal to his friend and honoring the woman who had loved and given to him came naturally. He had brought about their marriage and was always there to help them in times of need and loneliness. However, he never spoke of them. If they were ever in danger, he would give his life to protect them. To me, Senor Norris possesses the same stability, strength, and elements as the wild and rugged desert that surrounds us.

Vienna was enchanted by the soft-spoken, eloquent priest. His defense and praise of Norris, even if it had been expressed in the crude language of cowboys, would have been a source of pride for her. "Senora, please don't misunderstand my mission. Apart from my confession to you, I have a duty to tell you about the man who is your husband. But as a priest, I can read his soul. God's ways are mysterious, and I am only a humble instrument. You are a noble woman, and Senor Norris is a man of desert iron, forged anew in the crucible of love. Quien sabe? Senor Norris swore he would kill me if I betrayed him, but I'm not afraid of him anymore. He bears a great and pure love for you, and it has transformed him. I no longer fear his threat, but I do fear his anger if he ever finds out that I spoke about his love and his foolish paradise. I've seen his dark face turning toward the sunset over the desert. I've seen him lifting it to the light of the stars. Think, my gracious and noble lady, think about what his paradise is like."

To love someone beyond the physical realm, to know that they are your partner and yours alone, never to belong to another unless through sacrifice; to watch them with immense pride and joy, to protect them from harm, and to find happiness in serving them; to wait for the moment when you must leave them free and risk your own life to do so. Senora, these sentiments are beautiful, powerful, and terrifying. They have brought me to you today to confess my feelings. The ways of God are mysterious, and I cannot help but wonder about your influence on Senor Norris. He was once a brutish animal, but now he is a man unlike any other I have seen. As a priest and a lover of humanity, I implore you to consider that love may be at work here before you send Norris to his death. I have heard that you are a great lady in the Eastern cities, but to me, you are simply a woman, and Norris is just a man. Please do not dismiss his love without first being certain that you do not want it. You may be throwing away something precious and noble that you have created yourself.

Chapter Twenty-Four.

As if struck by lightning, Vienna Florentino dashed to her room, feeling like a wild creature. The dream she had created of real life was shattered, and she was left dazed. The incredible tale told by Danny Mains, the regret she felt for being unjust to Norris, and the shocking secret revealed by Padre Marcos were all forgotten in the sudden realization of her own love. Vienna ran away as if someone was chasing her.

With trembling fingers, she locked the doors and drew the blinds of the windows that opened onto the porch. She pushed the chairs aside so that she could pace the length of her room. Now alone, she walked with soft, hurried, uneven steps. Here, she could be herself; she needed no mask. The long habit of serenely hiding the truth from the world and from herself could be broken. The seclusion of her darkened chamber made possible that betrayal of herself to which she was impelled.

She paused in her swift pacing to and fro. She liberated the thought that knocked at the gates of her mind. With quivering lips, she whispered it. Then she spoke aloud: "I will say it here. I...I love him!"

"I love him!" she repeated the astounding truth, but she doubted her identity. "Am I still Vienna Florentino? What has happened? Who am I?" She stood where the light from one unclosed window fell upon her image in the mirror. "Who is this woman?"

She expected to see a familiar, dignified person, a quiet, unruffled figure, a tranquil face with dark, proud eyes and calm, proud lips. But no, she did not see Vienna Florentino. She did not see anyone she knew. Were her eyes, like her heart, playing her false? The figure before her was instinct with pulsating life. The hands she saw, clasped together, pressed deep into a swelling bosom that heaved with each panting breath. The face she saw was white, rapt, strangely glowing, with parted, quivering lips and great, staring, tragic eyes. This could not be Vienna Florentino's face. Yet as she looked, she knew no fancy could really deceive her, that she was only Vienna Florentino come at last to the end of brooding dreams. She swiftly realized the change in her, divined its cause and meaning, accepted it as inevitable, and straightway fell back again into the mood of bewildering amaze. Calmness was unattainable. The surprise absorbed her.

She couldn't trace back the countless, imperceptible steps that led to her current state. Her former ability to reflect, analyze, and even think had vanished in a pulse-stirring sense of a new emotion. She only felt the instinctive outward action that was a physical relief, and the involuntary inner struggle that was maddening yet unutterably sweet. They seemed to be just one bewildering effect of surprise.

In a nature like hers, where strength of feeling had long been suppressed as a matter of training, the sudden consciousness of passionate love required time for its awakening, time for its sway. Eventually, that last enlightening moment arrived, and Vienna Florentino faced not only the love in her heart but also the thought of the man she loved.

Suddenly, as she raged, something in her dauntless new personality took arms against the indictment of Gene Norris. Her mind whirled about him and his life. She saw him drunk, brutal, and abandoned. Then, out of the picture she had of him, a different man emerged: weak, sick, changed by shock, growing strong, strangely, spiritually altered, silent, lonely like an eagle, secretive, tireless, faithful, soft as a woman, hard as iron to endure, and at last noble.

She softened. In a flash, her complex mood changed to one wherein she thought of the truth, beauty, and wonder of Norris's uplifting. Humbly, she trusted that she had helped him climb. That influence had been the best she had ever exerted. It had worked magic in her own character. By it, she had reached a higher, nobler plane of trust in man. She had received infinitely more than she had given. Her swiftly flying memory seemed to assort a vast mine of treasures from the past. She saw vivid words from the letter Norris had written to her brother.

But oh, she knew. And while it may not have mattered before, it mattered now. She remembered the feeling of her hair blowing across his lips as he carried her down from the mountains. She remembered the way Norris had looked at her with pride in his eyes when she dressed in a white gown with red roses to greet her Eastern guests. These memories were fleeting, however, and her mind was restless. She couldn't find any peace. She was desperate and cast off her self-control, turning from her old self to face the truth. She listened to the ringing voice of circumstance and fate, and the whole story was revealed. It was a simple story with complicated details, beautiful in parts, but prophetic of tragedy from beginning to end. Norris had great love for her, but she had been blind to it. Vienna was like a prisoner in a cell, pacing back and forth. "Oh, it's all terrible!" she cried. "I am his wife. His wife! That meeting, the marriage, his fall, his rise, his silence, his pride! And I can never be anything to him. Could I be anything to him? Vienna Florentino? But I am his wife, and I love him! His wife! I am the wife of a cowboy! That might be undone. Can my love be undone? Ah, do I want anything undone? He is gone. Gone! Could he have meant...I will not, dare not think of that. He will come back. No, he never will come back."

Vienna Florentino was consumed with worry. The days that followed the emotional storm were excruciatingly long and seemingly hopeless. She spent countless hours lying awake, lost in passionate thoughts. Her mind was plagued with a growing fear that Norris had crossed the border to invite a bullet that would free her from her misery. Eventually, her fear became a reality. The news came to her in a sudden, unmistakable flash of certainty. She was devastated. The fire of her pain burned deep within her, and it was evident in her eyes. She withdrew into herself, waiting for confirmation of her worst fears. At times, she would lash out in anger at the circumstances that were beyond her control, at herself, and at Norris. "He should have learned from Ambrose!" she cried out in frustration, bitter with a pain that she knew was not consistent with her pride. She remembered Christine's straightforward account of Ambrose's courtship: "He told me he loved me; he kissed me; he hugged me; he put me on his horse; he rode away with me; he married me." But in the next moment, Vienna denied the insistent clamor of a love that was slowly breaking her spirit. She was constantly haunted by feelings of remorse, for she had failed to recognize a man's honesty, manliness, uprightness, faith, and devotion. She had been blind to love and nobility, which she had herself created. The wise words of Padre Marcos echoed in her mind, and she struggled to overcome her bitterness, to reject her intelligence, and to quell her pride. As she weakened, she gave in more and more to her yearning, hopeless hope. She had avoided the light of the stars and had forcefully dismissed every memory of Norris's kisses. But one night, she deliberately went to her window, and there they were shining bright.

Oh my stars! They shone beautifully, as always, but there was something different about them. They seemed closer, warmer, and spoke a kinder language. They were more helpful than ever before, teaching her that regret was pointless. In their grand, blazing task, they revealed to her the supreme duty of life - to be true. Those shining stars made her yield. She whispered to them that the West had claimed her, Norris had claimed her forever, whether he lived or died. She surrendered to her love, and it felt as though he was there with her, dark-faced, fire-eyed, violent in his actions, crushing her to his chest in that farewell moment, kissing her with one burning kiss of passion, then with cold, terrible lips of renunciation. "I am your wife!" she whispered to him. In that moment, throbbing, exalted, quivering in her first sweet, tumultuous surrender to love, she would have given her all, her life, to be in his arms again, to meet his lips, to put forever out of his power any thought of wild sacrifice.

The next morning, Vienna went out onto the porch, and Stillwell, haggard and stern, handed her a message from El Cajon. He spoke in a husky, incoherent voice. She read the message with a heavy heart: El Capitan Norris had been captured by rebel soldiers in a fight at Agua Prieta the day before. He was a sharpshooter in the Federal ranks and had been sentenced to death on Thursday at sunset.

Chapter Twenty-Five.

"Stillwell!" Vienna's cry was filled with agony, more than just a broken heart. It was the crumbling of a false sense of pride, old beliefs, and bloodless standards. She had finally conquered her doubts and found herself, her love, her salvation, and her duty to a man. Her unquenchable spirit blazed out of the darkness, and she refused to be cheated. The old cattleman, Stillwell, stood silently before her, staring at her pale face and fiery eyes.

"Stillwell! I'm Norris's wife!" Vienna exclaimed.

"My God, Miss Princess!" Stillwell exclaimed. "I knew something terrible was wrong. Oh, it's such a pity-"

"Do you think I'll let him be shot when I know him now, when I'm no longer blind, when I love him?" Vienna interrupted with passionate fervor. "I will save him. This is Wednesday morning. I have thirty-six hours to save his life. Stillwell, send for Link and the car!"

Vienna swiftly made her way into her office, her mind racing with clarity and speed. She devised a plan in a single moment of inspiration, which required the careful wording of telegrams to Washington, New York, and San Antonio. These messages were intended for senators, representatives, and people of high public and private status, people who would remember her and would work tirelessly to help her. Never before had Vienna's position meant anything to her in comparison to what it meant now. Never before had money seemed as powerful as it did in that moment. She dispelled heartbreaking thoughts and focused on the power she had at her disposal. She had wealth and influence, and she would use these resources to save Norris. Though she felt the suspense and strain almost beyond endurance, she would not entertain the possibility of failure.

When Vienna emerged from her office, the car was waiting with Link, helmet in hand, a cool, bright gleam in his eyes, and Stillwell, losing his haggard misery, beginning to respond to Vienna's spirit. "Link, drive Stillwell to El Cajon in time for him to catch the El Paso train," she said.

"Wait here for his return," she said, handing Stillwell the telegrams to send from El Cajon and drafts to cash in El Paso. "If any message comes from him, telephone it at once to me." She instructed him to go before the rebel junta, then stationed in Juarez, to explain the situation, to inform them to expect communications from Washington officials requesting and advising Norris's exchange as a prisoner of war, and to offer to buy his release from the rebel authorities.

After hearing her out, Stillwell's huge, bowed form straightened, and a ghost of his old smile just moved his lips. He was no longer young, and hope could not at once drive away stern and grim realities. As he bent over her hand, his manner appeared courtly and reverent. But either he was speechless or felt the moment was not one for him to break silence. He climbed to a seat beside Link, who pocketed the watch he had been studying and leaned over the wheel. There was a crack, a muffled sound bursting into a roar, and the big car jerked forward to bound over the edge of the slope, to leap down the long incline, to shoot out upon the level valley floor, and disappear in moving dust.

For the first time in days, Vienna visited the gardens, the corrals, the lakes, and the quarters of the cowboys. Though imagining she was calm, she feared she looked strange to Nels, Nick, Frankie Slade, and the boys best known to her. The situation for them must have been one of tormenting pain and bewilderment. They acted as if they wanted to say something to her but found themselves spellbound. She wondered if they knew she was Norris's wife. Stillwell had not had time to tell them; besides, he would not have mentioned the fact.

The cowboys gathered on the porch were aware of Norris's impending execution. They knew that if Vienna hadn't been angry with him, he wouldn't have crossed the border in a desperate mood. Vienna engaged them in small talk about the weather and the animals before abruptly changing her mind. "Nels, you and Nick don't need to go on duty today," she told them. "I may need you. I... " She trailed off, her eyes catching sight of Norris's black horse prancing in a nearby corral. "I've sent Stillwell to El Paso," she continued, her voice shaking. "He'll save Norris. I have to tell you all something. I am Norris's wife!" The cowboys were stunned into silence as Vienna left them and retreated to her room.

As she tried to occupy herself with various tasks, Vienna found that she couldn't stop thinking about Norris and his fate. Why had he become a Federal? She remembered that he had fought for Madero, the rebel, and had earned the title of El Capitan. But now Madero was a Federal, and Norris remained loyal to him. Had Norris crossed the border with any other motive besides the one he had hinted at with his mocking smile and words? "You might have saved me a hell of a lot of trouble!" Vienna remembered the shock of touching the gun she had dropped in horror. Did he mean the trouble of getting himself shot in a way that wouldn't be cowardly? Or was there something else going on, like Don Carlos and his guerrillas? The uncertainty gnawed at Vienna as she waited for news of Norris's fate.

Vienna couldn't shake the thought that Norris was out for blood. Don Carlos' blood. She imagined him as a vengeful, silent man, driven by wild justice, much like Monty Price. It was the kind of deed that Nels or Nick Steel might do, or even Gene Norris. Vienna regretted that Norris, who had risen so high, had not risen above seeking to kill his enemy, no matter how evil that enemy might be.

Vienna had never been interested in the local newspapers that arrived a day late from El Paso and Adam, but now she eagerly pored over any she could find, reading every word about the revolution. To her, every word was of vital significance.

The newspapers reported that American citizens had been robbed by Mexican rebels in Madera, Chihuahua, to the tune of $25,000 worth of goods. The rebels, under the command of Gen. Antonio Rojas and comprising a thousand men, were headed westward through Sonora to Agnaymas and Pacific coast points. They planned to pass through Dolores, where they would be met by 1,000 Maderista volunteers. The railroad south of Madera was being destroyed, leaving many Americans marooned. General Rojas had executed five men for trivial offenses. Meanwhile, somewhere in Mexico, Patrick Dunne, an American citizen, was in prison under sentence of death.

On July 31, the news continued to pour in from Juarez, Mexico.

Today, General Orozco, the leader of the rebels, announced that if the United States would remove all barriers and allow them to purchase as much ammunition as they needed, he could guarantee peace would be restored in Mexico and a stable government would take over within sixty days. The situation in Casas Grandes, Chihuahua has worsened as rebel soldiers looted the homes of many Mormon families living in the area. As a result, all Mormon families have fled to El Paso for safety. Despite General Salazar executing two of his soldiers for the robbery, he has made no effort to prevent his troops from looting the homes of unprotected Americans. Last night and today, many Americans from Pearson, Madera, and other areas outside the Mormon settlements have fled on trains. Refugees from Mexico have also continued to pour into El Paso, with about one hundred arriving last night, mostly men.

Vienna was reading about the war in Mexico with great interest. She knew it wasn't a traditional war, but a revolution that was causing starvation, looting, and burning. She was particularly disturbed by the news of five men being executed for minor offenses, as it made her fear for the safety of Norris, an American cowboy who was being held captive by the rebels. Vienna waited patiently for any news, but none came. As the sun began to set, she went outside and looked out at the desert, hoping for strength. The desert was red and mutable, shrouded in shadows, and it seemed to mirror her own terrible mood. The stars that had previously soothed her spirit failed her, and she felt completely alone in her torment. She knew Norris was out there somewhere, waiting for his fate to be decided, and the thought of the endless, insupportable hours he was enduring made her heart ache. Night fell, and the stars continued to be unresponsive to her pain.

She retreated to the refuge of her room, seeking solace in the darkness as she lay there with her eyes wide open, waiting, waiting. Night had always held a certain mystic allure for her, but now her mind was consumed by a vague and monstrous gloom. Despite this, she remained acutely aware of her surroundings, her senses attuned to every sound. She heard the measured tread of a guard, the rustle of the wind stirring the window-curtain, and the mournful wail of a coyote in the distance. The dead silence of the night eventually became oppressive, weighing down on her like lead. She waited in silence for so long that when the window

casements finally showed a hint of grey, she believed it was just
her imagination and that dawn would never come. She prayed
that the sun would not rise, that it would not begin its short
twelve-hour journey towards what could be Norris' fatal setting.
But the dawn came, swift and remorseless. Daylight had broken,
and it was Thursday.

Suddenly, the sharp ringing of the telephone bell broke the silence,
startling her into action. She ran to answer the call. "Hello, Miss
Princess!" came the hurried voice on the other end. "This is Link
speaking. I have messages for you. They're favorable, according to
the operator. I'll ride out with them. I'll be there soon." And with
that, the line went dead. Vienna desperately wanted to know more,
but was grateful for what little information she had. Favorable!
Stillwell had been successful! Her heart leaped with joy. Suddenly, she felt weak and her hands failed her as she struggled to get
dressed. Breakfast held no meaning for her, except that it helped
her pass the dragging minutes. Finally, she heard the low hum of
a car, quickly mounting to a roar and ending with a sharp report.
Link had arrived. If her feet had kept pace with her heart, she would
have raced out to meet him. She saw him, helmet thrown back,
watch in hand, and he looked up at her with his cool, bright smile,
with his familiar apologetic manner.

"Miss Princess, it took me fifty-three minutes to get here," Link
said, "but I had to ride around a herd of steers and knock a couple
off the trail." He handed her a bundle of telegrams. Vienna's hands
were shaking as she tore them open and began to read them with
quick, blurry eyes. Some were from Washington, assuring her of all

possible assistance, while others were from New York. The
Spanish messages from El Paso were harder to translate at a
glance. She searched for Stillwell's message, which was the last
one. It was a long message that read:

"I bought Norris's release and arranged for his transfer as a
prisoner of war. Both matters are official. He's safe if we can get
notice to his captors. I'm not sure if they received my wire, so
I'm afraid to trust it. You need to go with Link to Agua Prieta.
Take the Spanish messages with you, they will protect you and
secure Norris's freedom. Bring Nels with you and don't stop
for anything. Tell Link that we trust him and let him drive the
car. STILLWELL."

Vienna felt a surge of gratitude and joy as she read the first few
lines of Stillwell's message. But as she continued to read, she
felt a cold, numbing pain. When she got to the last line, she
cast aside her doubts and fears and faced the situation with a
determined resolve. "Read it," she said, handing the telegram to
Link. He read it and looked up at her with a blank expression.
"Link, do you know the roads, trails, and desert between here
and Agua Prieta?" she asked. "That's my old stomping ground,
and I know Sonora too," he replied.

"We need to get to Agua Prieta before sunset, long before, so
that if Norris is in a nearby camp, we can get to him in time,"
Vienna said urgently.

"Miss Princess, that's impossible!" Link exclaimed. "Stillwell's
crazy to suggest it."

"Can we drive an automobile from here into northern Mexico?" Vienna asked.

"Sure, but it'll take time," Link replied.

"We don't have much time," Vienna said, her eagerness growing.

"If Norris ain't found, he's as good as dead," Vienna said urgently to Link Stevens. The cowboy's demeanor changed suddenly, losing his usual confidence and appearing aged. "I'm just a cowboy, Miss Princess," he stammered. "The ride down to the border is treacherous. I could wreck the car and turn your hair gray. You wouldn't be the same after that."

Vienna revealed herself as Norris's wife, pleading with Link to help save him. Link's body jerked, mimicking Norris's own memorable reaction, and Vienna poured out her heart to him. "I love him. I've been unfair to him. I must save him. Link, please help me. I'll gladly risk anything to save him."

Link's response was beautiful in its selflessness. He didn't seem to think of himself at all, and Vienna felt a kinship with him that she couldn't explain. "Miss Princess, that ride is impossible, but I'll do it," he replied, his eyes shining with a daring spirit.

"I'll need about thirty minutes to go over the car and pack what I'll need," Link informed Vienna. She couldn't express her gratitude and only requested that he inform the off-duty cowboys, including Nels, to come up to the house. Once Link had left, Vienna took a moment to prepare for the ride. She placed her money and telegrams in a satchel and donned a long coat. She wrapped veils around her head and neck, forming a hood to cover her face if necessary. She even remembered to bring an extra pair of goggles for Nels. With her gloves on, she was prepared for the ride.

Upon reaching her home, she explained the situation to the cowboys and left them in charge. She then asked Nels to accompany her down into the desert. Nels turned white as a sheet, reminding Vienna of his fear of Link's driving. "Nels, I'm sorry to ask you," she added. "I know you hate the car. But I may need you so much." Nels replied, "Why, Miss Princess, that's surely a mistaken idea of yours about me hating the car. I was only jealous of Link, and the boys made that joke up about me being scared of riding fast. I'm proud to go, and if you're going down among the Greasers, you want me."

Despite Nels's cool, easy speech and familiar swagger, Vienna could see the gray still in his face.

Nels was inexplicably afraid of the massive white automobile, but he pretended otherwise. It was a strange manifestation of his loyalty. Vienna heard the vehicle's hum as Link approached, driving up the slope. He executed a brief, sliding turn and parked in front of the porch. Link had secured two long, weighty planks on either side of the car, and he had attached extra tires wherever he could. There was a huge barrel in one of the back seats and a collection of tools and ropes in the other. Nels could only just fit in the remaining space. Link placed Vienna next to him in the front, and then he hunched over the wheel. Vienna waved at the silent cowboys on the porch. There were no audible good-byes. The car left the yard, bounced from level to slope, and sped down the road, out into the open valley. The stronger gusts of dry wind in Vienna's face indicated an increase in speed. She took a quick look at the smooth, unobstructed cattle-road that disappeared into the distant gray. She glanced at the driver beside her, who was wearing leather garb and a leather helmet, before she pulled the veil's hood over her face and secured it tightly around her neck. The wind grew stronger and harder, pressing against her like a sheet of lead and forcing her back into her seat. The car's vibration was constant, intense, and incredibly rapid. Occasionally, she felt a long swing, as if she were about to be propelled into the air, but the car's effortless speed was undisturbed. The buzz and roar of the wheels and the heavy body in motion increased to a continuous droning hum. The wind became unbearable, moving towards her like a solid object, crushing her chest and making breathing difficult. Vienna felt as though time was flying by at the speed of miles.

Vienna felt a change in the car's movement and realized that Link was reducing speed. She took off her hood and goggles, grateful to be able to breathe freely and see clearly. The town of Chiricahua lay to her right, while the gray valley sloped to her left. The Guadalupe Mountains loomed in the distance, and Vienna couldn't help but think of Norris. Link turned the car south and picked up speed, and Vienna pulled her hood back over her face as the wind began to sting. It felt like she was riding at night as the car hurtled forward, wedging her back as if in a vise. The miles flew by, and Vienna felt the car accelerate to a certain swiftness before slowing again. She uncovered her face and saw another village passing by. She asked Link if it was Bernardino, and he confirmed that it was, 80 miles away. Vienna checked the time and saw that it was only a quarter to ten. Link had made quick work of the valley miles, and Vienna couldn't help but feel thrilled by the ride.

As they drove beyond Bernardino Link, he steered the car off the road and onto a long, sloping hill. Vienna noticed that the valley appeared to run south under the dark Guadalupe brows and they were headed southwest. The grass began to disappear as they climbed the ridge, replaced by dusty, white spots, patches of mesquite and cactus, and scattered areas of broken rock. Vienna had expected what she saw from the ridge-top, but the reality of the desert below still shocked her. She had lived on a ranch surrounded by desert, but this was different. This was the red desert, stretching far into Mexico, Arizona, and California, all the way to the Pacific. A bare, hummocky ridge lay ahead, down which the car was gliding, bouncing, and swinging. This slant seemed to merge into a corrugated world of rock and sand, patched by flats and basins, streaked with canyons and ranges of saw-toothed stone. The distant Sierra Madres were clearer, bluer, and less smoky than she had ever seen them. Vienna's faith held strong in the face of this daunting obstacle.

Gradually, the desert beneath them began to rise and condense its varying lights and shades, until it hid its depths and heights behind red ridges, little steps, outposts, and landmarks at its gates. As the car bounced along, Vienna noticed that Link was following an old wagon-road. When they reached the foot of the long slope, they struck rougher ground, and Link began to zigzag cautiously. The wagon-road would disappear and then reappear, but Link did not always follow it.

He maneuvered through cuts, detours, and crosses, all the while venturing deeper into a labyrinth of low, crimson dunes, flat canyon-beds lined with banks of gravel, and ridges that rose higher and higher. Despite the challenging terrain, Link Stevens pressed on, never once turning back or heading into a dead end. Vienna recognized that it was Link's incredible judgment of the land that made their progress possible. He knew the lay of the land like the back of his hand, never hesitating after making a decision on which way to go.

Eventually, they descended into a wide canyon, where the wheels of the car struggled to gain traction in the dragging sand. The sun beat down mercilessly, kicking up clouds of dust with no breeze to alleviate the oppressive heat. The only sounds were the occasional slide of rocks down the weathered slopes and the labored chugging of the machine. The slow pace of their journey began to test Vienna's faith, prompting Link to take over the wheel and call for Nels.

Together, they untied the long planks and laid them out in front of the wheels, allowing them to pass over the otherwise impassable sand and gravel. As they worked their way through the canyon, Vienna marveled at Link's foresight in bringing the planks along. Eventually, the canyon opened up into a vast expanse, affording them an unobstructed view for miles.

The desert stretched out before them in a series of steps, the mesas and escarpments bathed in the morning light. The landscape was a kaleidoscope of colors, ranging from gray, drab stone to vibrant shades of yellow, pink, and rust-red. Ahead lay a wind-swept floor as hard as rock, and Link wasted no time in rushing the car over it, eager to make up for lost time.

Vienna's ears were filled with a loud, persistent hum that sounded like a hungry bee. She soon realized it was the sound of gravel being kicked up by the car's wheels. The car was moving so fast that Vienna could only make out the colored landmarks ahead of them, and even those faded as the wind whipped past her face. Link began to climb a long, sweeping wasteland that was dotted with violet and heliotrope dunes. They followed a wagon-road that had recently been used by cattle, and the car steadily made its way up the incline. The sky was an intense, light blue that was almost painful to look at, so Vienna shielded her face until Link slowed down. From the top of the next ridge, they could see more of the red desert ruin. They came across a deep wash that forced Link to turn south. The space was barely wide enough for the car, and Vienna could hear the sound of gravel and earth sliding into the gully. As they crossed the sandy flat on the other side, rocks impeded their progress and had to be moved out of the way. The shelves of silt looked like they might collapse with even the slightest weight, and narrow spaces only allowed for a foot of clearance for the car's outside wheels. But none of these obstacles seemed to faze the cowboy driver, who kept going until they reached the road again. Once there, Link made up for lost time by speeding up.

As they ascended another peak, Vienna thought they had reached the top of a high pass nestled between two mountain ranges. The slope on the west side of the pass appeared to be rugged and un-even. Down below, a gray valley stretched out before them, and in the distance, a white speck twinkled in the sunlight. Link called it Adam, but Vienna knew that it was Agua Prieta, the neighboring town across the border. She peered out, wishing she could see it closer.

The descent from the peak was arduous. The front tires were punctured by sharp stones and cactus thorns, forcing them to stop and replace them. They laid planks across soft spots and even had to break a protruding rock with a sledge to continue. Eventually, a massive boulder blocked the road, and Vienna panicked. They had no room to turn the car around, but Link had a different idea. He reversed the car a fair distance and proceeded to the boulder on foot. After a brief moment of tinkering, he ran back down the road. Suddenly, a loud explosion rocked the air, and Vienna saw dust and debris fly everywhere. Link had used dynamite to clear the path.

Vienna marveled at Link's resourcefulness. She wondered how Nels, the silent cowboy, felt about the discovery of Link carrying explosives. But Nels reassured her, saying that nothing would stop Link. Vienna began to see Link in a different light. His fearless spirit and quick thinking were admirable, and she found herself drawn to him despite the danger they faced.

Nels responded in his own way, his face a shade of gray and his lips tightly pressed together. His eyes, however, mirrored the same cool, bright gleam as Link's. The road ahead was blocked by cacti, rocks, and gullies, but Nels approached each obstacle with a grim sense of humor. He knew that a small mistake on Link's part could spell disaster for the car and its occupants. Link had to use wooden planks to cross sandy washes, and sometimes the wheels slipped off. But he managed to make it across a deep ditch without incident, despite one of the planks sagging and splitting.

The road then led them around a narrow, rocky, and slightly downhill corner that was particularly hazardous. Link asked Vienna and Nels to walk around it while he drove the car. Vienna braced herself for the sound of the car crashing down into the canyon, but to her surprise, Link was waiting for them on the other side. As they continued on, the road became steeper and more treacherous. Link had to use ropes on the wheels and half-hitches on the spurs of rock to let the car slide down the inclines. At one particularly bad spot, Vienna exclaimed, "Oh, time is flying!" Link looked up at her, as if he had been scolded for being too careful. His eyes shone like steel on ice.

Vienna's words seemed to ignite something within him, unleashing his recklessness to its fullest extent. He pushed his car to perform seemingly impossible feats, navigating through gullies, hurdling over rising grounds, and leaping over breaks in the road. He made his vehicle cling to steep inclines like a mountain goat and rounded corners with the inside wheels higher than the outside. He even passed over soft banks of earth that crumbled beneath him as he crossed weak spots. Link continued on, weaving through tortuous passages strewn with rocks, sticking to the old road where possible, but abandoning it for open spaces when necessary. He always went down, descending further and further until he reached a mile-long slope, brown and ridged like a washboard, leading gently down to the valley floor where the sparse grama-grass struggled to grow.

As the road became clearer, Vienna's heart sank. It led straight across the valley, down to a deep, narrow wash that plunged on one side and ascended on the other at an even steeper angle. The crossing would have been difficult for a horse, let alone an automobile. Link turned the car to the right and drove as far along the rim of the wash as the ground would allow. However, the gully only widened and deepened, making it impossible to cross. He tried the other direction, but Vienna noticed the sun had already started its descent into the west. It shone in her face, glaring and angry.

Link drove back to the road, crossed it, and continued down the line of the wash. It was a deep cut in the red earth, worn straight down by swift water during rainy seasons. It narrowed, becoming only five feet wide in some places. Link studied these points carefully, looking up the slope and making deductions. The valley was now level, with only small breaks in the rim of the wash.

As Link drove on, he scoured the land for a place to cross, but to no avail. The southern path was blocked by deep gullies where the water flowed into a canyon, making it impossible to proceed. He had to reverse the car before he could turn it around. Vienna glanced at the stoic driver, but his face betrayed no emotion. When they arrived at the narrowest points, Link stepped out of the vehicle and scouted the area. After a small jump over the wash, Vienna noticed that the other side was slightly lower. She quickly realized Link's plan - he was searching for a spot to jump the car over the gap in the ground. He eventually found a suitable location and tied his red scarf to a nearby bush. Returning to the car, he muttered, "This ain't no airplane, but I've outsmarted that damn wash." He reversed up a gentle slope and stopped just before the steeper incline. His red scarf fluttered in the wind as he hunched over the wheel and gradually accelerated. The car leaped forward like a ferocious tiger, and the sudden gust of wind almost knocked Vienna out of her seat. Nels's strong hands gripped her shoulders as she closed her eyes. The bumpy ride gradually turned into a smooth glide. Suddenly, there was a slight bump, followed by a cowboy yell above the hum of the engine. Vienna braced herself for the inevitable crash, but it never came. When she opened her eyes, she saw the flat valley floor, unbroken. She hadn't even realized when the car had flown over the wash. She felt a strange sensation of breathlessness, which she attributed to the car's speed.

She pulled the hood over her head and leaned back in the seat, the sound of the car filling her world. The excitement and emotional highs were put on hold by the physical sensations. She struggled to breathe as the wind pressed against her chest, making her feel like she was floating and reeling at the same time. Her arms and hands felt heavy, like they were carrying mountains. Eventually, she lost consciousness, but when she came to, she felt an arm supporting her. The car was going slower now, and she could breathe again. They were on the outskirts of a city called Adam, near Agua Prieta. The sight of khaki-clad soldiers snapped her back to reality. They were at the boundary between the United States and Mexico, and Agua Prieta lay before her. A soldier came and said an officer would arrive soon. Vienna's attention was on the guard over the road and the dusty town beyond, but she could hear noise and people in the back. A cavalry officer approached the car and removed his hat.

"Do you have any information on Norris, the American cowboy who was captured by rebels a few days ago?" Vienna asked the officer. "Yeah," he replied. "There was a fight between a group of Federals and a large force of guerrillas and rebels over the border. The Federals were pushed west, and Norris was reported to have fought recklessly and was captured. He was given a Mexican sentence. Norris is known around here, and his capture caused quite a stir. We tried to get him released, but the guerrillas were afraid to execute him here and thought he might escape, so they took him to San Rafa with a detachment."

"He's supposed to be shot tonight at sunset?" Vienna asked. "Yes, and there are rumors that there is a personal grudge against him. I'm sorry I don't have more information. If you're a friend or relative of Norris, I might be able to help you," the officer said.

"I'm his wife," Vienna interrupted, handing him the telegrams. "Please read these and help me if you can."

The officer took the telegrams and read them with amazement. "I can't read these in Spanish, but I recognize the names signed," he said. He quickly went through the others. "These mean that Norris's release has been authorized. They explain the strange rumors we've heard here. The rebel junta's messages failed to reach their destination for some reason. We heard reports of an exchange for Norris, but nothing came of it. No one had the authority to take him to San Rafa. This is an outrage! Come with me to General

Salazar, the rebel chief in command. I know him, and maybe we can find out something."

Nels made room for the officer, and Link drove the car across the border into Mexican territory. Vienna's nerves were on edge.

The asphalt road stretched out before them, leading them straight into Agua Prieta. The town was a colorful sight with its walls and roofs painted in vibrant hues. As their car approached, goats, pigs, and buzzards scurried away from the commotion. Native women, dressed in black mantles, peeked through iron-barred windows, while men in oversized sombreros, cotton shirts and trousers, bright sashes around their waists, and sandals stood still, observing the passing vehicle.

Once they reached the end of the road, they found themselves in an enormous plaza, dominated by a circular structure that resembled a corral. It was the bull-ring where bull-fighting, the national sport, took place. However, at the moment, it seemed to be housing a considerable army of ragged, unkempt rebels. The square was littered with tents, packs, wagons, and weapons, with horses, mules, burros, and oxen wandering about.

Link had to drive slowly to navigate through the crowded plaza until they reached the entrance of the bull-ring. Vienna caught a glimpse of the tents inside before her view was obstructed by the pressing throng. The cavalry officer jumped out of the car and pushed his way into the entrance.

"Link, do you know the way to San Rafa?" Vienna asked.

"Yes. I've been there," he replied.

"How far is it?" she pressed.

"Not too far," he muttered.

Vienna knew he was lying, but she didn't question him further. The plaza was stifling and malodorous, with the red sun sinking low in the west, but still scorching everything in its path. A swarm of flies buzzed around the car, and low-flying buzzards cast their shadows across Vienna's vision. Then she noticed a row of black birds perched on a tiled roof, looking neither asleep nor resting, but waiting. She fought off a gruesome thought before it could take hold. These rebels and guerrillas were a sorry sight, with their lean, yellow, bearded faces, watching Link as he worked on the car.

Every man in the group was different, and none of them looked put together. Their eyes were bright and shiny, but sunk deep into their faces. They all wore big hats made of brown or black felt, straw, or cloth. Every guy had some kind of weapon in a belt or sash. Some had boots, some had shoes, some had moccasins, some had sandals, and some were even barefoot. They were all talking loudly and making wild hand gestures. Vienna couldn't help but think about how easily these poor revolutionaries could get caught up in a frenzy and start killing people. If they were fighting for freedom, it sure wasn't written on their faces. They looked like a pack of wolves on the hunt. Vienna was disgusted and even wondered if their leaders were of the same ilk.

But then, something caught her eye. Every single man in the crowd, no matter how dirty or torn his clothing was, had some sort of ornament or decoration on him. It could be a tassel, a fringe, a lace, a band, a bracelet, a badge, a belt, a scarf, or something else entirely. It was a sign of their vanity, their one poor possession that they treasured. It was a defining characteristic of their race.

Suddenly, the group split apart to let a cavalry officer and a rebel with a commanding presence through. "Ma'am, I had a feeling," the officer said quickly. "The orders to release Norris never made it to Salazar. They were intercepted. Even without them, we could have exchanged Norris if one of his captors hadn't wanted him dead. This guerrilla intercepted the orders and took Norris to San Rafa. It's a tragedy. He should be free right now. I'm sorry-"

"Who did this?" Vienna interrupted, feeling cold and ill. "Who is the guerrilla?"

"Senor Don Carlos Martinez. He's been a bandit, a man of influence in Sonora. He's more of a secret agent in the revolution than an active participant."

Vienna's heart raced as she heard the news of Norris being held captive by Don Carlos. She felt her strength falter until Nels, one of her trusted cowboys, placed his hands on her shoulders and spoke with a reassuring tone. Vienna knew she couldn't waste any time, and Nels promised to help her in any way he could. Link Stevens, another cowboy, agreed to join them on their mission despite the odds being against them.

Vienna asked an officer if she could get a permit to go to San Rafa, but he warned her that it was a long shot. However, he suggested that she take Senor Fernandez, a Mexican who outranked Don

Carlos and knew the captain of the San Rafa detachment. Vienna
agreed and thanked the officer for his kindness.

Nels and Link quickly prepared the car, and they took off with a
loud roar, causing the crowd to scatter. Vienna knew that time was
of the essence, and she couldn't afford to waste any more of it. She
had to save Norris, no matter the cost.

The car zoomed out of the plaza, gaining speed as it raced down
a street flanked by walls of white and blue. The rebels were busy
constructing barricades in a square as the vehicle whizzed past. The
railroad track was teeming with iron flat-cars that carried mounted
artillery pieces. Officer Fernandez was acknowledged by the guards
at the outskirts as the car sped by. Vienna secured her glasses tightly
over her eyes and wrapped veils around her face. She was in a
strange state of excitement, feeling a burning sensation that made
her pulse race, and she was determined to witness everything that
was feasible. The sun, which was sullen and red as fire, hung low
over the mountain range in the west. How far it had fallen! A
narrow, white road, dusty and hard as stone, stretched out before
her, a highway that had been in use for centuries. If it were broad
enough to allow vehicles to pass, it would have been a fantastic
course for automobiles. However, the car was brushing past weeds,
dusty flowers, mesquite boughs, and cactus arms as it accelerated.
The old, relentless force that pushed Vienna back and the constant
howl of the wind filled her ears. Link Stevens crouched low over
the wheel. His eyes were hidden beneath a leather helmet and
goggles, but his face was uncovered. He looked like a demon, with
his dark, stone-hard features that were strangely grinning. Vienna

suddenly realized how exceptional and remarkable a driver Link Stevens was. She sensed that Link Stevens could not have been weak. He was a cowboy, and he was genuinely driving the car, making it obey his commands, just as he was born to master a horse. He had never driven at a speed that satisfied him until now. His objective was to save Norris and make Vienna happy. Life meant nothing to him. This reality gave him the courage to face the danger of this ride.

With complete disregard for his own safety, Link expertly operated the machine, choosing the perfect power, speed, and guidance to get Vienna to San Rafa in time to save Norris. The white, narrow road flew by in a blur as they sped towards their destination. Even when Vienna noticed a clump of cactus in the distance, it seemed to shoot towards them and disappear in an instant. Despite the breakneck speed, Vienna knew that Link was holding something in reserve, taking the turns of the road as if he knew exactly what was ahead. He trusted in his cowboy's luck, even though a single wagon or a herd of cattle could mean a fatal crash.

Vienna never closed her eyes during those moments of danger. If Link was willing to stake everyone's lives on chance, she was willing to stake her own to save Norris. The car hummed and thrummed, darting around curves on two wheels like a bullet. But it wasn't all smooth sailing. Soft ground and cactus plants impeded their progress, causing the car to labor and pant and grind through gravel. Every leaf, blade, and branch of cactus bore wicked thorns that could easily puncture a tire.

Finally, it happened. The bursting report rang out, signaling a tire blowout.

The car jerked and stumbled, like a wounded animal, before finally coming to a stop under the control of the skilled driver. Link quickly replaced the tire, but even his speed couldn't make up for lost time. The red sun, darkening as it approached the horizon, seemed to mock Vienna, making her feel small and insignificant. With a burst of energy, Link hopped back in the driver's seat and the car surged forward.

The landscape around them changed constantly, from rolling hills to rocky terrain, with mesquite trees and other greenery providing a brief respite from the harsh desert. Vienna took in all the sights with a keen eye, but her focus was on one thing only – a straight, uninterrupted road. However, the road had other plans, winding lazily up a hill that grew taller and taller until it seemed like a mountain. The descent was treacherous, but Link kept up his speed despite the danger.

Just when Vienna thought they might make it, disaster struck again. A sharp spear pierced the tire, sending the car careening off the road and into a cactus. Link and Nels worked like mad to replace the tire, but the setting sun made Vienna feel like time was running out. Strangely, no one spoke during the entire ordeal, adding to the tension and fear.

Vienna was practically bursting with impatience, but she knew better than to try and rush Link. He was always lightning fast in everything he did. So she stood there in silence, feeling the heat inside her slowly dissipating, and watched with a growing sense of despair. She hoped and prayed that the road ahead would be long, straight and smooth. And then suddenly, there it was: a clear, narrow lane that seemed to stretch on for miles, disappearing into the distance like a thin white line against the greenery. Vienna's heart leaped with hope and she could only imagine that Link felt the same.

The car roared to life with a jerk, answering Vienna's silent call for speed. Faster and faster it went, until the roar turned into a whining hum that drowned out all other sounds. The wind rushed past them with such force that Vienna felt like she was being pushed down by a solid wall. She couldn't move, couldn't even hear anything over the sound of the wind. The desert plants along the road blurred together, becoming two shapeless fences that seemed to slide towards them from a distance. Objects ahead became streaky and blurry, and the sky took on a reddish hue. Vienna turned to look at Link one more time, realizing that this ride was just as much his as it was hers.

Link was hunched over the wheel, his face strained and rigid with concentration. He was a great driver, but the stakes were high. One wrong move and they would be done for. Vienna could see the millions of spikes on the cactus plants that lined the road, and she knew that if they so much as brushed against one of them, it would be the end. Link's cheek and jaw were bulging with the effort, and his lips were tightly shut. The smile was gone from his face, and Vienna could see that he was just as human as she was.

She felt a strange sense of camaraderie with him, realizing that he understood her soul just as Monty Price had understood it.

Link was the unstoppable machine, forged by lightning and driven by a woman's will. He was a man whose strength was fueled by a woman's passion. He stood as tall as she did, felt her love, and understood her pain. These qualities made him a hero. However, it was the hard life, the dangerous years spent in the wild desert, the companionship of ruthless men, and the raw elements that made his physical accomplishments possible. Vienna adored Link's spirit and gloried in the man he was. She had imprinted on her heart a memory of the little hunched, deformed figure of Link's, hanging onto the wheel with a fearless grip, his gray face like a stone mask. That was the last clear image in Vienna's mind during the ride. She was blinded, dazed, and succumbed to the demands on her strength. She fell back, only vaguely aware of a helping hand. Confusion overwhelmed her senses. She rushed through a dark chaos, under the wrathful red eye of the setting sun. She felt like she was being propelled through a limitless space, rushing like a shooting star. For moments, hours, or ages, she was pushed with the velocity of an automobile, hurtling down an endless white track through the universe. Giant cacti plants, as large as pine trees, loomed over her, piercing her with giant spikes. She became an unstable being in a shapeless, colorless, soundless cosmos of unrelated things, but always rushing, even to meet the darkness that haunted her and never reached her. But at the end of infinite time, the rush ceased. Vienna lost the strange feeling of being disembodied by a frightfully swift careening through boundless distance. She distinguished low voices, apparently far away. Then she opened her

eyes to blurred but conscious sight. The car had come to a stop.
Link was lying face down over the wheel.

Nels hollered for her, and she rubbed her hands together, eager
to see what he had found. As they traveled, a pristine house with
whitewashed walls and a brown-tiled roof caught her eye. Beyond
the house, she could see the silhouette of a mountain range, and
the final red glow of the setting sun.

Chapter Twenty-Six.

V ienna noticed that the car was surrounded by armed Mexicans. They were different from the others she had seen that
day, and she wondered why they were so silent and respectful.
Suddenly, a sharp order was given, and Senor Fernandez appeared,
walking swiftly towards them. Despite his dark face and strange
accent, he spoke her language politely and authoritatively. "Senora,
it is not too late!" he said. "You got here just in time. El Capitan
Norris will be free."

Vienna was shocked to hear that Norris would be free. She rose
from the car, but would have fallen if Fernandez had not taken her
arm. Nels supported her on the other side. Together, they helped
her out of the car. For a moment, Vienna's mind was spinning, but
soon she regained her composure.

As they walked through the hall and into the small room full
of armed rebels, Vienna scanned their faces, hoping to see Don
Carlos.

However, he was nowhere to be found. A soldier spoke to her
in Spanish, but spoke too quickly for her to understand. Despite
his shabby appearance, he exuded an air of authority and was

as gracious as Senor Fernandez. Vienna's attention was directed towards a man holding a bright red scarf near the window. "Senora, they were waiting for the sun to set when we arrived," Fernandez explained. "The signal was about to be given for Senor Norris's walk to death."

"Norris's walk!" Vienna repeated in shock. Fernandez then went on to explain that Norris had been court-martialed and sentenced according to a Mexican custom reserved for brave soldiers deserving of honorable executions. On Thursday, at sunset, Norris was to be set free and was allowed to walk in any direction he pleased. However, he knew that death was inevitable and that there was no escape from the men armed with rifles.

"Senora, we have sent messengers to every squad of waiting soldiers with an order that El Capitan is not to be shot. He is unaware of his release. I shall give the signal for his freedom," Fernandez declared ceremoniously. Vienna noticed his pride and realized that the situation brought out the vanity, ostentation, and cruelty of his race. She feared that Fernandez would keep her in suspense and let Norris walk in ignorance of his freedom, but she soon realized that he was simply barbarous.

Vienna couldn't help but feel a horrible fear that Fernandez was lying and that she would witness Norris's execution. But she knew that the man was honest, even if he lacked compassion.

In order to satisfy his primal instincts of sentiment, romance, and cruelty, Fernandez devised a plan to start Norris on a deadly walk. He reveled in the thought of watching Norris face death and seeing

Vienna's agony of doubt, fear, pity, and love. Vienna was on the brink of collapse, feeling weak and unsteady. "Senora! Ah, it will be one beautiful thing!" exclaimed Fernandez as he took the scarf from the rebel's hand. He was passionate and glowing, and his eyes had a strange, soft, cold flash. "I'll wave the scarf, Senora. That will be the signal. It will be seen down at the other end of the road. Senor Norris's jailer will see the signal, take off Norris's irons, release him, open the door for his walk. Norris will be free. But he will not know. He will expect death. As he is a brave man, he will face it. He will walk this way. Every step of that walk he will expect to be shot from some unknown quarter. But he will not be afraid. Senora, I have seen El Captain fighting in the field. What is death to him? Ah, will it not be magnificent to see him come forth to walk down? Senora, you will see what a man he is. All the way he will expect cold, swift death. Here at this end of the road he will meet his beautiful lady!"

Vienna faltered, "Is there no possibility of a mistake?" Fernandez replied firmly, "None. My order included unloading of rifles." She then asked about Don Carlos, and Fernandez informed her that he was in irons and must answer to General Salazar. Vienna looked down the deserted road, feeling the last ruddy glow of the sun over the mountain range. It had been torture for her to think of that sunset, but now the afterlights were luminous, beautiful, and prophetic. With a heart stricken by both joy and agony, she saw Fernandez wave the scarf. Then she waited.

The road ahead was desolate, not a single sign of life could be seen. The room behind her was silent. The wait felt like an eternity.

The pink, blue, and white houses with their colorful roofs were etched in her memory forever. The dusty road resembled a street from Pompeii, abandoned and forgotten for centuries. Suddenly, the door creaked open and a tall man emerged. It was Norris. Vienna's emotions overwhelmed her, and she had to steady herself against the window sill. She had saved him, and he was free. Life transformed in that moment, becoming sweet, full, and strange.

Norris greeted someone at the door before scanning the road. He rolled a cigarette, lit it, and leisurely began his walk down the middle of the road. Although he appeared nonchalant, the eerie silence, the red haze, and the charged atmosphere made everything feel unnatural. Norris occasionally stopped to survey his surroundings, but only silence answered his calls. He lit another cigarette, and then his pace quickened. Vienna watched with a mixture of pride, love, pain, and glory as he made his way down the road. It felt like an eternity, longer than her awakening, her struggle, and her remorse. She couldn't wait until he reached the end of the road.

Amidst the chaos of her emotions, Vienna experienced fleeting moments of panic. She wondered what she could possibly say to him and how she could face him. As she waited behind the window, she could see the tall and powerful figure of Norris approaching. His face was still a dark gleam, but she knew it wouldn't be long before she could distinguish his features. She longed to run and meet him, but fear kept her rooted to her hiding place. She imagined the terrible walk he must have taken, thinking of home, family, and life itself, knowing he was walking towards his executioners.

Despite the turmoil in her heart and mind, Vienna still felt the incomprehensible variations of emotion that are unique to a woman. Every step Norris took sent shivers down her spine. She had a strange, subtle intuition that he was not unhappy, and that he believed without a doubt that he was walking to his death. His steps began to drag, even though he had started off swiftly. The old, hard, physical, wild nerve of the cowboy was perhaps in conflict with the spiritual growth of the finer man, realizing too late that life should not be sacrificed.

As Norris approached, his face grew sharper and clearer. He was stalking now, and there was a hint of impatience in his stride. He couldn't believe how long it was taking these hidden Mexicans to kill him! Halfway down the road, in front of a house and directly opposite Vienna, Norris halted abruptly. He presented himself as a fair, bold target to his executioners, standing motionless for a full minute. But only silence greeted him. It was plain to Vienna, and she thought to anyone with eyes to see, that this was the moment when Norris should have been mercifully shot, since he had been spared for so long on his walk.

With no shots fired, Norris's demeanor shifted from rugged dignity to reckless scorn. He strolled over to the corner of the house, rolled another cigarette, and presented his broad chest to the window as he smoked and waited. Vienna found the wait unbearable. Though it was only a moment, it felt like an eternity. Norris's face was hard and scornful. Did he suspect treachery from his captors?

Did they plan to toy with him before murdering him? Vienna thought she saw an inscrutable, mocking smile pass over Norris's lips. He held his position for what seemed like a reasonable amount of time to him. Then, with a laugh and a shrug, he threw his cigarette into the road. He shook his head in disbelief at the incomprehensible motives of the men who had no fair reason for delay. He made a sudden, violent action, more than just straightening his powerful frame. It was an instinctive display of violence.

Then he turned to face north. Vienna knew he was thinking of her and calling her a silent farewell. He would serve her to his last breath, leave her free, and keep his secret. The image of him, dark-browed, fire-eyed, strangely sad yet strong, was etched into Vienna's heart. The next moment, Norris strode forward, boldly and scornfully, to force a speedy fulfillment of his sentence. Vienna stepped into the doorway, and Norris staggered as if he had been mortally wounded. His dark face turned white, and he stared at Vienna with a wild fear, as if he had seen an apparition and doubted his own sight. Perhaps he had called out to her like the Mexicans called out to their Virgin, or perhaps he imagined sudden death had come unawares, and she was his vision in the afterlife." Who you be?" he rasped. She made an effort to raise her hands, but they shook uncontrollably. On her second attempt, she managed to extend them towards him. "It's me, your highness. Your lady!"

THE END.

Printed in Great Britain
by Amazon

25666062R00218